The Shakespeare Sisters

Juliet Greenwood

Storm
PUBLISHING

Ebook ISBN: 978-1-80508-031-2
Paperback ISBN: 978-1-80508-033-6

Cover design: Eileen Carey
Cover images: Trevillion, Shutterstock

Published by Storm Publishing.
For further information, visit:
www.stormpublishing.co

Also by Juliet Greenwood

The Girl with the Silver Clasp

The Ferryman's Daughter

The White Camelia

We That are Left

Eden's Garden

To Margorie Jenkins, Aunty Margorie
With love and happy memories

Part One

Rosalind: There is a man haunts the forest, that abuses our young plants with carving 'Rosalind' on their barks; hangs odes upon hawthorns and elegies on brambles... he seems to have the quotidian of love upon him.

As You Like It. Act Three, Scene Two

Chapter One

Summer had come again to Arden House.

On moth-eaten tapestry rugs, spread out across the grass to keep stains from the pale cotton of summer dresses, Rosalind Arden turned to gaze across the lawn towards the crumbling Tudor mansion. With its rows of mullion windows, glinting, fractured, in the sun, beneath winding chimneypots in tiles as red as the rich English earth, the house appeared to have stood forever amongst the surrounding undulation of woods and fields.

When she was little, Rosalind's grandfather had told her the house would have been a familiar sight to Shakespeare himself, as he made the journey between nearby Stratford-upon-Avon and the theatres of London. Arden was a timeless place, Grandfather had declared. A world unto itself, untouched by what lay beyond.

She had so wanted to believe his words. To passionately cling to Arden's beauty and security, even as she grew into womanhood and Grandfather had been absorbed into the earth within the churchyard of the tiny village of Brierley-in-

Arden, a short walk away. But today – sitting with her sisters, just as they had on summer days for as long as she could remember – Rosalind felt an uneasy stirring in her blood. The world was changing.

'It's too hot to concentrate,' announced Kate, pushing back her jet-black hair, which, much to the horror of their stepmother, she had recently chopped into a short bob, imitating a photograph of American actress Louise Brooks in *Diary of a Lost Girl*. Not that any of them had been permitted to see so shocking a movie, of course. But even Alma had to eventually admit that the style set off her step-daughter's high cheekbones and olive skin, and emphasised the dramatic arch of her eyebrows.

Kate threw down her pencil, followed by her half-finished sketch of the small rise in the landscape between a scrub of oak and birch, known locally as the burial mound. 'I'm going to cool off in the lake.'

'We can't,' replied Cordelia, who was lying on her stomach, deep in inspection of an iridescent green beetle making its way through the jungle of clover. 'The boys are there. I saw them heading off earlier, and they had a friend with them.'

Rosalind frowned. 'It wasn't Henry Luscombe, was it?'

'I don't think so.' Cordelia abandoned her beetle and sat up. She was the youngest of the sisters, and more lightly built, her features delicate, despite being the only one of the Arden children to inherit their father's stern, green–grey eyes. Her long, honey-coloured tresses, which fell naturally into ringlets, were currently being held in place by a length of white silk, cut from the remains of an elaborate ballgown their Great Aunt Beatrice had worn when she had been presented as a debutante at the court of Queen Victoria.

Cordelia had a passion for refashioning the forgotten

dresses the sisters had discovered hidden in trunks amongst the endless attics of Arden House and which – given their ancestors' taste in the palest chiffon and muslin – tended to give her a deceptively demure appearance. Not that any of the four Shakespeare sisters of Arden House could ever be described as a pushover, as several young men – keen to ally themselves with one of the oldest families of Warwickshire (even England itself) – had discovered when attempting to lure them, deviously, into secluded corners.

'I only saw them from a distance,' Cordelia continued. 'But it didn't look like him. It must be Will's new friend, the engineer from Stratford he keeps telling Papa is so brilliant. Guy... Thomas? Thompson? In any case, I'm sure *the esteemed Henry Luscombe* isn't the swimming sort.'

'That's true,' said Rosalind, relieved. Of late, their father's pointed remarks to all his daughters about Henry Luscombe being heir to one of the largest estates in the neighbouring county of Shropshire had grown more pressing. She might have been initially dazzled by Henry's classical features and dark-gold hair – the skin on her arms had been sent prickling by his casual athleticism, born of hours spent at his rowing club and as a leading member of his university cricket team. But there was a way he looked down his Roman nose at all those around him, including her two brothers, that set her nerves grating.

'*I shall only ever marry for love,*' Rosalind murmured under her breath, a mantra she had breathed to herself regularly in the months after the King's abdication. Edward VIII's speech was still seared into her mind, even more vividly than the radio coverage of the coronation of George VI and Queen Elizabeth.

A flurry of snow had swirled against the windows that day, as the entire Arden household had paused in their traditional preparations for Christmas to gather around the wire-less in its much-polished art deco cabinet, set in pride of place in the less formal drawing room.

There had been a shocked silence throughout the crack-ling of the King's broadcast, broken only by the swoosh as a burning log collapsed to embers in the grate. Had a king really given up his kingdom for love? Rosalind had felt the realisation shooting through them all, seen the tightening of her father's lips, the tears welling up in her stepmother's eyes. This was not a play, not a Shakespearean romance, this was now, and this was real.

'I have found it impossible to carry the heavy burden of responsibility, and to discharge my duties as King as I would wish to, without the help and support of the woman I love.'

Edward VIII's words lingered in the air long after Papa had reached for the dial. Her father hated taking the cumber-some battery to the garage in Stratford-upon-Avon for recharging, so only permitted the radio to be switched on for performances of Beethoven and such solemn occasions as the King's broadcast to the Empire.

Could Rosalind herself ever be as resolute as Edward? It was a question that had haunted her ever since. She knew nothing of love, apart from the balcony exchanges of Romeo and Juliet, the inner longing of Jane Eyre, and the film *The Constant Nymph* that her stepmother had taken them to see in the Picture House in Stratford.

'Love is merely a madness,' declared her namesake in *As You Like It*. Even so, she'd rather be mad than spend her life married to Henry Luscombe, required to droop prettily and have no views of her own.

Rosalind returned her gaze to the table set under the shade of a large oak to one side of the house, complete with spotless white cloth and the second-best china. The quiet murmur of conversation drifted through the still air from where Bianca, far too dignified to sprawl with her younger sisters, sat with their stepmother, sunlight flickering over the sprigged folds of their skirts and the brims of straw sunhats preserving their complexions.

It was a vision of so many summer afternoons throughout her childhood, the kind she wanted to bottle and keep forever. Rosalind reached for her battered Kodak Brownie, tucked discretely under the pile of their discarded cardigans. As she unclipped the camera's leather case, she paused. Despite the heat, a sliver of chill travelled slowly up her spine. The scene before her could so easily have been from one of the sepia photographs displayed in Miss Parson's little museum of local history, set next to the church hall in Brierley-in-Arden.

Those pictures had been taken by Rosalind's Aunt Flora, in the summer before the Great War, using the huge wooden box of a camera that was now rotting quietly away in the cellars of Arden House. Several of the photographs portrayed the family sitting around the same table, under the shade of the exact same trees, the women in frothy lace and extravagantly feathered hats, the men stiff in their formal suits. All of them aunts and uncles Rosalind had never met, scattered in the war to end all wars, so many of the men lost forever.

Even more haunting was the single photograph of the estate workers, the men proudly perched atop the hay wain, scythes and pitchforks to hand, while children peered with open curiosity at the strange contraption capable of creating pictures out of light itself.

Rosalind shivered. Most of those lads grinning at the triumphant bringing in of the harvest had never made it home from the horrors of the Somme and Passchendaele, their names now etched alongside those of her uncles, Rupert Arden (aged

32), Arthur John Arden (aged 21), and Charles Arden-Phillips (aged 19), on the memorial next to the village green. Many of the girls in that sepia image had faced sorrows she could not imagine – a life without any hope of a family of their own. Aunt Flora herself, who must only have been Rosalind's age – twenty at most – when she took the photographs, had lost two of her brothers and her fiancé in France, only to elope to America with the son of one of the estate's stable hands, never to be spoken of again.

But that was then. The past. She was being silly. It was just the talk over the previous months of the possibility of war breaking out all over Europe. It had stirred up a lingering sense of unease in the village, too, sending the old men enjoying the sun (not to mention the beer) outside the White Hart pub to shake their heads over the foolishness of all politicians, declaring loudly that no good would come of that clown Hitler rising to be Chancellor of Germany.

It was just talk. It was only natural that her elders – who remembered the last war, for all they never mentioned the subject – should be nervous of a screaming madman and his regimented flag-bearers. But this was Arden House, calm, beautiful and timeless as it had ever been. It was just talk.

Rosalind removed the Kodak from its case and concentrated on positioning the camera. This was, after all, the vision of Arden her grandfather had held fast, even after the death of both Rupert, his heir, and Arthur, his youngest and most favoured son, leaving her father the unexpected inheritor of the vast Arden Estate. Had cousin Charles survived, it would have been the Arden-Phillips family installed in place of Papa – the middle son, the one who (for reasons unspecified) had never quite lived up to expectations.

Grandfather had been an uncomfortable presence to live with in his final years, having never hidden his view that his grandchildren, even the boys, had been tainted by Papa's inadequacies. It had been a relief when he finally relinquished all responsibility for the rambling estate, to become utterly absorbed in his passion for the noble history of Arden, stretching back to the beginning of time.

Rosalind's strongest memories were of the old man ensconced in his library, white hair unkempt, resembling illustrations of King Lear, his papers and books scattered in disarray. Whenever she had passed, she had heard the rapid scratch of his pen, in his increasingly desperate attempts to convince the academic world that the White Hart pub in nearby Brierley-in-Arden had been a favourite of Shakespeare's and a place where most surely he had sown his wild oats.

Where else but in Brierley-in-Arden, Grandfather had declared, could the playwright have observed all human nature in its rawness and its beauty? And wouldn't it have been the tramp between Brierley and Stratford, in all weathers and seasons, when the soul of the poet had absorbed the bank where the wild thyme grows, and the storms of the blasted heath, with its oak-cleaving thunderbolts racing across the fields? And didn't that make the White Hart the natural inspiration for the Boar's Head in *Henry IV,* and Prince Hal's encounters with Falstaff before the unruly prince became Henry V? It stood to reason, he thundered to every learned journal he could find, that this was the very tavern the great playwright had in mind, as he recalled his own transformation from wild youth to the greatest of men.

Sadly, not one of the journals had sought fit to print Grandfather's great discovery, nor even had the courtesy to acknowledge his years of scholarship. *Poor Grandfather,* thought Rosalind, as she pressed the camera shutter to capture this summer afternoon for eternity.

For all Grandfather's dedication to his cause, Arden House had remained in its accustomed obscurity, as had the dusty little lanes between the thatched and timber-framed cottages of Brierley-in-Arden, clustered around the green, with its pond and its ducks, and the squat little church rumoured to have been built in Norman times. She was sad for her grandfather's humiliation at being ignored by those he so admired, but she was rather glad her home had remained undisturbed by curious tourists and souvenir collectors.

Rosalind closed up the Brownie as the young men suddenly appeared, racing towards them from the direction of the lake, hair slicked against their heads, damp shirts worn open-necked, their jackets swung carelessly over their shoulders.

'We swam right across,' announced Will, the eldest of the Arden siblings, throwing himself down on the unoccupied rug.

'Twice,' added Jamie, attempting to control his shivering. He might only be a year younger than their brother, but Jamie was lighter in build – painfully skinny however much he ate. Rosalind resisted the urge to sweep up the blanket beneath her and wrap it tightly around him. Poor Jamie would be mortified to be treated as if he was a child.

Will – Arden's future lord and master – removed the wicker basket containing Kate's drawing materials from the rest of the blanket and flung it onto the grass.

'Plenty of room, Thompson,' he remarked to the fair-haired young man shrugging on a jacket of worn brown tweed, elbows neatly patched with ovals of leather. 'Come and join us. You don't have to stand on ceremony. It's only the Shakespeare sisters.'

'Charming,' said Rosalind.

'Idiot,' added Kate, throwing her discarded cardigan at their brother, leaving him struggling inside the enveloping sage-green of knitted lambswool.

'Some of us have manners,' put in Cordelia, in tones of mock primness, squinting up at the interloper in their midst, who appeared torn between embarrassment and an impulse to laugh.

'It's all right,' said Rosalind, taking pity on him. 'There's enough room for you and Jamie, Mr Thompson, we don't really confine our guests to sitting on the grass.'

'Thank you.' He folded his long limbs down into the space next to Jamie. 'I have sisters,' he added, breaking into a smile. 'Two of them.'

'Aha,' said Rosalind. 'So, you're familiar with the eternal squabbles of the lesser-spotted sibling.'

'Daily,' he replied, wryly. 'I'm hopelessly outnumbered. Besides, my sister Gwen never lets you forget a thing. She's the one who chases up Dad's creditors, so discretion is definitely the better part of valour.'

Rosalind laughed out loud at this, while a stifled hiccup escaped Cordelia, and even Kate turned away to hide a smile.

'The eternal what?' demanded Will, emerging red-faced from his prison. 'You do talk nonsense sometimes, Rosalind.'

'So, not all the time, then. You freely admit it. I shall hold you to that the next time we disagree.'

'That's not what I meant.'

'Rosalind's only teasing you, Will,' said Jamie quietly. 'You should know that by now.'

'Instead of falling for it every time,' added Kate.

Jamie grinned. 'You're probably wishing you were still

freezing in the lake, Guy. It's much more peaceful surroundings than the Arden family *en masse*.'

'Tranquillity is overrated,' returned Guy, good-humouredly.

'Brave,' said Cordelia.

'Or foolish,' added Rosalind, eyeing him curiously.

The friends Will had brought to stay when he was still at Oxford had been fresh-faced, schoolboy roundness still clearly visible even as they strode with the confidence of future masters of the Empire between the formal rose beds and the time-darkened panelling of Arden House. Guy's features, on the other hand, were sharper, more defined and, unlike the future lords of the city and viceroys of India, he was making no loud attempts to impress the females captive at his feet.

'I hope not,' he replied. His eyes were a clear sky-blue and in the brilliant sunshine, Rosalind's gaze lingered a little too long for politeness, caught in the intensity of their depths, impossible to tear herself away. Out of nowhere, a knot formed deep inside, an unfamiliar tugging in her belly. She could feel the blush starting in her toes, surging rapidly upwards, and turned away before it could reach her face.

'So,' said Kate, who was always the first to notice any discomfiture of her sisters, and just as quick to deflect attention away until they had recovered. 'Aren't you curious to know why we're the Shakespeare sisters, Mr Thompson?'

'Of course,' Rosalind heard him reply. Was that just the slightest tremor of emotion to his voice, or was she imagining it?

'It's a family tradition,' said Cordelia, returning to her beetle. 'Our grandfather was obsessed with Shakespeare. He insisted that we were named after characters from the plays.'

'Only the girls, thank goodness,' said Will. 'I'd rather be disinherited than answer to "Orlando".'

'Orlando?' A twitch caught the corners of Guy's mouth, hastily supressed. 'Oh, you mean from *As You Like It*?'

'It was one of his favourite plays,' explained Kate. 'That and *A Midsummer Night's Dream*. Although he became obsessed with *Henry V* just before he died. Papa is determined we should carry on the tradition, just as Grandfather would have wished. The village dramatic society, the Brierley Players, puts on a performance almost every year. They must know the plays almost by heart by now. We certainly do; Papa has made sure of that.'

'And does everyone do what your father says?'

'Yes,' said Kate, turning back to her sketchbook and concentrating on the perspective, to create the correct distance between the burial mound and the walls of Arden's kitchen garden.

'Even Will,' put in Jamie, whose shivering was easing in the heat. 'Even though he's the oldest and will inherit the Arden estate one day, it's Papa who decides everything.'

'I can understand about family expectations,' replied Guy, ruefully. He caught Will's scowl of annoyance at this mere suggestion of some kind of equality between them. 'Except mine's about running a factory rather than a grand estate.'

'Not *so* grand an estate,' said Rosalind, spurred back into joining the conversation by the superior expression returning to Will's face. 'Not anymore.'

'Oh, that's because of Papa,' said Will. 'He's just like Grandfather, he doesn't think anything should ever change and that Arden should stay just as it was when Shakespeare was alive. All this place needs is some modernisation to make the land more productive and for the villagers in Brierley-in-Arden to pay their rents on time.'

Pride soothed and the proper social order restored, he turned to Guy. 'I've been looking into purchasing a generator for the house and installing electricity. So many of the best houses have it now, and in London one gets quite used to the convenience. Papa won't hear of it, of course, but it's the first thing I'll do when I take over. And put in some decent plumbing.'

'I hope you'll be able to,' replied Guy. There was something in the tone of his voice that sent Rosalind looking back towards him, trying to read his expression.

'Don't be so pessimistic,' said Will, as if returning to a previous discussion. 'It's in no one's interest. Hitler's clearly completely deranged, especially with all that talk of a master race and a new German Empire to rival our own. I wouldn't be surprised if he's deposed before the year is out and it all comes to nothing.'

'I'm not so sure...'

'Germany's a long way away,' said Jamie, frowning.

'My dad's moving from producing cars to focussing on parts for spitfires and bombers,' replied Guy.

'Still doesn't mean it will happen,' said Will.

Guy traced the white blooms of clover pushing up through the neatness of the lawn next to the blankets, face troubled. 'Dad's business has contacts in Germany. So many people there are selling up and leaving. I've talked with some of the ones employed in the Birmingham factory. Even here, they are afraid of what might happen if Germany ever invaded. The things they say...'

He glanced towards the sisters.

'They never supported the Führer,' he added hastily, 'so they may well be exaggerating.' He returned to inspection of the grass, as if lost in his own thoughts. 'I can't imagine what it must be like to leave everything you have ever built, and the house your family has lived in for generations, to start again in a foreign land where you barely speak the language, let alone finding a way of supporting yourself. I have to believe they had no other choice.'

'Germany, invade here?' exclaimed Will. 'I'd like to see them try. One Englishman is worth ten of them. They wouldn't stand a chance.'

Will's voice was scornful, but Rosalind could hear the edge. Like all the boys she'd ever met, her brother had been raised for bravado and self-confidence, and to never admit to having been the small child who vomited with sheer terror when Papa flew into one of his rages, and ran through the corridors when the wind rattled the attics and stirred the drapery, in a bid to escape any ghostly Arden ancestor who, like the ghost in Hamlet, just might be lurking in the shadows.

'You mean you'd fight?' Jamie turned even paler, a bout of shivering taking hold once more.

'I'd volunteer like a shot,' said Will, staunchly. 'And Guy would, too.'

Guy pulled at the grass. 'Of course. Although I'm sure Dad would do his best to stop me. He fought in the trenches during the Great War. He never speaks about it, but we've all heard his nightmares, and it's always been Mum who's dealt with any rat that got into the coal shed.' He ignored Will's embarrassed shuffling at such an admission of family weakness. 'I'm his only son. He'd do anything to protect me.'

'Even if it prevents you from doing your duty for your King and country?'

Rosalind scowled at her brother. She hated it when he showed off like this, a pale imitation of Papa. When their father turned pompous, the house fell silent. Will, on the other hand, never could carry it off. He didn't have the power, the authority, the ruthless determination to bend them all to his will. It just made him sound hollow, a desperate clutching at something he could never be.

'Protecting each other is what families do,' she snapped, before she could stop herself.

Guy shot her a grateful smile, his eyes resting once more on hers, sending that strange sensation into her limbs. 'It's what I hope I'd do if I ever have sons.'

He turned to look over the lawns and the house, to the spire of the village church, safe in its hollow, and the patch-work of fields stretching towards the river and Stratford-upon-Avon. 'And I'd protect all this with the last drop of blood in my body.'

'Me as well,' said Jamie. The colour was returning to his cheeks. A sliver of dread went through Rosalind. Where Will led, Jamie would always follow. *Never show weakness, never admit to fear.* That was the lesson in required manliness she'd watched Papa instil into her brothers from before they could walk. At least, as a mere girl, whose only requirement was to find a rich husband to replenish the diminished coffers of the Arden family, this was one of her father's strictures she had managed to escape.

Her eye caught movement from the direction of the house. Lucy the undermaid appeared with a laden tray, followed by a large man with dark hair, slicked back after the manner of Clarke Gable in *Red Dust*, sporting a double-breasted jacket of the finest tweed and matching, sharply pressed trousers, topped off with a brown striped tie set perfectly in line.

'It's Mr Gorwell,' said Rosalind, trying to ignore the

anxious wave from their stepmother, indicating that they should join the party at the table.

'That's the third time this week,' said Cordelia. 'He must be keen.'

'Well, I don't know how Bianca can stand him,' announced Kate, with a shudder. 'He's so old, he must be thirty-five at least. And horribly pompous. I wouldn't touch him if he was the last man on earth.'

'Then lucky you don't have to,' said Will, grinning. 'He's immensely rich,' he added. 'He'll be a good match for Bianca. Then you'll be next, Rosy. You'll have to marry someone even richer, or Bianca will hold it over you for the rest of your life.'

'I'm not going to marry just to outdo Bianca,' she retorted.

'Then it will have to be Cordelia, and you can stay an old maid with Kate, if you prefer.'

There was a moment's silence. Kate pretended to be absorbed in her drawing, while Jamie flushed bright red, biting back angry words to save Kate from further humiliation in front of their guest. Guy, Rosalind saw, looked faintly embarrassed, as if sensing the tension crackling through the air. He must surely have heard the rumours about the not-quite-Arden – already signalled out by anxious mamas as '*that Italian girl*' – who had appeared from nowhere ('*and who's her family? I mean, really?*'). They weren't about to allow dubious foreign morals to sully the blood of the local gentry, nor that hint of darker skin than good Anglo-Saxon peaches and cream.

'I thought you were the one who wanted to spend a fortune on improvements, Will,' remarked Cordelia coldly, steely grey eyes fixing her brother with a glare. 'Perhaps you should be the one required to marry an heiress, however ill her temper.'

'I'll marry who I please,' he snapped, chin set in a stubborn line, in a conscious image of their father.

'I really think we should join them,' said Rosalind, sensing the outbreak of a familiar family skirmish, bound to get rapidly get out of hand. 'We promised Bianca we wouldn't let her down.'

Kate jumped to her feet and set off without a word. Cordelia looked as if she was about to reply to Will, but there was no point, especially not with the need to maintain his manly status in front of his friend, however lowly he considered Guy's station in life.

'Oh, all right then.' With a sniff of disdain, Cordelia followed her sisters, leaving the males of the party to stretch out on their abandoned blankets, luxuriating in the sunshine and the freedom from being expected to fulfil family obligations to keep a promising suitor suitably charmed.

When she glanced back, Rosalind saw they were deep in conversation, womenfolk already forgotten.

Chapter Two

'Ah, there you are my dears,' said their stepmother, smiling in relief as the three arrived to join the party under the trees. Alma, who at their father's insistence was always referred to as 'Mama', looked even more nervy than usual, the weight of not disappointing her husband resting heavy on her narrow shoulders. 'You remember my younger girls, Mr Gorwell, they're always pleased to see you.'

'A pleasure,' he returned, nodding stiffly in Rosalind's direction while barely acknowledging Cordelia and ignoring Kate's existence entirely. 'Of course, concrete is the thing, Mrs Arden,' he resumed. 'The Bauhaus influence is still very strong, and the Empire State Building in New York will have many imitators. I predict skyscrapers will soon be a familiar sight in Birmingham, and eventually in all major cities.'

'Yes, indeed,' murmured Alma politely.

'It will be increasingly used for domestic buildings as well. Take the Isokon building, near Belsize Park in London. A very fine example of the most forward-looking design for flats, very fine indeed.'

'I saw a photograph in the newspaper,' said Kate, as he paused to draw breath. 'I thought it looked a little soulless with all those concrete curves. I can't imagine living in a place like that at all.'

'Experts agree it's eminently practical,' he returned heavily, without so much as a glance in her direction. 'We can't keep on living in the past. The Arts and Crafts approach is undeniably charming for the layman, who generally favours the roses-round-the-door approach. But where is the progress? The innovation? We all need to make our mark, you know.'

Kate, who had never been known to resist an argument, opened her mouth and Rosalind trod on her foot, hard. Kate, for once, subsided, taking out her sketchbook and marking her objections by pointedly turning her back on the rest of them and shifting her attention to the branches of the over-hanging oak.

On the other side of the table, Cordelia slouched, glaze-eyed, barely able to conceal that her mind was most definitely elsewhere. Only Bianca, her dark hair smoothed into immaculate finger-waves after the manner of Bette Davis, hung on her suitor's every word, self-consciously adjusting the power-blue folds of her silk *crepe de chine* dress every now and again, to show her figure to its best advantage.

Rosalind sat dutifully straight in her chair, doing her best for Bianca's sake to look as inoffensive a prospective sister-in-law as possible. At least Alma began to relax a little as Mr Gorwell continued to inform them in great detail of his business empire, creating elegant houses (primarily of glass and concrete, naturally) for the wealthy in and around Stratford, with some of his larger projects being as far away as Birmingham.

Bianca smiled and nodded at appropriate intervals, but

Rosalind's mind soon drifted. It didn't feel right that Oswald Gorwell was sipping tea and calmly describing the innovative house with clean modern lines he had just been commissioned to build on the banks of the River Avon by a wealthy local artist, while her brothers discussed the possibility of having to kill their fellow men. They couldn't both be real, surely?

The conversation around the table might be tedious, but at least it was safe. Rosalind's world as it had always been – as it should be. Her glimpse into her brothers' possible fates was too terrifying to contemplate.

'Don't you agree, Miss Rosalind?' She was jolted back to the present as Oswald Gorwell addressed her directly. From the corner of her eye, she caught Alma's shoulders tense.

There was nothing for it. She had not the faintest idea of what he was talking about.

'Oh, yes indeed,' she replied, giving him her broadest, most enthusiastic smile.

Mr Gorwell leant complacently back in his chair. 'There, Miss Arden, your sister, at least, has excellent taste.'

'Yes,' said Bianca, through what could only be described as gritted teeth. As the object of her affections turned towards their stepmother for his cup to be refilled, the scowl she shot in Rosalind's direction was perfectly ferocious. Rosalind could have kicked herself. The last thing she wanted was an argument with Bianca, or even worse to be accused of trying to steal Mr Gorwell for herself. The mere thought left her feeling a trifle queasy.

She had never been so glad to see the distraction of their father striding from the direction of the walled garden. Alma sat up even straighter in her chair, nodding for her stepdaughters to do the same.

'Afternoon, Gorwell,' said Mr Arden, taking his seat at

the head of the table. 'I hope the ladies have been entertaining you.'

'Very well,' declared Mr Gorwell, gallantly. 'Most pleas-
antly. I couldn't have wished for better.'

'Good. Good.' Leo Arden, having married his first wife
late, and his second even later, was in his mid-sixties, his
thick mane of fair hair streaked with grey. He made an
imposing figure, over a head taller than Mr Gorwell,
browned from instructing the few remaining gardeners in the
walled garden, and even clambering up the tallest of ladders
to maintain the illusion of the Ardens still being able to
retain a small army of men to work on repairs to the house.

'Mr Gorwell has invited us to take a tour of the houses
he's building in Stratford,' said Alma. 'They sound very fine.'

'Excellent.' Her husband, never good in company, shuffled uncomfortably in his chair with the air of a man who
could not abide idling for any longer than was strictly necessary. 'Well, this is pleasant.' His eyes rested on the young
men, still deep in conversation on the higher part of the lawn.
'I don't know what they are doing, lolling around as if we
don't have guests.' He shot off, returning a few minutes later
with the three in tow.

As her brothers and their guest settled on the remaining
chairs, Rosalind leant back in her seat, this time taking care to
follow the conversation closely enough to avoid being caught
out again. For once she was thankful to be expected to be no
more than audience to manly discussions of land drainage
and the advantages of the new Alfa Romeo.

When the subject of conversation had been exhausted,
and their father proposed taking Mr Gorwell on a tour of the
grounds (still considered the finest this side of Charlecote
Park), Rosalind followed Cordelia and Kate, who had already
made their own bids for freedom and were vanishing inside

the house. She hastily grabbed the Wedgewood teapot on the pretext of helping Lucy taking the tea things back to the kitchens, where Cook could be heard declaring in a particularly strident voice that she had no time to waste if the family's dinner was to be sent up on time.

Rosalind had nearly reached the safety of the house, when her arm was grasped so tight she nearly dropped the teapot.

'How could you?'

'Bianca...'

'He came to see me. It's *me* he wants to marry. Not you. Only now he thinks you're wonderful.'

'Of course he doesn't!'

'He told me so himself, just now.'

Drat the man. Didn't he have an ounce of tact in his body?

'It doesn't mean anything. I'm sure he was just being polite, and anyhow, at least I didn't say anything unladylike and offend him.'

Bianca burst into tears. 'You might have just left me alone. You've already got Luscombe. Papa told me so himself.'

'Henry?' Rosalind blinked. 'I've no intention of marrying Henry Luscombe! From what I've seen of him, it would be even worse than...' She stopped herself just in time from saying the unforgiveable about Oswald. 'Worse than being an old maid, I mean.'

'You will,' said Bianca, blowing her nose. 'Of course you'll marry him. Papa will wear you down until you say yes. You don't think he'll let someone like him get away, do you?'

'Get away? You make Henry sound like a fish.'

Bianca hiccupped. 'A shark, more like it.' Her chin rose defiantly. 'Horrible man. And so vulgar when he wants to be. I don't mind that Henry obviously prefers you and never took so much as a second glance at me. You're welcome to him. Oswald may be a little... well, staid, but he's perfectly respectable and one day he'll be just as rich as the Luscombes. So at least Papa will be happy.'

'Bianca! You can't marry just to please Papa. Unless you really love Oswald, that is?'

'D'you really think we have a choice? Papa's only left you alone so far because Henry so obviously has his sights on you. I was always supposed to have the husband with a title because I'm the eldest girl, but it doesn't really make much difference, not as far as Papa is concerned, not so long as we all marry into money. Cordelia will be next, after you. He's picked out the wealthiest husbands he could find for us, from the day we could walk. Apart from Kate, of course.'

'Bianca—'

'You can do as you please, but at least I'm escaping this place. Papa thought it was alright for *him* to marry Alma even though she hasn't any money. That meant it was always going to be you and me and Cordelia who were going to restore Arden's fortunes. You know that all he cares about is the house and the gardens, and being rich again so he can pass it on to Will, and then everyone will remember him as clever and terribly important. Wake up, Rosalind! None of us have any money of our own – we're totally dependent on Papa for absolutely everything, and it will be the same with Will, when he takes over. If I marry Oswald I'll have a home and plenty of money, and I can arrange things as I wish.'

With that, Bianca strode off, back towards the shade under the trees, to where the source of her salvation was waiting.

Chapter Three

As the day wore on, the heat grew ever more stifling. Dinner that evening, under the vast high-vaulted ceiling, supposed to have once formed part of a Medieval banqueting hall, was a stiff affair. The pinkish flagstones, worn into undulating grooves and dents by generations of Ardens, gave off a welcome coolness rising from underfoot. All the same, unfinished arguments rumbled beneath the surface, as they often did by the end of the day, with appearances to be maintained in front of Will's friend, who had been given the rare honour of being invited to stay the night.

Or perhaps not such an honour, thought Rosalind, wincing in sympathy. It was rather that Papa didn't consider a manufacturer's son to move in high enough circles to notice the dilapidated state of Arden House. At least Guy had been given the one remaining guest bedroom still in possession of windows that opened without sticking, and lacking in sufficient damp to mar the ornate Victorian wallpaper.

With Papa's eagle eye on all of them, she did her best not to show she was following the male discussions of worldly matters. But with Guy seated opposite, she couldn't help her eyes wandering now and again towards him, despite the darkening of her father's face whenever he spotted her attention on the unattached young man in their midst.

The family had so few visitors these days, she'd forgotten how good it felt to have a stranger within the tight web of the Arden clan. And Guy brought with him a new way of looking of things, a quiet confidence in his own opinions, without the bluster of Will or Papa. His presence stirred up the restlessness she had once known as a child, a longing to traverse the wide oceans and snow-topped mountains she had only known in books, or to step into the painted scenery of the Brierley Village Players as they transported their audiences to the exotic surroundings of Venice and Bohemia, along with the terrifying witches' heath in *Macbeth*.

She glanced towards Bianca, who after the triumph of finally being able to announce as they sat down that she was engaged to become Mrs Oswald Gorwell before the year was out, was making no attempt to join the conversation around her, or conceal that she was waiting to leave the table at the earliest opportunity.

Rosalind couldn't help a brief twinge of envy at the ease with which her sister had escaped, in the only way open to her, and with the obvious approval of their father. Bianca was right, she could now look forward to being the mistress of a comfortable home, and the fulfilment of a family. Although that did include Oswald Gorwell for the rest of her days; Rosalind's envy vanished.

After dinner, Jamie quietly disappeared, as he often did when Papa wasn't looking, while Will announced he was taking Guy on an evening stroll to view the beauties of the countryside.

'The inside of the White Hart, more like,' said Cordelia,

settling down to finish sewing a costume for the next production of the Brierley Village Players, studiously ignoring their stepmother's hesitant suggestion that now might be a good time to help her start embroidering the new tablecloth.

Kate was nowhere to be seen. Rosalind suspected she'd shot off towards the fields adjoining the walled garden, to join Jamie in excavating the rumoured site of an ancient Roman villa. Kate, who shared Jamie's passion for investigating the ancient features of the landscape, had first been set on excavating the burial mound where, the gossips of Brierley-in-Arden had whispered for generations, there was buried treasure.

Jamie, who had heard enough of Grandfather's stories to be sceptical, had been firmly for the villa, where at least real ancient structures had been previously found, along with the coins and pieces of pottery turned up to the surface by each year's ploughing. Rosalind grinned. After all the arguments, the two of them had finally settled to do the villa first, then the burial mound.

Rosalind hastily took advantage of her stepmother's concentration on a particularly intricate bunch of forget-me-nots to slip out and make her way down to the cellar, set up by Will as a darkroom several years ago, when photography had briefly become his passion. Alongside the more basic sunlight enlarger in its wooden box, he had even installed a small generator to run a more modern electric version to produce the final prints. Her brother might have rapidly lost interest in mastering the intricate skill of balancing chemicals and timing, while manipulating light to create the final black and white printed version, then waiting for it to dry before being certain of the final result, but it was a process Rosalind found endlessly fascinating.

This afternoon's picture of the scene beneath the trees

had been the last on her roll of film, carefully developed before dinner, its length hung up to dry like a celluloid ribbon, ready for printing. Her little store of photographic paper was nearly finished. She peered at the negatives, looking for the most promising. That was the thing, you never knew until it was printed whether the picture was sharp enough, or if someone had moved too quickly for the available light, leaving their face a blur. The table beneath the trees definitely looked the most successful.

She fiddled with the enlarger, until she was confident the image was in focus, trimming it slightly to her satisfaction, then counting beneath her breath as the bulb did its work.

Her stomach curled into the familiar knot, part nerves, part excitement. She placed the exposed paper into the developing tray, coughing slightly at the chemicals catching the back of her throat. Slowly, the image began to appear, first splodges, resolving themselves into darkness, followed by the finer lines and the more subtle shading of grey. She knew, even before she had washed it several times to halt the development, that it was her most successful attempt yet. As the print dried sufficiently to take out into the light, she could see it was just as she had imagined it in her mind's eye, conjuring up a thousand teas in the garden on summer afternoons.

It wasn't often she was completely satisfied with her pictures, especially as the money she sneaked from her limited allowance for gloves and shoes was not nearly enough to allow her to keep on experimenting until she manipulated the image on paper to an absolute state of perfection. But this, she knew immediately, was one of those rare happy accidents that held the timeless quality of Grandfather's dreams.

She didn't want it hidden away with the rest, to gather dust, forgotten. It wasn't exactly history, but perhaps Miss Parsons, the village schoolmistress who had set up a small museum about the history of Brierley-in-Arden, might like the image to adorn the walls? After all, one day, Rosalind thought – the unease that had lingered all afternoon returning – it would be history. All that was left of people, and of days, long gone.

Shivering slightly, she returned the print to the darkroom to dry fully, and clambered back up the steep stairs back into the main part of the house. Opening a side door, she stepped out into the garden, breathing in deep the evening scents of lavender and tea roses, mingled with the distant hint of mown grass and summer meadows, until the vinegary sharpness of the developing chemicals were banished from her eyes and her hair, and the acid taste from her mouth. The light was beginning to fade, muted purples streaked with slivers of crimson hung over the horizon in all directions, darkening at the edges as day slid towards night.

She could not bear to return to the confines of the drawing room. Instead, she took the pathway alongside the walls of the kitchen garden, leading towards the wide stretch of field down to the village. An owl called from the direction of the burial mound, answered by another in woodlands far away. Bats flitted above her head, swerving and diving for the clouds of insects hanging in the still air. From the direction of Brierley-in-Arden came the woody scent of cooking fires, accompanied by laughter, as the inhabitants sat out late into the evening to enjoy the precious warmth.

'*Oh Danny boy,*' came a tuneful whistle from one of the paths through the field leading towards the hamlets and isolated farmsteads spread out of the far side of the Arden estate.

This, no camera could ever capture. Rosalind drew it all in, holding the scene inside her, suffused with the strange sense of fragility she had felt so strongly that afternoon. It was only natural, she scolded herself, given the boys' talk of a war that might never happen, and the more immediate breaking up of the world she had always known by Bianca's engagement to Oswald Gorwell. All the more so, because that raised the inescapable question of her own future. Bianca had warned her that with his eldest daughter settled, Papa could now turn his energies to making certain she accepted Henry Luscombe. Or rather his vast aristocratic wealth, which would compensate for the urgent necessity of accepting the manufacturing riches of Mr Gorwell.

She turned back towards the house, now a shadow against the first shimmering emergence of stars, with only a faint glow between the curtains of one of the upstairs rooms signalling that it was inhabited at all. Rosalind pulled the soft wool of her Fair Isle cardigan around her. She loved Arden, and all that it contained. She could not bear the thought of it continuing to crumble away until it was beyond saving, to be lost forever. On the other hand, her life was just beginning. She'd no wish to sacrifice her own dreams of love and happiness for Papa's vision of returning the estate to its former grandeur. And Papa was not the kind of man to give up. Like Bianca, she had very few options, but without any Oswald Gorwell striding pompously to her rescue.

'*Get thee to a nunnery*,' she muttered to herself, wryly.

'You gave me a fright!' She looked up to find Kate trudging towards her through the dusk, closely followed by Jamie. 'I thought for a minute the bull had got out again. It's so narrow here, it would have had to be the garden wall if it had been Malvolio on the rampage again.'

Rosalind laughed. 'Well?' she demanded, 'did you find anything?'

'Tiles.' Jamie was breathless but triumphant.

'Tiles.'

'Or possibly a mosaic, it's hard to tell in this light.'

'We got down quite deep this time. It could be floor,' said Kate, her voice echoing Jamie's excitement. 'It could even be Roman.'

'Bet it's just an old barn,' said Will arriving behind them.

'Take no notice, Jamie,' said Kate. 'Will never talks sense when he's had too many beers in the White Hart.'

'Rubbish,' said Will, pushing past them, stumbling slightly on the rough ground.

'Just don't let Papa catch you,' called Kate, as he rushed ahead, vanishing into the gloom.

As Rosalind turned to follow Jamie and Kate, who were walking towards the house in Will's wake, absorbed in discussion of their find, she found Guy falling into step beside her.

'Hello again,' she said, feeling suddenly and inexplicably shy. 'I take it Will has been showing you the village.'

'It's very pretty,' he said, in careful tones.

'It could be, you mean, if the windowsills of the cottages weren't rotting and the streets nothing more than mud when it rains?'

'I've seen worse.'

'I suppose.' He was being tactful, she could feel it. She dreaded to consider what he really thought of the Ardens with their swathes of land and their ancient manor house allowing their tenants to live in such squalid conditions, despite the householders doing their best to patch crumbling roofs and keep their gardens neat, and fill in the worst of the potholes when they could.

The two walked for a few minutes in silence, until the path opened out, allowing them to walk side by side.

Rosalind cleared her throat. 'You don't really think there will be another war, do you, Mr Thompson?'

29

'I hope not.'

'But you're afraid there may be.'

'I wish I could believe Hitler is bluffing, like all bullies do. But after his annexation of Austria in March...' Guy paused for a minute. 'I'm afraid the talk among the refugees in Dad's factory is that the Nazis mean it, and if it does happen, it's bound to be as messy as the last war and drag out just as long.'

'Several years, you mean?'

A chill crawled inside her scalp. A single year stretched out like a whole lifetime. Even last Christmas felt centuries ago. A war might last forever, or at least until her youth had gone. She had a sudden fear she might never get to live her life at all. It made her want to grasp everything now, while she could, catching at the shimmering brilliance of vanishing dreams.

They had nearly reached the house. The curtains in a downstairs room had been opened, allowing lamplight to streak across the grass. The photograph of Alma and Bianca sitting under the trees already belonged to the past, when life, for all its petty irritations, had been secure. Now, even Arden House felt as fragile as the spider's web clinging to the edges of the formalised swirl of Tudor roses of the gate allowing them into the gardens.

'Don't mind me,' said Guy, sounding a little guilty. 'I've been spending too much of my time with refugees lately. It still might not touch us here.'

'But it will, won't it?' She stopped in her tracks, trying to make out the expression on his face in the dusk.

The last of the light shone a luminous reflection in his eyes as they met hers. 'I've tried to hope for so long,' he returned, his voice losing all formality, all its previous consciousness of the social distance between them gone.

'There's so much I want to see, so much I want to do.' He gave a wry laugh. 'How utterly selfish that sounds.'

'No, it doesn't. It's only natural. I feel the same. I'm sure your refugees felt that as well. All of us only have one life, I can't bear the thought of it being obliterated on the whim of some madman. It feels so unfair. There, that's selfish too.'

There was a moment's silence. It had grown very still under the beech trees overhanging the little gate. She could barely make out the shadow of his features, but she could feel his warmth in the night air, and how close he was standing. There was a tightening in her chest, her limbs felt as if they were spiralling away into oblivion. The entire world, all of time, was held, like a perfect glowing orb, within the darkness beneath the branches. She did her best not to betray her body's sudden trembling.

Guy cleared his throat. 'I'll always be glad I accepted Will's invitation.'

'So will I,' she returned, moving so close she could feel the roughness of his jacket through the thin material of her dress. It felt daring, brazen even, to be quite so bold. Women who were brazen came to bad ends. But at this moment, not all the warnings in the universe could make her care. 'I hope you'll return.'

'It might not be for a while.'

'Oh.' She took a step back, hurt and bewilderment shooting through her. Had she misunderstood his meaning? Or had he remembered himself after all, and Papa, at dinner, fixing him with that stare, as if suspecting Will was being fooled by a ruffian with eyes firmly on the remaining family silver.

'I mean, I'm being sent to oversee my father's factory in Birmingham,' Guy explained hastily. 'Dad doesn't approve that that I've chosen to train as an architect, even if it is just

31

evening classes and he's hoping this might change my mind.'

'So that's why Will was talking to you about plumbing.'

He laughed, the tension between them easing. 'I'm afraid so.' He was silent for a moment. 'Dad's only trying to protect me. He believes people like us can't ever be more than we are now, and I'll never be accepted in high society, the kind I'd need to employ me to make my name as an architect. He's afraid my ambition will only lead to heartache.'

'But Will wants to use you here. And yes, I know it's because he thinks he won't have to pay you much, but he has plenty of far richer friends. That's a start, surely?'

He gave a low chuckle. 'You don't miss much. To be honest, that's what I'm hoping.'

Rosalind winced at the wryness of his tone. It couldn't have been easy for him to swallow his pride and agree to being exploited by Will's desire for personal aggrandisement on the cheap. Did she have that kind of fire to debase herself to achieve a higher goal? Within the safe surroundings of Arden House she'd never been tested.

She found Guy was still watching her. 'And you?'

'Me?'

'I couldn't help noticing the camera this afternoon, and Jamie said you're a fine photographer.'

'Just an amateur,' she replied gloomily.

'As I am an architect.'

'But you have ambition.'

'And you don't?'

'I...' She stopped. How did he know? They had spoken so little, how on earth had he managed to uncover secret deep in her heart, the secret she had told no one, not even Jamie, that one day she might even be able to make a living from her photographs. The secret she barely admitted to herself. 'What makes you think I have ambition?'

'I can see your passion,' he replied. She sensed the smile in his voice. 'I have a feeling passion recognises passion, wherever it's found.'

'Yes,' she replied slowly. 'I agree. But—'

'Hurry up, will you!' hissed Will, from near the house. 'Stop dawdling. Papa's on the prowl, if he catches us he'll find out we've been down to the pub and there will be all hell to pay.'

In the shadow beneath the branches, Rosalind felt the warmth of Guy's hand on hers. She returned the pressure, releasing it as they emerged onto the lawn.

Chapter Four

Once safely back inside, her companions quickly disappeared. Rosalind listened to their retreating footsteps, followed by the creak of ancient floorboards as they reached the bedrooms, sensing the darkness of the house settle around her.

Above, at the first landing of the mahogany staircase, a cracked Tiffany lamp in shades of green and blue illuminated the huge stained-glass window, the only serious alteration their grandfather had made to the Tudor fabric of the house before handing on the responsibility to Papa. The window had been commissioned from a follower of the pre-Raphaelite brotherhood and displayed scenes from Grandfather's beloved Shakespeare. The oval in the centre showing the magician Prospero, staff raised, commanding the world, surrounded by smaller panes of the fairies from *A Midsummer Night's Dream*, a pensive Viola from *Twelfth Night* and the balcony scene from *Romeo and Juliet*.

The window had been a source of wonder when they had been little, promising a world of fantastical stories where

all things were possible. Now, as the edges outside the
central glow faded into blackness, she had an uneasy sense of
the childhood promise of her life having been an illusion.
She could not banish from her mind Papa's suspicion at the
very presence of a young man so clearly lacking in Henry
Luscombe's more obvious pecuniary charms.

The distant creak of footsteps, combined with the faint
scratching of mice behind the panelling, became oppressive.
She could not breathe. The darkness held her prisoner,
draining the life from her.

Never. She shot outside, drinking in the cooling air, with
its lingering fragrance of honeysuckle and the first hint of
dew, fresh around her feet.

The cloud had cleared, leaving the sky closely speckled
with stars between the overreaching arc of the Milky Way,
lending the faintest illumination to the surrounding countryside. In the far distance, the lights of a motor vehicle moved,
vanishing now and again between hedges. Otherwise, the
fields and farmhouses were in darkness. Even Brierley-in-
Arden had no light to show.

She rounded the house, her nerves settling at last, to find
the French windows to the library standing open, curtains
swaying pale in the darkness. The rich scent of cigar smoke
met her.

'Rosalind?' The shadow seated on the steps leading
down from the French windows to the lawn stirred as she
attempted to retreat as soundlessly as possible. 'Rosalind, is
that you?'

'Yes, Papa. My room was too hot,' she improvised hastily.
'I came out for some fresh air.'

'Then spare a thought for Lucy, who sleeps right beneath
the eaves,' he returned with a grunt. 'At least you benefit

from a large room, with more than a single casement window.'

'I wasn't complaining.' *Why was it that whatever she said always came out in a way that was bound to offend him?* 'I'm very grateful for my room. It wasn't just that, it was also something Will and his friend were talking about earlier this afternoon.' Papa might have shut himself away in the country, but he still kept up correspondence with friends in London – members of parliament, even – and avidly read the newspaper each morning. She had to ask. 'About the possibility of another war.'

'Young fools. They should know better than to discuss such things in front of you. It won't happen. Don't distress yourself.'

'Won't it?'

He indicated the step next to him. 'You're not to concern yourself, you've plenty here to protect you.'

She took the seat, still holding a faint hint of warmth from the evening sun. His cigar glowed briefly, before he stubbed it out on the adjoining step.

'Please don't, not on my account.'

'Dreadful things,' he replied. 'I don't know why they bother importing them from halfway around the world just to choke us. Cuba can keep them.' He lifted a glass from the step next to him. 'Give me a good Cognac any day.'

'Yes, Papa.' She relaxed a little. It wasn't often that their father was in such a mellow mood. She wished she dared reach out and touch him, to have his physical reassurance that, whatever might happen in the great wide world beyond Arden's gates, within its walls they would always remain safe. Her heart opened up with a deep longing and the feeling that, despite his tempers and demands, there was a bond of love between them that could not be broken.

'He's no good, you know.'

'Papa?'

'Young Thompson. The sooner you put him out of your mind the better.'

Heat shot through her body. Had he seen them? Had he watched the way she and Guy had lingered by the gate? She had a sudden dread of not being allowed outside the house at all without a maid to chaperone her until Alma could marry her off to the first man prepared to take the responsibility off Papa's hands, whatever the state of his bank balance. 'I'm not sure—'

'I saw the way he was looking at you at dinner.'

She breathed an inward sigh of relief. If Papa was going to accuse her of disgracing the family honour, he'd have launched into it by now.

'He seems a pleasant young man,' she said mildly.

'That's as may be, but he has no prospects. Thompson & Son is, to all intents and purposes, bankrupt. Young Thompson might manage to turn its fortunes around, but that could take years. He won't be in a position to support a wife for a decade or more. And by then, who knows what might have happened? So do as you're told and don't give him another thought.'

He could instruct her all he liked, her mind was still her own. 'Yes, Papa.' She glimpsed his head turn, sensing the suspicious glance towards her meekness.

'I'm thinking of what's best. You know so little of the world. I don't want you to be taken advantage of.'

'I can learn.' She braced herself for the inevitable stricture about a woman being incapable of knowing her own mind and liable to be led astray by the first man who looked at her.

Instead, he remained a while in pre-occupied silence. 'I

will not allow the Arden estate to fail,' he said at last. 'That was my duty set out for me when I took over the custody of the estate, just as my father had taken it over from his. Generation after generation, keeping this house and the grounds safe, passed on from father to son, just as it should be, the Arden name forever kept alive.' He drained his glass. 'I won't have that endangered and the grounds parcelled up and sold off. Arden will be restored, and passed on intact to Will when the time comes. He's a fine young man is Will, the best of his generation. The estate will be safe in his hands.'

'Surely there are ways—'

'So put young Thompson out of your mind. Gorwell is suggesting the wedding to Bianca should take place at his mother's house in Bayswater. It seems to me an excellent opportunity. Henry Luscombe will be there, naturally, and Gorwell will be able to introduce your sisters to a far wider society than can be found in Stratford.'

A far *richer* society, was what he meant – and men who had inherited wealth beyond imagining and were now eager to use it to associate themselves one of the oldest families in the land. The Ardens' wealth might have slipped through their fingers over the past century, but they still possessed a family tree stretching back before Shakespeare's time, with a touch of royalty thrown in. It was a truth universally acknowledged (at least amongst her father's connections) that having an illegitimate son of King Henry VIII as part of the bloodline was better than no royal connection at all.

Rosalind returned inside, leaving him sitting in the starlight, empty glass in his hand, staring across the lawns towards the lake. Just as Grandfather had once done, completely absorbed in his dreams.

'Darling, there you are.' She found her stepmother on the landing, candlestick in hand. 'I was getting frantic.'

'I'm sorry, I was talking to Papa. I forgot the time.'

'At least you're safe.' Alma was already shooing her upstairs, with an anxious glance towards where her husband had not moved.

As she reached her room, Rosalind glanced back. Alma had closed the door to her own apartments, leaving the long corridor in darkness. Around her, the house settled into its night-time noises of scuttling in the wainscot and the movement of rafters. The faint star-sheen caught the ancient wood of the panelling with an eerie, timeless glow. A bat flitted across the window, followed by the call of owls in the woods. Something shrieked briefly in the distance, then was gone.

She wasn't sure she believed in ghosts, but tonight she could feel the generations of Ardens who had lived and died here, absorbed into the very fabric of the building, closing in around her. All those who had dreamed and whose dreams had faded into nothing, as the world turned relentlessly on its axis. *Out, brief candle,* indeed.

'Well, I'm not being snuffed out, not for anybody,' she muttered defiantly to herself, stepping inside the familiar security of her room and closing the door behind her.

Chapter Five

Will and Guy left early the next morning, long before breakfast. Rosalind heard the Ford roar into the distance, before most of the household was stirring, and jumped out of bed, charged with a restlessness like never before.

The light had a pure, just-after-dawn delicacy, promising the slanting beams of the first sun that created the most striking of effects on paper. Rosalind hastily pulled on her favourite plaid skirt, with enough give in its pleats to allow for stomping over the roughest ground, and its variations of dark green capable of hiding a multitude of grass stains. Covering her blouse with the matching woollen jacket, which had once been elegant, but was now worn into comforting softness with use, she grabbed her camera and tripod and hurried as silently as she could down the mahogany stairs. She sped through the kitchens, where Cook was berating yawning and drowsy-eyed maids into action, only just missing trampling over Lucy, who was retrieving a basket of vegetables left outside the door by the gardeners.

'Sorry!' mouthed Rosalind, hurtling past. Her father was

an early riser, but he generally remained immersed in a book before breakfast was called, and his rooms faced the rolling patchwork of fields and farms, divided by hedgerows and the distant hint of church towers on the far side of the Arden estate.

It was her stepmother's rooms that overlooked the garden and the steeple of Brierley-in-Arden, half hidden in its hollow, but Alma was too nervous of Papa's unpredictable rages to raise an uncomfortable subject so early – even that of one of her unruly stepdaughters wandering off unaccompanied. Papa had always delegated control of the female side of the household to his young wife, seemingly oblivious to the fact that, from the start, she had no control at all. It had given them a special kind of freedom, Rosalind was uncomfortably aware, which all four had exploited in one way or another, leaving poor Alma to take the blame.

As she reached the walled garden, and a safe distance from the house, Rosalind slowed. The garden door was open, allowing the sounds of spades, interspersed with voices, to echo from within, accompanied by a thin line of smoke. Mr Gloster, who had been head gardener since before she was born, had a habit of brewing good strong tea in the mornings in a battered old Kelly kettle, over a fire built from last year's prunings.

She slipped past the door and round the outside of the walls, until she reached the fields that stretched down towards the village. A large patch of ground had been cleared of meadow, revealing bare earth, from which boulders and the straight line of an ancient wall erupted, between deeper hollows dug into the ground. From the deepest pit there came the sound of scraping.

'I thought you'd be here,' she said, as she reached the edge of the excavation. 'You didn't go with the others, then?"

Jamie looked up from delicately removing earth from a small object with what looked like a paintbrush. 'They're meeting up with Henry Luscombe at Church Stretton to walk the Long Mynd.'

'I thought Will said you were going to Wales, to climb Snowdon?'

'That was the plan, but Henry sent a telegram yesterday evening suggesting we walk the Long Mynd first and then go on to Wales. He's got friends staying with him at Luscombe Hall for the summer. I've met most of them. They all want to be colonels in the army or run vast estates in Hampshire and marry some cousin of the King or the Russian royal family. Believe me, their conversation is very tedious.'

'Even after dinner?'

He coloured slightly. 'I don't particularly like that side of their discussions either... not that I'm a prude,' he added hastily, 'but they have less respect for their women than they do their racehorses. And no consideration at all for those they wouldn't dream of marrying. It's as if they don't see women as human at all.'

'Then I'm very glad you do.'

'The trouble is, Will feels he has to join in, and to be honest, I don't much like that side of him. Guy's different. Will likes him because he's got a reputation as being totally brilliant as an architect, even though he's not qualified yet, and he's got a real knack of finding ingenious solutions. Will wants him to do all kinds of things at Arden House. To be honest, I suspect that's why Guy accepted the invitation.' He nodded to a deeper hollow in the ground. 'I'd rather get on with this. Now I can see them in the light, I'm pretty sure it's a mosaic.'

'So it could be the remains of a Roman villa under the field.'

'Don't get your hopes up,' he replied.

'Oh ye of little faith!' called Kate, arriving breathlessly, lugging a knapsack bursting with trowels and a large sketch-book over one shoulder. 'There could be a whole Roman village under there as well, like the ruins found at Pompeii.'

'Don't,' exclaimed Jamie. 'You'll have half the village prospecting for gold coins up here, destroying the archaeology.'

Kate laughed, her face relaxing as it rarely did within the confines of the house. 'They're not that daft. If there were coins, someone would have found something by now. Most of the old men have worked the land since they could walk – they must know every inch of the place.'

'At least Miss Parsons will be pleased,' said Jamie. 'If there's a Roman villa, her museum will have the best exhibits in the country.' He looked down at the patch of tiny tiles forming themselves into a dusky blue coil of a shell. 'Strange to think there were people once walking on this floor, looking out on the very same countryside we're looking at now. Well, apart from the church.'

'And cars,' added Kate, flinging her bag onto the ground and jumping down next to him. 'You were right about it being a pattern.' She reached for her trowel and a paintbrush, to start the painstaking work of uncovering the remainder of the shell and the intriguing suggestion of a fish's tail. 'It's odd to think of all the stories beneath our feet, just waiting to be uncovered. Although I'm disappointed we haven't found human bones. I quite fancy sketching a human skull.'

'Well, I hope we don't find any such thing,' said Jamie, with a shudder.

As the two settled down to work in earnest, ready to make the most of the settled spell of weather and their father's summer preoccupation with the ordering of the gardens, Rosalind wandered further along the field, following the ancient pathways that crisscrossed Arden land, forging traditional routes between the village and the surrounding farms.

She set up her camera and waited until the clouds parted a little, allowing the slanting morning light to stream across the landscape, illuminating the dew-lined grasses in crystalline brilliance. A click of the shutter, and it was captured. She had caught the atmosphere of the moment, she could feel it. Her exposure and focus were right, and nature would do the rest. It would be one of those landscape photographs that had a touch of magic about them, wiping out the disappointment of the dull and out-of-focus attempts she had made while learning the camera's ways, and how it differed from the sophistication of the human eye, with its boundless ability to focus on specific aspects amidst an entire vista of green. A quiet exhilaration shot through her, as it always did when she knew she had succeeded in her mission.

Ambition. Yes, Guy was right. She held an ambition to create the most beautiful, the most startling, photographs within her power. She had a dream of packing her camera in her rucksack and making her way across Europe, maybe even beyond, capturing great mountains, ruins from ancient civilisations, and dusty villages untouched by time. Not that she was likely to get further than Stratford, if Herr Hitler had his way.

As she straightened up, her mind travelled back to under the trees by the little gate, to Guy's warmth next to hers, his breath so close she could draw it in and make it an eternal part of herself. That was what she wanted, she acknowledged. That warmth, that connection, that sense of a conversation flowing between them that would only deepen.

Rosalind pulled her jacket around her. She wanted to

live her life, not confined within the cage of a mansion, however gilded, however fine the grounds. She wanted to grow old, grow wise, to have eyes that had seen the world, skin wrinkled by the touch of sunlight and storms, and the violence of emotion. Of the few men she had met in the seclusion of her life in Arden House, Guy was the only one who gave her a sense such a life might be possible. Whatever Papa's objections, she wanted to get to know him more.

The sun was strengthening. They would soon be expected at the breakfast table, a summons that could not be disobeyed. Rosalind made her way back to the excavation, where Jamie and Kate were already abandoning their trowels and brushes, ready to return once the morning ritual was over.

'Did you find more of the mosaic?'

'It looks as if there may be quite a bit of it there,' said Jamie. 'It could even be an entire floor. It seems to be a water theme.'

'I still think that tail could be a depiction of Poseidon rather than a mermaid,' put in Kate. 'It would be just the thing for the god of the sea.'

'We'll soon find out,' replied Jamie. He smiled. 'And Kate found a brooch.'

'A brooch?'

'More like a pin of some kind, to hold up a dress or a cloak.' Kate fished inside her pocket, bringing out a small object wrapped in a slightly grubby handkerchief. 'It needs proper cleaning before I can sketch it, but it looks as if it might be Romano-British. Which could mean it was a local family who lived in the villa, rather than part of an occupying force. I like that idea. Especially as they must have been rich to build anything quite so grand.'

'You mean, not quite as oppressed,' said Jamie.

'Maybe self-made, even very important,' retorted Kate, returning the brooch to her pocket. 'After all, it was the Roman army that left in the end, and everyone here carried on perfectly well without them.' She snorted. 'They can look down their noses at me all they like, but I bet half the families round here are as Italian as they are Anglo-Saxon. And in the village, too. And it's the mix that makes them English.'

'That's true,' said Jamie, a wistful tone to his voice. 'This is the kind of place that always survives, no matter what happens.'

'Because it's real,' replied Kate. 'Not like all those stuffy old politicians in the newspapers, who think ordinary people don't matter and said women were too stupid to vote.'

'Or were more likely to vote for the other side,' said Jamie. 'Reading between the lines, I'd say that was their real objection.'

Kate giggled. 'You're sharper than you let on, Jamie dear. I wish you were going to inherit Arden instead of Will. He thinks no one else counts unless they're just like him.'

'I'm glad I'm not the one to inherit,' replied Jamie, with a shudder. 'I can't think of anything worse than spending my days chasing up rents from people who can barely afford to pay, for cottages I can't properly maintain, and wondering which bit of land I might have to sacrifice next so I can pass on the estate, in just the way it has always been, so as not to let down the family name.'

'I can't see family wealth is ever really free,' said Rosalind wincing as she remembered Guy's tactful lack of comment on the all-too-visible poverty of Brierley-in-Arden. When she helped Alma with her charitable work in the village, they took baskets of food to cottages where there was no money at all.

It always made her deeply ashamed that Papa and Will

were happy to take rent for places where the rain dripped in through the roof, leaving every surface with a sheen of damp and a pervading stench of mould. She'd heard them speaking of their tenants as if it were their laziness and lack of moral fibre that prevented them from keeping their home clean and their children free from constant colds, and worse, rather than the poor wages offered to agricultural workers and few opportunities for anything else. Little wonder that the younger villagers who could were drifting to the factories of Birmingham and Coventry, leaving a little less of Brierley-in-Arden each year.

'Like Bianca marrying Oswald Gorwell,' added Kate, gloomily. 'The trouble is, he sees eye-to-eye with Will, as well as being fearsomely rich. The two of them already get on like a house on fire. I can see them making mincemeat of the rest of us, once Papa is gone, just so Will can play lord of the manor in style.'

'I'm afraid Papa doesn't think I'm much to be proud of next to Will,' sighed Jamie, looking up at the house.

Kate frowned. 'Papa isn't still trying to tell you to study classics rather than archaeology, is he?'

'He's made it clear he'd rather I took up a place at Oxford, like Will, after Bianca is safely married, instead of studying with the Archaeology Department at Birmingham University. He thinks it would lead to better prospects, like being a diplomat.' He grinned wryly at Kate. 'Or a politician.'

'You can't! Jamie, you'd hate it, all that public speaking and jostling for position and toeing the party line.'

'Don't worry, I've no hankering after either.'

'So you'll still go to Birmingham University next year?' said Rosalind.

'I hope so.' Jamie sounded distracted. 'It's taken me long enough to get him to even think about it. I'll be years older than most of the other students. Papa says he doesn't want a professor who spends his life grubbing in the earth for a son. What he means is he'd be too embarrassed to introduce me as an academic rather than a general. He's quite convinced I'll inherit Grandfather's obsessiveness and become an embarrassment to the family.'

'Surely it doesn't matter what Papa thinks,' said Rosalind. 'You aren't a bit like Will, or Grandfather. Papa is stubborn, but he's not completely unreasonable.'

'Isn't he?' Jamie's eyes were travelling across the roof, bowed with age and soon in need of replacing, along with the rotting window frames, now too far gone to be disguised with paint. 'The thing is, it's not just that. I hate it when he thinks I'm not the kind of son I ought to be.' He shook himself. 'I shall just have to find a way to prove him otherwise.'

There was nothing more to say. From inside the house there came the gong summoning the family to breakfast. They had only just arrived in time. As they hastily hung coats and hats on the coat stand in the hallway, Rosalind slipped her camera and tripod behind the forest of umbrellas at its base, before following the others inside.

Chapter Six

A few days later, Rosalind set off with her sisters to take the brooch Kate had uncovered to Miss Parsons' little museum next to the village hall, at the centre of Brierley-in-Arden. Kate had carefully cleaned the fragile object, to reveal a delicately enamelled creature that looked as if it might have been intended to represent some kind of dragon, which she had sketched in meticulous detail from all angles.

'Well, I never,' exclaimed Miss Parsons, as she took the brooch reverently into her hands. 'No one's found anything quite as intricate as this, or so complete. Look, and it's even still got the pin to fasten it. I defy even the British Museum in London to have acquired such a beautiful find and this one most definitely belongs to Brierley.'

'You'll consider exhibiting it, then?' said Kate.

'It will take pride of place, and your drawings too – they will allow visitors to see how beautifully it is made at the back, as well as the front. In fact, I may well ask Mr Clarke if he'll make me a new display case, so the brooch and the drawing can be exhibited all on their own.'

'Really?' Kate coloured with pleasure.

'Of course, my dear. It's not every day anything so ancient and so beautiful is found. It's a miracle it survived, and that it was found by someone who took such care it was extracted without any damage, and has recorded it in such detail from every angle. You should be very proud.'

'Jamie's the one who knows all about excavating and is going to study at university,' said Kate.

'That doesn't mean you shouldn't continue doing it as well,' replied Miss Parsons, green-grey eyes as piercing as could be. 'You don't have to be a professor, or even a student, to follow a passion.'

Miss Parsons was a tall, wiry woman in her late fifties, with a faint hint of grey at the temples, but the rest of her hair had an abundant chestnut sheen and was continually escaping from the bun at the back of her head. As head-mistress of Brierley school, she was sufficiently respected for any minor eccentricities to be overlooked, such as rumours of her having travelled to far-flung places in her youth, in pursuit of her passion for history. Rosalind could just imagine her as one of those indomitable Victorian ladies, sailing through danger with an imperious manner and the confidence of being untouchable.

Rosalind had always rather envied the village school-children, as, from what she could see, Miss Parsons was a good deal more inspiring than Miss Matthams, the governess Papa had briefly hired to give his daughters sufficient accomplishments to be worthy companions to their future husbands, without becoming too intellectually endowed to scare them off.

Miss Matthams had lasted less than a year before admitting defeat, leaving Rosalind to continue ruining her hands with photographic chemicals, Cordelia to creating costumes

for the village production of *A Midsummer Night's Dream*
(which, like all theatricals, declared Miss Matthams, was
bound to slide into darkest immorality), and Kate to sit in the
mud with her sketchbook, undeterred by the damage
wreaked on her complexion by rain or frost.

'Uncontrolled and uncontrollable,' Miss Matthams had
announced to Alma, as she swept out of the front door with
dignity, suitcase in hand. 'I feel sorry for you, Mrs Arden. I
foresee a dismal future for all of them, I really do.'

It was a comment Alma had never confessed to her
husband, instead murmuring that Miss Matthams had been
suddenly called away to nurse a sick relative. A governess
was an experiment that had never been repeated, and left
Alma clearly convinced that controlling her stepdaughters
was quite beyond her.

Kate smiled. 'Very well. Then I'll make sure I find more.'

'I'm glad to hear it.' Miss Parsons smoothed down her
dress. 'Now then, while you're all here, all of you together,
there's something I've been keeping for you. From your
mother.'

'Our mother?' Rosalind stared. 'You mean, our real
mother?'

'Yes, indeed.'

Rosalind exchanged glances with Cordelia. They had
both been too young to have any clear memory of their
mother. Sometimes, when there was a particular hint of
spring in the air, and wild garlic sprawled through the woodlands, Rosalind felt sure she remembered the pressure of
warm arms holding her tight. Of being swung up, high,
against blue sky and apple blossom, amidst laughter and the
hum of bees. Bianca always swore she had no memory at all,
growing cross and tearful if Rosalind tried to ask. Jamie spoke
of their mother sometimes, haltingly, as if, even now, he

could not bear to recall the enormity of her loss, while Will's face shut down at the mere mention of her having existed at all, inevitably followed by being unpardonably rude to poor Alma.

Miss Parsons sighed. 'She trusted me to keep something safe for when the time came.'

Cordelia's eyes shone with excitement, edged with tears, while Kate turned away, as if suddenly absorbed in an inspection of the collection of flint arrowheads displayed in the nearest cabinet.

'It was her wish, when she knew she might not live. She worried about what might happen to you, especially...' She came to a tactful halt.

'As she knew Papa would most likely marry again?' put in Rosalind.

'Your stepmother is a good woman, don't get me wrong.' Miss Parsons coughed. 'To be perfectly frank, my dears, your father is not always the best judge of character, particularly where feminine flattery is involved, and as the heir to Arden, he was still quite a catch in those days. It could have been so much worse.

'In any case, Celia asked that I keep them safe, until your wedding days, or when you turned twenty-one, whichever came the sooner. But Bianca will be married before the summer is out, and with all this talk of another war in Europe, and the future so very uncertain... Well, I've been mulling things over, and it seems to me you should have them now, or you might never have the chance to have them at all.'

'And the boys, too?' asked Cordelia.

'No. These are just for you. William will inherit Arden, and your father will make sure Jamie is well provided for. Your mother didn't come from money, she had nothing else to leave you. She and your father married for love. In those days, your father was quite the romantic, you know, before the lessons instilled to him by that mad grandfather of yours took over. It broke Celia's heart to see the change in him.' She shook herself. 'Well, then, come along. And you too, dear,' she added as Kate hung back. 'I may have something for you as well.'

The three followed the schoolmistress through a small door and into a storage room at the back of the museum, passing between long shelves stacked high with boxes of various sizes, with intriguing labels announcing *Fossilised plants (various)*, *Arrowheads (flint)*, *Musket balls and Misc*, and *Ammonites (large)*. An upturned tea chest supported the vast leg bone of a dinosaur, another the blank-eyed stare of a Roman goddess carved from marble. At the far end, the shelves gave way to racks of brightly coloured costumes from the productions put on each year by the Brierley Players, giving off a faint aroma of mothballs and greasepaint.

With a faint tingling in her limbs, Rosalind recognised the green cap with its pointed ends from a riotous pantomime of *Robin Hood* she'd seen when she was very small, then the fur-trimmed cloak of King Lear from a few years ago, sending her instantly back into the performance that had terrified her with its madness and its cruelty, and the utter despair of its ending. She had still been too young at the time to contemplate that the princess in a story could die, rather than move on to her happily ever after.

She might be older now, but it was still a relief to pass the battered remains of the ass's head Cordelia had lovingly fashioned last year from a discarded fur coat for *A Midsummer Night's Dream*, and which was now disintegrating between the gossamer wings of fairies, the various shades of chiffon stirring gently in their wake. Cordelia stretched out her hand as they passed, gently caressing each gauzy fairy costume, as if greeting old friends.

'Here we are,' said Miss Parsons at last, reaching a sturdy-looking mahogany desk in a far corner. She retrieved a key from behind a line of books to unlock a drawer set to one side of the desk, lifting out a large rectangular parcel wrapped in tissue paper. She unwrapped three leather-bound books, with *Shakespeare* written in gold along the spine. 'Now let me see.'

She lifted out the first, putting it to one side. '*Histories*. That is intended for Bianca.' She lifted out the next. 'Ah yes, *Comedies*. That is for you, Rosalind. And *Tragedies*, that is for you, Cordelia. Don't look so alarmed, the comedies aren't all frivolity and the tragedies aren't all doom and gloom. You'll find there's a message in there for each of you.' Her eyes took on a particular gleam. 'And maybe more besides.' She reached into the tissue again. 'And this is for Kate.'

'It can't be.' Kate stepped back abruptly, sending the nearest rail of costumes shuddering, accompanied by the faint jingle of Morris dancers' bells muffled deep within the material. 'I remember my mother. My *real* mother.'

'I'm not saying Mrs Arden was your mother, my dear,' said Miss Parsons gently. 'Just that she loved you like one of her own. But this is still for you.' She held out a smaller volume than the rest. Kate hesitated, then grasped it, turning the pages in so much haste it was a wonder they did not tear. *Shakespeare's Sonnets*.

Kate slowed in riffling through. 'They're illustrated.'

Miss Parsons smiled. 'Like all of the volumes, and by the same hand. They were very famous illustrations in their time, almost as well-known as those of Arthur Rackham.'

'I always loved the Arthur Rackham drawings,' exclaimed Kate, 'especially the ones for *Midsummer Night's*

Dream. They were always so delicate, as well as whimsical. When I was younger, they almost made me believe fairies exist.' Kate was deep in the illustrations, oblivious to everything but the intricate dance of men and women surrounding the lines. 'These are less fantastical, but they are beautiful.'

'They are wonderful,' said Cordelia, opening her volume at the balcony scene from *Romeo and Juliet*. 'I'd love to see what Rosalind looks like in yours, Rosy.'

Rosalind turned the pages past *Love's Labour's Lost*, *The Taming of the Shrew* and *A Midsummer Night's Dream*, to *As You Like It*. There was a strange feeling back deep inside her, the kind stirred by the memory of the plays seen so long ago. The illustrations went past her eyes in a blur with an unmistakeable sense of familiarity.

'She even looks like you!' exclaimed Kate, as Rosalind paused on the head and shoulders of the smiling young woman looking out at her.

'So she does.' Cordelia hastily turned the pages of the tragedies past *Anthony and Cleopatra* and *Macbeth* to reach *King Lear*. She breathed a sigh of relief. 'Thank goodness for that. I was worried Cordelia might look like me. I don't particularly want to see myself strangled, even if it is only a drawing.' She turned back to Rosalind's volume. 'But those pictures of Rosalind really *do* look like you. It's unmistakeable. Is there a message?'

'Those are private. For you each to find,' said Miss Parsons.

Rosalind turned back to the opening pages. 'There's nothing there.'

'Don't worry, you'll find them, in your own way, and when you're ready. Those were the instructions I was to pass on to each of you when your turn came.' She blew her nose. 'It was never meant to be this way. Celia intended to give them to you herself, but she never fully recovered from the influenza she caught just after Cordelia was born. She was so relieved your father was too old to be conscripted to fight in the Great War – they were one of the few families left almost untouched by the slaughter. But the influenza pandemic afterwards took so many, both soldiers and civilians, rich and poor. There was barely a family this side of Stratford that didn't lose someone.'

'So that's how she died,' said Cordelia. 'No one ever talks about it.'

'You were little more than a baby, my dear, and Rosalind barely walking. The others were a little older, of course, but still far too young to lose a mother, not to mention being left with a father who could barely deal with his own grief. I'm not entirely sure Alma fully understood what she was taking on, but at least your papa had the sense to see her heart was in the right place.'

'You make me wish we'd been kinder to poor Alma,' said Rosalind.

'You were children, my dear, you had just suffered an unimaginable loss. I feel certain Alma understands that. And even if not, she was the adult in this, she made her own choices. You're not responsible for her, not in any way.' She smiled.

'These have been a weight on my mind, all these years. I'm glad to be finally handing them over. I'll give Bianca's hers as near to her wedding day as I can. Now remember, these are gifts from a mother to her children. You're each free to put them away and forget about them – they are free gifts of love, not an obligation. It's now up to you to do with them as you wish. Although... maybe don't mention them when you get home. Even in the closest of families, some things are better not shared.'

'I understand,' said Rosalind, fighting back tears. She could feel the silence from Cordelia, and see Kate fiercely clutching of her volume to her chest.

'I won't say a word to anyone,' said Kate, at last.

'Nor me,' added Cordelia.

'And I won't either,' said Rosalind, firmly. She caught Miss Parson's eye. There was pride there, as well as a lingering sadness – and something else. Anger? Fear? It was impossible to tell. There was so much she wanted to ask, but the schoolmistress was already leading them back towards the front of the museum and out into the sunlight.

Chapter Seven

The three returned in silence across the fields, none of them willing to raise the subject of the volumes, or their contents, particularly Kate, who hugged her book as if she could not bear to let it go.

When they reached Arden House, afternoon tea was already laid out under the trees in the garden, with Cook in a fine temper at their tardiness, her carefully timed scones drying out rapidly in the summer heat – an irritation she invariably took out on Lucy as the lowest of her minions. Rosalind raced upstairs behind Kate and Cordelia, hastily hiding her volume in her chest of drawers, deep amongst bodices and stockings, before hurrying down to join Alma.

'You were a long time,' remarked Bianca, sitting poised and elegant under the cool of the trees. 'I wonder that you could bear to walk so far in this heat.'

'It was only to the village,' said Cordelia. 'We took the brooch Kate found to Miss Parsons' museum. She was most impressed. And with Kate's drawings, too. She's going to display them.'

'Really, dear?' said Alma. 'That's quite a compliment. Now then, my darlings, there's a recital in Stratford next week. The boys won't be back by then, but there's no reason why we shouldn't go. I've spoken to Papa and he's agreed. He's even offered to drive us there in the Austin.' She set down the teapot without filling a cup. 'It's time we went out into the world, and I would like to see you all settled and happy. Besides, with all this talk of war, who knows what might happen?'

'Oswald says that all the stories in the papers are just scaremongering and tittle-tattle,' put in Bianca. 'And the French and the Germans are always fighting amongst themselves and it won't come to anything, not like last time.'

'Then let's hope he's right,' replied Alma, applying herself to the teapot once again. 'Now, if we're going to venture into Stratford, we'll need suitable gowns. There must be something in our wardrobes that doesn't look too shabby, and you have such a wonderful way with your needle, Cordelia. All those lovely costumes you've made for the Brierley Village Players, it's really very kind of you.'

'It's not charity, I enjoy the challenge,' replied Cordelia. 'I hate feeling aimless and just waiting around for some husband or other to carry me off.'

'Oh.' Alma blinked at her, as if Cordelia had suddenly announced she was inviting the author of *Lady Chatterley's Lover* for tea. 'Well, I've a copy of *Vogue*, showing the latest fashions,' she hurried on. 'I'm not having my girls overshadowed by any other young ladies. Just because we live in the countryside doesn't mean we can't be sophisticated. And besides,' she smiled encouragingly at Rosalind, 'there may be several young men there we haven't met before.'

'Yes, Mama,' murmured Rosalind, dutifully, ignoring the faint explosion that came from Kate's nose.

. . .

That night, when she was finally able to escape to the privacy of her own room, Rosalind took out the volume of Shakespeare's comedies, eagerly scouring through the pages for a message from her mother. There was nothing to be found. Emptiness opened up inside. She had hoped for something, a reaching out of love, even if only a few words to tell her the memories of warm arms around her, holding her safe, joyous in their laughter, were real. She could not bear to even look again at the illustrations.

She closed the book slowly, feeling the old loss taking hold of her as she lowered the leather cover. Rosalind ran her fingers over its intricate carving of a tree looking out onto a distant landscape, drawing in the faint scent of roses, feeling arms around her, the warmth of her mother's breath and the quiet beat of her heart. Loss never faded; it was as sharp now as it had been as a bewildered little girl, the loving anchor of her life gone forever.

'*Why should a dog, a horse, a rat have life, and thou no breath at all,*' she murmured beneath her breath, suddenly remembering the agony of King Lear's grief.

At the open window, the curtains stirred in the breeze. There was a crunch of footsteps on the gravel below, accompanied by the faint suggestion of a cigar. Papa on his evening inspection of the grounds, silent tonight, without Will to accompany him with their plans of improvements Rosalind was well aware the estate could not afford, and Will's grandiose schemes for the future.

A fox barked in the ancient woodland. An owl hooted, followed by one breathy reply, and then another, this time far away. From the direction of Brierley-in-Arden came the engine of a lone motorcar, roaring into the distance. Papa had moved away, leaving just the faintest hint of smoke, as if from the dampened cooking fires in the little village, now sleeping amongst its fields.

Despite the heat of the day, there was a chill in the air. Rosalind blew out her candle, moving as quietly as she could to replace the Shakespeare deep amongst her underclothes, before returning to bed, pulling the coverlet around her. Her feet felt as if they would never get warm.

The house was plunged into its night-time silence, broken only by the faint sound of crying from Kate's bedroom. Rosalind swung her legs out of bed, reaching for a shawl, ready to brave her sister's temper and investigate, but the sobs stilled as the front door banged shut, followed by Papa's heavy steps making their way up the staircase.

Rosalind placed her hands over her ears. She didn't want to hear whether he was heading for his own rooms, or the faint knock that signalled his occasional visitation to Alma's bed.

She might not know much about life, or the relations between husbands and wives, but tonight, more than ever, she knew she could not live in love's absence, waiting – or maybe even dreading – a knock on the door that was never a time of her choosing.

Love is merely a madness, Shakespeare's Rosalind declared, but the play made clear she didn't mean it, not when it came to true love, stripped of empty show and worldly considerations. It was the part of the witty exchanges between her namesake and her beloved Orlando that Rosalind had always instinctively understood from her youngest days, when most of the playwright's words had sailed past her, beyond her grasp. True love did exist. She had always felt sure of it, deep within her heart.

In *As You Like It*, Rosalind and Orlando found love

when both were exiled, cast out from all they knew, and in the most unlikely of circumstances. As she had grown older, Rosalind had loved their verbal sparring even more, as a man and a woman working out between them what it was to be truly in love, rather than caught up in a passing fancy. A love that lasts a lifetime, and allows both sides to grow. Every part of her longed to be the laughing-eyed young woman she had seen in the illustrations in her volume of plays, wearing her doublet and hose lightly as she countered Orlando's extravagant professions of passion by teasing him that '*men are April when they woo, December when they wed.*'

Rosalind sighed. Not that she was likely to be given the opportunity to explore her own heart in such a way. Her stepmother had not brought vast wealth to the household, and, if Miss Parsons was right, nor had her mother. Papa, for all his obsession with restoring Arden to its former grandeur, had followed his heart when it came to his own marriages.

'Well, he has no right to prevent me from doing the same,' she muttered, returning under the covers and rolling herself into a tight cocoon.

Alma might not have Cordelia's skill with a needle, but she had a flair for turning the drawings in the magazines into simple designs they could all follow, with the help of their existing packets of patterns from *Vogue, Simplicity* and McCall.

Rosalind hemmed layer after layer under Cordelia's instruction, transforming the musty and most moth-eaten ballgowns into sleek fitting dresses. At Alma's insistence, she added gardenias fashioned from silk to restore the original plunging necklines to respectability. Finally, the material was gathered under the bust into a tight-fitting waist, before flowing out again across the hips in widening folds that swayed to the floor.

With Cordelia delegated to a demure silk crepe of the palest apricot, and Kate directed, despite her protests, to a striking green satin, Alma turned particular attention to Rosalind.

'I've got the brown,' said Rosalind, alarmed by the look of determination in her stepmother's eye. 'I haven't worn it since last year, and no one will notice.'

'Far too severe and old-fashioned,' declared Alma. 'And cotton. Really, Most unsuitable. We can't have you looking like a blue-stocking.'

'Well, I am a blue-stocking, and I'd rather not hide it.'

'Nonsense, darling. First impressions count.'

'That's exactly my point.'

'We're about the same height,' continued Alma, choosing to ignore this. 'I've got that white silk I've barely worn since I was married.'

'Absolutely not!' exclaimed Rosalind. 'You can see every lump and bump in that. I'm not being put on display like a prize heifer for all of Stratford-upon-Avon to gawp at.'

'Darling, you look nothing like a heifer. It's a little old fashioned, I'll admit, far too drop-waisted and not at all like these more elegant modern styles.'

'And if it's clinging to every part of me, that will make it even worse!'

'Nonsense. It's all the rage to show your figure these days.' She considered Rosalind through half-closed eyes. 'On the other hand, I've also got that tulle I ordered from Derry and Toms that I was going to use for Bianca, but which didn't suit at all. It's a lovely dusky blue. Very subtle. There should be enough to go over the silk. Cut on the bias, it will do perfectly to give you a fuller skirt, and make charming open sleeves that will show off your arms while not appearing too forward. There's a photograph of an evening dress with short sleeves in *Woman's Own*, just like the one worn by Lady Hasting's daughter when she was in London for the King's coronation. She's about your age. Don't worry darling, I'll make sure you look suitably modest.'

'It's not my modesty I'm worried about,' growled Rosalind.

But Alma, when she set her mind to such matters, could be surprisingly stubborn. It was best, Rosalind had learnt, to give in over the small skirmishes and save her firepower for greater battles ahead. She had a distinct feeling that any callow Stratford youth in search of a wife, however penniless and unwilling she might be, was about to be the least of her problems. Particularly now Bianca was safely engaged to Oswald, and their father had made it clear his intention that one of his remaining daughters was to secure Henry Luscombe's wealth, not to mention becoming a future duchess.

Chapter Eight

The concert room in Stratford-upon-Avon was closely packed. Rosalind sat through poetry readings, interspersed with a recital of piano music, enjoying the change of scene, despite the conversations around her inevitably returning to the possibility of war and the young men who were already eagerly declaring they would sign up to fight for their country at a moment's notice.

At the interval, she slipped out from her seat before she could be directed by Papa towards the largest group of young men in the room, who appeared more interested in their own discussions than the young ladies being displayed by proud (or possibly desperate) mamas.

From the corner of her eye, she saw Cordelia being steered towards the familiar figure of young Frederick Wortley from Pershore House, just outside Coventry, who was clearly being prevented from beating a hasty retreat by his mama, resplendent (if a little out of place) in an emerald tiara. Kate had vanished, most probably related to the fact that Bianca was standing next to Oswald and his family and already scouring the crowd as if impatiently looking for her sisters to join them.

Rosalind dodged behind a large man in a shiny black evening suit and tuxedo, too engaged in adjusting his dapper bow tie to notice. Shielded from Alma's purposeful gaze, she headed for the safety of the back of the room. She wove her way between the groups of low-backed evening gowns, set off by long strings of glass beads and art deco-styled earrings, along with highly curled coiffures adorned with intricately beaded combs that sparkled like diamonds in the lamplight. Rosalind resisted the temptation to stare as she passed, careful to avoid the eye of any roaming male under at least the age of eighty.

Just as she reached a discrete corner, filled with couples too deeply fascinated by each other to notice her presence, she was stilled by a hand placed firmly on her sleeve.

'Ah, Rosalind. We guessed you might be here. Not the standard of London, of course, or even Birmingham... but then, what can one do?'

'Mr Luscombe!' She blinked in surprise at the pale eyes gazing down at her, the full lips curved slightly in enjoyment of her discomfort at being caught off guard. 'I thought you were still in Wales.'

'It rained. You couldn't see a thing. So we came back early.' His gaze ran over the dusky blue tulle, expertly layered by Alma to reveal just a hint of the white silk beneath, and rested a little too long at the intricate beading where the curve of her breasts began.

'Is Will here?' she demanded, squirming slightly as his eyes travelled downwards, undisguisedly evaluating the rest of her figure. Even with its diaphanous draping, the silk of Rosalind's dress felt like no protection at all. Until now, she had managed to avoid Henry as much as she could when he visited Will at Arden, much to the irritation of Kate, whose undisguised scowls and utter disdain for all of her brother's acquaintances had appeared to be viewed by Mr Luscombe as a challenge.

'I'm clearly not considered of marriable quality,' Kate had sniffed the last time Henry had been invited to join them at the dinner table. 'Just a passing entertainment. I'd tell him I was set on joining a nunnery, if I didn't think he was the kind to see that as even more of a challenge. He's got a mistress near Hyde Park in London, you know, and another in Birmingham. I overheard Miss Parsons telling Mrs Ackrite that they both know about each other, but neither of them are in a position to protest, or he'd have them out on the streets like a shot.' Her voice had lowered: 'She also said he had more children than you could count, and then she started talking about something else that was even more shocking, only then she saw me, so I didn't hear any more...'

Underneath the delicate tulle, Rosalind felt her skin crawl. It was no secret, Will had told them, that Henry Luscombe's father was demanding he secure a wife with as much speed as possible.

'He doesn't mind if she's rich or poor,' he had announced. 'All they are asking is that she's from a proper old family, is utterly respectable and has pleasing manners.'

'Ready to be trodden all over, you mean,' Kate had retorted. 'Wretched creature. I feel sorry for her already. They only want her for breeding. You can just imagine the kind of life she'll lead.'

'When Henry's uncle dies, he'll be a duke,' Will had returned, with the air of an argument won.

Kate had snorted. 'I'd rather be a penniless artist and live in an attic. At least my soul would be my own.'

'I'll find Will,' said Rosalind, dodging behind a group

deep in consideration of the new moving picture with Charlie Chaplin. 'Papa will want to know he's back.'

A few more turns between groups of concertgoers and she had lost sight of Henry. Any minute now, they would be called back to their seats. The safest course would be to join Alma, who had already retrieved Kate and was currently introducing her to a dark-haired young man who, even from a distance, was looking decidedly nervous at being in such close proximity to Mr Arden's least acceptable daughter, or indeed any young woman at all.

Rosalind hesitated. She spotted Will at the far end standing next to Papa. Her eyes moved back, to rest on the figure paused at the door, eyes scanning the room.

Her heart beat fast. This was no time to be coy, in a minute he would disappear. She dodged round the group in front of her, stomach churning at her own boldness.

'Hello, Guy. I heard Will was here, I thought I might find you.'

'Rosalind.' The pleasure on Guy's face told her without any doubt that hers was the face he had been seeking. He was browned and healthy, fair hair bleached by the sun, despite Will's complaints of rain. 'I was hoping I'd see you before I left.'

Already, the clanging of a bell announced it was time to resume their seats. Around them, the concertgoers were already beginning to move back into the main part of the hall.

'We'd better go,' she said regretfully. 'My family will be looking for me.'

'Of course.' He hesitated. 'If I may, I'll make an excuse and come up to the house tomorrow? I'd like to continue our conversation.'

This was definitely no time to be coy – or to risk Papa's

outraged wrath at one of the lower orders demonstrating ideas above his station. 'Come to the excavation outside the garden walls instead. All you need to do is follow the path across the fields from opposite the village hall. Jamie and Kate are there most mornings. I'll make sure I'll join them.'

'I'll see you there.' His eyes lingered on her face in a way that sent her insides turning somersaults and her knees beginning to shake. Across the room, her name was being called. She caught a glimpse of Alma abandoning Kate and making her way between the thinning crowd towards them.

'I must go. Until tomorrow.'

'Tomorrow,' he replied, as she wove her way back between the lingering groups of friends, coming across Alma as if by accident.

'Are you feeling quite well, my dear?' Alma peered at her. 'You're terribly flushed.'

'It's hot in here, that's all, Mama,' said Rosalind, taking her arm. 'I didn't want to worry you. The fresh air from the window soon revived me.'

'Yes, of course.' Alma's eyes strayed past her, in close inspection of the few concertgoers still left in the room. To Rosalind's relief, Guy had vanished. 'Did you see Will was back?'

'I thought I caught sight of him.'

'Apparently the weather was vile, and most of the people in Wales didn't even speak English. He was thankful he managed to get a ticket for tonight...'

Alma was still inspecting their fellow concertgoers. Rosalind had never been so grateful to hear her father's imperious tones summoning them back to their seats.

. . .

69

The next morning, Rosalind waited until after breakfast to join Jamie and Kate at the excavation, thankful that the rain still held off, and Alma was preoccupied by Bianca's demands for a suitably ornate wedding dress, made up by a proper dressmaker, rather than the simpler McCall pattern suggested by Alma. All of which clashed uncomfortably with their father's requirements that it should not be ruinously expensive, unless the groom himself chose to foot the bill. A prospect that had left Bianca mortified and their stepmother in an unenviable dilemma, caught between the conflicting tempers of her husband and eldest stepdaughter.

On the field leading down to the village, Jamie was deep in uncovering the Roman mosaic, which now included several dolphins surrounding a variety of fish and a rather annoyed looking octopus, tentacles akimbo as if to shoo away the invaders of his peace. Kate, on the other hand, had abandoned the excavation in favour of sitting on the grass at the very edge, making a detailed drawing of Jamie's find.

To Rosalind's relief, they were both too absorbed in their separate occupations to take much notice of her arrival, or show much surprise when, a few minutes later, Guy appeared. He greeted the three of them equally, admired Kate's handiwork, and listened while Jamie pointed out the suggestions of walls and fallen masonry bulging from beneath the earth, before joining her. As Jamie returned to his scraping and Kate to her drawing, Rosalind began to move away, across the field.

'Guy would like to see the burial mound,' she called, indicating the small hill rising between its scrub of trees. 'It's got the best view of the excavation, as well as the area.'

Neither looked up, seeming to have barely heard.

'Is it really a burial mound?' asked Guy, as they began to move away, as casually as they could manage.

'That's what it's always been called in the village. There was supposed to be a gold bracelet found up there, years ago, when I was little, only no one seems to know where it has gone.'

'I'm surprised it hasn't been completely dug out.'

'I'm not sure anyone from the village would dare. There's a legend that the land here was protected by a powerful ruler during the time of the Anglo-Saxons and Alfred the Great.'

'The king who burnt the cakes?'

'That's the one. And his daughter Æthelflæd, who became Queen and kept the kingdom safe for the rest of her reign and the Vikings at bay. Some of the villagers even think it was also a woman who protected Brierley, too. I like that idea. I expect it is just a local story, but it's always been a place treated with respect, if you know what I mean.' She smiled. 'Although Kate is determined she's going to try and excavate it one day.'

They had by now reached the edges of the trees, and safely well out of earshot, while remaining respectably in view of their companions.

Guy stared up towards the burial mound, as if fascinated by its every detail. 'I'm glad you found me last night. I wasn't sure... I didn't like to presume.'

'Presume?'

'That you would want to see me. Will made it quite clear I wouldn't be welcome to Arden House again.'

'Oh.' *She should have known.* 'Papa.'

'I can see his point. I don't want to ruin your prospects. Will told me you're promised to Henry Luscombe.'

'Did he now,' said Rosalind, darkly. 'Well, he was lying. I'm not promised to anyone. And I'd rather run away to the circus and become a lion tamer than have anything to do with Henry Luscombe.'

71

At that, he finally turned to meet her eyes. 'Thank goodness. That is, I don't mean—'

She didn't care if they were seen, she grasped his hand. 'I'm not stupid, Guy. Besides, Kate's told me enough stories to convince me I'd be safer in the company of a crocodile than Henry Luscombe.'

She watched the relief ease the taught lines of his face, and felt his hand tighten on hers. 'I've seen enough of him to know I wouldn't want anyone I cared for to ever be in his power.'

Cared for. He'd said it. He'd spoken the words out loud for her to hear. Warmth rushed through her, taking her breath away.

He took her other hand, holding them tight. 'Dear Rosalind. You've been in my mind every hour of every day since we met. But even if...' He cleared his throat. 'The truth is, I've nothing to offer you.'

'I don't need riches,' she exclaimed in dismay. 'I'm not like Papa, I don't want to mix with royalty.' There was no time for beating around the bush, it might be months – years – before they would meet again. If war came, maybe never. It was now, or not at all. She took a deep breath. 'I'd rather be happy, with you.'

His eyes searched her face. 'It's all I want too, believe me, with all my heart. But I could barely support a wife now, and if the transfer to making armaments doesn't succeed, Thompson & Son will be finished. You've got your life to live, Rosalind. I could never ask you to throw your future away on me.'

'It's *my* future,' she said fiercely. 'And besides, I don't want to be supported. I can stand on my own two feet. I'd far rather take the chance of poverty with someone who offered me a lifetime of seeing me as I am, passion and all, than a man who will obliterate that passion, the very core of me, in moulding me to his requirements.'

'Rosalind—'

'Only... not until my sister is safely married. Cordelia and Kate will always go their own way, but Bianca would never forgive me if I put her future at stake.'

He laughed at that, drawing her gently within the cover of the nearest trees. 'Never change,' he murmured against her lips. 'You're perfect as you are.'

'Then you don't know me very well,' Rosalind returned, slipping her arms around him. 'But I can safely promise never to be perfect.' She drew in his breath, the gentle probing of his tongue against hers. The warmth of his arms held her so close her breathing came fast, and she no longer knew, or cared, where she ended and he began.

The moment was all too brief, then they were walking back, as slowly as they dared, towards the others. Far enough apart for decorum, close enough for their hands to brush each other, as if by accident.

'Well, what did you think?' demanded Jamie, pulling himself out of the excavation to sit on the grass, wiping earth from his hands.

'Even to my untutored eye it looked as if it could be a burial mound,' said Guy, his voice not completely steady. Jamie's eyes slid from one to the other.

'Guy was eager to see more of the mosaic,' said Rosalind quickly, squashing down the blush at the thought of the soft bruising of her mouth being all too visible, not to mention the delicious sensations racing through her body at the touch of his hand travelling slowly down her back.

'We've uncovered so much already!' Jamie's enthusiasm for his subject overcame any suspicion that might have been stirring in his mind. Kate, she was thankful to see, was still concentrating on the disgruntled octopus, oblivious to anything else.

Guy stayed for a short while for form's sake, conversing with Jamie and admiring the emerging mosaic. Then he was gone, striding back towards the village through the fields. At the kissing gate he turned back. Rosalind did not dare give any sign that she had seen him, but she knew that he caught her gaze, just as she did his. She held that image of him, warmed by sunlight, so it might last in her mind forever.

Chapter Nine

Winter 1938

Over the next few months, as autumn sent the beech trees into a glorious russet, followed by the encroachment of low-lying mists along the fields, it seemed the possibility of war was drawing ever closer.

At the start of October, Alma expressed a more cheerful hope as the newspapers reported Chamberlain's triumphant return from Munich, with an agreement signed with Hitler, followed by the Prime Minister's declaration from the windows of Downing Street that 'this is the second time in our history that there has come back from Germany to Downing Street peace with honour. I believe it is peace for our time'. He finished by telling the assembled crowds to 'go home and sleep quietly in your beds.'

Despite this declaration, the preparations for conflict continued, with more reports of gas masks being produced, along with rumours about the wisdom of households storing additional supplies over the winter months and the drawing up of plans for rationing.

With the production of armaments gathering pace, there

was little opportunity for Guy to make even the short journey from Birmingham to meet her. Besides, to her frustration, Rosalind soon became aware of being even more closely watched than before, which limited her freedom to continue practising her photography, let alone conduct any illicit assignations.

As winter approached, with its promise of deep snow and impassable roads, Rosalind took matters into her own hands and wrote to Guy, addressed to the offices of Thompson & Son in Birmingham, under the pretext of sending printed photographs of the mosaic, and suggesting the reply went to the Post Office in Brierley-in-Arden, rather than her house.

From then on, the delight of each week was finding an excuse to walk into the village, to retrieve his precious letter and post her own replies. Mostly, the days passed in an endless routine of helping Alma with her charitable work, which, though welcomed by those barely getting by in the poorest cottages on the estate, was little more than patching over the cracks rather than confronting the underlying issues of insufficient means and walls running with damp.

The rest of the time was largely spent visiting neighbouring families, or at least those sufficiently grand for her father to consider them suitable acquaintances for his womenfolk, with the added attraction of coming into contact with the most promising young men available this side of Coventry.

Determined not to attract any suspicion that she might have other plans, Rosalind tried her best to sit politely, terrified of marking the mahogany furniture with her teacup, or knocking over priceless vases brought all the way from China to adorn windowsills and sideboards. She always found herself with woefully little to add to exclamations over the latest fashions and was that American actress Mae West really as outrageous as she made out? While Rosalind's own prospects of becoming a debutante (*nil*) left her simply an audience for discussions of suitable gowns, and was the new Queen Elizabeth as gracious as she was said to be, and would they catch a glimpse of the little princesses Elizabeth and Margaret Rose?

'I mean,' remarked Mrs Patricia Barnes, from Hambledon Manor, set on the banks of the River Avon, just outside Stratford, who was anxiously preparing her own daughters for their presentation at court before any outbreak of war could prevent them from enjoying such a social advantage, not to mention hopes of being photographed by Cecil Beaton and appearing in magazines such as *Vanity Fair* and *Vogue*. 'Can you imagine? They are such sweet little princesses, they always seemed to have such a happy child-hood with their mama and papa. An ordinary girlhood, just as it should be.' She inspected the gold and diamonds adorning her fingers with a complacent air. 'Or at least as ordinary as any connected to royalty can be. I can't imagine how Princess Elizabeth must feel, being thrust from that domesticity to becoming heir to the throne, with all that entails. And overnight, at that. Such a burden for so young a girl.'

'Yes indeed,' murmured Alma with the faintest of sighs. 'I hope they look after her.'

'Of course they will,' returned Mrs Barnes severely, bristling at any hint of a suggestion to the contrary. 'The King and Queen are devoted to their daughters. Always were, always will be. Besides, it's high time the Empire was ruled by another Queen. It hasn't been the same since the old queen left us. Not that you and I shall most likely live to see such a thing, Mrs Arden, but we can live in hope that our girls can have the pleasure of seeing in a new Victorian age. An Elizabethan Age, so to speak.'

'I hope so,' rejoined Alma, sounding even more hope-lessly out of her depth than her stepdaughters at this nodding acquaintance with royalty. Rosalind squashed a grin. Kate and Cordelia were even less adept than her at hiding their desire to escape from the obligatory constriction of girdles – not to mention the responsibility for making sure no ladders appeared in their silk stockings – to resume their customary traipsing about the countryside in walking boots, with not a headscarf between them.

Much as she loved her home, the world around Arden, with its hierarchies and rigid expectations, would never change. Guy was a breath of fresh air, a voice from a larger world. Even on paper, their conversation flowed as easily as it had done the brief times they had met. Unlike the stilted discussions around the dining table, which were inevitably between Will and Papa, with the rest of them an appreciative audience to their wit and wisdom.

Each evening, when she could finally retreat to the privacy of her bedroom, she pulled a blanket around her and sat on the armchair next to her bed, scouring through her volume of Shakespeare's comedies. She went through, play by play, speech by speech, trying to find something that might be from her mother. But there was nothing. Perhaps, she was beginning to think, it had never been there. Maybe her mother had intended to leave a message, but between the influenza and having small children to raise, along with the appearance of Kate, brought from Italy for heavens knew what reason, she had never completed the task.

Rosalind couldn't even ask her sisters, as neither Cordelia or Kate showed any sign of discussing their own books. Cordelia remained tight-lipped when she had tried to broach the subject, while Kate marched off into the November drizzle, returning only just in time for the ritual of dinner, eyes red, her hair shimmering with droplets of moisture.

Despite the uncertainty over Herr Hitler's intentions, Christmas that year was much the same as it had ever been in Arden House. As the damp chill of December settled, delicious smells of mincemeat and Christmas puddings crept through the house. Much furtive knitting of socks and scarves took place in corners, while Cordelia disappeared with lengths of old dresses and the lavender heads harvested during the last summer days to make fragrant lavender bags and pillows. Will and Jamie vanished to the barns, to the sound of sawing and sanding as they created the sturdy wooden boxes made from odd pieces of timber that were presented to each member of the family each Christmas, along with Jamie's delicate carving of the ends of fallen branches into deer and squirrels for their amusement.

On Christmas Eve, Will took charge of sourcing a suitably noble tree from the forests on the edges of the estate. As dusk crept in, Rosalind abandoned the pinning up of long lines of red, white and green strands of crepe paper, twisted into a festive pattern across the ceilings of every room she could manage, along with garlands of ivy, interspersed with the red berries of holly and the white of mistletoe. Amidst flurries of snow, she traipsed with Kate and Cordelia to watch as her brothers dragged back the enormous spruce, which filled the hallway almost to the roof, much to the despair of Lucy, who was tasked with sweeping up the needles each morning.

The annual ritual of placing decorations, many passed

down through the generations, took most of the evening. That was the part Rosalind loved best, retrieving delicate orbs from her Victorian grandmother, the glass glistening in the lamplight, to accompany brightly painted tin robins and reindeer, and the clipping on of metal candle holders, all ready for the candles that came out each year. Finally, the presents in their brown wrapping paper were hung in place, ready for the morning, followed by their father clambering up the highest ladder to light each candle and complete the effect.

Later, after Cook's mince pies and the obligatory sherry, served in tiny coloured glasses with the most delicate of stems, the family walked through the fields to the performance of *As You Like It*, carried out with zest by the Brierley Players in the village, followed by carols at midnight in the village church.

As the quiet of anticipation finally settled over Brierley-in-Arden, they left the warmth and laughter and took the familiar walk back through the fields. The darkness was punctuated only by Will's torch, revealing snow spiralling steadily down out of the blackness, as the family hurried towards the delicious warmth of logs kept burning in the grate, ready for their return.

Rosalind drank in the clean chill of the air as she lingered behind the others as far as she dared, watching the glow of starlight sending the fields of snow shimmering in the darkness, the sky milky with myriad points of light. Sights her ancestors must have glimpsed from this very position, stretching back to time before time.

'What?' demanded Cordelia, as they passed by the distant shadow of the burial mound, drawn towards the soft glow of Arden, welcoming them home.

'Oh, nothing,' said Rosalind. Laughter burst out of her

again, echoing, muffled amongst the feathery falling of snowflakes. 'It's always the same on Christmas Eve, a moment ago I was longing to escape and live a more exciting life, and now I wish it could stay like this forever. It feels so idyllic.'

Next to her, Cordelia swung in gleeful circles, coat flying in a circle around her. 'I want it to stay like this, too.'

Up ahead, a torch was swung impatiently towards them.

'Keep up, can't you,' chided Will's voice. 'I'm not coming back out to find you both.'

'We're following,' returned Rosalind.

'As we always do,' added Cordelia, as, giggling, they slid and slipped on the ice hardening the snow beneath their feet, racing to catch up with the others.

Chapter Ten

The first weeks of 1939 brought more persistent snow to the countryside around Arden, clogging up the lanes, drifts rising in places above the hedgerows. Rosalind escaped as much as she was able into the frozen wonderland, marvelling at the tiny splayed imprints of birds, interspersed with the large prints of rabbits and foxes, and the occasional passing of a deer.

But she could not avoid the preparations for Bianca's wedding, due to take place in August. While Bianca had succeeded in gaining her wish for the finest wedding gown money could buy (tactfully framed as a gift from Oswald's mother, rather than motivated by any suspicion that the bride might not appear suitably grand), her step-mother and sisters had been pointedly left to fend for themselves.

'All that money on a single dress,' exclaimed Alma, one particularly icy day, when even Rosalind balked at the needle-like penetration of the wind, despite the clarity of sunlight sending the mounds of snow on the fields glittering, and finally submitted to the fitting of her dress for the big day.

Alma set about adjusting Rosalind's skirt. 'You look lovely, my dear. You all do. But I can't help wishing they'd thought to offer the three of you new gowns to match Bianca's, even if they were only half as fine. After all, you are her sisters, and being in London will be such an opportunity. If only they had invited us to stay, that might have given you more time to attend parties and join in gatherings, rather than demanding your father book a hotel. I'm sure they don't mean it, but it makes me feel that we're not welcome.'

'I really don't mind staying in a hotel, Mama,' said Rosalind gently. 'We'll see Bianca, that's what matters.'

'It's you I feel for,' sighed Alma, through a mouth full of pins. After much sorting and choosing, and dismissing of possibilities of velvet and satin, she had finally unpicked a voluminous ballgown of silk chiffon in a dusky shade of pink, which had been fashioned by Cordelia into a delicate fall of ruffles, sweeping down into generous folds.

Alma finished fitting the silk slip to go underneath to preserve decency, and lifted over the finished dress, standing back to observe the effect. 'Perhaps it should go in a little more in at the waist.'

'It's perfect as it is,' said Rosalind, trying not to wriggle. 'Cordelia said it was supposed to flow naturally as I walk. Please don't make me wear a corset, Mama. Girdles are bad enough when we're dressed up for best. I quite like breathing as an occupation.'

'I wouldn't expect you to wear any such thing, my darling,' said Alma, kissing her. 'You have a perfectly elegant figure. You all do. Very well, we'll leave it as it is.' She positioned Rosalind in front of the long mirror in the second-best guest bedroom, long ago commandeered by Cordelia as a sewing room, to spare the blushes of any passing males. 'There, my dear, you look lovely.'

'Do I?' Rosalind scowled uncertainly at the unfamiliar figure draped in diaphanous pink froth. 'I'm worried I'm going to splash tea all over it, or tear the hem. I'm such a naturally grubby creature, pale colours always make me nervous.'

'Of course you won't.' Alma smiled, pushing Rosalind's thick auburn hair into a loose chignon at the back of her head. 'We can wave the rest to frame your face – that will set it off to its best advantage. You've grown into quite a beauty, you know.' She retrieved an ornate comb from the table, formed of a stylised spray of flowers and leaves in silver, set around a large oval amethyst, and experimented with its position amongst Rosalind's unruly auburn locks. 'Yes, that will work perfectly. I've a matching necklace to complete the look.'

'Mama, I can't wear those. They are your favourite, and besides, they match your dress.'

'Oh, I've others that will do just as well. I'm lucky my grandmother left me her jewellery, and good taste never goes out of fashion. Don't look so worried, darling, these aren't real jewels, only paste. They've become all the rage amongst Hollywood movie stars, you know. I've plenty of hair grips to keep it in place.' Alma fussed at the fine curls at Rosalind's temples that could never be corralled, however hard anyone tried. 'Did Will tell you Henry Luscombe is definitely going to be at the wedding? His family have a pretty townhouse in Kensington, overlooking Hyde Park, as well as a summer home near St Ives in Cornwall, with its own private beach. He's from such a very good family, my dear. Your papa would so like to see you settled and secure.'

'It doesn't sound as if anything is secure while there's a

possibility of war any moment. That's all the men talk about when we're invited to dinner these days.'

'They are the ones responsible for keeping us safe,' said Alma, returning to the positioning of the comb. 'You're very lucky Henry has so clearly signalled you out for his attentions.' She paused, meeting the reflection of Rosalind's gaze in the mirror. 'My dear, you're young, you should grasp happiness while you can. So many women waited too long during the last war, so certain the emergency would last only a few months and we could then be together for the rest of our lives. Miss Parsons wasn't the only one to lose an adored fiancé in Flanders' mud, you know, many others were left with no hope of ever having a home or a family.'

'Miss Parsons has her work and her museum. She never strikes me as being unhappy.'

'Miss Parsons was fortunate that her family was sufficiently wealthy to give her a university education, and secure her the post of headmistress. Not everyone is that lucky. There's nothing dignified about ending up a poverty-stricken old maid.'

'Yes, Mama,' murmured Rosalind. Her stomach curled into the tightest of knots. Alma had only spoken the truth plain to see in Brierley-in-Arden, amongst the elderly widows and the middle-aged women who had lost sweethearts during the Great War. Rosalind had always pitied them when she accompanied Alma on her missions of charity with the Women's Institute, taking hot meals and other necessities to those eking a living, barely clinging to the most tumble-down of roofs over their heads.

Rosalind swallowed. Even if she had never met Guy, she could never obey her father's demands, currently being transmitted through Alma, to agree to marry Henry. His regular appearance in the months since the concert hadn't changed the effect he had on her. If anything, it had only enforced it. Henry was making no secret that his family was demanding more urgently than ever that he was settled, with the requisite son already on the way, before he went off to secure fame and glory on the battlefield.

A brood mare I am not, Rosalind told herself. Henry's proximity gave her none of the intensity that raced through her body at the memory of Guy's hand gently tracing the line of her back, as if to know every part of her, or the desire that had consumed her senses at the exploring of his tongue in her mouth. The thought of any such intimacy with Henry, with hands that pushed away his deerhounds with impatience and smile that exuded the confidence of unquestioned possession, left her feeling distinctly queasy.

'And now Lucy is leaving us,' sighed Alma, as she removed Rosalind's dress to be finished to perfection, before starting on those destined for Cordelia and Kate. 'I'm sure I could have persuaded her to stay, but she and Albert are determined to marry as soon as possible.'

Rosalind blinked. 'Albert the undergardener?'

'And after I'd persuaded your papa to overlook their obvious attachment. I thought that might persuade them to put it off for a little longer. I know your father disapproves of relations between staff, but Lucy and Albert were always very respectful; there was nothing ever untoward. It would have been cruel to have forbidden them. Now she will have a home of her own, and children to look forward to.' Alma sighed. 'I don't know how we're going to replace her, girls seem to prefer to find work in factories these days. But I can only wish the two of them all the happiness they deserve.'

. . .

A few days later, Rosalind escaped Alma's fussing over Kate's dress, leaving Cordelia snipping creamy silk expertly, to form the modest impression Alma wished to convey. The wind had got up in the night, sending drifts of fresh snow high above the hedgerows. It had blasted against the kissing gate, impacted so hard it was impossible to open and she was forced to clamber over the top, slivers of cold wedging themselves in her boots, sending a chilly dampness into her socks.

Despite the unexpected hurdles, she arrived in time to see Lucy and Albert emerge from the church. Lucy in her best woollen coat of deep blue, a bunch of tiny, brave early primroses in her hand, and Albert in his best suit, both of them beaming.

'Those two have been sweethearts since they were knee high to a grasshopper,' remarked Miss Parsons, joining Rosalind to watch the bride and groom making their way through the path trodden into the snow of the village green, past the frozen pond with its disgruntled ducks hovering at the edges, and followed by guests in their Sunday best. 'They're the kind to be happy for as long as they live. If they are given the chance,' she added, straightening her hat. 'There's been so many marriages already this year, you'd think it was going out of fashion.' She coughed. 'I understand you yourself are to be married before the summer is out.'

Rosalind started, her boot slipping on the ice, only saving herself from sprawling at the headmistress' feet by clinging to the railings. 'Certainly not! What on earth gave you that idea?'

'Mrs Arden seemed to think it was imminent. I was given to understand young Henry Luscombe was the lucky man.'

'I don't see how he can be, since he hasn't asked. And besides, I've no intention of accepting him if he does.'

'Good for you.' Miss Parsons chuckled. 'Well, and don't

look so surprised, my dear. I'm as good a judge of a man as the next woman. Why do you think I've remained single for so long? I'm not saying I didn't dream of a similar happiness once.' She sighed. 'But it was not to be, and I have never found a man to match my Phillip. A true meeting of body and soul is to be grabbed with both hands, my dear.'

The bride and groom had reached the other side of the snowy green and were vanishing into alleyway, leading to the cottage inhabited by Albert's mother, where the newlyweds were to begin their married life.

'They look so happy,' said Rosalind.

'So they do. It might make me an old fool, but I'm with Mr Tennyson that it is better to have loved and lost than never to have loved at all. I find my heart is always warmed by the sight of two young people who are so clearly made for each other.'

'Yes,' agreed Rosalind, absently.

That night, she brought out once again her volume of Shakespeare's comedies, turning the pages, as she so often did, to open on *As You Like It*. Her mind was too filled with Lucy and Albert, the childhood sweethearts, whose life was just beginning, to seek in vain for any message that might have been left for her. Instead, she let her eyes drift over the illustrations. Rosalind grieving her banished father, living uneasily in her uncle's household, tolerated only as a companion for her cousin. Her meeting with Orlando, escaping from the machinations of his own wicked brother. Then dressed as a boy escaping with her cousin into the Forest of Arden...

Rosalind's eyes paused as they fell one again on the illustration of Rosalind teasing Orlando's profession of love-sickness, the gentle mockery of her smile. *No, no, Orlando,* went the caption. *Men are April when they woo, December when they wed.*

The candle flickered. It caught something. Rosalind held it close to the page. Was there something there? A shadow. Surely there was the just the slightest of indentations beneath the remainder of the quotation: *maids are May when they are maids, but the sky changes when they are wives.*

Was that the message from her mother? It couldn't be, surely? She shut her eyes, remembering the love and happiness on the faces of Lucy and her new husband. Lucy was nobody's fool and had known Albert all her life. She wouldn't have walked into a marriage that diminished her. Surely not all wives were unhappy or constrained, or forced to subserve their every desire to that of a husband?

She opened her eyes again. Her sisters were right. There was something in features of the Rosalind of the illustration that resembled her own, those odd quirks of the shape of a nose or eyebrow that speak indelibly of a blood shared and an ancestry reaching back through the generations. Then it was gone. The face of Shakespeare's heroine one of playful longing, surrounded by the stylised forest of dreams, and with no special relationship to her own. Any indentation below the caption, if it did exist beyond her imagination, was invisible.

Rosalind closed the volume, hiding it away and picking up a much-read volume of *Pride and Prejudice* instead. But even as she chuckled over Mr Collins' pomposity and obsession with Lady Catherine de Bourgh and the superior furnishing of Rosings, unease remained, lingering at the back of her mind.

Chapter Eleven

'Oh, my lord,' whispered Cordelia, as the Daimler transporting them from the church swept through the imposing gates of the Gorwells' London house, set just off Park Lane. 'Bianca is going to be far too grand to ever talk to us again.'

'Well, I'm glad we don't have to live here,' said Kate, gazing up at the gleaming white façade, with enough columns and porticos to rival nearby Buckingham Palace. 'It looks like the kind of place where you daren't touch anything.'

'The Luscombe's house is almost half as large again,' remarked Alma. 'And the grounds are reputed to be quite as charming as St James' Park.'

'Oh,' said Rosalind, at whom this was directed. Under her extravagantly feathered hat of blue velvet, fashioned by Cordelia from the remains of a moth-eaten coat, Alma had the strained look she always wore when Papa had given her strict instructions she dared not fail.

As they joined the other guests making their way up the

steps to the doorway set between rows of columns, Rosalind had a strong urge to flee. Her refashioned gown left her feel uncomfortably exposed. Despite her protests, Alma had chosen the last of the real pearls to place around her neck, leaving Kate and Cordelia to make do with paste. Her step-mother had even unscrewed the diamonds from her own ears, tightening them on Rosalind's lobes, where they hung uncomfortably heavy, burning into the soft flesh. But she dared not remove them, not when Alma had nothing more to adorn her own ears than clip-on drops that, in the absence of candlelight, were making heavy weather of pretending to be genuine emeralds.

She was most definitely on display. Cinderella, encased in fairy-dust, ready to dazzle. In the London heat, the silk of her dress clung to every part of her, as Alma propelled her in front of their party, the most visible of the Arden females.

They were shown into a large room, walls lined with paintings, their gilded frames lit brilliantly by the electric lamps along one wall, despite the reflected glow of the intense heat outside. The furniture consisted of Louis XV armchairs, equally gilded, with seats of palest blue satin, so elegant Rosalind wondered at anyone daring to sit on them.

'One of the finest houses in London, Miss Rosalind,' remarked Henry Luscombe, appearing at her side.

'It is?'

A complacent smile passed over his narrow features. 'Apart from my own, of course.'

'What about the King?'

He laughed. 'I'm sure we can allow the King to outshine us.' He leant a little closer. 'Witty, as well as charming.'

'Hardly.' *If he thought that was the height of wit, heaven help us.* At the far end of the room she could make out Papa, holding forth to a group of elderly men, who were nodding in agreement. Will was standing in a circle of a rather younger variety of suited manhood, deep in serious discussion, no doubt of the possibility of adventure overseas, should war arrive.

'A fine wedding,' said Henry. 'You must be proud to see your sister so well settled.'

She followed his gaze to where Bianca stood in the middle of the room, basking in greeting an endless stream of ladies dressed in silks and satin, with low-cut backs, and jewels in their hair, and not a hint of paste between them.

'I'm glad she's happy.'

'I'm sure it must make you wish to find similar contentment of your own.'

She glanced at him. Despite his gallant words, he sounded faintly bored, as if he would rather be elsewhere, no doubt with the group of young women giggling loudly by one of the open windows, the tallest of whom was sending frequent glances in their direction. She moved slightly away from the others, showing a devoré silk velvet gown in dark gold that closely followed the curves of her slender frame. A long string of silver interspersed with turquoise beads hung around her neck, echoed by a smaller version wound in amongst her fair hair. Henry's eyes followed her, mesmerised.

Rosalind squirmed uneasily in her dress, feeling childish and old-fashioned amongst the elegantly tailored robes around her, of which the gold was deliberately striking. Henry, she couldn't help but notice, was not the only male in the room whose eyes were drawn to the fair-haired young woman, and who was now feigning indifference to the attention, though her eyes slid in their direction at every pause in the conversation.

Is that Henry's mistress? Heat went through her. If she

was, no mere wife could possibly compete with her elfin beauty, so clearly conscious of her power. The young woman turned her head, attention directed away from Henry towards a slightly older man, who bent to speak to her with every sign of deference.

No, of course she wasn't Henry's mistress. Such a woman would never be allowed within such an august gathering. This was for wives and daughters, the respectable aspect of a man's life. The girl in the clinging dress was now focussing her gaze, and her full concentration, on her male companion, the other young women surrounding her already drifting away, forgotten.

'She's very beautiful,' Rosalind said aloud.

'Exquisite,' said Henry, unable to tear his eyes away, irritation in his tone. 'If you'll excuse me...' The next minute, he had joined the young woman and her admirer, launching himself into their conversation.

'She won't marry him, you know,' said a new voice. Rosalind turned to find a woman in her thirties, who, she was relieved to see, had nothing diaphanous about her, eyes fixed on the little trio.

'Won't she?' The fair-haired girl still had her eyes firmly on the older man's face, but Rosalind could see her conscious of Henry's every move, every gaze, the curve of her body moving instinctively towards him.

'Miss Darlington is one of the richest heiresses in London,' said the woman. 'You mark my words, she'll never settle for being a mere duchess. She'll find some foreign prince or other, before the season is out.' She gave a dark chuckle. 'Whatever her animal passions may prefer.'

'You mean Mr Luscombe?'

'Henry Luscombe is a very attractive man,' said the woman. 'The kind who can have anyone he wants.' She reached into a capacious bag slung from her shoulder. 'Thank goodness I was blessed with plainness and a lack of any fortune, and so am quite beneath his notice.'

Rosalind laughed at the dryness of her tone. It was true her new acquaintance was handsome rather than fashionably pretty, with sculptured cheekbones and a prominent nose, set off with a pair of sharp brown eyes. But she could under no circumstances be described as plain.

'I can't argue with that,' she replied. 'I don't think he finds me particularly attractive, either.'

'Luscombe always did go for the delicate types.' The woman's tone hardened. 'Easier to break, if you know what I mean? Believe me, I've watched him. There's a way a man can destroy a woman's spirit, even more than poverty, or pain. Broken from the inside. That's almost impossible to heal, even if you're lucky enough to find a way of escape.'

Her eye focussed on the new arrivals making their way into the room. 'I had a feeling Chamberlain would be here, it wouldn't be a Gorwell wedding without the Prime Minister present. Well, well. Mr Churchill too, even better. And I'm certain I spotted the Sackville-Wests earlier. Excuse me, I've a commission to fulfil and once the official photographer arrives, I'll stand no chance...' With that, she strode over to the arriving dignitaries with a determined air.

Rosalind watched in growing admiration as the photographer button-holed the solid figure of Mr Churchill, smiling and conversing, bringing every charm to bear without once fluttering her eyelashes or appearing faint, until she had her photograph, and headed off in pursuit of the bridegroom's mother, standing next to the Prime Minister.

The atmosphere in the room was stifling. Papa and Will were still in their separate discussions, while her siblings were nowhere to be seen. Kate and Cordelia were no doubt being introduced to any acquaintance in close proximity to a young man and Jamie, who hated such gatherings, was likely to have taken himself off into the garden for a cigarette. Henry was still monopolising Miss Darlington, much to the annoyance of her elderly admirer, who looked as if he wished he were bold enough to give young Luscombe a bloody nose for his impudence. The remainder of the groups remained deep in conversation, with a few outliers like herself lingering awkwardly at the edges.

Rosalind moved closer to the tall casement, with its view between roofs towards the distant greenery of Hyde Park. The window was slightly open, allowing in the distant sound of voices, the passing of horse-drawn vehicles and automobiles and the steady tramp of men and women hurrying along the pavements, heading towards their destination with a set purpose. She itched to join them and explore the city, to walk past the Houses of Parliament and see Big Ben, and even find her way to view the grandeur of Buckingham Palace. But she had no idea where to start and Papa had given Alma strict instructions not to let any of his girls out of her sight. Besides, she had the feeling that even in London, where more women were beginning to take up paid employment, an unaccompanied young lady swathed in silks was unlikely to pass unnoticed.

From the corner of her eye, she could see Henry now had the full attention of Miss Darlington, and, having achieved his purpose, was already beginning to lose interest. Which meant it was high time she braved the nearest group, before he remembered her existence.

'Wait there a moment longer.' It was the photographer, who had returned to stand a short distance away, adjusting her focus. 'Thank you. You looked so wistful, standing there by the window, and the light was so perfect I couldn't resist. I hope you don't mind?'

'Not in the least,' said Rosalind. 'I'm flattered.'

'Good. I didn't think you looked like the fluttery kind, or filled with false modesty. You won't object if I use it? I work for a lady's magazine. They will be most interested in the bride, naturally, and what the usual society ladies are wearing, but I'd like to submit the one of you. If it works, that is.' She grimaced. 'I suppose I feel it rather captures the mood of the times. None of us can be completely carefree, these days.'

'I know what you mean, and I really don't mind,' said Rosalind, colouring slightly at the thought of being even more exposed than in the Gorwells' reception room. Even the occasional copy of *Vogue* that Alma allowed herself from her much-stretched housekeeping told Rosalind that many thousands, maybe even hundreds of thousands, would be reached by each magazine. 'May I see your camera?'

'Of course.' The machine was placed in her hands.

Rosalind gazed intrigued at the rectangular object fronted neatly by a round lens surrounded by the familiar exposure numbers, and turning easily to bring the scene in front into focus.

'No bellows?'

'Not on this one. Isn't it a relief? The beauty of the new Kodaks lies in the lenses, and that they take 35mm film, which is much easier to use, and can be loaded in daylight. Far simpler than having to load film in a darkroom, or carrying around one of those light-proof bags. Mine inevitably tear just when I need them. I love this camera. It's so easy to handle, and generally doesn't need a tripod either, thank goodness, unless you're confined to very low light. It allows you to be far more spontaneous and catch the moment, than those old-fashioned box things my dad used to use.' She sent a curious glance in Rosalind's direction. 'You've an interest in photography?'

'A little.' She kicked herself. That was what modest young ladies were brought up to say, as they slinked back into obscurity. 'Yes,' she said, in a firmer tone. 'I use my brother's Kodak Brownie. It's much older and clumsier than this to carry around.'

'At least you're persisting. Good for you.' Her companion took back the proffered camera, tucking it away into its leather case.

Emboldened, Rosalind couldn't resist. 'You said you worked for a magazine. Do you mean you earn a living from your photographs?'

'Well, I wouldn't call it exactly a living. But yes, it's how I support myself. And you?'

'I've had few pictures exhibited in the local museum.'

'I see.'

Rosalind felt herself turning scarlet with mortification. The photographer clearly had her down as a wealthy woman playing idly at photography, as others took up painting to ease the tedium of their comfortable existence.

'But I'd like to try and see if I could sell them.'

'Then you should. The world could benefit from being seen more from a woman's point of view. The male vision is so impossibly limited, don't you find?' She smiled. 'I may be restricted to society ladies and fashion to earn my keep, but I have other projects few of the male sex would find worthy of recording, if they noticed them at all.'

Reaching into her pocket, she pulled out a business card. 'If you're serious about selling your work, this is the magazine I work for. *Woman's Time* is one of the few that will consider work by women. I'm hoping they will use the photograph of you by the window, but if not I'll try it with others. Always best to keep your options open in this life.'

The card was knocked from her hand, skimming along the floor, ending up half under the ornate gilded leg of the nearest chair.

'You're not here to make sales, Ginny. And Miss Arden is not interested in your wares. Now make yourself scarce, like a good girl, before I'm forced to inform Mr Gorwell that you're proving a nuisance to his guests. You can do that for me, can't you?'

The photographer finished securing her camera with care, before placing it deep inside her shoulder bag.

'I have no intention of affronting any guest, Mr Luscombe.' When she looked up, her eyes were frosty in the extreme. 'And it's Miss Blake to you, as it always was, and always will be.'

Henry smiled. 'Unless you find some other unfortunate soul like Gordon Knight to take you on, despite your... shall we say, ramshackled, past.'

The frost extended to the remainder of Miss Blake's body. 'As the judge in my case made it clear, Mr Luscombe, an abused wife who barely escaped with her life is never ramshackled. The shame should be on the husband alone, whatever some in society might choose to believe. I refuse to wear Gordon Knight's cruel misdemeanours for the rest of my life. I've wiped him entirely from my existence.' There was a distinct glint in her eye. 'You might do well to remember that yourself, one day.'

She nodded towards Rosalind, expression hardening. 'Good day, Miss Arden. My apologies for any offence, it was not intended.'

'There's no need—' began Rosalind, but Miss Blake was already striding through the room, her plain linen coat –

which would have looked more in place behind the wheel of a car than a grand house – flying out behind her.

'Dreadful woman. They wouldn't allow her anywhere near the place if it wasn't for old Arthur Gorwell's wife having an obsession with making an appearance in ladies' magazines. I trust she wasn't troubling you?'

'Not in the least.'

'I should have a word with Gorwell. They must be able to find other photographers in future, even if Mrs Gorwell does insist on having some female for the less formal portraits.'

'Miss Blake was perfectly courteous,' said Rosalind. She was about to give vent to her irritation when her eye rested on the business card still sticking out a little from the chair. 'She was telling me the name of the magazine she was working for,' she added, 'I was certain my sisters would like to know, so they can get copies.'

'They all look the same to me. And filled with trivia. My dear Rosalind, you really are quite above such things.'

'Well, I'd rather like to find that out for myself,' she retorted, moving towards the chair and placing her shoe firmly over the little card.

'Ah, the official photographer has arrived,' said Henry, as a stir announced the entrance of a rotund little man, followed by his assistants lugging the impressive tools of his trade, including a large box of a camera and several tripods, followed by an oversized flash lamp. 'We'd better go and join the others. These are the photographs that will appear in the newspapers. Forget some silly little magazine, these will be in *The Times* and *The Strand*.'

'Of course,' said Rosalind, bending as if to adjust a buckle, slipping the card neatly inside her sleeve. As soon as Bianca's official photographs were done, she would visit the

Gorwells' famous marble bathroom, set aside for the ladies of the party, and transfer the card inside her bodice for safe-keeping.

She accompanied Henry to where the photographer was marshalling the wedding party for the formal pictures, her mind racing. Miss Blake earned an income from her photographs, just as a man did. Even if it wasn't much, she had said it was enough to support herself. The very thought made Rosalind dizzy. To be able to marry where she wished, to choose a soulmate, rather than be pushed and harried towards a man who was, at heart, indifferent to her, and would, she was more certain than ever, stifle the life out of her.

Doubt set in. Miss Blake was bold and decisive. Rosalind had seen with her own eyes how the photographer clearly knew what she was doing and the kind of pictures she needed, and wasn't afraid to direct a stranger, or even the Prime Minister himself, to get what she wanted. Rosalind swallowed. Could she really do that? The photographs she had taken had mostly been of landscapes, for her own satisfaction rather than considering the requirements of a sale. What if her work wasn't good enough for a magazine? Or sufficiently interesting, like Miss Blake and her society clients.

But even Miss Blake must have started somewhere. And from Henry's casual insults, she was clearly no society lady herself, having pulled herself up from the social disgrace of divorce and being dragged through the courts, no doubt every lurid detail fodder for newspapers and *Tit-Bits* magazine. Despite that, an influential family like the Gorwells, who rubbed shoulders with prime ministers and minor royalty, had chosen her as one of the photographers for the society wedding of the year.

In any case, Rosalind thought, as Henry placed a proprietorial hand on her arm, directing her to stand next to her sisters, what had she to lose?

'Ah, Miss Katerina.' Henry installed himself on the other side of Kate, leaning towards her with every sign of admiration, while sending a sly glance towards Miss Darlington, who was watching proceedings with the remainder of the guests. Kate glared, but under Papa's eagle eye was unable to do little more than turn her face away to engage Cordelia in conversation.

Rosalind ignored him.

The least she could do was try to make a living from her photography. If she could manage to earn only a small amount, it would still mean it wouldn't be all up to Guy to provide for them. She could ensure they could earn enough to support themselves while Guy was making his name as an architect. They wouldn't need to wait. They could elope to America if necessary. They wouldn't need Papa's approval, or his permission.

Next to her, Rosalind found Henry abandoning his fruitless attempt to engage the exotic beauty of her sister as a means of piquing Miss Darlington's attention, and, under the purposeful gaze of his father, turning his efforts back towards herself.

After all, thought Rosalind bleakly, *what did it matter to Henry?* Marriage to please his family would not make the slightest change to the way he lived his life. Henry Luscombe knew all too well that Miss Darlington would always be there. Like numerous other young women, both in London and the wider world, he was clearly confident Miss Darlington and her animal passions would wait. Even Rosalind had heard whispers of the goings-on of the aristocracy, with no questions asked at the gatherings at great houses when bedroom doors were quietly opened for secret assignations in the middle of the night.

Rosalind gritted her teeth. She couldn't live like that. She could never be the little country mouse wife, opening fêtes and providing the requisite sons, while her husband openly pursued every pretty young woman he chose, without even feeling the need to hide the fact to spare her humiliation.

The sky changes when they are wives, came the quotation from As *You Like It*, unbidden, into her head. Maybe it had been marked as a warning, after all; there for her to find if doubts in her own mind led her eyes to linger on Shakespeare's words long enough to see the faint indentation. All she would wish for her own daughters would be to see them happy, and to find a true and fulfilling love, not walk blindly into the prison offered by Henry Luscombe, however richly furnished with gold and velvet.

Whether the quotation had been signalled out as a message for her or not, it was a truth she could not ignore. The moment they returned home to Arden House she was going to do everything she could to start selling her photographs. Then she would never have to see, or hear, Henry Luscombe, ever again.

Chapter Twelve

August 1939

As soon as they had returned home from Bianca's wedding, Rosalind had wasted no time sorting through the best of her photographs.

Now that she did her best to examine them as if she were the reader or editor of a magazine, she saw that their range was far too limited. They were mostly landscapes around Arden: the view looking over the fields towards Stratford, some of the prettier cottages and one or two of the village grocers. The sturdy figure of Mrs Ackrite positioned in the doorway, a row of serving staff standing stiffly in front of the shop window accompanying her, surrounded by advertisements for Kellogg's Rice Krispies, Bisto gravy granules and Campbell's soup.

They might have been crisp and clear and with a reasonable eye for positioning and the qualities of light, but were all too obviously the work of a lady amateur photographer. One amongst many. She needed something to grab the attention and make her stand out.

Since there were no Hollywood actresses to hand, and

she had a suspicion Mrs Patricia Barnes would not allow her daughters to risk being shown in an unflattering light by trusting their portraits to any but the most expensive of photographers, she took pictures of the ladies from the WI sorting out donated piles of children's clothing for those who had not a shoe between them, and cooking up great vats of soup.

She spent many evenings standing at the back of the hall, photographing the Brierley Village Players rushing in after a day's work to throw themselves into rehearsals of *Twelfth Night*, ready for the following Christmas, and the choir practising for September's harvest festival, with the yearning of the chorus of the Hebrew slaves from Verdi's *Nabucco* lingering amongst the rafters, between rousing renditions of 'John Barleycorn', 'Men of Harlech' and 'The Barley Mow'.

As August drew towards September, the talk of war increased. Even in out of the way Brierley-in-Arden the old men, cradling their pints on the benches in front of the White Hart, increased the shaking of heads, while deep in reminiscences of Passchendaele and the Somme, faces lined with memories never spoken of in more settled times.

Rosalind had so many more villagers she wanted to picture, from the baker with his huge ovens, to the women gossiping around the village pump, but she had a sense, as they all did, of time running out. If a war was to come, it might be too late to attract Miss Blake's attention.

Rosalind hesitated over her most recent photograph of Clive Leverson from the village tannery, whose promising tenor voice had recently earned him a scholarship to the Birmingham School of Music. Despite trying on several occasions, she hadn't quite caught the earnestness of his face, without it appearing contorted, as he practised with the pianist his passionate rendition of 'E lucevan le stelle' from

Puccini's *Tosca*. She wanted to get it right, to do full justice to the love and loss held in every note of the young man waiting in starlight for dawn, and certain death.

Rosalind tried one last time, waiting as Clive stayed behind after the choir's rehearsal to practise his solo, hoping the light had remained strong enough to freeze the image she had in her mind, and that she had finally done him justice. As she slipped out of the door into the late August evening, she felt the first touch of autumn chill in air edged with the scent of ripe apples and the first bonfires. Even her fear of attracting attention to her activities by being late home couldn't prevent her from pausing, as Clive ran through the aria once more. This time, there were no faults, no hesitations from singer or pianist. Clive's liquid tones hung in the air, cracking slightly on the high passage, before deepening into the final anguished notes.

'Exquisite, eh?' said Miss Parsons, who had paused in returning from her customary evening stroll across the fields to listen.

'Very,' replied Rosalind, fighting down the catch in her own throat, echoing the tears in the older woman's eyes.

'The final hours of a man who has everything to live for,' said Miss Parsons. 'It always reminds me... Well, never mind, my dear. Let's hope the world comes to its senses, and we don't have to go through all that again. Damn all madmen who demand the blood of young men to fill their own emptiness, and leave the rest of us with little choice.' She blew her nose in a defiant manner. 'Luckily survival is a powerful thing. Highly underestimated. Take no notice, my dear. I'm just tired. I'll be as right as rain once I've got the kettle on. You get home while there's still light to see.

Rosalind hurried through the dusk, following the pathway across the fields. As she reached the mosaic, she found Jamie and Kate still packing up their trowels and brushes, deep in conversation.

'You'll come with us, won't you?' called Kate, as she joined them. 'We're setting off tomorrow morning, it'll be the last chance.'

'Where?'

'East Anglia.'

'East Anglia?' Rosalind stared at her. Even with her fairly hazy knowledge of the world outside Arden, she suspected that must be at least a day's car journey away. 'Why would you want to go to East Anglia?'

'Some of the fellows from the Birmingham Archaeological Society are visiting a place near Ipswich,' said Jamie. 'There's a farm nearby where we can camp, I'd go on my own—'

'Don't you dare,' put in Kate. 'I'm not missing this for anything. There aren't any other women going, and they won't let me go without a female companion.' She sniffed. 'In case I tempt the students into my tent with just one glance, I expect. As if that's all women think about. And anyhow, they must be pretty poor archaeologists if they are that easily distracted. You'd think it was something out of Jane Austen, needing a chaperone.'

She brightened. 'Come on Rosy, who knows when we'll be able to escape again. You said you wanted to take more interesting photographs. Well, this is a perfect chance. There's a couple of women who have taken photographs, but we need some of our own. I'll sketch as much as I can, but we won't be there more than a few days, and I'm useless with a camera, and Jamie will be too busy talking to the archaeologists.'

'What am I supposed to be photographing?' asked Rosalind, warily.

'The archaeology. The dig. The boat.'

'Boat? What kind of boat?'

'The one found at Sutton Hoo,' explained Kate impatiently. 'It's been in the papers. You must have seen it. Even Papa has heard about it.'

'They think it's Anglo-Saxon,' said Jamie. 'It's a burial, probably of some kind of king. There doesn't appear to be any sign of a body, but the archaeologists have found some amazing artefacts, beautiful pieces of gold, as well as the imprint of a ship. Professor Wilson from the Birmingham Archaeological Society is already saying it has to be the most exciting find since the tomb of Tutankhamun in Egypt. He's got permission to visit. It's the opportunity of a lifetime.'

'And besides,' said Kate, swinging her rucksack over her shoulder. 'It might lead to something closer to home.'

Rosalind followed her sister's gaze up to the burial mound, looming with its surrounding trees in the encroaching dusk.

'Doesn't mean there's anything there,' said Jamie, who was clearly trying to sound calm and rational, rather than excited as a child hovering in anticipation, one hand on the sticky handle of a favourite sweetshop. 'Just because it's called a burial mound doesn't mean it has to be one.'

'But it could be. And it could be Anglo-Saxon,' returned Kate. 'That's how Mrs Pretty at Sutton Hoo knew to dig the mounds on her land, because she'd been to plenty of archaeological sites and knew that's what they must be. If Mrs Pretty and her amateur archaeologist Basil Brown found the burial of an Anglo-Saxon king, even before they called in the professionals, why shouldn't we find one here? It might not be as rich, but it would still be something.'

'In that case,' said Rosalind. 'I'll definitely come with you. I'm quite sure Papa wouldn't let either of us go so far on our own, not if we wanted to see a wonder to rival Egypt, and even with Jamie as a protector.'

'It would certainly cramp poor Jamie's style if he was expected to chaperone his sisters every hour of the day,' said Kate. 'He'll be covered in mud the moment we get there, just you see.'

'It's getting dark,' said Jamie, turning towards the house.

Rosalind followed as they hurried towards the glow of the lamp shining in the library window. She hadn't finished her roll of film, and she couldn't afford to waste any, which meant she wouldn't be able to develop the pictures of Clive before they left. The rest of her prints were ready, carefully placed in a strong envelope with her even more carefully composed letter to Miss Blake, in her best handwriting. She could seal it up and ask Jamie to stop in Brierley just long enough for her to post it, so at least she would know it was on its way.

On the other hand... She scoured her memory for any mention of the finds at Sutton Hoo. Papa had mentioned something about an Anglo-Saxon king, but they had all been caught up with the wedding, and since then she had focussed every hour of every day on drawing up her portfolio to send to the address on the business card. If the finds were that impressive, then sending photographs of such a newsworthy item would surely be the very thing to catch Miss Blake's eye. It would prove she wasn't an amateur lady photographer, contenting herself with summer fêtes and the minutiae of village life.

Her strongest instinct was that she would only get one chance at this. If her pictures were dismissed out of hand as too ordinary and parochial, however many more she sent, they would be rejected before they were opened. A few more days wouldn't hurt. She would wait until they returned, and take as many photographs as she could at Sutton Hoo, and hope there was at least one that came out well enough to take pride of place in the waiting envelope.

The three set off the next morning, before any objections could be made, the Austin piled high with tents and cooking equipment, squashed in amongst sleeping bags and blankets. They were waved off by Cordelia, who visibly shuddered at the mere thought of a night under canvas, and was already deep in refashioning the costumes for *Twelfth Night*.

The drive was long, as they made their way along winding lanes and almost empty roads, caught behind tractors trundling between fields and buses making frequent stops to pick up and let down passengers, as well as the occasional van, loaded to the gunnels with furniture or supplies for the local grocery stores. For the first twenty miles, Jamie took the wheel, while Kate directed him from the map, but from then on they took turns.

Although uncertain at first, having never driven more than five miles from Arden House under Jamie's patient instruction, Rosalind soon got the feel of keeping the vehicle the best distance from the hedgerow to avoid scratching the paintwork, while allowing cars coming from the other direction to pass. With her attention focussed on every bend or corner, in case of meeting cows being moved between pastures, or delivery boys on their bicycles, she could still delight in the freedom passing through the countryside with effortless speed. She soon took off her headscarf, enjoying the wind buffeting around her through the open windows.

That night, they made camp in a meadow near Cambridge, setting off again with the early light to catch up with the Archaeological Society, who had set off several days before.

'It's near the sea,' exclaimed Kate, as Jamie followed the final lanes towards a field, just a short distance from a shingle beach opening out into an expanse of blue water, where a motley collection of canvas tents had already been set up.

'It's beautiful,' said Rosalind, looking up from scouring the map to make sure they didn't miss the way. She jumped out as they reached a wooden gate set across the entrance to the field, breathing in deep the salt-edged air as she opened the gate for Jamie to pass through. Between the green of the grass and the blue of the sea, separated by a long stretch of shingle, it felt as if she could see to the very edges of the world. It was so different to the rolling pasture and poppy-strewn crops around Arden. The great oceans and mountains she had read about in books suddenly felt a little more real. It seemed, she thought as she closed the gate and followed behind the car bumping slowly over the grass, as if she was stepping on the edge of a new world.

While Jamie went to speak to the archaeologists drinking tea around a camp fire, Rosalind worked with Kate to erect their tent in its designated place, discretely apart from the masculine quarters, with Jamie's placed nearby to deter any young men who might find themselves distracted from the archaeology by the prospect of female company.

'It's strange hearing the sea again,' said Kate.

'I've never thought of the sea having a sound,' replied Rosalind.

'No. You wouldn't.' Kate's voice was tight.

'I didn't mean...' Rosalind looped the front guy ropes around the front tent pole, pulling them away from the canvas until they were taut, before pushing the mental tent pegs into the ground for Kate to pound in place with her mallet. 'I only meant I'm glad I've finally seen it. I never imagined it would be so vast.'

'I didn't bring my bathing suit,' said Kate, bashing away with the mallet.

'We can always go in our underwear, when the boys aren't looking,' said Rosalind. 'What else are vests for?'

'I bet it's cold, not like—' Kate struck the second peg so hard the metal bent.

'There's another one here, we can easily straighten that out.' Rosalind glanced at her sister's closed-down face. 'You mean, the water must be colder here than the Mediterranean.'

'There, that one's in. I'll do the rest, then we can get the sleeping bags.'

She should let it all out. But Kate rarely opened up to any discussion about herself, and especially her origins, unless she was away from the house.

Rosalind took a deep breath. 'I remember you were only a small child, no older than me, when you came to join us from Italy.' There, she had said it, the subject they had all skirted around for as long as she could remember.

'Yes,' said Kate shortly, turning away, her usual means of avoiding any such discussion. Then she paused, mallet poised above the tent peg pulling the canvas into shape over the groundsheet. 'But I remember it.'

It was like a dam bursting, the words tumbling over themselves. 'Sometimes, it comes in my dreams. There's a long stone walk, with statues on either side, and a grape vine hanging above. The light seems much clearer and stronger than any I've felt here. I can remember sunbeams travelling through the grapes, turning them from black to a reddish glow, and the scent of flowers – a kind of dry scent, like the lavender bags Cordelia makes, but so much stronger. And the sound of the sea. It must have been close, I can remember the water was so warm and clear, and I could watch shoals of tiny fish nibbling at my toes.'

'It sounds idyllic,' prompted Rosalind, as her sister resumed the banging of tent pegs into the stony ground. She had never heard Kate say nearly so much about her childhood. Papa never mentioned anything about being in Italy, or even having family there. The subject of Kate's origins, and for her absorption into the Arden clan, only months before the death of Rosalind's mother, was always closed.

'I'm going back there one day,' said Kate abruptly. 'I'm going to find it, the place by the sea.' She looked up to meet Rosalind's eyes. I don't know who I am, or why I was taken to Arden. I don't remember anything about the journey, except that there was a boat. And a train. I remember the steam when we arrived at the station. Papa won't tell me anything, and Alma would never go against him, even if she knows. I need to find it, and find out why. You can't stop me, you know. Nobody can.'

'I wouldn't want to. I'll help you, if you'll let me.'

Kate smiled. 'I always thought you'd hate the idea. I was planning to just run away. Except I wouldn't know where to begin.'

'Didn't the book of Shakespeare's sonnets contain a clue?'

'None that I could see. I so hoped... But maybe I'm just too stupid.'

'No, you're not.' She hesitated. She still wasn't certain the quotation from *As You Like It* was truly the one she was meant to find, and the sentiment went so deep it wasn't something she wanted to discuss, not yet at least. 'I'm still searching through my volume, and I'm sure Cordelia would have said if she had found something in hers. Besides, if

Bianca had found something, she wouldn't have been able to resist telling us. But Miss Parsons said there were messages, so they must be there. We just haven't recognised them for what they are, yet.'

'I suppose,' said Kate, turning away again as Jamie returned to attend to his own tent.

Chapter Thirteen

The next morning, trails of white mist hung over the coast, clearing as the sun rose to a late summer's day of slow sailing clouds chasing bursts of sunshine. Rosalind took as many photographs as she dared, saving most of her precious film for the excavation. Before long, she joined Kate and Jamie, who drove them behind their companions through the lanes to the burial mounds at Sutton Hoo.

'Oh my goodness,' whispered Kate, as they left the cars and walked the short distance over grassy fields undulating with mounds, stopping at the edge of the excavation. 'I'd no idea it would be so huge.'

'I don't think there's a ship beneath the mound at Arden,' said Jamie. 'It's not nearly large enough.'

'And too far from the River Avon,' said Kate, thoughtfully. 'I can't imagine anyone dragging something so huge over land.'

'Stonehenge?'

'That's different, that's stone. Surely the wooden planks of a boat, even such a large one, would be bashed to bits. If there's something underneath the one at Arden, it has to be something smaller.'

'A coracle,' suggested Jamie, grinning.

'Don't be daft, I bet you couldn't even lie down in a coracle. I wish we could find something like this. It's incredible.'

Rosalind left them arguing the point, and moved as unobtrusively as she could among the visitors gazing down at the length of a boat, the ghosts of ribs and planks clearly marked in the ground, the men still brushing away the earth dwarfed by the uncovered remains. The astonishing treasures found inside the ship might have been removed to safety, but the ghostly imprint was enough.

As she reached the far end, away from the archaeologists observing the work, she paused to take one last frame. The fall of the light caught the sweep of the ship. It was a strange sensation, standing there, feeling so close she could almost touch the men and women who had last seen the buried vessel, and who had created the objects found inside. It was the same sensation as seeing the Roman mosaic at Arden. Their eyes would have seen the very same sights she was viewing now; they would have worked the fields, fished to the rise and fall of the sea. In the ghost of the ship, she could feel their presence all around her. Not so very different, after all.

'Beautiful, isn't it?'

For a moment, she froze. *She must be dreaming.* 'Guy!' It was like a vision, conjured out of the memories contained within the earth. He was standing so close she could reach out and touch him. 'What on earth are you doing here?'

'I bumped into Jamie in Birmingham, when he was visiting the Archaeological Society to arrange the visit. He said Kate was going to persuade you to come with them.' He smiled. 'I suggested I'd do my best to join him, however briefly, as this could be the last chance to see the famous ship uncovered before this stage of the dig ends.'

'Come and see it then.'

'I'd rather spend the time with you.'

Rosalind glanced back. Jamie and Kate were gazing into the ship, conversing eagerly to someone contained within its depth. They had a short window before she would be missed.

'Come on.' She grasped his hand, pulling him towards the rises and indentations in the grass, until they found one large enough to collapse behind, out of sight.

'I only have a few hours,' he said regretfully, as they caught their breath. 'I need to get back to Birmingham tomorrow.'

'You drove all this way for just a few hours?'

He kissed her. 'Believe me, it was worth it.'

'Then I'm glad you did.' She could see his face was drawn with exhaustion, thinner than she remembered. A tight knot formed itself amidst the excitement in her belly. She pushed it to one side. He was here, not the memory of him spilling through the pages of his letters, but flesh and blood, his warmth so close she could feel it. 'I've missed you.'

'I wish—'

'Don't.' She kissed him, stilling the words on his lips. 'How many times do I have to tell you that if you were wealthy enough, and connected enough to please Papa, then you wouldn't be you. And then I might not love you half as much as I do.'

His arms tightened around her. 'So you do love me?'

'Of course I do.' She wanted to hold him safe and never let him go. 'Always and forever.'

'I'll always love you, Rosalind. Whatever happens. You have to believe that.' In the short time they had, she wanted to breathe him in, feel the rapid beat of his heart against her.

She wanted— The look in his eyes stilled the longing building up inside her. His gaze held love, but also a wistfulness bringing silent shadows of regret.

'Guy, what is it?'

'Nothing. It was good to see you pursuing your passion out there at the dig, and so completely absorbed. It's good to have a calling in life. A passion.'

The knot was back, tightening this time in certainty. 'You're enlisting.'

'Not yet.'

'But you will do.' His expression told her all she needed to know. 'Guy!' She grabbed the lapels of his jacket, shaking him in despair. 'I remember you said the factory would be an exempted occupation if there was conscription, especially now it's making armaments. You'd still be contributing to the war effort. It's selfish, but at least I'd know you were safe.'

'Dear Rosy.' He kissed her gently. 'I'm afraid none of us are safe, not any more. After Austria and the Sudetenland, it sounds like Hitler has his eyes on Poland next. That means war. I've heard too much of what happens when his armies roll into a land from the refugees working for me to just stand by and watch others lay down their lives to protect us. I couldn't live with myself.'

Her joy in holding him so close turned to grief. 'So you came to say goodbye.'

'I might never get another chance, and I couldn't bear to leave without seeing you again.'

From the direction of the dig, her name was being called, coming ever closer.

'Come back, you hear,' she said, folding into his kiss. 'Just come back to me. I don't care how, or why, but just come back.'

. . .

The rest of the day passed in a blur. It was, thought Rosalind, like standing on the outside looking in, watching them all, like puppets making their customary gestures, unaware of the storm about to break and tear their existence apart. *Surely it could not be real?*

Everything was so normal she sometimes forgot, coming back to herself with a jolt. War, that had seemed so far away, in countries she only knew on a map, might soon overtake them. The security of land and occupations being passed from generation to generation, of the quiet routine of their lives, however much she might kick against it at times, could soon be gone forever. To be replaced— She shut her mind to what might replace the councils and the mayor, the school governors and the government in Westminster itself. It was the only way to keep sane. All she could do was to hope it never happened.

Guy was preparing to fight – and die – to keep the country safe. Is that what Jamie and Will, and all the young men around her, were planning to do? Or maybe, with the talk of men under forty being conscripted into the army, they would have no choice.

She swallowed, remembering the names carved into the monument in Brierley-in-Arden to the men lost in the Great War. Posies of wildflowers still appeared to mark a birthday, or a wedding day, interspersing the wreaths on Armistice day, and the single lantern left burning each Christmas Eve until the candle finally flickered to nothing.

She tried to keep as close as she could to Guy, her hand brushing his whenever she passed, camera forgotten, every inch of her focussed on the sound of his voice, the way he moved, the faint lines that creased his face when he smiled. The look in the brilliance of his eyes when they sought out hers.

As evening crept in, heralding their return to the campsite, she heard Guy take up Jamie's offer of a place in his tent, rather than sleeping in the car, with a spare sleeping bag and battered canvas camp bed rapidly found. At least they would have a few more hours.

Under a clear sky, a bonfire crackled on the beach, with the delicious smells of bacon and sausages soon rising into the air. As dusk eased into darkness, Rosalind quietly joined Guy at the very edges of the little gathering, where they could be close together under the cover of darkness.

There was little opportunity for conversation. In truth, what was there to say? All she wanted was to hold him close and feel his living, breathing being until the very last moment. As the bonfire began to die down to ash, its last flames reflecting an orange glow in the slow rise and fall of waves, the sky filled with a myriad of stars, crossed every now and again with the brief flight of a shooting star. A chill rose from the pebbles, as the group fell silent, the faces revealed by the dying embers pensive, each lost in their own thoughts.

As they made their way slowly back to the campsite, Guy gave a final press of her hand and was gone into the darkness. All through that night, Rosalind felt the chill of the night air entering within her bones. She curled, wakeful in her sleeping bag, unable to get warm. As she finally began to doze, the sound of an engine rumbled towards her. She sat up instantly, wide awake. Through the canvas sides of the tent came the undulation of headlights making their way over uneven ground.

Rosalind scrambled out of the cocoon of her sleeping bag, untying the doors to the tent with shaking hands, to emerge into the faintest hint of light before dawn, just as the car made its slow way out through the entrance. She could just make out the shadow of Guy shutting the gate, followed by a brief pause, as if, even now, he could not bear to tear himself away, before he vanished into the driver's side and the car set off once more.

Rosalind followed the beam of headlights streaking through the lanes, illuminating hedges and the occasional roof of cottages, as the car headed in the direction of Cambridge, and the long drive back to Birmingham. Finally, all signs vanished and even the sound of the engine was lost in the vastness of air and land.

Rosalind could not bear to tear her eyes away from where she had last seen the car taking Guy away from her. She tried to hold him next to her, the warm reality of him close in the darkness, as if she could keep him there forever. As perfect sky appeared over the sea, and the dew formed around her, she crouched in the strengthening light, hoping beyond hope that day would never come.

Chapter Fourteen

September 1939

Within hours of returning to Arden House, Rosalind hurried down to the basement to develop her photographs of the dig at Sutton Hoo. As soon as the film was dry, she selected the three best of the images to print, along with those of Clive Leverson practising his arias.

She peered critically at the black and white prints as she hung them up to dry. They weren't perfect. The one of the archaeologists working in the skeleton hull of the boat at Sutton Hoo could really do with a bit more cropping to make it more dramatic, and she could definitely improve the shading on the view from the front of the funeral ship, showing the entire dramatic length. But it was growing late. The household were already in bed, and she dreaded Papa coming down to investigate the rumble of the generator if she attempted to use the enlarger again. They would have to do. She would just have to pray that those in the envelope were sufficient to demonstrate her skill and her versatility, as well as her eye for a subject, and that Miss Blake would recognise that she was eager and professional, and would improve over time.

The following morning, she escaped Alma, who was deep in discussions with Cook about where to store the larger than usual delivery of sugar and flour from Mrs Ackrite to keep it safe from mice and weevils. As she passed the site of the Roman mosaic, she found Jamie and Kate had not yet resumed their painstaking work. Through the low mist hanging over the fields, she could hear the echoes of their voices, muffled in the damp air, coming from the direction of the burial mound. Clutching her precious envelope, she brushed past the hedgerows of glossy blackberries glistening with dew and the fine networks of spiders' webs, interspersed with the swelling blackness of sloes.

She emerged through the kissing gate into Brierley-in-Arden with damp creeping through her shoes and droplets of mist in her hair. The winding lanes of the village were quieter than usual, with none of the usual bustling to and fro, or groups of housewives gossiping outside Mrs Ackrite's, wicker baskets with meat from the butcher's over one arm, string bags bulging with leeks and cabbages in the other. Even the queue in the Post Office was subdued, with only Mrs Evans from Woodfield Farm quietly asking after Mrs Cooper's youngest, who was still recovering from a bad case of the measles.

Her precious envelope safely on its way, and having determined there was no letter from Guy waiting for her, Rosalind emerged into the deserted street. As she passed the newsagents, she came to a halt, eye caught by the headlines on the boards outside. *Hitler's Order to the Army!*, declared one, *German Offensive in Poland! Warsaw Bombed: Many Reported Killed*, said the other.

'Bad, ain't it, Miss,' came a voice behind her. 'Never thought even that Hitler would really go and do it.'

'Lucy!' exclaimed Rosalind. 'It's good to see you.'

'And you, Miss.'

Rosalind smiled at Arden's erstwhile maid. She had not met Lucy since her wedding day, when her marriage had instantly freed her from her lowly position in the household to becoming a wife with a home of her own to rule. With a pang of guilt, Rosalind could see how Lucy had filled out from the skinny girl nervously glancing round corners for any ambush from Cook or the housekeeper to accuse her of slacking, to the bloom of a pretty young woman. The hair piled at the back of her head was thick and glossy, there was colour in her cheeks, browned from tending her own little vegetable patch, and her eyes were no longer permanently bagged from lack of sleep.

'I'm glad to see you looking so happy,' Rosalind said.

'Yes, Miss. I am, Miss.' Abruptly, Lucy's eyes filled with tears. 'At least, I was. But Albert says now Hitler is invading Poland there really will be a war. He's such a gentle soul, I can't bear to think of him being sent off to fight.'

'He might not be,' said Rosalind, grasping her hand. Lucy returned the pressure.

'That's what I hope, Miss. That's what we all hope. All I ever wanted was a home and my Albert to look after. It isn't so much to ask, is it? I don't know what I'd do, if he was taken away.'

'Let's hope it never happens,' replied Rosalind. Deep inside, her stomach twisted itself into a tight knot. *It couldn't be happening. It couldn't.* This was now, not the Middle Ages. The scene around her had been reassuringly familiar all her life and yet silently, imperceptibly, that security had shifted, like the thick sheets of ice on the lake at winter's end, that one day vanished to nothing.

Rosalind said her goodbyes to Lucy and made her way home across the fields, the knot inside her tightening further until she could hardly breathe. This must have been how her mother and father – along with all the other villagers whose lives were about to be changed forever – had felt all those years ago, when they were young, with a small son, and another on the way.

Little was said when she arrived home. There was the same tense quiet, with no one, not even Papa and Will, discussing the only subject on all their minds.

A few days later, she gathered once more with the rest of the household around the radio, just as they had done for the king's abdication, but this time to listen to Neville Chamberlain's solemn declaration:

'This morning the British Ambassador in Berlin handed the German Government a final note stating that, unless we heard from them by eleven o'clock that they were prepared at once to withdraw their troops from Poland, a state of war would exist between us. I have to tell you now that no such undertaking has been received, and that consequently this country is at war with Germany.'

As soon as they could reasonably escape, Rosalind joined Cordelia, who was following Kate as she headed towards the archaeological dig.

'Will and Jamie are bound to be called up, or volunteer to fight,' said Kate, as the three sat sombrely at the edges of the excavation, feet dangling above the mosaic floor. 'It's all Will's talked about for months. He's dragged Jamie away from here so many times so he could listen to him.'

'I can't imagine Jamie fighting,' said Cordelia.

Kate pulled at the rough grass next to her. 'He might if he thinks it would give him a chance of getting away from Papa. After all, that's why Will's doing it really. And to prove to Papa that he's as brave and heroic as Papa is always telling people he is. He'd probably even risk being killed to get a medal.'

Cordelia shuddered. 'I hope he won't risk anything.'

'They might not get to the front,' said Rosalind. 'Surely they'd have to do some kind of military training first?'

'Yes, that's true.' Cordelia brightened. 'Declaring a war doesn't mean there's definitely going to be any fighting, at least not over here. Hitler might be bluffing.'

'I suppose,' said Rosalind.

'I bet women will volunteer to do their bit too,' said Cordelia.

'Don't be silly, women don't fight,' retorted Kate.

'Not to fight, you goose. There are plenty of other things that need to be done. Remember Miss Parsons telling us how the women took over during the last war and did the jobs there was no one left to do?'

'Then Papa can't stop me from going to volunteer with Aunt Phyllis in Birmingham,' said Cordelia. 'She told me in her last letter that she has so many orders for uniforms, her factories need all the machinists they can get. I can use a sewing machine, and I'm familiar with how to make all kinds of clothing – I've even made uniforms for when the Brierley Village Players put on Mr Shaw's *Arms and the Man*. She's looking for women to help with the war effort, wherever she can get them.'

Rosalind frowned at her. 'What does Papa say?'

'I haven't told him.' Cordelia kicked at the side of the

excavation with her heel, sending a rivulet of dried earth onto the mosaic. 'I'll tell him tonight.'

There was, Rosalind saw, a particularly stubborn look on her sister's face.

'Papa might not let you.'

'It's for the war effort. I'm not staying here and knitting socks in the village hall with Alma. If I'm making uniforms, at least I know I'm doing something useful, and Aunt Phyllis has a spare room, so it would be perfectly respectable. And if he tries to stop me, I'll find another factory and rent a place of my own.'

'Pay rent?' Kate stared at her. 'With what?'

'My earnings, of course, you goose. You don't think I'd be expected to work for nothing, do you? You two can stay here if you want, but I'm not waiting to be married off by Papa to whoever he finds convenient, just so Will can inherit the estate and a fortune and do exactly as he pleases. He'll be a rotten landlord, even worse than Papa.'

'Cordelia!' Kate was shocked.

'Don't look at me like that. It's the truth. I'm embarrassed to show my face, especially when it's winter. I know Alma does her best with the charity ladies at the village hall, but even hot soup doesn't make up for rain coming through the roof and a broken chimney. So many of the children die, it's horrible. There has to be a better way.'

She gave the earth a particularly vicious kick. 'At least if I'm making uniforms I'll be doing something real, and I'll be taking charge of my own life. The longer I stay here without saying anything, the more Will and Papa think I see things the way they do. Not that they listen if I try and say something – Papa just says I don't understand economic realities and I need a husband who does. I don't *agree* with his economic realities, is what he means, as if there aren't any other kind.'

The three sat for a while in silence. Rosalind stared gloomily at the mosaic at her feet as a touch of sun came through the cloud, illuminating the now fully uncovered fish-tail god, surrounded by the leap of dolphins.

She thought of the photographs she had sent off to Miss Blake. Did magazines survive when there was a war? It was utterly selfish when there was so much suffering taking place in places like Poland, but she had sent her work off with such hopes that she might be taking a step towards her secret dream of independence – and now it looked as if those hopes were to be dashed. What other skills did she have?

'Well, I'm not staying here,' announced Kate.

Rosalind frowned at her. 'What will you do?'

'I don't know. But I'm going to do something.' A thoughtful look came over her face. 'I could be a spy behind enemy lines.'

'Kate! What a thing to say!' Cordelia was horrified.

'Why not?' Kate replied. "Madeleine Wentworth from Stratford, the one who comes to sing solos with the village choir, has an aunt who was a spy in the last war. She even took wounded soldiers and civilians who needed to escape from France right over the Alps, through the snow, and into Switzerland. I met her once when she was visiting from London. Madeleine said she still works for the War Office. She sort of hinted that Aunt Lydia has been training women to be spies in case there was another war. She's a tiny little woman, you'd never think.'

Kate stared down at the mosaic at her feet. 'Papa is bound to find someone to marry me, too, before long, and you can bet it's the kind who would never let a wife of theirs get their hands dirty with archaeology. He'll just make sure I have hordes of children and pander to his every whim, and never have time for painting and drawing. I know other women have to give up things like that when they marry, but I can't. It would kill me, I know it would.'

'Don't say that,' exclaimed Rosalind.

'I might not have any choice.' Kate's face had shut in on itself. 'I'm not like you and Cordelia. You know this is your family and they'd never disown you because blood is what counts. Papa has never said he's my real father, so I might not be a blood relation at all. It's not the same.'

'That doesn't matter,' said Cordelia, hugging her. 'You'll always be one of us, dearest Kate. You'll always be a Shakespeare Sister.'

'Papa might not feel that way. You should have heard the way he called me an ungrateful minx when I tried to ask about my mother. I've never seen him look so angry.'

'I'm sure he didn't mean it,' Rosalind reassured her hastily. 'You know what Papa is like. He loses his temper with Will all the time. You can see he's often sorry afterwards, only he's too proud to admit it.'

'He's the same when he knows he's really in the wrong, even though he swears he isn't,' sighed Cordelia. 'Poor Papa, he can be so horribly stubborn, and thinks he can make the world be just as he likes, and then he complains that nobody tells him anything.'

'Then I won't tell him,' said Kate. 'If Madeleine still comes with her mother for the choir practice this week, I'll ask her to mention me to her Aunt Lydia. I bet they're desperate for volunteers.'

The three fell silent again. A chill went through Rosalind's veins. This felt horribly like a parting of the ways. She had expected it, the natural course of things as they grew older. But she had always assumed it would be as they married, followed by regular visits to each other's homes, especially when children arrived, the shared experience drawing them back together again.

It was the way of things. Even in the grand houses, few women moved more than a short car drive away, and many no more than a few minutes' walk, once they were married. The women in the village often settled a few doors down from mothers, sisters and aunts, in and out of each other's houses to help with looking after children while the household chores were done, and if any troubles arose.

From time immemorial, rich or poor, those living around Arden's ancient lands had remained all their lives within a settled circle of friends and acquaintances from their own class, their lives, it seemed to Rosalind, little changed from those of their ancestors.

This felt different, especially with the uncertainty of a war. One that might overtake them all, and turn even Arden into the bleak ruins she had seen in newspapers, with only mud and the burnt skeletons of trees left of the rich and productive landscape that had spread out in crops and pasture for as far as the eye could see.

A faint panic bubbled up inside. It might be supremely selfish, but she was envious of Cordelia and Kate, who were planning their escape, just as she was feeling her own opportunity was fading. She might, after all, be the daughter kept at home to keep Alma company, to be safely married off to Henry Luscombe once the war was over.

'Men are April when they woo, December when they wed...' If what she had already seen of Henry was his April, she wasn't staying around to feel the chill of his December on her skin.

'Over my dead body,' she muttered under her breath.

Chapter Fifteen

1940

The following months remained eerily quiet. There was no threat of instant invasion, no obvious signs of shortages. Will and Jamie dutifully registered for service, but after a few tense weeks heard nothing. Maybe, Will opined gloomily, the war would be settled before they were even trained. Rosalind found that both Cordelia and Kate disappeared regularly to their rooms and visited the Post Office in Brierley more than usual, but neither mentioned any more about leaving and when she asked either of them, the subject was definitely closed.

As autumn progressed, several of the men from the village received their call-up papers and were sent off for military training, but for the most part life continued much as it had always done. The preparations for winter were more elaborate than usual, with little time for Jamie and Kate to work on the mosaic, let alone investigate the intriguing possibilities of the burial mound. Jamie and Will were employed ensuring there was sufficient firewood and helping their father mend windows and exclude as many drafts as possible. Rosalind was sent out with her sisters to collect blackberries and rosehips to join apples from the orchard, as Alma and Cook toiled in the steaming kitchen making more jams and preserves than in previous years.

Throughout the turning of the trees from green to gold, and then to the rustling dryness of leaves crunching beneath her feet, Rosalind made her way to the Post Office in Brierley-in-Arden, torn between hope that Miss Blake might yet reply, and dread that Guy's letter would tell her that he was leaving to start his military training. Each time there was nothing.

Christmas came and went, with rather more subdued celebrations. At times, Rosalind found herself forgetting there was a war at all, then a headline in the papers about battles in Europe would bring it back with a jolt.

She found herself looking less at her copy of Shakespeare as the months progressed, still unable to decide if the quotation beneath the illustration of Rosalind was truly marked, or if it was merely a trick of the light. Besides, with such uncertainty in the air, she dreaded finding an even more unwelcome message. She had never smiled so wryly at the illustration of Rosalind before setting out on her adventure, dressed in a stylised Tudor gown, flowing skirts embellished with entwined violets and columbine between the wandering delicacy of wild roses, a long sweep of hair streaming out behind her as she sighed ruefully '*how full of briers is this working-day world!*'

January 1940 brought the start of rationing, with each member of the household doing their best to make sense of the coupons in their ration books.

'Thank goodness we got in all that sugar when we could,'

remarked Alma, returning from registering with Mrs Ackrite's and the butcher in the village. 'We have a good supply of jam to last us. I don't know how Cook is going to make the meat ration stretch with two young men still at home, and your father isn't going to be happy about not being able to spread so much butter on his toast. But at least we have the land. I must speak to your papa about turning over more of the walled garden to the growing of vegetables, and ploughing up that field going down to the village.'

'Not the one where the mosaic is!' exclaimed Kate. 'You can't destroy that.'

'Of course not, darling. We can rope that part off, but really the rest should be used for potatoes and carrots, that kind of thing.'

'Potatoes,' sighed Cordelia, who had remained gloomy over the small amount of cheese (to which she was particularly partial) designated by her coupons, especially as most seemed to be allocated to the men of the household who, as Alma regularly reminded them, needed to keep up their strength.

One day, as the snows of winter began to melt with the first hint of spring, Rosalind made her customary journey into the village to find the group of women clustered outside the grocer's fell silent as she passed, before resuming their discussions once she was at a safe distance.

'He only bloody went and volunteered,' she heard one of the women exclaim.

'Not your boy Edmund?'

'And just when I'd talked my brother into taking him on as an agricultural worker. Protected occupation, that. The young fool. He could have stayed in Brierley and sat it out. It's all right for him and his ideas of going up in the world and ending up rich as blazes, but what am I supposed to do on my own, and with a husband who can barely move for his rheumatism? That roof will never get seen to now.'

'He'll be back, Mrs Ford,' said Miss Parsons, emerging from her museum to join them, cup of tea in hand.

'Ay, but to what?'

'He's a bright lad,' replied Miss Parsons. 'One of the brightest we've had in the school.' She sipped her tea thoughtfully. 'I still think it's a pity he couldn't take up that scholarship. He might not have ended up wealthy, but he'd have had more of a chance of fulfilling those dreams of following a profession he loved if he'd been able to attend Birmingham University.'

'You know I agree with you, Miss Parsons,' replied Mrs Ford. 'I did my best to persuade my Tom to let him go. I'm sure you're right and he'd have made it to study at Birmingham. But his dad had plans for Edmund to take his place as undergardener at Arden. Tom were so sure he had every chance of rising to become Head Gardener one day. But now the other gardeners have already been called up and Edmund swore he wasn't staying to do the work of three men.'

'Cook won't be happy if she's forced to send a maid to dig the day's potatoes,' said Lucy, appearing next to Rosalind, with a basket over one arm.

'She'll be as cross as anything,' replied Rosalind, with a smile.

'Yes, Miss.' Abruptly, Lucy's eyes filled with tears.

By the grocer's, Miss Parsons abandoned her cup and moved towards them.

'Lucy!' exclaimed Rosalind. 'What is it?'

'It's Albert, Miss. He's been called up, too.'

'I'm so sorry.' Rosalind came to an awkward halt. *What was there to say?*

'It's all right, Miss. Don't get me wrong, I'm proud of him, going off to serve his country. And Albert's never been beyond Stratford. At least if he sees France he's more likely to settle down when the kiddies come along. Not that I'd think he'd stray,' she added hastily. 'But he gets restless sometimes. He's hoping this might lead to something.'

Something better was what she meant. Like Edmund Ford. Something better than working all hours, and in all weathers in Arden's walled garden, for barely enough to keep a roof over the family's head and food on the table. Hard, backbreaking, repetitive work that would leave Albert crippled with arthritis by the time he was fifty, dependent on his own children for his subsistence.

It was no secret that Lucy took in washing to make ends meet. Rosalind could see it now in her hands, already roughened and swollen with hours plunged in hot water, alongside the hours of hard physical work it took to keep a household, and one day she would also have small children around her feet.

'I hope it does,' Rosalind said, humbled.

'The thing is...' Lucy hesitated. 'The thing is, Miss. I hope you don't mind me asking...'

'Anything.'

Lucy blushed. She glanced uncertainly towards Miss Parsons, who nodded encouragingly.

'Go on, my dear. Like I said, there's no harm in asking, and I'm sure Miss Rosalind will be only too pleased to help.'

'Of course I will,' said Rosalind. 'Anything I can do. Anything.'

Lucy took a deep breath. 'The thing is, he's leaving in a few days for training. I was wondering, well, if you wouldn't mind...' She glanced towards Miss Parsons again.

'Go on, spit it out,' said the headmistress.

'If you wouldn't mind taking our picture,' said Lucy in a rush.

'Your picture?'

'Photograph,' said Miss Parsons. 'Of the two of them.'

'So Albert has something to take with him.' The blush deepened. 'The thing is, we were going to have a photograph taken for our wedding, only...' Mortification took over.

'You didn't get round to it,' said Rosalind gently.

Lucy nodded. 'We were going to. I kept my dress, special, I've not worn it since, except for church, of course. We can pay,' she added, chin going up. 'There's a photographic studio in Stratford. Only, well, it's a long way.'

And a bus fare to add to the amount the two of them had painfully saved to be able to afford a precious wedding photograph. Rosalind could have kicked herself. There she had been last summer, enjoying the simple happiness of Lucy's wedding, with never a thought that the least she could have offered her would be to take her wedding picture.

'Of course,' she said. 'It would be a pleasure.'

'Thank you.' Relief went over Lucy's face and she could no longer hold back the tears.

'I could always come and take the photographs in your garden tomorrow, when Albert's home from work. Or maybe we can use the village hall. It won't take long. I can get them back to you the next day.'

Lucy nodded. 'Thank you, Miss. We'd like that. And like I said, we can pay.'

'There's no need.' She saw the pride rear up on Lucy's face. 'That is, there's no need to pay me, Lucy. It's my way of doing something for the war effort. How about we set up a fund to pay for other families to have their portrait taken before their men go to war? I'll do as many as I can, but it would help if they know there's a small fund to help them if there are too many and some need to go to the studio in Stratford.'

'I agree,' said Miss Parsons. 'I'm sure the WI will be happy to contribute. Not many people have cameras in Brierley, and if the men are going to go and fight for their country, it's the least we can do.'

'Thank you, Miss,' said Lucy. 'And tomorrow will suit. I'll make sure Albert manages to get away early. They can hardly stop him.' With that, she disappeared down the road, blowing her nose on a spotless handkerchief.

'Good thinking,' said Miss Parsons, approvingly. 'About the fund. Lucy would have refused otherwise, not a girl who likes to take charity, that one.'

'I don't like taking money from her at all.'

'Don't worry, I'll deal with it. I'll make sure it's as little as possible, and I'm sure we can find a means of getting it back to her, in a way she won't notice.' She sighed. 'I know it can be a comfort, but I'm afraid I'm hoping she hasn't got a little one on the way. She's enough to do, being a young wife on her own.'

She brightened. 'And you're right about others wanting to have their portraits taken. Those who have the money or a camera have a photograph already, but there are plenty others who haven't the means, or the time to travel to Stratford. Why don't you set up a studio on the stage in the village hall? There's plenty of light if we pull the curtains right back, and you can use the scenery as a backdrop, like they do in proper photographer's studios. If these were normal times, I'd suggest we put out a rail of costumes so they could dress up as who they pleased, but I'm not sure any will want to, under the circumstances.'

'Although some of the women might like a fine dress or a hat,' said Rosalind.

'That's very true.' Miss Parsons grinned. 'That's something else the ladies can donate, some of their old gowns, so we have a variety of styles and sizes, as well as the ones from the Players. I'll speak to them this evening.'

At least she was doing something practical. A new energy went through Rosalind as she set up a small studio space on the stage of the village hall the following day, using the backdrop of gardens and a fountain, with a large stately home in the distance that had been used by the Brierley Players for an adaption of *Pride and Prejudice.*

'Now what you need is an aspidistra,' announced Mrs Elphick, a compact little woman with greying hair and a taste for the full skirts and high-necked blouses of her Edwardian youth, who directed the amateurs of the Brierley Players with as much severity as if they were to perform at the Birmingham Repertory Theatre, or even the Adelphi in London. She wiped down an armchair that had taken centre stage for the appearance of Banquo's ghost in her blood-curdling production of *Macbeth.* 'That will look very elegant. There's one in our hallway, I'll get one of the men to bring it. And there's a palm you might find useful. Great overgrown thing.'

'I wouldn't want to damage them, Mrs Elphick.'

'Don't worry, my dear. The aspidistra requires constant dusting and the palm is threatening to take over the hallway. My father-in-law had an obsession with them, and the family just won't have them trimmed. I've been attempting to kill them both for years.'

'Thank you,' said Rosalind, swallowing a smile.

'I'll have them sent over tomorrow. I'll check with my sister-in-law too. I seem to remember my nephew recently went through a phase of being obsessed with photography,

I'm sure there must be photographic paper and other materials you can use.'

She sighed. 'He was called up in November. Turned down for his chest, but now he's insisted on working in the War Office in London and never a consideration of how his poor widowed mother is to manage at home. Not very patriotic sentiments, I know, but it's always the women left to deal with the practicalities. Men are so often driven by their emotions, you'll find, and are simply thoughtless about anything else unless there's a woman to tell them what to do.'

'Indeed,' murmured Rosalind.

'Ah, your first clients, I believe.'

Rosalind turned to find Lucy hesitating in the doorway in her Sunday best, arm tucked inside that of her husband as if she could not bear to let him go for a single moment.

'You could come back tomorrow,' remarked Mrs Elphick, eyeing the stage critically. 'Miss Arden's set will be fully finished by then.'

'That's quite alright, Mrs Elphick,' said Lucy, polite but firm. 'We'd rather have it done this minute, if that's all right with Miss Rosalind?'

'Yes, of course, Lucy. I promised I would do it today, and it's a pleasure.'

'Only, I'm off tomorrow, see,' said Albert, his round face weather-beaten with sun and rain, overcome with his customary shyness.

'Yes, indeed, very well.' Mrs Elphick's generally severe expression softened as the two drew nearer, Albert hastily removing his cap, stuffing it awkwardly under his free arm. 'You must be proud, Lucy.'

'Yes ma'am, I am.' Lucy's eyes held a sheen of tears. 'Very proud.'

'As are we all,' declared Mrs Elphick, beaming at Albert

who blushed to the roots of his hair, with the air of a man wishing the ground to swallow him up instantly. The two were ushered up to take their position, with Mrs Elphick clearly intending to remain in charge of proceedings. 'Now then, if Lucy takes the chair, and Albert leans over the back, like so...'

'Ah, Mrs Elphick,' said Miss Parsons, appearing on stage and forestalling the manhandling of Albert into a suitably dignified pose, to the undergardener's deep mortification. 'There are some costumes here I'd like you to inspect. I understand Miss Cordelia has volunteered to alter several to be suitable for use in the photographs, but I need to check with you, first. I am sure you'd like to keep back any you think might be needed for your next production. I understood it hadn't been decided yet.'

'*A Midsummer Night's Dream,*' announced Mrs Elphick, in tones that brooked no argument. '"*I know a bank where the wild thyme blows,*"' she declaimed, striking a pose. Mrs Elphick had, despite her directing duties, insisted in taking the part of Oberon in the Brierley Players' previous production, and clearly had her eyes on repeating her triumphant portrayal of the fairy king. '"*Where oxlips and the nodding violet grows, Quite over-canopied with luscious woodbine, With sweet musk-roses and with eglantine.*"'

'Grecian or Elizabethan?' persisted Miss Parsons.

'I... Very well, I shall come and see what's what.' Mrs Elphick strode towards the museum, followed by Miss Parsons, who winked broadly as she closed the door behind them.

'Thank the Lord for that,' said Lucy, easing her bolt upright pose and leaning against the back of the chair. 'And I'm not playing no fairy, neither. I've had enough bossing about at Arden House to last a lifetime. Begging your pardon, Miss.'

'Not at all,' said Rosalind. 'I don't much fancy being Peaseblossom, either.' She smiled. 'And Cook scares the living daylights out of me, too.'

Albert, being on his manly pride, didn't dare admit to such weakness, but grinned in sympathy, visibly relaxing now Mrs Elphick was nowhere in the vicinity.

'That looks far more natural,' said Rosalind, as she checked the strength of the light with her light meter and set the speed of the shutter. 'And the sun has come out. All I need you to do is to smile and try not to move too much. Now, what have you grown in your vegetable patch?' She chatted to them both until their expressions eased, and the sunbeams streaming through the windows sent the dust in the air hanging in gilded clouds bathing them both in a warm light.

Photographs taken, all Rosalind could hope was that she had got all her settings correct and there was at least one where neither of them had closed their eyes.

'I'll bring the finished versions over to you as soon as I've developed them,' she said. 'They won't take long to dry, I'll get them to you before it's time for you to leave, Albert, I promise.'

She watched them through the window, arm in arm, holding each other tight as they retraced the steps they had made so joyfully with their wedding guests, as they made their way back to their little cottage. She couldn't help but envy their closeness, but also felt for Lucy's fear, that had now become all of their fears.

'Excuse me, Miss.' She turned to find a lad from one of the small hamlets tucked away around the village, whom she knew from the summer haymaking on Arden land. He was twirling his cap nervously around in his hands.

'Nice to see you, Billy.'

'And you, Miss.' He cleared his throat. 'It's Mum. Oh, she's not poorly,' he added quickly. 'Only, she won't stop crying. I were called up last Friday, you see... only, well, I thought it might help. If she had a picture of me, like. They said in the White Hart that you were doing pictures'

'Of course.' She smiled at him. 'I'm glad you came, I've some film I need to use up. Hop onto the stage.'

A look of alarm went over his features and he instinctively adjusted his jacket. 'You mean, now? Like this?'

'Of course. Your mother won't mind you not being in your Sunday best, this is how she remembers you. And if she doesn't, you can always come back.'

Billy grinned and clambered up onto the stage. 'I'll miss the plays,' he remarked, throwing his arm over the back of the chair with the air of a country gentleman. 'Although not a lot else, begging your pardon, Miss. When I get back from the war, I fancy trying the London stage, or even being in one of them moving pictures. Beats working all hours for Dad on the farm, any day.'

By the time she had coaxed Billy into looking more like himself than Mark Anthony holding forth, several other young men, who had clearly been making the most of a Saturday afternoon by speculating on a brighter future in the convivial atmosphere of the White Hart, appeared.

Rosalind finished her film and loaded her spare, photographing each, one by one, in various dignified poses, while Mrs Efflick, attracted by the joshing and the slightly tipsy laughter at the door, reappeared with a comb and demands for a contribution to the village photographic fund.

'Since you can clearly afford a pint,' she retorted to a half-hearted attempt at protest, 'you can afford to put something in the box. And any buttons in there, and I shall be round to see your mothers, quick as a flash. All of them.' With that, she held out a small wooden collection box, pointedly watching as each meekly put in the required amount, with a satisfying clink of metal.

Rosalind returned home with her mind filled with Lucy and Albert and all the other young couples in the village facing an equal uncertainty, along with whole families watching a beloved son or brother, the hope for their future, heading off to war. The most precious thing for any of them would have would be an image of those who had gone, just as she had seen the longing in Albert's eyes for an image of his new wife to keep with him.

Papa had several photographs of Will, taken in a large studio in Birmingham, as well as a portrait in oils, commissioned from a leading artist from London. There must be so many in the village like Lucy and Albert who hadn't been able to afford a wedding photograph, let alone a portrait.

Chapter Sixteen

Early the next morning, Rosalind slipped out into slanting spring light, amongst the glistening of heavy dew and the white network of cobwebs stretched across the lawns.

Clutching her precious prints, she hurried into a just-stirring Brierley, the winding alleyways echoing with horses' hooves and the rumble of carts, along with workers making their way stiffly towards the fields.

As she knocked at the door of the tiny cottage at the edge of the village, it was opened by Lucy, eyes red-rimmed with the effort of keeping cheerful.

'Thank you, Miss.' Her face lit up with pleasure as she lifted them out of their protective brown paper. 'Do I really look like that? I suppose I must. They are beautiful. Albert will make a frame for the big one when he comes back, and the small one will go with him.' She blew her nose. 'He's having a proper breakfast. Proper. I'm not much of a cook, mind, but I can do bacon. That'll set him up for whatever they want him to do.'

'So it will,' said Rosalind, gently. She had a feeling the

generous portion of rashers sizzling in the pan meant that Lucy would have used up all her meat ration and be facing lean pickings for the rest of the week. She would see if the WI ladies could find a food parcel for her, to tide her over. Surely they could be tactful and say it was for every wife and mother whose men went off to serve their country?

'I'd better go,' she said, at the sound of footsteps creaking down the stairs. It didn't take much to guess that Lucy and Albert would want all the time they could spend together before he set off.

Over the next few weeks, Rosalind settled into a routine of taking photographs of the young men preparing to leave for war, followed by printing them up at night. Despite the circumstances, she enjoyed the challenge, and as even Alma agreed she was doing her bit for the war effort, it kept her free from the WI knitting circle. It kept her busy, far too busy to think. Besides, it gave her an excuse to slip to the Post Office each afternoon before she returned home. She had not quite given up on a reply from Miss Blake, however unlikely it seemed now, but most of all she longed for a letter from Guy, an ache of worry permanently at the back of her mind the longer she heard nothing.

Finally, a letter arrived. She could see Guy's handwriting as she took it from the post mistress, but her joy was tempered by the uneven slope of the address, the air of it being scribbled in haste. Resisting the urge to tear it open, she hastened to the kissing gate. Secluded from the curious eyes of the village, she took a deep breath.

It was as she feared. Guy was heading for military training within days. Rosalind held the paper tight against her, breathing in the faint hint of carbolic soap and cigarettes, as if they could form his essence and become part of her. Fear went through her, jabbing at her stomach, followed by a spurt of anger. *Why had he signed up? Why hadn't he remained safe in a reserved occupation?* How many of the young men she had photographed – most likely, for some of them at least, the very last image of them their families would ever have – would have given everything to be able to play their part in the war at home.

But there was nothing she could do. Guy had to follow his own path, as did all the men heading off to war. Her role, as with the rest of the women left behind, was to wait, never knowing each day if he was still alive, uncertain of the future, while working to keep the fabric of everyday life intact. She read through his words again, before folding up the letter, replacing it in its envelope and thrusting it deep in the pocket of her coat for safe keeping before slowly making her way home.

As she reached the house, Rosalind saw Will striding towards her.

'Henry is waiting.'

She dragged her mind back to the present. 'Henry?'

'Henry Luscombe,' he said impatiently. 'He arrived over an hour ago. Alma is attempting to keep him occupied, but it's you he wishes to see.'

'It can't be that important, surely he can come back tomorrow?'

'Of course he can't. He's joining his regiment in a few days. This is his last chance to talk to you before he leaves. So now it's up to you, Rosy.'

'To me?'

'To settle things with Henry. It'll make things so much easier.'

'I don't see what difference it will make.'

'Not to Henry,' said Will impatiently. 'To Papa. To Arden.'

Charming. She did her best to keep her temper. 'I thought Bianca's riches were enough, for now at least.'

'It's not a matter of riches. Not entirely. The thing is, Henry is one of us, his family go back nearly as far as the Ardens. They're not new money, like Oswald Gorwell, made from manufacturing.'

'The Ardens must have made their money from something once,' remarked Rosalind, dryly. 'And manufacturing sounds more dignified than rape and pillage and selling off your daughters to the highest bidder.'

'He'll help Papa,' continued Will, as if she hadn't spoken. 'At least I'd know Henry would look after the place, should anything should happen to me. The thing is, Rosy, the way Oswald has been talking since his marriage to Bianca, I don't trust him. He's already been trying to persuade Papa to use the bottom field, and the one Jamie is always messing about in, to build several villas in this new Bauhaus style, all glass and concrete. He's telling Papa they'll make a fortune as summer homes for families from Birmingham or London who don't want to travel as far as Cornwall.'

'Papa would never agree to that!'

'He might if that's the price of Gorwell investing in the house and the rest of the estate. I always said we couldn't trust him, especially now he can claim association with the Ardens of Arden House. He's quite impossible to talk to, all he can see is profit. At least Henry'll be reasonable.'

Rosalind fell into step beside her brother. She knew him too well to delude herself that there was any point in trying to argue. Will was as stubborn as their father once he had an idea fixed in his head. But, Rosalind told herself, they could hardly lock her in her room and throw away the key until she agreed to marry for their convenience. It was simply a matter of sticking to her guns, and refusing to throw her life, or any hope of happiness, away. She could understand the lads in the photographs she had taken earlier being so eager to take the only opportunity they might ever get to escape the destiny set out for them in Brierley by generations of their forebears, and get away.

Rosalind gritted her teeth as they reached Arden House, bracing herself for the inevitable battle ahead.

'Ah, there you are, my dear.' Alma had clearly been watching for their arrival. Impelling Rosalind away from the front door, she ushered her through the kitchens, causing even Cook to lower her dignity to stop and stare, and up the twisting servants' stairs to her own bedroom.

A pale rose muslin dress, with demure folds and set off with a collar of finely-worked lace, lay waiting for her on the bed. 'Now clean your face, there is warm water and a flannel waiting. If only we had thought to wash your hair last night, but it will have to do. I take it Will told you Henry Luscombe is waiting for you downstairs?'

'Henry has seen me on several occasions,' said Rosalind. 'He knows what I look like; it's a bit late to try and persuade him I look like a princess now.'

'You'll always be a princess in my eyes, darling,' said Alma, kissing her. 'But you can't possibly see him with dirt on your hem. You're going to look your best. You can leave your things here; the maid can take them back to your room.'

Washed and scrubbed until her cheeks shone, her long

auburn hair removed from its customary plait and pinned into a neat chignon, Rosalind was firmly buttoned into the dress.

'There, you look lovely,' said Alma, head on one side. 'I know what you need.' She retrieved a cameo brooch from her dressing table, adorned with a suitably bashful-looking Grecian maiden surrounded by a delicate line of tiny seed pearls. 'My grandmother gave it to me, when I was a girl. I was wearing it when I first met your father. It brought me luck. I feel sure it will do the same for you.'

'I'd rather make my own luck,' growled Rosalind under her breath.

'What, darling?'

'Nothing.' Poor Alma, she would be the one blamed for not raising her step-daughters correctly if they didn't follow Papa's wishes. 'Thank you, Mama, it's very beautiful, I'll take care not to lose it.'

Henry was waiting for her in the drawing room, standing at the window, gazing out over the lawns.

'Ah, Rosalind.' Truth to tell, he didn't look best pleased. Henry Luscombe was clearly not a man accustomed to being kept waiting. Or indeed, be disappointed in anything. Having spent much of her life cursing the need to be chaperoned each time she ventured into the company of young men, she wished she had Alma, or at least one of her sisters, safely installed in the corner of the room, to be appealed to if required.

Don't be a fool, she scolded herself. The stories in the newspapers told of women in occupied France having to endure far worse things than a disappointed lover. Particularly, she reminded herself firmly, one she had done her best to discourage. The sooner this was over the better.

'Good afternoon, Mr Luscombe.'

'Henry.'

The tone of instruction set every nerve that wasn't yet on edge jangling violently. Well, if he thought that would bring her to heel, he had another thing coming.

'I'd no idea you were visiting today.' She smiled blandly. 'Perhaps you'd like a walk in the grounds?' The urge to escape was irresistible. 'I'm supposed to be meeting Jamie,' she improvised hastily, half an eye on the nearest window. 'He's been teaching me to drive.'

'Unseemly,' pronounced Henry.

'I beg your pardon?'

'Women driving. My father considers it to be a first step to a lost reputation, a woman dashing round the countryside like that on her own. He has expressly forbidden my sister to engage in such an occupation. I trust you won't mention it to him.'

Since she'd no intention of ever being in the same room as Mr Luscombe senior, the promise was easy. 'I'll take care not to.'

'Thank you.' His face relaxed a little, turning from irritation towards a sentimentality. 'Dear Rosalind—'

'I hear you're leaving.'

'Tomorrow. I may not get the chance to speak to you before I go, which is why—'

'Then let's hope the fighting won't last.'

'It's bound to be over before long. The old man isn't happy with me going, of course, but he's resigned to me doing my bit. It's only what anyone would expect.'

'The same with Papa. I can't help thinking that it might be

best for none of us to make any decisions, at least until we all have a clearer picture of what is happening. There will be plenty of time in the summer, when hopefully the war will be behind us—'

'Which is why I wish to have things arranged before I leave for France.'

That settled it. She was accustomed to Papa and Will assuming she wasn't worth listening to, but she was not about to exchange a further word than was necessary with a man who had been instructed to spend his life with her and didn't care enough about anything to refuse.

'I hope you manage everything to your satisfaction,' she said brightly. 'I won't keep you. I wish you well, Mr Luscombe.' She turned towards the door to make her escape. 'Perhaps we should join the others.'

'Rosalind.'

She glimpsed returning irritation, mixed with a dogged determination to have the task at hand done. She saw herself through his eyes. It was not exactly flattering. Of reasonably good stock, a family eager to connect their name with his. A young woman pretty enough, but not renowned as a beauty, not known for attracting male attention, and who had been shielded from the world by the seclusion of Arden. As unsophisticated and innocent as her virginal attire. One accustomed to having her life directed by a forceful father.

She swallowed. One who would be absorbed into his family in a docile manner, provide the required sons, and be in no position to question his life – his real life – in London and fascination with conquering ladies such as Miss Darlington. The country mouse, who would maintain his veneer of the country gentleman, always there in the background but with no say over her own existence, even her sons dispatched to boarding school when they were barely old enough to tie their own shoe laces, instructed to deny their own distress, taught to view her with equal disregard.

'I think it's best we join the others,' she said loudly. 'I've no wish to embarrass you or hurt your feelings Mr Luscombe, but my mind is set on contributing to the war effort in any way I can, so it's best if we didn't discuss this further. Good day, Mr Luscombe, and my best wishes for you, wherever you're posted.'

'You little...' She was spun round to face him. 'Who else is going to take notice of you? The stench of those vile chemicals is enough to put anyone off. Let alone the rest of it.'

'Then you should be relieved that I've saved you from your obligations.'

'Obligations?' The eyes fixed on hers were hard and cold. A man who needed to be master. A man who would not be made a fool of. There was nothing there, behind those eyes. No empathy, no humanity. No feeling, apart from irritation that she hadn't fallen into place, and so had caused him trouble.

She was pushed unceremoniously against the wall, hands either side of her, blocking her in, until there was just his face, filling her world, and the hardening of his excitement against her thigh.

'I'll teach you obligations you won't forget, you little bitch.'

Over my dead body. Her hand reached the handle, turning it, jerking the door towards her, catching his outstretched arm. He yelled in surprise as much as pain, grip barely relaxing, but enough to pull herself free. Diving through the doorway, she raced along the empty corridor, turning a corner in the direction of the kitchens. Dodging between hangings, she took the winding steps of the servants' stairs, and raced up to the safety of her own room. She pulled the door behind her, manoeuvring a heavy chair against it, legs shaking.

Downstairs, she could hear raised voices, Henry's and Papa's amongst them, with Alma doing her best to soothe both, followed by the slam of the front door, and the roar of an engine racing down the driveway.

Only then could she breathe. Hands still trembling slightly, she removed the rose-coloured dress, pulling on her skirt and blouse, waiting for the knock on the door, the demand that she attend Papa in his study. Instead, nothing. The silence downstairs was distinctly ominous. Even Cook had refrained from her customary banging of pots and harrying of her underlings. If keeping her on tenterhooks was Papa's way of intimidating her into submission, she wasn't going to give him the pleasure. She laced up her walking boots and reached for her coat.

It wasn't there. It must have been left in Alma's room when the rest of her clothing had been returned.

A cautious glance into the corridor showed no one in sight, and the door to Alma's room open. To her relief, the coat was there, flung carelessly over the metal bedframe, where it must have been forgotten.

It was still quiet in the rooms below, but she was taking no chances. She raced down the servants' stairs and out into the grounds, shrugging on her coat as she went. It wasn't until she had reached the far side of the walled garden, where the Roman mosaic lay and abandoned, waterlogged from last night's sudden burst of rain, and oozing with fallen mud, that she stopped to draw breath. She reached into her pocket for Guy's letter, aching for his words to steady her, to draw in the scent of him, feel him close once more.

It was empty.

She searched again, then through all her pockets. There

was no sign. She must have dropped the letter in her haste. She quickly retraced her steps, eyes scouring the ground for any sign. Nothing. As she reached the front of the house, she came to a halt. In that case, she could have dropped it inside for anyone to pick up. Or Alma had come across it when she was folding up her clothes after hurrying her away towards Henry Luscombe?

She took a deep breath. This had to be faced at some time or other. The French windows to the library stood open. She stepped warily inside.

'Ah, there you are, darling.' Alma was standing next to the unlit fire. 'I knew you wouldn't have gone far.'

'I'm not going to marry him.'

'There's no need for any hasty decision. Henry explained it to Papa, it was too much of a shock for you, without time to prepare you as he would have wished. He was very under-standing about it.'

'He wasn't to me. He did his best to force himself on me.'

'Nonsense.' Alma's customary pallor turned to a deathly white. 'He truly cares for you, my dear. He said to Papa that he regretted frightening you, but that it was understandable given your innocence, and that was the very quality that had first attracted him to you, and he was prepared to give you more time...' Her voice trailed off into silence.

Rosalind watched the eyes that wouldn't meet hers scur-rying over the antique Chinese rug, as if her stepmother couldn't tear herself from the pattern of waves surrounding a serpentine dragon.

'Not even you believe that,' she said.

'He's very well-connected.' Alma's voice was thin, a woman clutching at straws.

'I thought love was wanting the best for those you loved,'

153

retorted Rosalind. 'Not sacrificing them, simply to keep peace with your husband.'

'Darling, isn't that a little over-emotional? You've had a shock, that's all. Of course I care for you. And so does your Papa. Why else would he have taken so much trouble to find you a good match?'

It was like a blow to the stomach, robbing her of breath. Somewhere, throughout her life, there had been the sense that Alma was doing her best to be a good mother to all her stepchildren, that she had placed herself as the buffer between them and Papa, because she was the adult, and that's what adults did. But now it had been tested, it was an illusion stripped away before her very eyes.

Alma was back to following the dragon on the carpet, a rare piece, old when it had been brought half way around the world by some Arden ancestor simply to prove his wealth and his ability to stride the globe. Fury shot through Rosalind, followed by contempt. Alma may have sold her soul for material comfort, along with kindness and human understanding, but she was never going to do the same. Whatever it took.

'There, that's the bell for dinner,' said Alma, turning towards the door. 'There's no time to change, but your papa will understand. He knows that you needed to get some fresh air to calm your nerves, and you were thoughtful enough not to ruin your beautiful dress. Best not to say anything, my dear, just let it blow over. Henry has promised he won't try and speak to you again until they all return from training. We'll have plenty of time to talk it over. You know you can come to me with any worries.' Her voice faltered. 'With any... questions that you may have. About the relations between husbands and wives. That kind of thing.'

This time, pity went through Rosalind, catching her by surprise.

'I saw a shadow of myself,' Rosalind tried to explain to Cordelia, as they escaped into the garden in the cool of the evening, following the excruciating ritual of dinner, with Papa keeping up a conversation as if she did not exist and Henry had never visited that afternoon.

'What do you mean, a shadow?'

'I suppose I saw what I might be if I really did give in and married Henry. He'd wear me down, until that's how I would become, too.'

'You'd never be like Alma!'

'I hope not. But we know what Papa is like – he's at us all the time. At least we have futures to look forward to, and the possibility that we can escape. I tried to hate her, but I can't. Alma has nothing. She might live in a big house, but really she has nothing. Not even her own mind. I suddenly saw how that could be, being worn down year by year, with no hope of anything different. I don't expect Alma thought that would be her future when she married Papa. At least I've seen enough of hers to know what would happen to me. That means I've nothing to lose.'

'Rosalind!'

'Don't be silly, I'm not planning to throw myself in the river. What I mean is, I know Alma won't side with me, she daren't. And anything is better than having a life like hers, which is no life at all.' She took a deep breath. 'So I'm going to make sure I escape, before Henry has a chance to come back.'

'You could come with me to Aunt Phyllis. She's almost persuaded Papa to let me work with her, now there's talk that women might be conscripted too. He began to soften the moment I told me I would be torn between volunteering for the air force or the navy. You could see the thought of any of us let loose in the WAAF or the WRNS made his hair stand on end. She says she's desperate for machinists, and her workshop isn't in the centre of Birmingham, so it'll be almost as safe as here, even if there is any bombing.'

Rosalind shook her head. 'Too close.'

'Where, then?'

'I don't know. London, I suppose. That's the obvious place.' And where she could brave the offices of Miss Blake's magazine in person, stole the thought into her mind, or any other newspaper or magazine she could find. Besides, wouldn't Guy be likely to travel through London when he came home on leave? So far away, where nobody knew her, they might finally be free to meet.

'But Rosy, women and children are being evacuated in case Hitler bombs the city. And what if the Germans invade?'

'There hasn't been any bombing and it says in the papers plenty have already returned.'

'That doesn't mean it's safe. I've seen the posters telling mothers to leave their children in the countryside.'

'I'll take my chances,' said Rosalind, stubbornly. 'And if there's an invasion, we're all sunk. None of us would be safe, not even here. I'm sure I could find work of some kind in London, and it's too far for Papa to come and bully me until Henry finds someone else.'

'Don't look at me!'

'You won't be here.' Their eyes met. *And Kate is safe from him*, went the unspoken acknowledgement between them. Olive skin and jet-black hair, along with the high cheekbones that set her apart from them all, wouldn't be considered right in the drawing rooms of Mayfair, even without the question mark over her birth.

'You can drive,' said Cordelia. 'Miss Parsons said so many men have been called up, there's a shortage of drivers.'

'Is there now?' said Rosalind, thoughtfully. At this point, she didn't care what she did. She had to take any chance to escape before Henry could have a chance to return. Papa was utterly determined, and she had seen that Alma would put her loyalty to him first. Her instinct was stronger than ever. She had to get away while she could.

Something stirred in her mind. This time, she knew exactly where to look. As soon as she reached her room, she took out her volume of Shakespeare, turning the pages of *As You Like It* until she found the illustration she wanted. This time it was Rosalind in the Forest of Arden once more, hair cut short, with a loose tunic over her breeches, giving her a passing resemblance to Robin Hood. There was a definite challenge in her expression as she gazed down at her Orlando, propped up against a fallen tree, gazing up at her as if mesmerised.

She turned the page in the candlelight, until she could make out the slight indentation underscoring the quotation. It was there. It surely wasn't a coincidence? And even if it was, she had found the answer in Rosalind's words. *'Make the doors upon a woman's wit, and it will out at the casement; shut that, and it will out at the keyhole; stop that, 'twill fly with the smoke out at the chimney.'*

'Thank you,' she breathed, kissing the figure of her name-sake. 'I know I've wit enough to make own my way in the world, and I will escape, however much anyone tries to stop me.'

Chapter Seventeen

Rosalind worked late into the night, developing the portraits. While she waited for the finished prints to dry, she retrieved Papa's most recent newspapers from the kitchens, where they were destined to clean windows and light fires.

Cordelia was right. There were plenty of appeals for drivers, along with clerical staff and munitions workers. She had nothing to lose. Hastily fetching her best writing paper from her room, she answered each one, stating that she was organised and that she was an experienced driver. Thank goodness for her drive with Jamie and Kate to visit the ship at Sutton Hoo – at least that was reasonably accurate. The last one written and safely sealed inside its envelope, she returned to the basement.

'I thought you might be here.' She found Jamie inspecting the line of photographs dangling from the lines stretched across the room. 'These are really good, Rosy. You're getting better and better, you know. You've got a real knack for capturing expressions.' He shuffled his feet, a certain sign he was feeling profoundly uncomfortable.

Rosalind's stomach lurched. She wasn't ready for another fight with a member of the family – she was still feeling too raw from the confrontation with Alma. 'I'm under instructions to make you see sense.'

So that's what this was about. Not that she could blame Jamie. It was the story of their lives: Papa gave his orders, and none of them had yet dared to come out in open rebellion.

'I'm not going to change my mind about Henry,' she replied, stubbornly.

'I don't expect you to. It's all right, Rosy. I didn't come to persuade you to accept him. He may be Will's friend and rich as blazes, but I've seen enough of him to know I wouldn't want any sister of mine near him.'

'I wouldn't marry him if he was the last man on earth.'

'Good for you. And don't let Papa nag you into changing your mind. I hate the thought of him having anything to do with you or Cori, or any woman I know.' He paused. 'And don't let yourself be anywhere alone with him. I've seen what he's capable of.'

She longed from the bottom of her heart to tell him of her narrow escape, of what Henry had tried by way of mastery to ensure her compliance, of the terror that still lingered on her skin at the thought of his touch, his intent to break her apart. But, although Jamie might be quiet by nature, she had seen the flash of temper when he'd see something he thought wasn't right. Heaven knew what might happen if he attempted to confront Henry.

If it came to fisticuffs, Jamie was light and fast, and would give as good as he got, with fury on his side to make any blows count. But from what she had seen of Henry Luscombe, he wasn't the kind to engage in a fight with an equal. He was more the kind to use his wealth and social standing to ensure any blame was placed squarely on his accuser. And then to pay a couple of thugs to do his dirty work for him.

'I'll take care,' she murmured.

'And Cori and Kate?'

'We'll stick together whenever he's here.'

'Good.' The relief in his voice was unmistakable. 'It's the way he talks about women. All women. As if they are chattels, and he can do anything with them and it doesn't matter, because they don't matter. Papa just sees that he's rich, and Will thinks being associated with him will make people think we're still rich and powerful. The way they were talking just now, they made it sound as if you were too scared of men to accept him, and you were just a silly girl. I know that's not true. You've more sense than that.'

'I have. Thank you.'

'I haven't done anything.'

'You believed me when I said I didn't want to marry Henry; you looked at it from my point of view.'

'It's the least I could do,' he muttered gruffly. 'I did my best to raise the fact that there are quite a few families around – wealthy and respected ones too – who won't let their daughters anywhere near Luscombe Hall. But Papa just informed me it was all envy and I shouldn't listen to gossip. It didn't do any good, I'm afraid.'

'But at least you tried. I won't ever forget that.'

He turned away, towards the photographs again, but she could sense he didn't see them at all. 'To be honest, Rosy, I can't wait until my call-up papers arrive. I'll be glad to get away.'

Rosalind gazed towards the rigidity of his back. Something fell into place. 'You're not intending to come back once the war is over.'

'I can't.' It came out in a rush. 'Rosy, I just can't. I'm not like Will, and I never will be. And Papa can't bear it. I'm not the kind of son he wants. He wants someone good in business like Oswald, who will make Arden rich again, or with royal connections, like Henry, who will make him feel part of the aristocracy again. I can't think like that.'

'Jamie, Papa still loves you, just as we all do.'

He shook his head, face still turned away. 'But it doesn't matter. Don't you see? We all know that, in the end, it's Papa's vanity that rules us. He's blind to the fact that Oswald sees us as brainless for having lost the Arden riches, and Henry despises us for being unable to have a house in London and a summer place in Cornwall, and that not even Will has been on a grand tour of the continent, as if we were still in the time of Lord Byron. Papa's living in the past. I'm not sure it's a past that even really existed, except in his mind. I want the future. And I've a feeling I can only do that away from here.'

'As an archaeologist?'

'Ironic, eh? Studying the past, to be free for the future. Even if Papa refuses to pay for me to go to Birmingham, I'll find a way of earning enough so I can study under my own steam. It's like your photography, Rosy. It's my passion, it's how I make sense of the world.'

'Then that's what you should do.'

'Even if that means I can never return here again?'

'Papa wouldn't do that!'

'Wouldn't he?' Jamie finally turned to face her, voice cracking with emotion. 'None of us have ever stood up against him. Not really. Will daren't, and Alma never does. I dread to think what he'll do when he finally has to accept I'm going to study archaeology with or without his permission. He doesn't believe me for now, but he's going to have to when this war is over. I'm going to give him no choice. Dear

Rosy, you're worth more than this, too. I promise that when I'm settled and have a place of my own, there will always be room for you, so you can escape if Papa tries to marry you off. And a darkroom too.'

'I'll hold you to that,' she said, smiling sadly, slipping her arm affectionately through his, as they left the prints to finish drying and made their way up the stairs into the main part of the house. Everything was still and silent. Even the maids had gone to bed.

'Still, I might not be called up,' said Jamie, with an attempt at cheerfulness, as they paused on the first landing. 'And this war could end before any of us are sent to fight.'

'It will be alright, you'll see.' There was a forlorn air about him she couldn't bear. 'I promise, Jamie, we'll work something out.'

'I hope so.' He vanished up towards his own room on the higher floor, where she could hear his footsteps creaking over the floorboards.

Chapter Eighteen

Over the next weeks, Rosalind continued to work in the village hall, taking photographs of volunteers heading off for training or able to escape home for a brief visit before heading to join their regiments. Then there were wives and sweethearts desperate to send their own portraits out to a loved one working away from home, and a rush of marriages, each grateful for the opportunity of a wedding photograph.

There was no sign of the lost letter from Guy. Each time Rosalind walked the path past the Roman villa her eyes scoured the grass and the hedgerow, trying to find any trace of paper, but there was nothing. There was no sign at Arden House, either. For the first week, she braced herself for the call into Papa's study, but it never came. Perhaps it had simply been lost, after all. Or, if it had been found, a careless – or even understanding – hand had destroyed it in the nearest fireplace. Slowly, she began to breathe more easily.

Finally, not even Papa could resist Cordelia's insistence on volunteering her skills. On a rare escape from Arden House, Rosalind accompanied her sister on the train journey to Birmingham, where they were met by Aunt Phyllis to take them to her terraced house, a short tram ride away. Rosalind couldn't help but envy the tiny room under the eaves which Cordelia would have all to herself.

'I'm glad I've a way of helping to support myself,' said Cordelia, as they returned downstairs to the neat drawing room, overlooking a narrow strip of garden. 'I don't like the idea of depending on Papa for my allowance.'

'Neither do I,' said Rosalind, gloomily. She had given up any hope of hearing back from Miss Blake, and she had received no reply to any of the applications she had sent, not even the munitions factory in Liverpool she had applied to in desperation.

There are plenty of openings for women to find paid work in Birmingham,' said Aunt Phyllis, 'I'm sure I can find you something, Rosy, if you're set on contributing to the war effort. I know of several places desperate for drivers. It's a rare skill you have there, you know, now so many of the men have left. We'd need to obtain your father's agreement, of course.'

'I don't mind sharing my room,' said Cordelia, eagerly. 'It would be fun.'

'I'll think it over,' said Rosalind. The temptation was agony. Perhaps charities in London were too overwhelmed with volunteers to consider a country bumpkin like herself? The prospect of easily finding work in Birmingham gave at least some prospect of freedom. But that still left the problem of being close enough to be dragged back at any moment...

She turned the question over and over in her mind as she took the train back to Stratford Railway Station, where she had parked Jamie's car for the short drive home. She was still deep in thought as she parked the Austin in the barn, where it was kept safe from rain and wind, along with the boys' bicycles.

'Ah, there you are, my dear.' From the way Alma shot out from the front door as she approached, it was clear she must have been looking out for her. With a sinking heart, Rosalind saw an unaccustomed look of determination on her step-mother's face. 'Your father is asking for you. I'll take your coat. You go straight there. He's in his study.'

Rosalind's mind was whirring as she made her way along the corridor. *Don't be silly,* she told herself. He was most likely to want to know how Cordelia had settled in to her temporary home. The door was open, waiting for her.

'Ah, Rosalind.'

'Papa?' She froze as he rose from his seat, picking up an envelope from his desk. At least he wasn't waving it at her, forbidding her to darken his door again.

'This came for you this morning. Who can you be corresponding with in London?'

The envelope was sealed, the address in an unfamiliar hand. The blood rushed to her head in relief. Even from here, she could see it was not from Guy.

'I'm sure it's perfectly respectable, please open it if you prefer, Papa.'

He handed the envelope over without a word. Rosalind tore it open, devouring the neat handwriting. She read it twice over to make sure the message sank in.

'I've been offered a position with a charity in London. As a driver, taking supplies to and from feeding stations for the troops and soup kitchens for poor families.'

'A driver?' said Alma, appearing in the door behind her. 'Darling, surely you have more than enough to keep you occupied here. I'm sure we can find charitable work for you in the village, if that's what you wish. London is so expensive, and wasn't there talking about possible air raids?'

'It's a paid position. I'm replacing men who have been called up. They'll teach me to drive a truck as well. I'll be able to support myself, as well as contribute to the war effort.'

Barely, but that was not the point. She had never earned anything in her life, she'd never had money that didn't require lists and notes of expenditure, with a snort from Papa on the rate at which she went through gloves, as she tried to hide as much as she could of anything spent on film or photographic chemicals. And she would be in London. Her heart began to beat fast. *She would be free to meet Guy when he was home on leave…*

Shakespeare's Rosalind was right. *Make the doors upon a woman's wit, and it will out at the casement; shut that, and it will out at the keyhole; stop that, 'twill fly with the smoke out at the chimney.*

'But, my dear, where would you live?'

'It says here I'll be sharing with other young women working for the war effort. It'll be perfectly safe.' She held out the letter. 'Lady Millicent Stanley has secured rooms to accommodate us, as the daughters of respectable families, with no male visitors permitted. And with cooking facilities,' she added as Alma opened her mouth to protest. 'I shall have to get Cook to show me some simple dishes, although I expect some of the girls there must know how to cook. I feel so lacking, not even knowing how to feed myself.'

'Lady Millicent *is* highly respected for her charitable work…' said Alma uncertainly, scanning through the letter. She looked up as her husband took the paper from her hand, inspecting it closely.

'Is this why you were so off-hand with Luscombe before he went away, Rosalind? Because you planned to go to

166

London? Are you aware how much embarrassment it cost us? Cost me?'

'I didn't expect to hear back from Lady Stanley. I promise I didn't set out to hurt Henry Luscombe's feelings. I've never given him any encouragement. I was simply honest with him, Papa.'

'Hmm.' He returned to his perusal.

'I want to do what I can for the war effort, Papa. Plenty of other girls are volunteering. At least I can do something if I'm working for a charity looking after those in need, and London isn't so very far away.' Desperation gave her imagination wings. 'Besides, Henry will be in France. If he's home on leave, isn't he's more likely to stay at the family's London home than travel to Church Stretton?'

She found her father had turned his inspection to her face. 'You're not quite so set against Luscombe, then.'

She gritted her teeth. What was a small untruth, if it was her only chance of getting away? 'No, Papa.'

'I'm glad to see you've come to your senses, now you've had time to think it over. He's a good match. You'll be far richer even than your sister, and that's saying something, given Gorwell's wealth. But your connections will be of the highest rank. You could have a title yourself, one day.' There was a moment's silence. 'Very well. I'll see if my acquaintances can vouch for the character of this Lady Stanley.'

'But, my dear, London,' protested Alma. 'So far away. With the danger of enemy attacks. And with so much work to be done here. Are you determined to leave me on my own, with no help at all?'

'You'll have Kate.' There was a thoughtful expression on Papa's face. 'This could well prove an opportune way of Rosalind being introduced into a far wider society. In the meantime, even with so many young men having left, she's bound to be introduced at social gatherings, which could open excellent opportunities for her sisters. And the Luscombes could well take her under their wing.'

'I'm sure they will,' said Rosalind demurely, earning herself a glare from her stepmother.

'Very well, I shall consider it,' said Papa. 'You will still have Kate as a companion, my dear Alma. Perhaps we should take this opportunity to ensure that Rosalind is settled.'

'Thank you, Papa,' said Rosalind, fleeing before he could change his mind.

As she hurtled into the corridor outside, she almost crashed into Kate, who was hovering just outside the open door, a look of thunder on her face.

'You're going to London?' Kate's voice was tight. 'Papa is allowing you to go to London?'

'I've been offered a position to help with the war effort. I don't expect it will be for long.'

'But he wouldn't give me permission to go even to Stratford! The most he'll let me do is to go with Alma to knit socks in the village hall.'

'I'm sure you can find something else.'

'Easy for you to say. Now he definitely won't let me go anywhere. You know Alma can't manage on her own. She gets into a panic if the slightest thing goes wrong. He's always made it clear he wants one of us to stay and help her. Cordelia managed to escape and now you. You've made sure the one who stays is me.'

'I haven't! When I'm in London I've a much better chance of finding something you can apply to as well.'

'You won't,' said Kate, sounding close to tears. 'You'll be too busy enjoying yourself and doing exactly what you please.'

'You know me better than that.'

'Even if you do, Papa will stop me. Will and Jamie are both determined to go on their great adventure as soon as they are called up, and Cordelia is doing what she wants. And you're going to be mixing with Lady this and Lady that in London, and preparing to be a duchess, and I'm left here to look after Alma until I'm an old maid and no one wants me.'

'I'll be Lady Stanley's employee, not her protégé,' said Rosalind. 'Besides, whatever Papa thinks, I'm sure I'll be too busy driving a van loaded with vegetables for soup kitchens to meet high society, even if they considered inviting me, which I doubt. I don't want to know the Luscombes and I bet no one has ever heard of the Ardens in London. I'll be back before you know it.'

'No, you won't,' said Kate angrily. 'Once you've escaped this place you won't be coming back. Who would? And Cordelia won't either, she'll be famous designing ballgowns for society ladies. I'm the one who's being left behind to rot. Well, I'm not staying, you hear? I'm not.'

'Kate—' But her sister had already fled, sobs echoing around the silent house.

Chapter Nineteen

Rosalind replied the next day to accept the position, waiting with baited breath while Papa telephoned acquaintances in London, with the newly installed telephone – a gift from Oswald – that now took pride of place in his study. So far, so good.

To her relief, her father's first informants confirmed that Lady Stanley did indeed have an impeccable reputation for charitable work, having run a field hospital near Calais in the last war, one whose reputation for effectiveness and efficiency had been second to none. His further enquiries, he announced at dinner that night, had established that her Ladyship was of irreproachable respectability, despite – according to his friends in the House of Lords – being rather too forthright in her manner for a female, even one with 'Lady' before her name. Several of these illustrious acquaintances had already offered to spirit Rosalind away to their country homes at the first sign of Herr Hitler daring to threaten the capital. Besides, many of their own daughters had already volunteered to assist with the war effort. He positively beamed.

Despite her father's approval at her presumed imminent elevation to being the darling of high society, the atmosphere in the house remained tense. Alma avoided her, while Kate refused to engage in any kind of conversation, leaving a silence you could cut with a knife at mealtimes, even when Bianca, by now visibly pregnant, swept in for one of her brief visits. Matters were not helped by Cook giving in her notice to take advantage of the opportunity to up a position in a large hotel in Birmingham, followed days later by the girl who had replaced Lucy finding better paid work in a munitions factory, where at least her evenings were her own and no one could forbid her to step out with any young man she wished.

One afternoon, while the family were gathered outside the front door as Oswald took Bianca home, a bicycle made its way up the driveway, swerving to miss the Bentley.

'I hate telegrams,' sighed Alma. 'They're never good news.'

Papa strode down to meet the cyclist. 'It's for you, Rosalind.'

'Probably another offer of marriage from Henry,' sniffed Kate, slinging her knapsack over one shoulder, ready to beat a hasty retreat with her sketchbook.

'It's from Lady Stanley,' said Rosalind. 'She's sending her chauffeur to fetch two other young women from Stratford. He's staying tonight in a guesthouse so they can start early tomorrow. She says he can pick me up as well on the way back.'

'She just expects you to jump to attention, then?' exclaimed Alma. 'And I thought petrol was rationed! We've hardly been able to use the car at all.'

'That's for private use,' said Papa, reaching for the telegram. 'Rosalind is embarking on important work. I have to admit, I didn't think you'd go quite so soon...'

Rosalind clutched her hands so tight the nails bit into her skin, terrified that he might, now it came to it, change his mind.

'It means we don't have to travel by railway, Papa, with all those soldiers, and search for our rooms once we get to London. It's by far the safest way, which is why she has taken so much trouble.'

He grunted. 'Very well. In that case, I shall telephone Lady Stanley immediately and let her know that you will be ready for when her chauffer arrives.'

As he strode back to the house with his customary sense of purpose, Rosalind remembered to breathe. It was going to be all right. She was about to take her first step towards freedom. Her stomach gave a lurch of excitement. She would write to Guy as soon as she got to London, telling him of her new address. She felt certain he would find a way to meet her. It might be only weeks, even days, before she saw him again.

Early the following morning, Rosalind unpacked and repacked her suitcase. She had been through what she would take several times, to make sure she could fit in everything she needed, but her heart was beating fast as she arranged her neatest skirt and blouse one last time among underclothes and her precious volume of Shakespeare. Finally satisfied nothing was forgotten, she put it next to the bed, and placed her camera in her large canvas shoulder bag, where she could keep it with her at all times.

It was real. Now it came to it, her excitement turned

towards terror. In just a few hours, she would be travelling to a new life, with two young women she had never met. She ran her fingers along the ancient wood of the window looking out over Arden's grounds, with the roofs of Brierley-in-Arden peering between the trees. This was something she would miss, with all her heart. It held her memories, her sense of herself. Memories of her mother, of impossible grief, all mixed with the magic of frosted mornings, cobwebs lacing the lawns as the sun lit the melting droplets into shimmering jewels and the soft light of summer evenings, with rabbits sneaking in at the edges of the grass and the distant scent of roses.

Strange how, only a short time ago, home had grated with its constrictions, and been the place she'd have given anything to escape. Now it came to leaving, she clung to the familiarity, the world that had made her. Whatever happened, the next time she stood here as the afternoon light bathed the walls of the kitchen garden, she would have seen things, experienced things, she could barely imagine. However short her time in London might be, this was the end of childhood. When she stood here again, she would be inevitably changed.

'Rosalind?' It was Alma hovering at the door that drew her back to the present. 'You're here. Didn't you hear me calling you?'

'I'm sorry, Mama. I'm coming down now.'

'Your father wishes to speak to you. You'll find him in the library – you'd best not keep him waiting.'

'Yes, of course.' She hastily grasped her bags and, with a final glance at her room, headed downstairs. It was only as she was placing her luggage in the hallway, ready for the arrival of Lady Stanley's chauffeur, that she felt the silence. There was no sign of Kate, and the clatter of pots and pans from the kitchens had been stilled, as if Cook's imminent departure had paralysed all activity. Even Alma had vanished. With a twinge of unease, she headed for the library.

'There you are.' Her father was standing at the window, looking out over the lawns.

'Yes, Papa.' She stood waiting. The line of his back gave no hint of his mood, but it brought back all the times she had been sent to him as a child to answer for her misdemeanours. Her throat constricted. She hoped Lady Stanley's chauffeur would arrive before long. Now it had come to it, all she wanted was to be on her way.

'Did you think I wouldn't know?'

'Know?'

He turned back to the desk, face tight with anger. 'Did you really believe I wouldn't find out? What kind of fool d'you take me for?'

'I don't know—' Her mind was back to every occasion she had waited, knees trembling, to discover what exactly had caused his ire. Her eyes scrabbled around for some clue, resting with a horrible certainty on the paper lying on his desk in front of her. Guy's letter.

She braced herself.

'This was handed to me this morning.'

'But... who?' she demanded. Who on earth had found it? That meant someone in the household, someone she loved and trusted, had kept the letter all these weeks, knowing that it was a weapon to use against her when the time came. A wave of nausea swept over her.

Her father ignored her interjection. 'So, this is why you're so insistent on going to London. Nothing to do with helping your country, but instead finding a way to disobey my wishes.'

'I told the truth when I said I was volunteering for the war effort.'

'But you intend to meet up with Thompson, after I'd expressly forbade you do any such thing.'

'That wasn't why I volunteered.'

'Then you'll promise me you won't make any attempt to see him.'

'Papa!' She stared at him in despair. A moment ago, she was revelling in her anticipation of freedom, now it seemed she would never escape his rule.

'Promise me you won't see him.'

She couldn't lie. Not this time. Not when asked so directly. Not about this. It was a promise she could never keep, had no intention of keeping. To lie now would mean there would never be any way back, and that she could not bear. She had to try to make some kind of compromise.

Rosalind took a deep breath. 'I won't refuse to see him, Papa.' A glance at his face revealed it was like thunder. 'But if we did ever meet up, it would only be briefly, as I would any other young man of my acquaintance. You trusted Lady Stanley would keep me in check, like the rest of the women working for her. She says in her letter that no men are allowed inside the door of our accommodation.'

'Young men can be devious to get what they want and persuade young women to anything.'

'Then you can't think much of me,' she retorted angrily. 'And I would never waste my time on any man who didn't respect me, or wish to cause me harm for his own amusement.'

'Really? When it's clear from this that you've been conversing for some time, after I'd told you he was not suitable.'

'They are letters, Papa. An exchange of views and opinions, much as I have with Cordelia, now she's in Birmingham. If you've read what he says, you can see Guy isn't trying to trick me into anything. He's perfectly respectful.' Thank goodness she didn't remember anything in the letter on the desk of the kind that sent a shiver down her spine and heat rush through her. At least this time, with Guy heading off for military training, he had been too preoccupied with the war and what might happen to stray into more personal exchanges.

The thought of Papa reading about holding close the memory of those brief moments within the shadows of the trees at the burial mound would have confirmed his worst suspicions and left her wanting to crawl away and hide beneath the nearest stone. Papa clearly had no intention of getting to know Guy. His wealth and social standing – or rather the lack of it – was what counted.

In the distance, came the sound of an engine in the lane leading from the village, followed by the deepening roar as the gears changed to accommodate the final hill up to the house.

Her father had returned to the letter, oblivious to anything else. 'I take it this is the real reason you turned down Luscombe?'

'Of course not. Papa, please, Henry would make a terrible husband. I wouldn't have agreed to marry him if he was the last man in the world.'

'But you're set on Thompson.'

'Not necessarily, Papa. It's true he's the only man I've met that I'd consider marrying, but I'd still want to know him better before I'd ever think of tying my fate to his. If I was going to do anything stupid, I'd have fled to Gretna Green by now. Surely you know me well enough to know I'm not going to make a fool of myself, or do anything that could endanger my future. Or the family reputation,' she added, as his eyebrows snapped together. 'I'm not a silly little girl whose head is easily turned.'

'You did this behind my back.'

'A few letters, Papa. What harm could they do?'

'Hmm.' He thrust the letter under a sheet of blotting paper, as if he could bear to see it no longer. She could sense it from the tightness of his face, from his suppressed fury, that he had read it – perhaps more than once. A twinge of sadness went through her. There might be no hint of anything improper, but Guy had still been a grown man pouring his heart out to her as a grown woman. It had been different with Bianca. She had forged her escape from his control without ever challenging his authority, without him even noticing. Desperation went through Rosalind.

'Very well, I'll promise not to make any attempt to see Guy Thompson, Papa. You can instruct Lady Stanley that I should be accompanied at all times, if that will reassure you.'

'You'll stay here. I'll inform Lady Stanley's man that you have been detained and that your mother and sisters need you.'

'No! Please, Papa.'

'Your stepmother needs you. I made an exception for Cordelia in respect of her talents being so clearly needed for the war effort, and Bianca has responsibilities of her own that will only grow. As for Kate...' A look of pain crossed his face. 'You can't expect to leave your stepmother to deal with her and run the household, especially now Cook is abandoning us and there's not domestic staff to be had for love nor money.'

The engine was slowing to almost nothing as the motorcar negotiated the gateposts set either side of the entrance. Within minutes it would arrive at the front door.

'But if I don't go with them now, Lady Stanley will assume it was because I'm too afraid, or that I'm flighty and can't be trusted. I'll never be given the chance again.'

'Your place is here. That's my decision. I'm not having you make a fool of me. There is plenty the volunteers in the village hall are doing to support our brave soldiers, if that's what you wish.'

'I don't want to make up food parcels and knit scarves! I want to do something more real. I—' She stopped herself just in time. But she could see he could read her mind, she could see it in his eyes. *I want to live my own life. Make my own choices. Live as I choose. Not be subject to you, or, by proxy, the man you choose to fashion me into the quiet, docile version of a woman you intend me to be.*

His gaze flicked away from hers. 'You will stay here and help your stepmother. If you leave now, you leave this house and this family. If you choose to follow your own path, out of some foolish infatuation, you have no place at Arden House. I will wash my hands of you. Don't believe I won't.'

'Papa—'

This time he heard it too, the drawing up of a heavy vehicle outside the door. 'There's no more to say on the matter. I shall expect to see you at dinner tonight, with no sulkiness, in consideration of your stepmother, and prepared to see reason.'

Rosalind hesitated. He meant it. She knew him well enough to know he was deadly serious. Take one step, and there would be no way back. Grief shot through her, combined with terror. Everything she had ever known, her entire world, her security, the place where she belonged, teetered on a cliff edge in front of her.

Out in the driveway, a door slammed, followed by foot-steps making their way towards the front door. Alma must have heard them too. Rosalind heard her greeting the new arrival, followed by a lowering of voices, leaving only the odd word floating along the corridor toward her. *Apologies. Indisposed. About to write to Lady Stanley.*

'Please, Papa.' But he was refusing to look in her direction, to even acknowledge she existed. That was how it would always be from now on. No more mellowing of his moods when she was present. No more choices. No more being able to slip away into the village and some sense of her life being her own. She had defied him, shown an independent streak, one that challenged his authority. One that could not be allowed to continue. She felt the breath being crushed from her body.

Rosalind fled, hurtling down the corridor, the walls swaying crazily either side of her as she went.

'Darling,' said Alma, as she reached the hallway. 'I was just explaining to Mr Stewart here, and that you will write to Lady Stanley tonight to apologise.'

Her bags were still there, tucked beside the hatstand. Her stepmother either hadn't seen, or hadn't had the presence of mind to remove them. Her stomach heaved.

'I knew you'd stay, in the end,' said Kate, appearing at the top of the stairs. 'Next thing, Cordelia will be back and we'll all be a family again.'

'Then you thought wrong,' said Rosalind, squashing the nausea. She swung her bag over one shoulder, grabbed her coat and hat from the hatstand, and shot past Alma, suitcase in hand. 'I'm quite ready, Mr Stewart. My stepmother is mistaken. I'm perfectly well, and eager to go.'

The chauffeur glanced uncertainly towards Alma, who dithered just enough for Rosalind to reach the car and greet the two young ladies already inside, who were watching agog at the drama unfolding in front of them. The dark-haired young woman nearest to her gave a grimace of understanding.

'Families,' she mouthed silently through the open window, raising her eyes to the heavens.

Rosalind found a hand placed on hers, taking her suitcase and loading it into the boot. There were voices behind her. Papa had arrived at Alma's side. Shutting everything out, all sounds, all feelings, she clambered inside, to take the remaining place on the back seat.

As the car reached the end of the driveway she craned her head to look back. The house stood blank and still in the morning light. She could make out Alma was still in the same position on the top step, Papa next to her. Kate was standing halfway down the driveway, as if she had made an attempt to run after her. They were like statues, visions of something that had once been. As Mr Stewart turned the Rover into the lane, heading towards Brierley and the road to London, they vanished from view between the trees.

Rosalind's vision blurred. Grief went through her. But what was done could not be undone. She would never see Arden, or her family, again.

Part Two

Rosalind: Oh, how full of briers is this working-day world!

Celia: They are but burs, cousin[...]if we walk not in the trodden paths, our very petticoats will catch them.

Rosalind: I could shake them off my coat: these burs are in my heart.

As You Like It. Act One, Scene Three

Chapter Twenty

London, September 1940

The wail of an air raid siren filled the air.

Rosalind cursed beneath her breath as she inched forward the van filled to the brim with vegetables and other supplies for the soup kitchens and centres for those made homeless in the bombing of London. She made her way along the street of darkened terraces as carefully as possible. In the uncertain light making its way through the slit of her headlamps, she was terrified of knocking down any unwary pedestrian braving the blackout.

'Not now,' wailed Mabel, her passenger. 'Please, not now. How the hell are we going to find an air-raid shelter?'

'There will be one somewhere,' Rosalind reassured her. The two had been late leaving the supply depot after collecting their delivery, leaving them perilously close to nightfall and the now nightly attacks by German bombers that sent all those who could in the capital heading for shelter. They would have made it back to Lady Millicent Stanley's headquarters, had it not been the need to change a tyre punctured by the remains of last night's raid, only to find themselves in an unfamiliar part of London as darkness fell.

Over the past weeks, since the first bombing raids at the beginning of September, Rosalind had grown accustomed to the routine of heading to the underground station a few minutes' walk from her lodgings the moment the siren sounded, or, more recently, with no let-up in night-time raids, as soon as darkness fell.

She urged the van on. There had to be a shelter of some kind nearby. The streets were deserted, no sign of the usual rush of people heading for the nearest place of safety once the air raid sirens sounded. The public shelters must be already full, everyone else already in their basements or Anderson shelters.

In the distance came the low rumble of approaching aircraft.

'Bloody Jerry,' exclaimed Mabel, voice shaking. 'We'll be blown to smithereens.'

'It doesn't mean they are going to drop their bombs here,' said Rosalind. 'They usually head further east.'

'I don't want to be the one to find out,' retorted her passenger.

'There's something over there.' Rosalind pulled the van under the shelter of a large shadow of a building, with the faint outline of a painted sign. She made out the flare of a match beneath the faint image of a swan, followed by the glow of a cigarette.

'Turn off them lights,' came a man's voice. 'You want Fritz to see?'

'Certainly not,' replied Rosalind, killing the engine and jumping out, followed by Mabel stumbling out of the passenger door.

'It'll be the docks again,' said the man, taking a deep draw of his cigarette. 'Poor sods.' The roar of the bombers was growing closer. With a final sucking in of smoke as if his life depended on it, he stubbed out his cigarette, placing the remains in his pocket. 'The tube's in the next street. You'll never get there. You're best staying the basement with the rest of us, I've got half my regulars down there, and all. My missus'll look after you.'

'Thank you,' said Rosalind in relief.

'Well, don't hang around then,' returned the publican, ushering them through the door. 'Jerry don't always end up where he's aiming, not even with the Thames all laid out to lead him right to them docks.'

A second door led them to a flight of steep stairs, lit by a single bare bulb hung from the ceiling. They were only half way down, following their rescuer, when the first explosions rocked the walls, sending mortar dust cascading down around them and plunging the basement into complete blackness.

'I told you not to go back up there!' came a woman's voice. A match was struck, this time bringing a kerosene lantern to life, revealing a young woman with two small children clinging to her. Arrayed on chairs and mattresses around them sat a motley selection of men and women, some still with their pints in their hands, squashed between kegs of beer and long racks of wine bottles. 'You're a fool to risk it Dylan, it'll be the death of you one day. Then what'll we do?'

'No need to fuss, woman,' replied her husband, ducking instinctively as a second, louder, explosion shook the cellar, sending the wine bottles in a far rack rattling wildly.

'It'll be all right,' said Rosalind, holding Mabel tight as the vibrations from several further thuds, one after the other, reached them from above.

'We've had worse,' said a white-haired woman, arms

184

around two older children, one on each side. She smiled reassuringly at the boy, who could not have been more than twelve, and was doing his best not to cry. 'They won't get us this time, dearie. And they won't get us ever.'

The next explosion sent great clouds of dust flying through the air, extinguishing the light. Rosalind tightened her grip on Mabel, who was shaking violently, fighting down her own nausea that threatened to overwhelm her. The smell of damp and human sweat filled her nostrils. She shut her eyes to blank out the darkness closing around her like a tomb.

There had been too many stories in the newspapers over the past weeks since the bombing began of people being trapped in their bedrooms as flames licked around them, their charred remains only found the following morning, or pinned under fallen rubble for days. She had been carefully through this in her mind, and less carefully in her nightmares, but this was the closest she had been to facing the reality of her own extinction. She gathered the memories of her life tight around her, as a protection.

Somewhere out there, Arden House remained as it had always done, for generations, surviving the destruction of war and civil war. She hoped with all her might that the bombers droning overhead would never find it, or the thatched rooves of Brierley, which had already lost too many of its sons in fields far away, not even their bodies returned to burial in the soil that had made them.

She might never know if Guy survived the fighting out in France, or Will and Jamie, who had both finished their training and were headed out to join the conflict. She might never know the fate of Cordelia and Kate, now both engaged in war work far away, with only letters from Cordelia, hastily scribbled between the bombing raids devastating Birmingham, to let her know they were still alive.

Light flickered against her lids. Rosalind's eyes flew open to the steadying flame of the lamp. A trickle of mortar slid down the wall beside her, loud in the silence. A thud echoed in the distance, further away.

'Let's hope there ain't no more of the bastards, and that lot don't come back this way,' said one of the older woman, grimly.

A second lamp was lit, as the patrons of The Swan in Clover resumed their evening. Several of the older men returned to their interrupted game of dominoes. A young man peered short-sightedly through his round spectacles as he worked on the intricate innards of a portable radio, while his elderly neighbour patiently glued the broken wheels of a slightly moth-eared toy, its brown fur worn off in bald patches, but still making a valiant attempt to resemble a Lakeland terrier.

The group of middle-aged women propped up between the wine racks took up their steady click of knitting needles and crochet hooks as they exclaimed over the dog-fights they had watched over the Thames earlier that week, the plucky little Spitfires downing the cumbersome bombers before they could reach their destination. In a far corner, the publican's wife settled her children into camp beds, before picking up her mending of small trousers and tiny romper suits, head nodding towards sleep every now and again.

Finally, the all-clear sounded, bringing with it relief, tempered by dread of what lay waiting for them in the world above. Rosalind followed the night's companions as they emerged warily, into the first light of dawn, and a scene of utter destruction.

'At least the van's still there,' exclaimed Mabel. 'Lord knows how. I didn't fancy walking home.' Their van had survived with little more than a cracked windscreen and a covering of dust and rubble, its back door swung open to reveal the emptiness within. The rest of the narrow terrace, however, was lit with the glow of fires, showing the front of several of the buildings gone, the survivors staggering aimlessly in the street, shocked and white with dust.

Without a word, Rosalind followed Mabel in joining the improvised line removing buckets of rubble, passed from hand to hand. Further down, firemen tackled one blaze after the other, as those lucky enough to be unscathed helped free neighbours trapped beneath the ruins of their homes. As the light strengthened, the sense of urgency eased a little, as a family trapped deep in their cellar were safely pulled out, one by one, dusty and bloodied, but grateful to be alive.

With the final child placed in the arms of his weeping mother, Rosalind stepped away from the line. Rage bubbled up, replacing the night's fear, as her eyes took in the devastation around her, and lives that had been quietly lived without harm to anyone were broken so violently, so needlessly, apart. She reached for the camera in the shoulder bag slung across her body, which she never let out of her sight, using the rest of her roll of film, as well as those tucked away in a side pocket, to capture the broken houses, the children with roughly bandaged heads and limbs, and the tiny forlorn shape beneath the covering of a sheet.

'Are you sure you don't mind?' she asked of a young woman surveying the ruins of her home, the front almost completely destroyed. Wallpaper showing pink stripes interspersed with bunches of roses hung from the jagged remains of the living room walls. In the room above, an iron bedstead perched on the edges of a cliff, next to the bathroom whose sides had been sliced away to reveal an untouched cistern and washbasin, the family's toothbrushes still neatly stored in a glass tumbler.

'You go ahead,' said the woman, swinging up a sobbing child into her arms, two more, only slightly older, clinging to her skirts. 'You show them what it's bloody like.'

'I'd like to take a picture of you too, if you don't mind? You'll just be a silhouette against your house. I'll make sure no one can see your faces.'

'You take our faces.' The woman's voice broke. 'You show everyone what Jerry leaves behind. I've a husband at the front, and Mum's driving the trams all hours. How am I supposed to get to work and look after this lot with no home to go to? The firemen won't let us in to find anything, says the whole roof might come down at any minute. Took us years, did that house, and every penny we earned. All we wanted was for the kiddies to grow up right and not in that filthy slum we left behind. Now it's all gone. We've nothing. So you bloody show them.'

'I'll do my best,' said Rosalind, balancing her camera on a kitchen chair flung carelessly into the road by the blast, praying that there was no shake on the low light and the image would come out clear. She took picture after picture in the surrounding destruction, until there was no film left, shutting her senses to the sight of a baby's shoe in the rubble, the twisted remains of a rusted perambulator and the stench of fire, which left a lingering edge that caught in her throat and she did her best to tell herself was not the singeing of human flesh.

When she returned to the van, Mabel had swept away the debris and cleared the remains of the windscreen so they could see out.

'I don't like to leave them,' said Rosalind.

'Me neither.' Mabel pushed her hair, almost completely escaped from its pins, away from the grubbiness of her face. 'But the firemen say they want this moved, and at least we can let Lady Millicent know what happened, before she starts telling our dads we didn't make it back last night. I'm not being dragged back home to sweeping floors and helping Mum in the shop, not for anybody's business.'

Rosalind pulled herself into the van and set off gingerly, avoiding the detritus of lives and shards of broken glass. Once free, they headed back into the just-stirring streets, with men and women making their way through the gloom, plodding wearily, but determinedly, to work.

'You wouldn't think anything had happened,' said Mabel. She shuddered. 'Funny how it's started to feel normal.'

'I suppose we've all got used to it.'

'Like them lads at the front,' added Mabel, who waited in a permanent state of anxiety for each letter from her sweetheart, fighting in France.

'I expect so.' Rosalind did her best to shut out the sights and the sounds of just a few hours ago, her treacherous imagination taking her to the front line where those she loved must be under constant bombardment and the imminent possibility of death.

The two returned to the little depot of the charity collecting food and other necessities for the poor and the displaced, arriving as the lady volunteers were sorting out the day's deliveries under the eagle eye of Lady Stanley.

'Good grief!' Lady Millicent Stanley was a well-built woman with greying hair and a non-nonsense approach. She had spent the years between the wars terrorising the local school board into submission and running a charity hospital for sick children with a firm hand. She now abandoned her supervision of freshly laundered babies' napkins and tins of National Dried Milk to hurry towards them.

'I can see you've had a night of it. We could hear the bombing from here. I was almost certain I might be composing letters to your parents this morning... Thank goodness. I could never have forgiven myself, sending you out like that, so far, and so late in the day.'

'The van's in more or less one piece,' said Rosalind. 'Apart from the windscreen and there's a slight rev on the engine when it goes uphill. And I had to change a tyre – the old one's slashed, I'm afraid.'

'No need to worry about all that, my dear.' Lady Millicent's usually severe expression had softened a little, the lines of her face deepened with weariness and anxiety. 'You're both safe, that's what matters. I'll get one of the girls to look at the van, we'll have it back on the road in no time. Now, I take it neither of you have had breakfast?'

They were given cups of tea, accompanied by toast with generous servings of marmalade, brought in from Lord Stanley's country estate in Wiltshire by Lady Millicent's husband, a mild-mannered man who generally followed his wife's instructions with good-humoured adoration.

When they both began to nod off, Rosalind and Mabel were driven back to their lodgings by Lady Millicent herself, with instructions to take a bath and rest as much as they could while daylight kept them reasonably safe from any further raids.

While Mabel could barely keep her eyes open, Rosalind found herself unable to sleep. Horrible as it had been, she was aware of having been in the right place at the right time to obtain a unique picture of an event as it happened, the kind of thing a photojournalist might dream of. Besides, she could not get the image of the woman with her three young children out of her head, any more than the baby's shoe amongst the rubble. As quietly as she could, she made her way to the small cupboard under the stairs she had made into a makeshift darkroom, with a thick curtain to block out the light.

Jamie, bless him, had retrieved the contents of the basement at Arden house during his last leave, arriving with it hidden beneath blankets in the boot of his motor car. He didn't say so, but she suspected he had attempted to intervene on her behalf with Papa and got nowhere. She could feel the undercurrent of anger as he brought her precious equipment, and his even greater determination to make his life elsewhere once the war was over. Whatever happened, she had understood, with a feeling of profound sadness, the Arden family would never be the same again.

With the film developed, she inspected it carefully. Her printing equipment was limited, but she had enough to give an idea, and reveal if the photographs were clear. Some she could see were blurred from movement in the low light. She printed the ones that appeared to be in focus, and were most striking. The shoe in the rubble told its own tale, one that still caught in her throat. The woman with the three small children stood forlorn, but dignified, the epitome of resilience in the face of despair.

Once the prints were dried, she took them out into the light to inspect them closely. Laid out, she could see they told a powerful story. She might have failed in her attempts from Arden House to have her pictures and articles accepted by a magazine, but she was not going to give up on these without a fight. Despite her exhaustion, which had by now become a normal state for everyone she knew, Rosalind spent the rest of the day writing and rewriting her impressions of the night under the air raid, until finally it felt right.

Their adventure meant that Lady Millicent did not expect either her or Mabel to resume their deliveries the following day. Rosalind slipped out while Mabel was still asleep, and the others had left for their day's work, following her map through the streets to the address on the battered little business card she had retrieved from Henry Luscombe's scorn.

Finally, she found herself in front of a tall building, containing several offices. The *Woman's Time*, the door announced, was on the first floor. Taking a deep breath, she made her way inside.

'I wish to see the editor, please,' she announced, doing her best to emulate the self-confident tones of Lady Millicent.

The young woman sitting at the nearest desk with a roll of fair hair swept up high above her head, and wearing an expensively tailored jacket, complete with a broach centred with a large sapphire, looked her up and down, with the air of assessing her for good maid potential. 'She's in a meeting. Do you have an appointment?'

'No.' Rosalind held out the parcel with her article and the photographs. 'But I do have something here she'll wish to see.'

The girl clearly decided she would not make the level of scullery maid. 'Leave it on the desk. We'll see she gets it.'

This year, next year, sometime, never…

The door of the inner office was open. 'As I said, it's urgent,' Rosalind said, as loudly as she dared. 'I'm offering it here first, as I'd prefer to support the reputation of a women's magazine for serious reporting. Or would you rather I went to *The Times*? I'm sure they'd love such a scoop.'

The young woman's lips compressed. 'As I said, leave it on the desk.'

'What kind of a scoop?' called a voice through the open door of an inner office.

'The air raid last night,' returned Rosalind. 'I was in the middle of it.'

'Photographs?'

'Several. And an article giving a first-hand account.' She concentrated on persuading the unseen woman, throwing doubts and female modesty to the winds. 'There were no reporters on the scene and anyone who did get there won't have been able to gain nearly so vivid an impression. I sheltered in a pub basement through the raid and spoke to plenty in the street immediately afterwards.'

'I've plenty coverage of air raids.' The voice wasn't totally indifferent, but clearly on the point of dismissing her. 'As have my rival publications. I need things that are unique.'

Unique. Rosalind dug her heels in. 'This is unique. The women talked to me in ways they'd never do to a male reporter, and especially because they knew I'd shared the danger with them. I wasn't some man dashing in afterwards looking for a story, without caring to understand things from her point of view. You can't get more on the spot than that.'

'You'd better come in, then.'

The disdainful young lady sighed loudly and returned to her desk, leaving Rosalind to sweep past her into the office.

Inside the door, she came to a halt.

'Oh.'

'Well, I never. I thought the voice was familiar. I didn't expect to see you here, Miss Arden. Unless, perhaps, you're visiting family?'

Rosalind cursed inwardly. The gaze meeting her was less than welcoming. She squared her shoulders. 'Good morning, Miss Blake. And no, I am not meeting my family.' Before the editor could say another word, Rosalind hastily spread out the photographs on the desk.

Miss Blake turned away, busy lighting a cigarette. 'And how is Mr Luscombe, these days?'

'I wouldn't know. And I most certainly don't want to know.'

'Really.' She didn't believe her. Miss Blake gave the photographs a cursory glance. 'I take it he sent you here?'

'Of course not! That's utterly unfair. I don't spend my life just doing some man's bidding, any more than you do. Besides, he's a vile little man I intend never to see again.'

'You've some sense then.' The gaze returned to the photographs, this time lingering on each one in turn. 'The printing could be better.'

'It's the best I could manage, under the circumstances.'

'Circumstances?'

'A cupboard under the stairs in my lodgings. I've brought the negatives as well.'

'I see.' Miss Blake's attention was focussed on the image of the young woman and her small children, framed against the ruin of their home. 'You took these yourself?'

'Yes. And like I said, I've written an article, too. A first-hand account.'

'Have you now.' Miss Blake reached out to take the paper, scanning it rapidly with her eyes. Halfway down the first page, she placed the cigarette in a large cloisonné ashtray, the smoke rising unheeded from its deep turquoise decorated with an abstract pattern of flowers, as she remained absorbed in reading.

'I've others too. I've taken photographs of the work women are doing.' Rosalind reached into the envelop. 'Like Lottie Evans here, acting as a fire warden, and Mary Ellis who drives a fire engine. I've plenty more.'

'I see.' Miss Blake eyed her. 'So why now?'

'I beg your pardon?'

'I take it you were unaware I'd been promoted to the post of Editor. But why approach the *Woman's Time* now?'

'My brother only recently brought my photographic equipment so I can make a proper darkroom. I don't have access to a studio. And I thought... surely this subject is of interest?'

'This subject?'

Rosalind felt the heat rise from her toes to the top of her head. 'I've submitted articles before. Before the war, that is.'

Miss Blake sniffed. 'My dear Miss Arden, it's not my responsibility if you change your mind.'

Rosalind stared. 'Change my mind?'

'I don't take the risk of commissioning work from a young woman only to find her lose interest. I'm not likely to risk such a thing again.'

'What commission?'

'The village near Stratford-upon-Avon. The singer. The female archaeologist and her find. The work at Sutton Hoo. I have to say, those prints were of better quality than these.'

'Because I had a proper darkroom, not a cupboard!' retorted Rosalind. 'And you didn't commission anything. I never heard a thing back.' She met Miss Blake's eyes. They were irritated, convinced of their truth. 'Oh my lord! It was addressed to the house...'

'Arden House.'

'Buggeration,' said Rosalind, ignoring the raised eyebrows. 'I should have given the direction as the Post Office. Only—' She stopped.

'Only?'

'I already had letters directed there.' She failed to fight down a blush. 'I was afraid if there were too many, someone might say something. And no, it wasn't Henry Luscombe,' she added, as the eyebrows were raised higher. She took a deep breath. 'I'm sorry, Miss Blake. I never received any communication from you. Do you think I wouldn't have jumped at it if I had? After all, you've just had first-hand evidence I'm prepared to humiliate myself in person to follow my ambitions.'

Miss Blake was still watching her, as if trying to make up her mind. 'Marriage to Henry Luscombe would give you a far more secure future.'

'Never!' It must have been lack of sleep and the shock of last night catching up with her. To her mortification, tears sprang to Rosalind's eyes and her legs shook uncontrollably. She sat down hard.

'Veronica!' Miss Blake's voice echoed through the building, followed by the appearance of the superior young woman.

'Yes, Miss Blake?'

'Tea.'

'Tea?'

'With sugar.'

'Sugar?'

'Oh, for goodness sake, girl, use the stash in the tin marketed "Lentils".'

'Yes, Miss Blake,' murmured Veronica, through delicately gritted teeth.

Miss Blake waited until the tea arrived, with the smallest possible bowl of sugar. 'Thank you, my dear. And shut the door behind you, will you? Miss Arden and I have a considerable amount to discuss.'

'Yes, Miss Blake.' The door slammed so hard the frame shook.

'Does her good,' remarked Miss Blake. 'I'm giving her the training in life skills her governess and Swiss finishing school never managed. All Veronica needs is the corners knocked off her, along with the conviction that the world owes her a living, and she might make a journalist yet.' She took out the remains of fruitcake, heavy with real raisins, from a tin in her desk. 'I take it you don't wish to discuss Henry Luscombe then?'

'No.'

'Nasty piece of work, especially where young women are concerned.'

'Very.' She caught the look on Miss Blake's face. 'Oh, he didn't hurt me. Not in that way. He tried to but, well, I bashed him with a door.'

Miss Blake chuckled. 'So that's what it was. I have my sources, so I'm well aware he couldn't use one of his arms for weeks. He told acquaintances he'd damaged it heroically stopping a runaway horse, but I so hoped there might be a woman involved.' Her eyes returned to the photographs. 'Good for you. You clearly have more sense than I did at your age, or I would never have looked twice at Gordon Knight and his veneer of charm.'

'I'm not sure about the sense,' replied Rosalind gloomily.

Miss Blake gave a faint smile. 'I'm glad to hear it. You can have too much of a good thing. If I'd any sense, I'd be married to the nearest vicar by now and digging for victory in the deepest countryside. You had the presence of mind to use your camera when caught in an air raid. That shows courage and an ability to keep your head in the most distressing of circumstances.'

'Very well, Miss Arden, I'm interested now. I liked your photographs of village scenes. I was disappointed when I heard nothing back. I so nearly destroyed them, now I'm rather glad I chose to keep them on the off-chance you might change your mind. I'd like to look at them again. What with all the shortages, and war raging above us in the skies, not to mention bombings of our major cities by night, my readers appreciate reminders of the life they once took for granted, and are fighting to have again. I'm always on the lookout for photographs of women working for the war effort, and any articles to accompany them. That will interest my readers, and reminds them that we are all doing our bit, in everything we do, even if it doesn't feel very heroic at the time.'

'I can certainly get more pictures,' said Rosalind. 'And stories. As many as you wish.'

Miss Blake lit a fresh cigarette and eyed Rosalind through the smoke spiralling upwards in the light, making its way through windows crisscrossed with brown tape to protect from the danger of flying glass. 'I'd also like to cover more of how people are coping after the bombing, particularly the women. How they are rebuilding their lives in the face of hardship and tragedy. Women of all ages, mind, not just the pretty girls my male photographers can't seem to see beyond, however much I nag them.'

'Definitely,' said Rosalind eagerly. 'Until last night, I'd no idea of what it was really like in the places that see the worst of it. Or the courage it must take just to keep life going.'

'It's an angle I feel is still too little covered, particularly from a woman's point of view, with all her responsibilities for housing and feeding and keeping generations of her family safe.' Miss Blake placed a slab of cake in front of Rosalind. 'Now, Miss Arden, I hope you're not squeamish when it comes to business. I suggest we discuss terms.'

Chapter Twenty-One

Rosalind returned to her lodgings in a daze. The payment for her photographs might not be much, but her work would finally appear in a magazine, and she had the promise that Miss Blake would look at any pictures and articles she sent in. It was a start. She hated the thought that it had been the destruction of houses and lives that had given her the opportunity, but that made her even more determined to show the resilience she had found amongst the ruins of everyday lives.

She still couldn't quite believe her earlier photographs of Sutton Hoo and Brierley-in-Arden had not been destroyed. She had left Miss Blake looking through them again, as a source of welcome distraction from the grim news from France.

Rosalind could have kicked herself. She should have given her correspondence address as the Post Office! She'd thought that if Papa saw that she'd received a letter from a magazine, he might be forced to take her ambitions more seriously. Instead, it had wasted so much time. If it hadn't been for the chance of being caught in the air raid, she might never have known.

She turned into the street leading to her lodgings deep in thought. As she drew closer, her attention was caught by the figure in Khaki leaning against the railings alongside the front of the house, absorbed in hasty scribbling in a notebook. Her heart beat fast.

'Guy!'

He looked up, face breaking into a smile. 'Thank goodness. I thought I'd missed you.' He closed the notebook, shoving it into his pocket. 'I was leaving you a note. I only just managed to get away – I didn't get the chance to let you know.'

'And I wasn't here.' She could so easily have missed him altogether.

'I knew it was only luck that you weren't out at work, but I had to take the chance. I've only a few hours.'

Rosalind glanced up at the house. Visitors were strictly forbidden, but a blind eye was turned now and again to girls with sweethearts on leave, or heading for the front. All the same, she had an uncomfortable sense of curious eyes watching their every move.

'Come on.' She took his hand, hurrying him out of sight, to the iron gates of the nearby park. They joined pathways filled with uniformed nannies pushing perambulators and mothers with small children, all enjoying the sunshine, merging amongst the other couples walking slowly, finding the nearest thing to isolation, away from family or lodgings and the need to observe the proprieties, absorbed in precious moments with each other.

'A few more minutes and you'd have gone,' said Rosalind, her stomach twisting at the thought. 'I so wish I'd been back sooner.'

'You were there. You're here now. That's what matters.'

They walked in silence for a few minutes, heading towards a more formal part of the gardens, where benches were set between trailing arbours of roses, giving a touch of privacy. They took the one remaining bench, among couples huddled together. From the bench next to them came the sound of a woman's muffled crying, a man's voice comforting her.

Rosalind held Guy tight. 'I was so afraid I might never see you again.'

'I'll always come back to you,' he replied, meeting her kiss. 'Your letters are the only thing keeping me sane out there.'

'I know it's not the same, but yours keep me sane here.'

He pushed tendrils of curls away from her face. 'I've heard it's bad with the bombing.'

'Not a bad as being on a battlefield, or in a country that has been overrun.'

'All the same, I can't help wishing you were somewhere safe.'

'Just as I wish you didn't have to be in the midst of the fighting.'

'Touché.' He smiled, his old familiar smile, and yet one that was changed, as the tightening of the flesh over the cheekbones lent a gauntness to his face that had not been there before, and the shadows behind his eyes spoke of things he had seen that she would never see. Just as she had seen sights amongst the rubble of the bombing raid she had locked away in her mind as the only way of keeping horror at bay.

It felt a thousand lifetimes ago that she had last seen him in the unchanging landscape of Sutton Hoo. Already, despite the letters they exchanged when they could, and with consideration of the censors, they had been through experiences too profoundly visceral to share, even with each other. A sliver of fear went through her. She had been so focussed on the physical reality of him, willing him to simply stay alive, it had not occurred to her that there might be more than one way for love to be lost. But now, more than ever, she could not extinguish herself, even if it meant losing him forever.

'I don't want you to protect me, Guy. This is where I want to be.'

'So I can see.' His hand touched her cheek, travelling slowly down the exposed flesh of her neck, to where her jacket began, expelling the breath from her body.

'Come with me.'

'What?' *Had he heard nothing at all?*

'Not now. I wish with all my heart it could be. I mean when this is over. One of the men I'm stationed with has a cousin with an architectural practice in New York. He's put in a good word for me. I could finish my training there. It's a respected practice, once with branches all over America. We could start a new life there. A good life. Dearest Rosy, I can't imagine being without you beside me, as my wife.'

She could no longer think, no longer feel, except that he was with her now, and she could not bear the thought of ever letting him go.

'Of course I'll come with you. I can't imagine life without you either.'

His arms tightened around her, his mouth on hers, and she was lost in his warmth, the closeness of him. If she lost him, her life was over. Her body might live on, but inside she would be empty. She didn't even have a photograph of the two of them together. She had taken so many portraits of men about to be waved off by wives and mothers, sweethearts and daughters, knowing that black and white image might be all they would ever have left and they would never see them again. The thought of never seeing his face again was unbearable agony.

'Just come back,' she said, voice cracking.

'I'll always come back to you, darling Rosy. You're the love of my life. I so nearly didn't join Will's invitation to swim in Arden Lake that day. It's haunted me ever since, how close I came to never meeting you, and how much poorer my life would have been. You're all I ever want. I can't imagine existing without you.'

She held him as his lips found hers once more, drinking in the clean smell of him, the faint beginnings of stubble brushing against her face, the beat of his heart against hers. Desire swept through her, startling in its intensity, with urge to entwine him ever closer, until there was nothing between them, or ever could be again.

But it had to end. Slowly he released her, kissing each part of her face as if to draw it in to become part of him, so he would never forget. The sound of the subdued voices around them crept in, along with the distant rumble of the city and the scent of damp and fallen leaves.

They rose and, still holding each other tight, emerged to join the other couples making their way as slowly as was humanly possible, towards the iron gates, and out into the street.

Chapter Twenty-Two

London, Spring 1945

Rosalind had never thought the war would last for almost six long years. By the spring of 1945, she was, like everyone she knew, bone-weary, worn out by the tension of not knowing what might happen from day to day, the daily struggle to overcome the ever tighter rationing and shortages and the grief of loss all around. Even with the growing certainty over the past year that Hitler would eventually be defeated, and the war was finally drawing to its close, there was little sense of celebration, more a feeling of utter numbness.

As she finished the final photographs for her series following the work of the female police, and returned wearily to her motorcycle, propped up against iron railings, Rosalind patted the letter buttoned safely inside an inner pocket. Jamie's letters had become briefer over the past year. He had seemed distant, shut away, when she had last met him on leave, as he stopped briefly in London on his way to Arden. But at least he gave give her news of Will, and the hope that the fighting would soon be over.

Guy still wrote to her regularly, each letter a precious

sign that he was still alive. Like Jamie, he told her very little of the fighting, filled instead with memories of summers in the Warwickshire countryside and wondering if the Roman mosaic in the fields at Arden had revealed any more of its secrets. They had only managed to meet a few times over the past years, precious moments in a park or café, snatched between her next deadline for Miss Blake and his visits to his family in Stratford.

Rosalind sighed and packed her camera securely in the pannier on the back and set off along the river towards home. The Triumph had been the best investment she could have made with her first earnings from her commissions from Ginny Blake. It allowed her to travel quickly to places beyond the reach of the even more ancient bicycle she had first used to seek down opportunities to show the communities surviving the destruction.

Her journalism work had gradually begun to take up more of her time over the past year, as she had gained a reputation for being the first on the scene when disaster struck. Her photographs of the destruction left behind, of soup kitchens and temporary shelters, and of Londoners pulling together in the worst of circumstances, had appeared in magazines and newspapers, along with a series showing the families sheltering in tube stations, deep in the London underground.

Thankfully, the Blitz had been abandoned during the second year of the war, leaving her to concentrate more of her energies on articles following the work women had taken on to replace the men at the front, just as they had done in the previous conflict. She had covered everything from munitions factories, and the driving of trams and buses, to the young women like Princess Elizabeth joining the Auxiliary Territorial Service. She had tried her best to show mothers juggling work with finding some kind of childcare, not to mention keeping their houses in order and their families fed. Little wonder so many of them were worn down and couldn't wait for the men to come home and life to return to normal. But she had also interviewed some who, despite the constant anxiety and bracing for the worst, were enjoying the freedom and the sense of abilities stretched far beyond their own expectations, let alone anyone else's.

As Rosalind reached her lodgings, the cloud handing over the city lifted, sending shafts of spring sunlight onto ruined buildings and revealing the hint of clear blue above.

'Did you find them?' called Amy, the nurse who lived on the floor above, pausing in her rush for the bus to take her to her shift, as Rosalind wheeled her motorcycle towards the safety of the back yard.

'Them?

'There was someone looking for you. A woman.'

'A woman?' It must be one of her London friends. Despite herself, her heart sank. How many times had her hopes been raised that it was Guy, back on leave, or Will and Jamie returning as the triumphant heroes Papa dreamed of welcoming home?

'Didn't give a name,' said Amy. 'Just said she'd find a café and wait for you. I suggested she went to the British Restaurant in the old Dawlish furniture shop, as it's so close.'

'When was this?'

'About half an hour ago. I'd have let her in, but I hadn't seen her before, and you can't be too careful these days, can you?'

'No,' said Rosalind, her initial disappointment turning to unease. She only knew a handful of women outside those in her lodgings, mostly they were all too tired and working too long hours to meet, and they would have written or telephoned to make arrangements. The only friend Amy didn't know by sight was Barbara, who also worked as a freelance journalist, but Barbara's husband was still on leave, so it was unlikely she would take the time to come over to this part of London, and especially unannounced.

Amy shot off in search of her bus, while Rosalind left the motorcycle in the protection of its outhouse, removing her helmet and shaking out her hair, closely cropped for ease. She headed off on foot to the abandoned furniture shop that had been turned into a British Restaurant, serving hot meals without the need for coupons, including to those who had been bombed out of their homes and owned few means of cooking a hot meal.

Rosalind paused at the door, scanning the hotchpotch collection of tables donated by businesses and the surrounding houses, searching for a familiar face. Being lunchtime, the restaurant was full, a haze of smoke and steam hanging over the place. The lady volunteers who ran the Dawlish had gained a reputation as being excellent cooks, able to turn even the most frost-bitten of turnips and a handful of dried beans into a delicious pie. Her visitor could well have been too late to secure a table. She had most likely gone to the more pricey, and decidedly less popular, café a few doors along...

'Rosalind!' She paused at the familiar voice, so unexpected she didn't trust her ears. But the slight figure in a dark linen suit, now hurrying towards her between the tables, was unmistakeably that of Alma. One glance at her stepmother's face, and the world tilted on its axis.

'Who?' she demanded.

'I'm so sorry, my dear. Perhaps we should find somewhere a little quieter.'

'Who?'

'Will.' Alma's voice cracked. 'The telegram arrived a few days ago. He died in a hospital in France. We didn't even know he'd been wounded. And yesterday the message came that Jamie is missing, presumed dead.' Her face collapsed. 'I'm sorry, my dear. One would have been bad enough, but to lose both of them, and over so short a period...'

The murmur of the diners around them had become more subdued, no one looking in their direction, while every ear focussed with an irresistible fascination on their own worst dread unfolding before them.

Rosalind reached into her pocket, forestalled by the waitress, who shook her head at any suggestion of payment for the untouched pot of tea grown cold on the table. 'Thank you,' she mouthed, her unnatural calm of knowing that she had to get them both to a safe place before her brain could take in what she had heard, threatening to crack apart. Blinded by tears, she led Alma into the street, and the short walk to her rooms.

At least most of the girls in her lodgings were out at work, apart from the small group of nurses from the floor below making toast in the little shared kitchen, who had just returned from their shifts and were heading for bed.

She couldn't believe it. Rosalind made tea in silence, tactfully ignored by the nurses, who knew when not to ask questions – particularly when someone appeared with red-rimmed eyes. *Will was gone.* She would never see him again. He would never lord it over her. His grand schemes for Arden House would never take place. Their shared memories of childhood had vanished forever. She would never hear his voice or see his eyes, ever again. All that time she had been irritated by his grandiose gestures, by his awareness that he was the chosen one who would one day inherit the mantel of Arden – she would have taken it back in a blink of the eye. She would have given anything for him to drive her to fury.

And Jamie. Her mind froze, blocking out the thought. It was horrible enough to know that Will was most likely already part of a land far away, among rows of crosses, but the thought of Jamie laying in the mud for rats and crows to feast on was unbearable. Or maybe he was, as she had read, one of those left in a crater, lingering in fear for days, as life ebbed agonisingly away.

Would Guy be next? She couldn't help the thought creeping in between her grief. She had interviewed mothers who had lost more than one son to the fighting and a husband to the bombing, some left with traumatised grandchildren to support, the rest of the family gone.

Rosalind took the teacups to her room, where Alma was sitting in the armchair by the window, gazing listlessly over the rows of roofs and chimneys. They must be practical. There would be time for them to grieve, long years ahead. But for now they must be practical.

'Does Papa know you're here?'

Alma shook her head. 'I couldn't tell him I was leaving, even for a short time. The news broke him, my dear. You should have seen him. Both sons lost with days of each other, and his daughters scattered heaven knows where, and Bianca and the children are staying with Oswald's friends in the lakes for the summer.'

Alma took the cup, abandoning the saucer to the windowsill, instead curving her hands around the little vessel, as if to warm her blood. 'Lucy is looking after him. Bless her, I don't know what I'd have done without her. You know she lost that poor, sweet husband of hers?'

'Jamie told me Albert had been killed at El Alamein,'

said Rosalind, fighting back tears. The papers talked of glory, but all she knew was loss and grief.

'I don't know what I'd have done without her,' repeated Alma, slowly. 'But it's too much for her, on her own looking after us all. Especially now. What your papa needs now is his family around him.'

No! Rosalind's heart and mind screamed with the sudden understanding of what came next.

'You can stay here for the night,' she said. *Stay on the practical. Shut out the future.* Her mind could take in nothing else. 'There's a telephone box opposite, I'll let Lucy know you're here.'

Alma's eyes remained on the faded pattern of rosebuds decorating her teacup, with no signs of listening. 'So you will come back with me. This is the time when your father needs you the most.'

'He told me I could never return.'

'But things are different now. Cordelia is working with refugees in France and I haven't heard from Kate in months. Your papa has no one left, only you and me. He's taken this so hard. I didn't want to say, darling, not with everything else, but he has not been in the best of health as it is, and the doctors think he may well have had some kind of seizure when he heard the news about Will. One side is very weak...'

Rosalind could feel the trap closing around her. The particularly feminine prison of empathy and family bonds, both taking the best of her and wiping away any life of her own.

'But in that case, aren't I likely to make it worse?'

'No, of course not, darling. He'd love to see you. He misses you.' Alma dissolved into tears. 'The thing is, he's not easy at the best of times, and since he's had this seizure... My dear, he needs his family around him.'

'Jamie told me Oswald and Bianca have built a house just outside Brierley-in-Arden.'

'Darling, I can hardly ask Bianca, even when she returns from Windemere. She has her two boys and a husband to consider, and a household to run.'

'And I have nothing?'

'I didn't say that.' Rosalind caught her stepmother's teacup as it toppled. There was a moment's silence. Alma straightened, as if bracing herself. 'The truth is, my dear, I'm a little afraid of what they might do.'

'They?'

'Oswald and Bianca. Oswald is so very, well, forceful and your father listens to him. And when he doesn't agree immediately, Bianca has this way of talking him round to agree with Oswald's point of view. I'm not blaming her. Of course her loyalty is bound to be with her husband.' Alma was shaking violently all over. 'The thing is, I'm there on my own. Lucy does her best, but no one is going to listen to a servant. I'm so afraid of being steamrollered into doing something that isn't in mine, or your father's, best interest. Or that of Brierley-in-Arden.'

Rosalind swallowed. *Had Will been right, after all?* He had been set on her marrying Henry as the most effective way of keeping their father from falling under Oswald's influence and being swayed by his plans. She had assumed at the time that Will was just being disdainful about Oswald coming from the wrong kind of money. But what if that very snobbishness had pointed her brother to a truth about Oswald after all? What was it Will had said? Something about Oswald trying to persuade Papa to grow rich giving over fields for summer houses for the aristocracy, running roughshod over Arden's past, its history, perhaps even its future.

She might have been banished and done her grieving for never being permitted to see the place of her birth again, but it was still a part of her. The recognition was so visceral it was like a blow to the stomach, sending her dizzy. Arden's ghosts were her ghosts, the long bloodline of ancestors, stretching back until before time began. The water of Arden's streams flowed in her veins, her very bones were made from the green fields surrounding the estate.

She couldn't just walk away and leave the house and the village to their fate. It felt a betrayal of the Roman family, maybe themselves her forebears, who had walked over the mosaic Jamie and Kate had uncovered in the field between the house and the village. An undoing of all those who had lived and died loving the rich red earth of Arden's fields, the deep green of its trees.

She couldn't go back. She couldn't. She had broken free of the past. She had made a new life. Love Arden as she might, she couldn't go back. And Papa? Rosalind shut her eyes. For all his faults, for all his selfishness and his irrational rages, the strong bond of shared blood was still there, an unhealed ache in her heart. If she had learnt nothing in the years of war, as she faced nightly bombardment and the suffering of those who lost everything, it was that, in the end, when all things are gone, when all the differences and vanities of everyday life are stripped away, there is only love.

Somewhere, deep inside, her heart was torn into a thousand pieces, breaking her apart.

Alma returned home to Arden House the following day, unwilling, until the moment they reached the entrance to Euston Station, to leave without her. With the plea in her stepmother's eyes to follow as soon as she could make the necessary arrangements impossible to ignore, Rosalind could not settle to anything for the rest of the day.

Her mind was dazed from the bone weariness of grief, compounded by a night of fitful sleep on the camp bed kept for visitors approved by Lady Millicent as suitably respectable. And running through her thoughts, like an endless thread, was the decision she could not escape. All through the day, she paced the streets that had become home, not caring where she went. She wove between the lunchtime buzz of workers enjoying a few minutes of fresh air on the banks of the Thames, their customary weariness displaced by rumours that, now Hitler was dead, an announcement of the war ending was bound to come within days, maybe even hours.

'This is where I found my true self,' she said aloud, as she found herself on Westminster Bridge. She turned her gaze from the battered Houses of Parliament and the distant dome of St Paul's Cathedral, rising high above the Luftwaffe's attempts to destroy the city. This was the place where she had been tested, where she had faced her own destruction, and had seen sights so terrible they were beyond imagination. It was where she had found inner strength she had never suspected to be hers, along with the unexpected satisfaction of being able to support herself, of taking charge of her life and being answerable to no one. The place where she had found her calling. The place that held her hard-won freedom. With the grief of what had been lost inhabiting every cell of her body, she felt the urgency of life flowing through her veins.

I can't just let that go.

And yet... Around her, women hurried past, heading for home, to turn from doctors, police officers and office workers into wives and mothers, the centres of their home, with all its joys and frustrations, the beating heart of life itself. Three young women, similar enough in appearance to be sisters, paused next to her, laughing as they gossiped together, the war momentarily forgotten in the joyous oddities of existence. All of them bound together by family ties, weaving together the public and private aspects of their worlds as only women do, without fuss, or a demand to be noticed.

As she finally returned to her lodging in the late afternoon, Rosalind came to a halt, her preoccupation breaking apart. Walking towards her, silhouetted against the slanting sun was a soldier in uniform.

She wanted to cry out, to will it to be the miracle, for it to be Jamie to come home, after all. But the soldier was too tall, his gait, although familiar as her own, could not be mistaken for her brother.

But it was still a miracle she had longed for, hoped against hope. For all her grief and anxiety, life folded round her again; the world glowed with light.

'Guy,' she exclaimed, as she walked into his arms. His coat reeked of dirt and engine oil as it came around her. She had never smelt anything so good.

'I told you I'd return,' he said, releasing her at the passing of an elderly gentleman clucking disapprovingly at such damned disgraceful behaviour, war or no war.

'Have you heard...?' She could not say the words.

'About Will? Yes. I'm so sorry, Rosy.'

She leant against the roughness of his uniform as his arms came around her. 'And Jamie, too.'

'No.' He released her, cupping her face in his hands. 'Don't cry, Rosy. At least, not for Jamie. That's what I came to tell you. I've seen him. He's badly injured, but he's alive.'

'Alive?' She didn't dare believe it. The blow of grief for Jamie hitting her again would be too hard to bear.

'He's in a hospital in France. It was only by chance that I heard from a doctor about a British soldier with no identity tag and no memory of who he was. From the description, I prayed it was Jamie. I didn't dare believe it myself until I saw him with my own eyes.'

'You've seen him? You're sure it's Jamie?'

He kissed her. 'Yes, it is really him. I've spoken to him. He didn't remember my name, but he had a sense of who I was. He asked after you. He was worried you might have been killed in the Blitz.'

Doubt shot through her. 'But... I've seen Jamie since the Blitz.'

'I know.' He kissed her gently. 'He's still confused at times. He remembered after a while – he talked about you riding around on your motorbike and glad it was a Triumph.'

Finally, relief went through her. 'That's what he told me to get. I should phone Arden House, Alma should be nearly home by now.'

'The telegram to let them know where he is should already have arrived.' Despite his smile, his eyes were grave.

Her relief evaporated. 'You said he was confused.'

'The doctors are hopeful he will recover, at least to some degree. But Jamie has suffered a severe head injury. It will take time, even after he returns home.'

'I see,' said Rosalind. Several of the nurses from the rooms above hers turned into the road. She was too raw, too torn, to speak to them. Even their chatter, letting off steam after the unrelenting suffering of the day, went through her like a knife.

'Let's get out of here,' said Guy, steering her out of their way and towards the little park. Rosalind slipped her arm tightly through his as they returned to the privacy of the little arbour.

'Will you go back to France?' she asked as they sat down on the bench, a new fear shooting through her. She could not lose him now. Not after all this time. Not when peace would come any day.

He shook his head. 'Looks like I'm to be stationed in Dover, as part of the evacuation of the wounded. This is the final stage. Everyone knows it's over.' His voice shook slightly. 'To be honest, I can't wait to be demobbed.'

She should have been joyful. Guy, at least, would be safe. And yet... This was different. Every time they had met during the war, in fact ever since they had met, it had been in snatched moments, lived intensely in place of a future that might never be. Now that future was here, stretching out in front of her, the simplicity of such intensity gone, the complexity of a whole life to be lived gradually dawning.

'Are you planning to take up the post with your friend in America?'

'The offer is still there.' His eyes were fixed on the ground in front of him, lost in thought. 'Dad is insisting I go back to managing the factory in Birmingham as soon as I'm demobbed. But I can't. Not after everything. It would kill me.' He looked up, a new light in his eyes. 'The chance to become a qualified architect in America is the kind that might never come again, Rosy. It's our chance to build a good life together.'

'It's a huge change,' she said. 'And so far away from everything I know. And you said it would take Jamie a long time to recover from his injuries.'

'He has your family to look after him. Once he's well enough to be released from hospital they can take him home to heal.'

'Except it's not that simple.'

There was a moment's silence.

'Rosy, they can't expect you to throw your life away...'

'Is it? Throwing my life away, I mean. It's my family. Doesn't that matter?'

'Of course it does.'

'But my loyalty should be to you, you mean.'

'No, of course not.' He frowned. 'That's not what I meant.'

But he did, she saw with a jolt. He might not think it, but deep down that was his assumption, that she would follow where he led, even if that was half a world away. That's what a woman did when she married, transferred her loyalty from one family to another, leaving the ties that had formed her to create new ones, using her infinite resilience and adaptability.

Rosalind closed her eyes. Once, she had said yes to such a wrench without a second thought. But that was before she had built a life for herself. Confusion went through her. She remembered the girls in Brierley-in-Arden who, like Lucy, married the boy from the next street, remaining in the same place with the same family bonds, mothers helping daughters with childbirth and the raising of children, taking over from each other when illness or disaster arrived, a firm unit against the world. They might not escape the constraints of the life they had been born into – the one that stretched back largely unchanged throughout the generations – but she finally understood that their tight network of female support meant not being totally dependent on one person for everything.

'I can't just leave my work behind,' she said.

'There are magazines in America.'

'But it's here that I've started to make my reputation.'

'All the more reason for being able to find someone to take your photographs there.'

She swallowed. She had never fought Guy on anything.

She had not needed to; they had always understood each other, even when the words were not spoken. This was different. This was to do with the life she had built without him. He understood more than most of the men she had met that her photography was important to her, but he still saw himself in the role of provider. After all, when children came along, she would be too preoccupied to pursue a career.

Panic shot through her. Maybe she didn't know him at all, any more than he knew her – not in the 'live every day together for the rest of your life' kind of knowing. The kind that counted.

'Guy, I love you, but I can't just leave, not now, or in a few months' time. Papa and Jamie have never been close. Alma is afraid that Oswald and Bianca have too much influence over Papa as it is, and from what I've seen of them, I'm worried they will want to keep it that way. I'm not sure Oswald will have Jamie's best interests at heart, and where Oswald leads, Bianca will follow.'

She caught the faint bewilderment he was trying to hide, and her heart began to break. Was this a reality they had never faced? But she could not efface herself, she could not be absorbed into his existence, as if she had no inner life, and no ties of love and loyalty, that were hers alone.

Men are April when they woo, December when they wed: maids are May when they are maids, but the sky changes when they are wives.

'Jamie has always looked out for me, Guy. I need to make sure that he's strong enough to stand up for himself.'

'Are you asking me to return to the factory?' He sounded hurt.

'Of course not! That's the last thing I want, to stand in your way. I understand that this is your chance, and I want you to take it with all my heart. I want you to follow your dream, but I also want to find a way to follow mine. And I can't make a new life without making some kind of peace with my family. I don't want to lose you, but please understand that I can't go with you to America, not yet.'

He was silent for a minute, lost in thought. Around them, evening mist was beginning to curl in from the river, sending the surrounding trees and shrubs into ghostly figures, looming out of the whitish-grey of damp, bone-aching chill. Even the bricks of the little arbour were oozing moisture, along with the mushroom smell of last year's rotting leaves, turning back into earth.

'Then I'll go first, and make a home for us,' he said at last. 'And you can join me when you're ready.'

'Thank you.' She met his smile. There was love in his eyes, but something else. Maybe a touch of disappointment? Had he been dreaming through the horrors of the fighting about their perfect life together when the war was over? When they could live as one mind and one body? Doubt shot through her. She had dreaded losing him all this time. Had she now, in her unfeminine selfishness, sent him to a new world where he might form a new life, new ties – even new loves – without her?

She longed to take it all back, to say she'd go with him as soon as he was free to leave. But an even stronger instinct stilled the words on her lips, the self-preservation she had developed weaving her motorcycle between crumbling buildings and the remains of bombing raids. If she bowed now to what was expected of her, how could she ever ask for anything of her own in the future? More to the point, if love couldn't survive this, how could it ever survive the twists and turns and inevitable stresses of a lifetime?

She held on to his warmth for as long as she dared, aching for his kiss to last forever. He was still Guy. She could feel it in the familiar gentle exploration of her mouth, of the fingers lingering down her spine, of her body's instinctive opening up as he pulled her closer against him. He was still the only man she would ever love, as his kisses travelled slowly down her neck, towards the warmth between her breasts. He paused, defeated by her myriad of buttons, just enough for her to recover her senses.

'Write to me,' she said, gently disentangling herself, trying to sound rational and unmoved, and not betray the rapidity of her breathing. One more touch and her resolve would melt, and there was a small suspicion at the back of her mind that he knew all too well she would not be able to resist him for much longer.

'Of course,' he replied. There was still a touch of hurt pride in his voice.

Fear stirred that, once far away from her in a new world and a new life, with sights and sounds she could not share, he might move even further away from her in thoughts and experience. Changed again, as he had been by war, until he no longer had any links to the world he had left behind.

She was still torn apart, stretched thin by conflicting loyalties, as they rose, making their way once more through the deserted park.

On one of the benches, a rose had been tied to on arm with a crimson ribbon. Every time Rosalind had passed that spring, there had been a fresh flower. First the glossy cups of tulips, later the generous blooms of roses, always tied in the same place with a silk ribbon, sending heavy scent out into the surrounding air, reminding her of the couples lingering close together the day she had said goodbye to Guy as he went off to war. This one was the palest pink and faded around the edges, with no scent left, the inner petals already starting to rot. Some griefs could last a lifetime, with only memories left to cling onto, however painful, to prevent them drifting out of sight.

She tightened her arm on Guy's, absorbing every part of him, the feel of his warmth next to hers. As they reached the metal gate and emerged into the mist-obscured street, she had a sudden fear that she could well have lost him, after all. That, once gone, she would never see him again.

Part Three

Rosalind: O coz, coz, coz, my pretty little coz, that thou didst know how many fathom deep I am in love! But it cannot be sounded: my affection hath an unknown bottom, like the bay of Portugal.

As You Like It. Act Four, Scene 1

Chapter Twenty-Three

Brierley-in-Arden, August, 1945

Summer cloud cleared to sunshine as Rosalind reached the outskirts of Brierley-in-Arden. A group of boys playing in the evening warmth turned to stare as she pulled her motorcycle onto a patch of empty ground, just before the tumbledown cottage where the High Street began. She swung herself wearily from the seat, removing her helmet before glancing up to where the twisting chimneys of Arden House peered between the trees. For the first time since leaving London, her courage began to fail. This was the world she had never thought to see again.

Rosalind took a deep breath and turned her gaze towards the village. Brierley was smaller than she remembered, and even shabbier. The thatch of the nearest cottages was in urgent need of replacing, and potholes littered the road. Unlike the cheerful bustle of before the war, the winding lanes between the houses appeared almost deserted.

Doubt shot through her. In a moment of nostalgia for her childhood world, she had appeased Ginny Blake's irritation at her desertion by suggesting she use her time in Arden to write a series of illustrated articles showing how a traditional English village was returning to some kind of normal life after the traumas of war. What better complement to her pre-war scenes of the amateur dramatics and the blacksmith that made up the peaceful existence that had been threatened by Hitler's jackboots?

'I would focus on the women,' she had added, as her final shot. 'The village schoolmistress once told me how hard it was for women returning to domestic life after the Great War, after all those years of taking on a man's responsibility and status, and earning an independent income. I'm sure it would be of interest to your readers to see how women adjust this time to a civilian life.'

'Possibly,' Ginny had conceded thoughtfully, pouring coffee from the percolator that lived almost permanently on the little stove in her office.

'If you give me six months, I can cover Christmas as well. The news has been so terrible for so long, and there are such vile things coming out about what happened in the occupied countries, and the unspeakable things human beings did to each other in the concentration camps, surely what your readers need now is warmth and joy and kindness.'

'That is true...' Ginny's voice had been thoughtful as she handed her one of the tin mugs that had long ago replaced the teacups smashed when a bomb had crashed through next door, narrowly missing the precious printing equipment. 'Christmas?'

'Choirs, amateur dramatics, carols at midnight in the church, that sort of thing. The children always put on a nativity play, and the villagers decorate a tree on the village green. I'm sure they'll want to continue that.'

'Hrmph.' Ginny had sipped her coffee, black, no sugar, as they had all grown used to since rationing began. 'Very well,' she said at last. 'Up until Christmas, it is. Then I want you back here. I'm not losing my best reporter now.' Her eyes had glinted. 'I understand you wishing to do the best for your brother and your family, but I never accept martyrdom as an excuse from my female staff.'

'I'll bear that in mind,' Rosalind had replied, trying not to show her relief at not being dismissed out of hand.

Looking at it now, Brierley was much the same as the many villages she had passed through on her way, each clustered around the spire of its church. All had shown the same forlorn air, like an animal hunkered down, not daring to move until its wounds had healed, or it took its last breath, to fold back into becoming earth once more. Maybe, crept in the doubt, there was nothing left of the old life, and no optimism, or returning to normality, to report.

'Must be speedy, that.' She found herself surrounded by a collection of small boys, closely inspecting the sleek black curves of the Triumph. The girls playing hopscotch with the aid of squares chalked onto the rough ground paused in their game, chanting fading into undisguised curiosity.

'This yours, Miss?' demanded the largest of the boys, thrusting out his chest in an attempt to sound casual. Every one of them, Rosalind realised with a jolt, would have either been babies, or not even born, when she had last been in Brierley. A new generation. It made her feel old.

'Yes it is. I can move it, if it's in your way.'

'That's all right,' said the boy gruffly. Having signalled that she was the approachable rather than severe form of adult, Rosalind found herself surrounded by eager faces.

'So, does it go fast?' asked a grubby-faced boy sporting the most threadbare of shoes.

'It can do, if there's a straight piece of road. I was told it could get up to fifty miles an hour, although I've never quite dared to quite reach such a speed.' A collective intake of breath went through the boys.

'D'you drive it a long way, then?' demanded a girl with thick plaits tied neatly either side of her head, a skipping rope dangling from her hands.

'From London, that's where I live.'

The collective intake was louder this time. She might, Rosalind realised, have announced she had come from the moon.

'D'you drive it all the time?' asked a small girl, who was staring at her with undisguised admiration.

'I do now. I began to use a motorcycle when I became a magazine reporter during the war.'

'A reporter!' The remainder of the girls clustered around, closely inspecting every part of her, several touching her jacket to assure themselves that she was real, as if she had indeed sailed down from some celestial body.

'Well, I'd drive a motorcycle all the time,' announced the largest of the boys.

'No you wouldn't,' retorted the girl with plaits, 'you can't even keep a tractor on a straight line, how'd you manage with only two wheels?' She turned to Rosalind. 'You going to have one of them big houses, then, Miss?'

'Big houses?'

'The new ones. Like that one.' She pointed towards a large mansion standing on a small rise on the opposite side of the village, its curved white concrete interspersed with rectangular windows. So there was change in Brierley, after all. With all the shortages, and everything focussed on the war effort and surviving the destruction, Rosalind hadn't thought of houses being built during the time she had been away. She had admired the clean lines of the art deco and Bauhaus-inspired houses she had seen in London, while the expanse of glass had been inviting with its hint of light flooding in to a less crowded interior. But there was something stark, almost brutal, about the way this one dominated the countryside, with whole swathes of ancient oak scrub having been cleared to accommodate grounds so new they were still bare earth.

'Who owns it?'

'Mr Gorwell.'

She might have known.

'He built it. He's going to build more.'

'Mum says he's a greedy bu—' began the smallest of the girls, instantly shushed before she could repeat such disgraceful language before a respectable lady.

'You mean, on that hillside?'

'Don't know.' The boy thrust out his chest again. 'But my dad says they are going to build a road, right through the village so the motor cars of posh people from London can get there.'

'Right through?' Rosalind stared at him. 'You mean right through the middle?'

The boy nodded. 'Aye. Dad says they can't go round, 'cos of the water meadows on the other side, and he ain't letting them have none of his grazing land, however much they offer, because money don't last forever, and that's the best of his land and if the cows don't give milk we can't pay the rent. And half the houses is falling down anyhow, and even Mrs Ackrite's grocers is on its last legs, after the war and all the rationing, and all.'

'But what about the ducks?' exclaimed one of the younger girls, to whom this was clearly news. 'They can't go through the pond.'

'We'll just have to eat them, all at once.'

'Oi, you lot!' The resulting shrieks of protest were

silenced by an elderly man appearing from of the houses, spade in hand. 'Leave the lady alone. She don't want none of your nonsense.'

The children scattered.

The man gave Rosalind a look as if he half-recognised her, then thought the better of it. Clearly the woman in wide-legged trousers and leather motorcycle jacket, hair cropped for ease of management and curling around her head like a boy, bore little resemblance to the flowing hair and skirts of Mr Arden's second daughter he had been accustomed to see before the war.

What am I doing here? She fought down panic. She was here for Jamie, to build bridges with Papa and the rest of the family. She was here to fulfil a commission from her employer. She was not trapped in Arden, not unless she allowed herself to be. She had the Triumph. She had her petrol ration. There were no physical constraints keeping her here.

It's not the physical ones I'm worried about.

'Sorry about that, Miss,' the elderly man was continuing. 'No manners, these days, don't know what the parents are teaching them. Or them teachers. You'd have thought with Miss Parsons as headmistress they'd get some kind of sense. Time I had a word with her again.'

'Thank you,' said Rosalind, 'but I'm sure they didn't mean any harm.'

The man sniffed his disagreement and set off down the street with an air of purpose.

Rosalind glanced back up towards the glass-fronted house. Was Oswald really planning to erect similar build-ings, when several of the cottages on the edges of the village appeared to be deserted, their rooves falling in, windows boarded up? But the children must be repeating conversations overheard between adults, and Brierley-in-Arden was the kind of place where no secrets could be kept for long, not even the most hidden, or belonging to those considering themselves the village's social superiors.

A sense of unease lingered in the sunshine. The new house definitely had an air of dominating the village. It was exactly the kind she imagined her brother-in-law building for himself, following the fashion of the times, but in a manner designed to impress, rather than have any regard for its surroundings. So much for his once-vaunted plan to build his home on the banks of the river, on the outskirts of Stratford-upon-Avon.

She couldn't make out any other patches of ground being cleared, and the meadows in their summer richness seemed much the same. Ears of ripening wheat and barley, speckled with crimson poppies, sprang up through the red Warwick-shire earth, the network of hedges untouched. There was nowhere obviously being prepared for building, and, unless Oswald bribed or bullied all the farmers away from the land they had farmed for generations and was in their blood, she couldn't see where he could put a large number of smart new houses with the grounds expected by a wealthy clientele, and especially not so many as to warrant a road to accommodate their cars.

Her gaze travelled back over the rolling grounds surrounding Arden House, largely given over to meadows and the lake, with scrubs of ancient woodland in between. The land looked as rich and fertile as it had ever been, its fields still crisscrossed by the pathways leading to and from the marketplace, and the close networks of families, centred upon Brierley-in-Arden. It still held the village, and its tight-knit community, safe within its embrace. Surely Papa would never allow the ancient surroundings to be taken over by mansions for the wealthy, destroying everything he would once have sacrificed so much to preserve, including, as she knew only too well, his daughters' happiness?

Rosalind began to walk down towards the green, ignoring the curious glances from the women with triangles of head-scarves covering their hair and baskets on their arms, who emerged from the church hall as she passed, and tried not to hear the whispers that followed her. They recognised her, alright, despite the changes in her appearance. It would be round the village by evening that one of them Arden girls had returned, after all.

An unexpected warmth went through her. She had little doubt she would be awarded at least one faithless lover and an abandoned love-child by the end of the day, along with a secret marriage to dashing Prince Phillip of Greece. Not even war could remove Brierley's relish for the most outrageous of gossip.

Her body began to relax as she felt the familiarity of the village close around her. She reached the green, with its swathe of grass and the ducks enthusiastically bobbing their heads, to send water all over them with much flapping and preening. Moorhens scurried hastily away as the ducks spotted the newcomer and noisily pushed their way to the edges of the pond to await any booty that might be on offer.

'Some things survive, after all.'

'Miss Parsons!' Rosalind smiled at the headmistress, resisting an overwhelming urge to embrace her, something the older woman's dignity would never allow.

'I thought it must be you, Miss Rosalind, when I was opening up the museum just now.' Miss Parsons looked older, thinner, with more lines on her face, but her eyes were as sharp as ever. 'So you're back.'

'For a while. Until Jamie is on his feet again.'

'That can't have been an easy decision.' She coughed. 'I hope you know what you're doing.'

'So do I,' said Rosalind, fervently.

Miss Parsons laid a hand on her arm. 'I'm so sorry about Master Will, my dear. A terrible loss.'

'We're not the only family to have lost brothers and sons.'

'But no less painful, for being shared.' Miss Parsons concentrated on fussing with the buttons of her coat. 'I'm sure Jamie will find a way through, once his injuries are healed.'

'Alma seemed to suggest in her letters that the doctors felt it wasn't just his physical injuries that were keeping him from returning to full health.'

'Try not to worry, my dear. I knew so many men who came back from the last war with minds that could not deal with all that they had seen and done. Shell-shock, they called it. Some of the most effective cures tended to allow them to focus on practical projects. I volunteered at a hospital for a while, it was like a miracle, seeing men who came in unable to see or speak, or even hold their hands still, finding peace once they became absorbed in gardening or woodworking. You'll see, that brother of yours will recover.' Her eyes turned, as if irresistibly drawn, towards the Gorwells' house. 'And he will find a way of keeping Brierley safe.'

Rosalind watched the headmistress as she returned inside to her evening occupation of tending to her little museum. *Keep Brierley safe.* From Jamie's letters during the years of the war, she knew that Oswald was reputed to have made a fortune building factories and repairing the damage to buildings caused by the bombing of Birmingham and Coventry on behalf of the War Damage Commission. Now, it seemed, he had his sights on Arden.

How she wished Guy was by her side! She had never felt

so alone. Papa did not consider any female opinion worth listening to, and she had an instinct that Oswald's plans for the village were unlikely to include the inconvenience of the heir to Arden regaining his strength. With Papa incapacitated, what better time for Oswald to make himself indispensable, to tighten his influence, as the son-in-law to take Jamie's place, and so do as he wished?

Rosalind gritted her teeth. This might not be war, but it was a struggle for survival of a more subtle kind, for both the inhabitants of Arden House and the village. There might indeed be nothing physical holding her in Arden, but this was the land that lay deep in her heart, deeper than she had ever suspected when she had lived here. She could not just walk away.

Chapter Twenty-Four

On the surface, Arden House showed little sign of being touched by war. Rosalind parked the Triumph on the gravel driveway and swung down to the ground, gazing up at the familiar imposing façade of red brick, with ivy clinging to its chimneys and mullioned windows. All the same, there was a silence, a lack of activity, that was unnerving.

She reached the front door, still the familiar relic from the Arden's long-gone Tudor grandeur, vast and heavy, carved wood deeply cracked and darkened with age and set within the protection of its high stone arch. Squaring her shoulders, she tugged the bell pull, the familiar deep note echoing within the house.

The door opened to reveal Lucy peering at her with a harassed expression on her face, maid's cap askew and a deep frown on her forehead. 'Oh my goodness. Miss Rosalind. You did come after all. You're brave.'

'Or foolish,' returned Rosalind with a smile. 'Dear Lucy, it's good to see you again. Jamie told me about Albert. I'm so very sorry.'

'Thank you, Miss.' The maid's eyes filled with tears, quickly blinked away again. Only the ring on her wedding finger remained of the smiling girl Rosalind had seen at the church with her Albert beaming proudly at her side, or the contented wife, blossoming in her own home. She might have lost the scared look of her previous years at Arden, when she'd been terrorised on a daily basis by Cook, but she was thin and lined, her face that of a much older woman. 'You'd better come inside. Mr Arden's in the library.'

'And my brother?'

Lucy glanced up the stairway towards the bedrooms. 'Mrs Arden is with him. She's spent most of her time reading to him since he was brought here. She hardly goes downstairs at all except when Mr Arden calls for her.' She swallowed. 'Miss—'

'It's all right, I know,' said Rosalind, gently. 'Mrs Arden has written to me regularly since he was returned from France.'

'Oh, thank goodness.' Lucy wiped her eyes. 'I'm sorry, Miss Rosy, I don't mean it like that. But that was so on my mind that you didn't know. Mrs Arden is trying so hard to understand, but Mr Arden...'

'Acts as if nothing has happened?'

The tautness of Lucy's face eased. 'I'm so glad you're here, Miss. I don't know quite what to say to them.'

'Don't tell me you're here on your own?'

'I'm not complaining.'

'I didn't think you were.'

Lucy sighed. 'I were grateful to have a job back here after my Albert were killed. The other girls, well most went to work in factories in Birmingham during the war, even the ones who came back don't want to come back into service no more.'

'It was the same in London,' said Rosalind. 'I can understand why.'

'Keeps me busy. I'm glad of that. I'll bring the tea,' said Lucy, hurrying back towards the kitchens, blowing her nose.

Rosalind took a deep breath. She could feel the ancient walls closing in tightly around her, just as they had always done, heavy with generation upon generation of expectations of its womenfolk to pick up the pieces, pushing their own hopes and dreams aside.

The corridor leading to the library was lit only by the faint light from a distant window, a deep cold rising from the ancient flagstones, worn into their familiar shoe-worn dips. The echoes from the wooden panelling brought back memories of winter days when as children this had been their playground. Now Will was gone forever, and Kate and Cordelia were far away, maybe never to return. For all its familiar surroundings, loneliness crept inside her heart. Taking a deep breath, she tapped on the carved wood of the door at the far end.

'Come in.' Her father's familiar voice, more abrupt than ever, wasn't exactly reassuring.

She stepped inside the library to find a fire crackling in the grate, sending flickers of warm light over the shelves with their row upon row of leather-bound books. There was no movement from the armchair set at one side of the fire, illuminated by the reflected sun stealing in through the windows and supplemented by the glow of a small lamp.

'It's good to see you again, Papa.'

He looked up from the large volume on his knees, peering at her beneath heavy brows, now turned white and more forbidding than ever.

'Hrmph.'

'I'm sorry you've not been well.'

236

'Nothing wrong with me.' He turned to his book, as if to shut out her presence.

There was an awkward silence as Lucy appeared with a tray, placing it on a small table next to the fire, setting china cups and saucers rattling, before shooting out with the air of a woman with too much to do and too little time.

With only two teacups and saucers, there was no indication that Alma was expected to join them. Rosalind poured milk from the little silver jug into each of the cups, waiting for the tea to steep in the same blue and white Wedgewood teapot she remembered from her childhood, worn with age and slightly chipped.

'Thank you,' he muttered, as she handed him a cup.

His air of being shut up tightly within himself unnerved her more than if he had sent her immediately packing. Was there no way through?

'Papa—' But she was silenced by the sound of rapid footsteps tapping towards them on the flagstones.

'In that case, Lucy, you can bring another cup,' came a brisk voice that most definitely did not belong to Alma. Papa's shoulders shrank even tighter within themselves. 'And a fresh pot of tea.'

'Yes, Mrs Gorwell.'

'Well, Rosalind,' said Bianca, appearing in the doorway. 'So you did come, after all this time.'

'It's good to see you again.'

'And you,' said Bianca, tautly. Not exactly the warmest of welcomes. Rosalind's heart sank. She'd had no communication with her sister since the day she had left for London, with the tentative letters she had sent to the Gorwells' home in Stratford upon Avon, the family's London residence being abandoned for the duration, remaining unanswered. Now, like Papa, Bianca seemed determined to show that she was neither needed or wanted.

'And how are you today Papa?' Bianca headed for the armchair.

'Can't complain.'

'Papa's so much stronger than he was.' Bianca briefly met Rosalind's eyes, the hostility in their depths unmistakeable. 'He almost died, you know. We nearly lost him.'

'I wasn't that bad,' he muttered. 'And there's no need to treat me like a child, woman. There's nothing wrong with my brain.'

'Not in the least,' said Bianca, soothingly. 'Oswald's businesses have been expanding, especially since the war. But he's still found time to assist Papa.'

'That's very generous of him.' From the corner of her eye, Rosalind saw her father shuffle uncomfortably in his chair.

'If we're going out for our walk, we should go now, Papa. It'll get too cold again later.'

'Yes, yes of course.' He pushed himself upright. 'I can manage.' He knocked Bianca's helping hand away, instead leaning heavily on the support of his armchair, transferring his weight to the solid wooden wheelchair set next to the window. He sat down heavily, as Bianca busied herself tucking a woollen blanket in a tartan of blues and greens around him.

'No need to join us,' Bianca remarked, unlatching the French windows. 'It will give you time to settle in.'

Rosalind watched them go, following a clearly customary routine, the way families do, Bianca bending over their father, the slight movement of his head as he answered. As they reached the wider paths leading between beds of straggling rosebushes towards the walled garden, Bianca halted to adjust the blanket, before setting off again.

Arden House was quiet as Rosalind returned the tray to the kitchens. Lucy was nowhere to be seen. The whole place felt abandoned. She took a deep breath. This had to be faced sometime, the silence that lay at the heart of the house, the subject that none of them had touched upon and yet was there at the centre of it all.

She washed out the cups and saucers and made a fresh pot of tea. Holding the cup carefully, she made her way upstairs, stomach knotting, despite herself.

As Rosalind reached the landing, Alma emerged from Jamie's room. 'Darling, I thought I heard your voice just now. It's so good to see you.'

'And you, Mama.' She returned her stepmother's embrace, fighting down unexpected tears at one member of the family welcoming her presence.

'You'd better come in, my dear. Jamie will be pleased to see you. He's a bit tired today. Don't worry if he doesn't say much.'

'It's all right, Mama.' Rosalind kissed her. Jamie's head injury was healing, Alma had told her in her letters. His memory appeared to be gradually returning, but he was still locked inside himself, as if unable to return from the dark place his mind had sent him. Alma's face was paler than ever, Rosalind saw, lines of strain and exhaustion making her appear, like Lucy, to have aged beyond her years. 'I can stay with Jamie. I'm sure you can do with some fresh air, and Bianca is keeping Papa company.'

'Is she?' A look of desperation overtook her stepmother's face.

'So why don't you have a walk in the grounds, while you can.'

'Yes, yes I suppose I could. Although I should see Bianca. She has been very good, she comes nearly every day, even though George is still young and Hubert only a baby. They hired a nanny the moment your father fell ill, you know, so she could be here as much as she could.'

'You mean they had no intention whatsoever of employing a nanny beforehand?'

'I...' A touch of colour appeared on Alma's pale cheeks. 'It did strike me she might be exaggerating a little.'

'I seem to remember Bianca rather liked to play the martyr when we were children,' suggested Rosalind gently.

'Oh, I'm sure...' Alma's protest came to a halt. An unexpectedly mischievous grin lit up the weariness of her face. 'I'm very glad you're here, my dear. And yes, I think I may take a little walk, it would be good to clear my head.'

As Alma disappeared, Rosalind made her way into the room. She found Jamie sitting in an armchair positioned next to the window, face turned away. He made no move, or sign of being aware of her presence. Her stomach twisted into a tight knot. She had expected to see him changed; she had been prepared for his fragility, but not this blankness. Perhaps, crept the doubt inside her, Alma had been more optimistic about his condition in her letters than the truth warranted, so as not to alarm her.

Rosalind set the cup down on the small table at one side of the armchair, supporting a glass and a jug of water protected by a much-washed cover embroidered with roses, weighted down by beads, along with a leather-bound copy of Dickens' *Bleak House*.

'I've brought you some tea, Jamie. Alma has just gone out for a few minutes.'

It was the silence that was the worst. The not knowing

whether he could hear her, deep inside in the place where he was lost.

'I'll read to you, shall I?' she said, taking the chair placed near to the table. In the absence of any protest, she opened *Bleak House* at the carefully placed bookmark and launched into the creaking Chancery proceedings of Jarndyce v Jarndyce. Jamie remained without moving. Footsteps passed below on the gravel, accompanied by the crunch of wheels. At Bianca's voice, loud and insistent, he shuffled slightly in his chair, before subsiding back into stillness.

Rosalind read on, until the heavier crunch on the gravel alerted her to the arrival of a car, followed by Oswald's resounding voice in the hallway.

'She's upstairs with Jamie,' came Alma's reply, sounding flustered. 'I'm just going to take over from her, she'll come down now.' A tap of shoes on the stairs, signalled their step-mother's return. As Rosalind stood up, a hand reached out to grip her arm tight, like that of a drowning man.

'I'll be back, Jamie dear,' she said. 'I'm staying. They won't get rid of me that easily.' Nothing else of him moved, but slowly his hand released its grip.

'I'll be back soon,' she said, fleeing before the tears overcame her.

The rest of the day passed in agonisingly stilted conversation. Oswald, having greeted her with a less than complementary sweep of his eyes over her short hair and clearly shockingly masculine attire, proceeded to ignore her, focussing his attentions on Papa.

Rosalind gritted her teeth, stubbornly determined not to submit to his disapproval by donning the one skirt she had brought with her, and certainly not by resorting to the dresses that Alma had reassured her remained in her closet, awaiting her return. The sprigged cottons, and even more so the delicate silks, were a memory of a world that had vanished, of a Rosalind who could not have imagined the horror she was soon to see in the bombed-out houses of London's East End. A Rosalind who had lived safe within Arden's time-washed grounds, and who was also gone forever.

She was thankful when Oswald finally ran out of descriptions of the mansions he was building on the banks of the River Avon, within easy reach of Stratford-upon-Avon. A lord and a famous artist had already chosen those in the prime position, adjacent (or almost) to Holy Trinity Church, the burial place of the bard himself. In the somewhat battered silence that followed, and with Papa's admiration reduced to a glazed look in the eyes and mutterings about dinner, even Oswald was unable to overlook Bianca's tentative hints about it soon being too late to wish the boys goodnight.

Rosalind couldn't help but feel the very bones of the house breathe a deep sigh of relief as the large Bentley finally lumbered down the drive in the direction of Brierly-in-Arden.

'Fine man, Oswald,' remarked Papa, somewhere in the direction of the portrait of an Arden ancestor sporting an extravagant ruff and bejewelled velvet doublet, who had looked down upon generations of his descendants with the utmost disdain. 'Very fine. Highly respected, you know.'

Keep the peace. At least he was acknowledging her presence, that was a start. 'Yes, Papa.'

'A good match for Bianca, a very good match. And for Arden, too. He has some excellent ideas about how to make the most of the unused fields between here and the village. The kind of thing to put Arden on the map.'

'Do you mean houses, like the ones he's building in Stratford?' she ventured.

He turned to contemplate her. 'You've cut your hair.'

'Only for practicality during the war,' she replied.

'It was far more fetching when it was long.'

'It will grow out, Papa.'

Over her dead body. But he wasn't to know that, and at this rate he was unlikely to keep her in Arden long enough to find out, she thought, sadly.

The face that looked back at her had aged, even more so than Alma and Lucy. Apart from a little drooping of the mouth on one side, she could see no other obvious effect of his seizure, but there was a fragility about him she had not known before. He was no longer the man she had held in her memory through the years, the man in the prime of life with everything he surveyed at his command. He had always been such a large and overwhelming presence throughout her childhood, she had never considered the world existing without him. But the face before her wore its mortality all too clearly. She wanted to reach out and touch him, to make some kind of peace before it was too late. She could not bear the thought of losing him.

'You know Luscombe is back?'

She came back to reality with a jolt. 'Luscombe?'

'Henry,' he retorted, impatient at her slowness. 'Henry Luscombe. His uncle is seriously ill, you know. It's only a matter of time before Henry inherits the title, and the wealth, of course.'

'Indeed,' she murmured politely, the old anger and hurt at him bulldozing over her life returning in a hard knot, deep within her belly. She had an urgent desire to jump on the

Triumph and roar off through the night to places unknown, where at least she could breathe freely.

'He's taken up with business in London for the next few weeks, Oswald informs me, but I'll forward an invitation as soon as he returns to Luscombe Hall.' His eyes sharpened. 'If he hasn't changed his mind, that is.'

'It's been such a long time,' she ventured.

'Quite. None of you are growing any younger. You'll be thirty in a few years, high time you were settled. You're fortunate Henry didn't find some other young lady to marry during the war.'

I so wish he had. She did her best to banish the thought from her face. Ginny had been right about Miss Darlington, who had finally settled for a Russian prince and was now living at a safe distance from Henry's charms, in the sophisticated heart of Manhattan. Not that Rosalind would wish Henry Luscombe on any woman. She would just rather he wasn't free to settle on herself, due to no one else being foolish enough to take him on a permanent basis.

She was glad of Alma appearing to join them for the evening meal, taken as it had always been in the vast dining room, made even more drafty and echoing by the lingering awareness of Jamie eating in the seclusion of his room. With the further tightening of rations since the end of the war, dinner consisted mainly of potatoes and carrots, enlivened by Lucy's delicious omelettes, made with fresh eggs from the hens scratching on the lawns, so different from the powered egg variety Rosalind had grown used to enduring in London.

Afterwards, Alma returned to attend to Jamie, while Rosalind kept her father company in the library, trying to ignore the hurt of the brief grunts he sent in her direction whenever she attempted to start a conversation that steered him away from the subject of Henry Luscombe. The evening seemed to drag on forever, until she could finally escape to her old room, laid out much as it had always been. Her instinct was still to take to her motorcycle and flee. But she could not abandon Jamie, or poor Alma, who was clearly taking the brunt of everything.

Rosalind woke early the following morning, after a night filled with uneasy dreams of crossing wild seas on an ocean liner, waves rising above her head as the Statue of Liberty came in sight. She shot up straight in the darkness, for a moment forgetting where she was. It was the silence that caught her. The stillness of no cars or vans, no sound of trams and no footsteps in the street below. No voices calling to each other as the business of the day began.

She was back in Arden, and Guy would be safely in New York by now, and had promised to write to her, addressing his letters to the Post Office like before, to make sure they didn't disappear, or find themselves mysteriously passed on to Papa.

Pushing the nightmare away, she pulled on her blouse and slacks, covering them with the leather jacket, and slipped down the servant's staircase to the kitchens. She found Lucy, bleary eyed and yawning, attempting to bring the recalcitrant range back to life.

'You're up early, Miss. They'll be a cup of tea in a bit. Mrs Arden's still asleep, best thing for her. You go and sit down, there's a fire in the dining room for when Mr Arden starts to stir, and I'll bring it in.'

'I don't expect you to do that, Lucy! I'm used to looking after myself. I'll come and help you. I just wanted to have a quick look around before anyone starts getting up.'

'Very well, Miss.' Lucy was already back to coaxing the range.

Rosalind pulled an ancient pair of wellington boots over her socks and headed out into the clear dawn, with a sheen of dew over the lawns and a pale, flawless sky. She breathed in the clear, earthy smell, edged with the scent of roses and greenery, the air filled with the chatter of swallows arguing over some disagreement or other.

How she had missed this sense of space and the absorption into the natural world! Unable to escape the city during the war, she had instinctively used her brief free time to seek out Hyde Park, which, despite being partly given over to the growing of vegetables, allowed her to follow the changing seasons, along with the trees lining Constitution Hill on the way to Buckingham palace and the bird-filled ponds of St James' Park. She had to admit that, much as she adored the speed and energy of London, there was a part of her that would always remain a country girl at heart.

Rosalind followed the path skirting the edges of the walled garden, until she reached the grassy expanse of meadow curving gently down towards the church spire of Brierley-in-Arden.

To one side, she could make out the remains of vegetable beds, mainly the heaped-up rows where potatoes had been grown during the war, the odd strangling stem lying collapsed and frost-bitten on the ground. To her relief, the excavation appeared to have been maintained untouched, mounds of earth piled up, the stones of ancient walls still showing through. *If she could just manage to get Jamie back here...*

'It's very old, you know.' She nearly jumped out of her skin as a tousled head of dark hair appeared a little way along, followed by a young man no older than herself pulling himself out of the ground, to sit on the edge looking down.

'The Roman mosaic, you mean?'

'Ah, you know about that.' He looked up, showing a deeply tanned face with a small white scar touching the side of his temples, marring the even shape of his brows. 'It's a fine example.'

'Are you an archaeologist, then?'

He grimaced. 'Amateur, I'm afraid. I'm an engineer by trade.' He retrieved a corduroy jacket from the pile of stones next to him, pulling it on over his worn, and now slightly earthy, jumper. 'It's a pity really.'

'Pity?'

'From the timeframe Mr Gorwell is talking about, there won't be nearly enough opportunity to attempt a full excavation.'

She followed his gaze down towards the village. 'You mean, the road.'

'I can see Gorwell's point. And he's right, there's little enough to keep anyone in the village, especially with so much of the work before the war gone. New houses of the kind he's contemplating would provide work for months, if not years, and could help to revive the village shops. I've no idea how they struggle on.'

'They won't go on at all if the road goes straight through them,' she retorted.

'Mrs Ackrite will be retiring before long, I can't see anyone taking over the grocers.'

'They may do. Then there's the museum and the school. Those and the church hall are the heart of the village. As far as I can see, it must be hard enough for people to stay. What'll be left if those go?'

'I'm afraid there's no way round that. Displacing the

graveyard is quite out of the question, of course.' His eyes rested on her face. 'I expect you don't remember me, Miss Arden. Edmund Ford. My dad used to work as an undergardener here for Mr Gloster, before the war.'

'I remember,' said Rosalind, his features resolving into the sullen-faced lad who had been delegated much of the heavy work around the grounds.

Edmund looked older, more assured, the deference demanded of Papa's underlings most definitely gone. The maids, she recalled, had used to blush and giggle at his passing resemblance to Errol Flynn, despite the lack of pencil-thin moustache. Windblown and dishevelled from his exertions, he most definitely sported a rakish appearance. 'It must be you who's been helping Lucy bring in the vegetables.'

'Maybe.' He was wary. 'When I can. In an unofficial capacity, you understand. Albert was a good friend, and it seems to me Lucy has quite enough to do without digging potatoes every morning.'

'So I can see.'

'The trouble is, no one wants to return to working the grounds. We've all had enough of mud. I suppose you knew Ted died at Dunkirk.'

'Yes, I heard. I still can't believe he's gone, as well as poor Albert.'

'Dad is convinced Fred and Alistair have both found work in factories near Birmingham and won't be back. Not that I blame them. No one wants to work the land anymore.' He gave a wry smile. 'I expect that's what I should have been doing, if things had been different. Dad was so set on me taking over his place, but then the war came, and I had a chance to train as an engineer.' He shot her a sharp glance. 'I understand Master James is back at Arden House.'

'I should have remembered there are no secrets in Brierley.'

'Absolutely none.'

There was a moment's silence. There was nothing to say. Brierley-in-Arden would have grieved for Will as the heir to Arden, knowing that it sent its own future, so tied up with the estate over generations, into uncertainty. And now the only remaining male heir had returned from the fighting a man so broken he was unlikely to ever be able to take up the reigns.

Edmund took a squashed cap from his pocket, pulling it over his unruly curls, giving him even more an air of rushing off to rescue Olivia de Havilland from a fate worse than death. 'But none of us can live in the past.'

'That's true,' said Rosalind. She eyed him. 'The road won't begin soon, surely? There still might be time to uncover the rest of the mosaic. I was hoping it might help my brother regain his strength. Perhaps if someone with a similar interest were to join him now and again...'

'My work takes all my time.'

'All of it?'

He hesitated. She couldn't miss the look of longing he sent back towards the mosaic. 'I'll consider it,' he said, gruffly. 'No promises, but I'll consider it. Good day, Miss Arden.'

She watched as he strode back down towards the village, with the long-legged energy of a man confident in his own capabilities, master of his future. She could understand his ambition not to remain an undergardener on a minor country estate, destined for repetitive, back-breaking work in all weathers until arthritis settled into his bones and he became just another one of the white-haired men dependent on a daughter or daughter-in-law for a roof over his head, limping out on summer days to catch the warm to ease his aches and pains.

She looked again at the mosaic and up at the burial mound within its protective circle of trees. Surely this must be the place where Jamie could regain his physical strength and the visions that haunted his mind. Damn Oswald, with his straight-lined view of the world, who was prepared to flatten everything in his path to fulfil his ambition to create grand houses for the richest clients he could find, with a road crashing carelessly through the heart of an insignificant English village to service them.

She shouldn't be sentimental, she should be looking to the future. But she couldn't help feeling – in a deep sense she couldn't entirely explain – that in obliterating the ancient stories of the landscape, Oswald was taking away a part of herself.

Chapter Twenty Five

As Rosalind reached the driveway on her return, the front door opened to allow Alma to step out, turning to guide Jamie, who was muffled in a blanket and leaning on a walking stick. Rosalind's heart squeezed painfully in her chest as her brother emerged slowly, hesitantly, placing his feet as if afraid he would fall over the edge of a bottomless pit. As they reached the lawns, he stopped, clearly nervous of going any further. Alma waited patiently, until he began moving forward again, body straightening as he stepped a little more confidently towards the grass.

'What the hell d'you think you're doing?' Before she could call to alert them to her presence, Oswald appeared at the doorway. 'He could catch his death, let alone the danger of a fall.'

'I'm sure the fresh air will do him good,' said Alma, sounding defensive. 'Jamie's feeling a little stronger today.'

'And who are you to decide?' Rosalind saw Jamie wince painfully at the harshness of Oswald's voice. 'Are you a nurse? What qualifications do you have to make such a choice? If he falls, you could have caused him irreparable harm.'

Anger shot through Rosalind at the whip of contempt in her brother-in-law's tone, at Alma's white-faced silence, followed by the increasing distress on Jamie's face as he turned, as if in an attempt to protect her, throwing himself off balance.

'It's all right,' Rosalind called, speeding towards them, steadying Jamie as he stumbled.

'Rosalind.' Oswald coloured, discomfiture in every pore. 'I'm acting for the best.'

'Mama has been looking after Jamie since he returned, I'm sure she knows what she's doing.'

'We'll have to see what Dr Andrews says.' With that, he returned inside, the click of his boots on the flagstones fading into the distance.

'He shouldn't,' muttered Jamie.

'It's all right, my darling,' said Alma gently. 'It doesn't matter. Besides, it's time to get back inside the warmth.'

'He shouldn't,' he whispered, voice stronger this time. 'Unfair.' He turned back towards the house. 'Bully.'

'I've met plenty of those,' replied Alma, with more spirit than Rosalind had seen before. 'They are generally not nearly as powerful as they consider themselves to be, or they wouldn't need to assert their influence.'

Jamie gave a low chuckle, descending instantly into a fit of coughing. Rosalind helped Alma guide him back up the stairs with painful slowness. By the time he reached his room, he had only the energy to collapse into his chair, stick tumbling to the floor as he fell instantly into a death-like sleep.

'He'll be like that for a while,' whispered Alma as she covered him with a quilt before following Rosalind out into the corridor. 'That's the furthest he's ventured so far. Fresh air is what he needs, most of all. Hopefully the exercise will do him good and give him more of an appetite.'

'Does he always talk to you like that?' asked Rosalind, as they escaped onto the lawns in front of the house. 'Oswald, I mean.'

'I'm sure he means well.'

'And I'm quite certain he doesn't.'

Alma gave a faint smile. 'He's right, I'm not a nurse.'

'Then he should persuade Papa to hire one.'

'No.' A stubborn look came over her stepmother's face. 'I'm afraid Oswald's idea of a nurse... Jamie is better here.' Her eyes filled with tears. 'I'm not having him sent to an asylum.'

'An asylum?' Rosalind stared at her horrified. 'Is that what Oswald is suggesting? Papa can't agree with him, surely?'

'I'm not certain. He sees it as simply weakness, and Oswald is good at playing on the idea. They are wrong, both of them. Jamie can get well. Men do. After losing Will, the least we can do is give him a chance.' Alma started at the sound of the front door opening. 'I'd better help Lucy attend to breakfast,' she muttered, as Bianca appeared, walking towards them in a purposeful manner.

'Isn't it a beautiful morning,' called Rosalind, as Alma hastily dodged round the side of the house, making for the kitchen door.

Bianca came to a halt, frowning at her in a less than welcoming manner. 'What are you really doing here, Rosalind?' she demanded, abruptly.

'To help you and Alma with Jamie.'

'I see. So Oswald was right to warn me that you think you can just swan in, after I've done the hard work, and play the perfect daughter. Then Papa will think you're marvellous and make you one of the family again, especially now Cordelia is insisting on continuing her working with refugees in Paris and Kate has gone off in search of some ancient buried town near Naples, and they've clearly both totally abandoned us.'

'Of course not! And anyhow, Papa isn't likely to change his mind about me, you know what he's like.'

Bianca ploughed on without listening. 'Have you any idea how impossible he can be? Who do you think has been here, all this time, making arrangements, putting up with his tempers? Have you any idea how difficult it's been? And then him insisting Jamie should be looked after here, instead of the institution where everyone can see he belongs, where he can be cared for properly. Papa just thinks he can make him pull himself out of it and replace Will. Well, he can't.'

'I'm sure Jamie has no intention of replacing Will. He just needs time to be able to get well again.'

'What would you know about it?' Bianca's voice wobbled with anger, laced with frustration. 'While I've been here, dealing with it all, you've been doing just as you wish, riding round London on that motorcycle, just like a man, and meeting all those famous people.'

'What? I don't know anyone famous!' exclaimed Rosalind. 'It's just my job, Bianca. Believe me, the people I photograph don't even notice I exist. Miss Blake, my employer, says that it's my ability to remain in the background that makes me good at my work.' She grinned. 'So there are some uses to being born a girl, after all.'

Bianca ignored this. 'You've photographed Churchill, and the King and Queen visiting bomb damage.'

'In the street, along with a dozen other reporters.'

'Miss Parsons goes on and on about your picture of Princess Elizabeth in uniform during the war.'

'That was just luck, Bianca. I'd been commissioned to do a piece on the young women joining the ATS; I'd no idea the princess would be there that day, nobody did. I only spoke to her briefly, to ask if she minded me taking the photograph. She was gracious and kind, but I was just another photographer.'

'But you met her. You talked with the future Queen of England, while I was here, in the middle of nowhere, stuck with Papa and all the rationing, and no hope of going to London with all the petrol shortages, or any parties. And all the time Oswald was spending all hours building that great big house for us in Brierley – Brierley of all places – which is always freezing, and even worse than here.'

'You have your boys,' said Rosalind, gently. 'Isn't that worth more than anything?'

Bianca burst into tears. 'Oswald is already teaching them to despise me. He keeps on telling them I'm a silly woman who doesn't know anything. He's put both of them down for some ghastly prep school, where I'm sure they'll be bullied, just like Jamie always said he and Will were. I can't bear the thought, but he won't listen.'

'Oswald might change his mind?'

'He won't. He never does. He plans for them to go to Eton and Cambridge and then be members of Parliament before they are thirty, and George will be Prime Minister before he's a day over forty. He's only five, poor love, and all he's known is planes flying overhead and people talking about how they could see Coventry burn. He still has night-mares about how there might be tanks and aeroplanes coming to get us at any minute.' She blew her nose. 'And now I hardly ever see them – even Hubert, who's no more than a baby. Oswald insists I spend all my time with Papa, just so he can—' She came to an abrupt halt, a slow flush spreading over her features.

There was a moment's silence. The sense of unease that had remained in Rosalind ever since her return, sharpened, twisting her insides. From the stubborn look on her sister's face, there was no point in questioning her further on the subject. Besides, what could Bianca tell her that she hadn't already observed in Oswald's contemptuous undermining of Alma, the one who had insisted that Jamie would recover and that he was best looked after at home?

She swallowed. She and Bianca had never been close, but she could not believe her sister had become one of those women she met in London, who put their loyalty to their husband above everything – family, friendship and the even the best interests of their own children. Some, she had understood, had been enduring a violent marriage in the only way they could, but for others it had seemed to be in response to a need for male approval and the reflected glory emanating from their lord and master's importance.

Which was Bianca? She no longer knew her well enough to guess. And neither, she suspected, boded well for her sister's future happiness, let alone the damage such blind loyalty could do to Arden. Rosalind knew she had to at least try and build some kind of bridge between them.

'Why don't you bring the boys with you?'

'Papa won't like to be disturbed.'

'Have you ever known anyone able to resist small children?'

Bianca's face relaxed a little. 'I suppose not.'

'It'll do Papa good to see his grandchildren, however noisy, and I can't wait to meet my nephews.'

'I'm not sure if Oswald would approve. He's convinced I can't control them.'

'Is Oswald with them all the time?'

'He spends most of the time in London, and even when he's here, he's working. That's why he brought me here so early today, before the boys were properly up. He doesn't think of anything else.'

'Well then.'

'I can't hide something like that!'

'If he objects, you can always lie and tell him Papa insisted.'

'Rosalind!' Bianca was shocked.

'You said Oswald wanted you to please Papa. Seize the moment. Use it to your advantage. It's not very feminine, but that's what I've learnt to do, and I don't feel any less of a woman, despite the haircut.'

Bianca gave a smothered kind of a giggle. 'I suppose I could...'

'You could always tell Oswald you'd rather spend your time with your children than with Papa, you know. He has Alma to take care of him, and if she needs help, wouldn't it be easier to hire a woman from the village?'

'You don't know what Oswald's like. He goes on and on and doesn't listen, and when he sets his mind to something...' She trailed off.

'What sort of thing?'

'It doesn't matter.' Bianca was back to her brisk, no-nonsense self, as if shutting out their conversation. Her face resumed its martyred look. 'I'd better see to Papa.'

Over the following weeks, as August turned into September, Rosalind did her best to fit into the routine at Arden House.

Papa was still not really speaking to her, apart from the occasional mention of Henry Luscombe, but at least Jamie seemed to be taking more notice of his surroundings.

After a while, she abandoned reading him *Bleak House*, telling him instead of dashing between cars and trams on the way to report on some story or other, from the communities formed underground in the tube to escape the bombing, to the women flying spitfires between bases, with little training or instrumentation and no means of protecting themselves should they be unfortunate enough to cross the path of enemy aircraft.

'Brave,' he remarked one afternoon, when the clarity of sunlight clearly heralded the approaching autumn, the air heavy with the scent of ripening apples and distant bonfires.

'There are many ways of being brave,' she replied. 'And most of the women pilots confessed they were terrified, especially when the clouds came down unexpectedly and they'd no idea where they were.'

He turned his head, his eyes finally meeting hers. 'And you, too.'

'I'm not sure it was bravery. It's what we did, what all of us did because we had to. I didn't think. None of us did. You can't when you might be killed at any moment, or an enemy might invade. I never used to even dream of what I'd seen. But I dream of it now.'

'Yes.' He turned his eyes away again, but this time his gaze, rather than blank, followed the lines of the landscape set out below.

Strike while the iron is hot... 'I met Edmund Ford at the excavation, just after I arrived.'

He didn't reply, but she could feel him listening.

'The mosaic is still there, you know. It was kept safe when the rest of the ground was turned over to cultivation. I had the enlarger sent back from London and I've finished setting up the old darkroom again. I've been commissioned to take photographs of Brierley, to show how life has changed. My editor gave me a few weeks to settle in, but now it's time I got to work.' He was still listening. 'I like the idea of picturing the work on the mosaic starting again. Maybe even the burial mound, if there's anything there. Remember all the plans you had to dig a trial trench after we visited Sutton Hoo?'

'Kate,' he muttered.

'Kate's in Italy. Alma said she went there straight from Cornwall, as soon as the war ended, to help with the excavation of Pompeii, and no one knows when she'll be back. But Edmund seemed keen to work on the mosaic. I suspect he's troubled by dreams, too. Perhaps you could find a way of working together?'

'Maybe.'

'I've promised I'll help Alma dig up enough potatoes from the walled garden tomorrow, so poor Lucy isn't always traipsing down there, with everything else she has to do. So we'll be there, anyhow. You could always come and join us. I'll unlock the door onto the field.'

'Maybe.' This time his voice was stronger. 'You said the mosaic was still there?'

'Yes, it is. Someone took care that it survived. It seems a pity to abandon it now.'

'Yes, that's true,' he replied, thoughtfully.

Chapter Twenty-Six

'You didn't have to do that, Miss,' said Lucy, the following morning, looking up from kneading potato bread to eke out the available flour, as Rosalind pushed her way through the half-open door balancing the laden tray with the breakfast dishes.

'I wanted to. Besides, I can see how busy you are.' She placed the tray next to the sink, filling it with hot water from the kettle gently burbling to itself on the range, and set to cleaning the plates and bowls. 'I don't know how you manage to prepare such delicious meals, with rationing being worse than ever.'

'You get used to it,' replied Lucy, dividing up the dough into baking tins, covering them with a large cloth to prove, before reaching for a large earthenware mixing bowl, balancing it on her hip as she resumed the creaming of a small amount of butter and sugar, in preparation for the bottled cherries, glowing deep crimson in their glass Kilner jar, to take the place of hard-to-find sultanas and raisins. 'To be honest, I like the challenge, and at least we can get more things from the farms and the hedgerows, being in the country. Cakes are a nuisance, but Mr Arden insists there is always one when Mr Gorwell comes to tea.'

Rosalind paused in swilling out the teapot. While Bianca remained a daily visitor since her return, Oswald had been mostly away on urgent business in London, far too busy to even come back at weekends to see his wife and children.

'Is that often?' she asked.

'Two or three times a week, when he's in Brierley. Mr Arden likes Mr Gorwell's company. He says it's a man to talk to, instead of just being surrounded by women all the time.'

'That's a lot of work for you, especially with everything in such short supply.'

'I don't mind Miss, honest. Not when it gives Mr Arden so much pleasure. He won't allow any other visitors, see, especially now.' She gave the cake mixture a particularly vicious beating.

'Because of Jamie.'

'Yes, Miss.'

Rosalind put the plate she'd been scrubbing clean of grease to dry on the wooden rack above the sink. 'Why do you stay?'

'It's a roof over my head.'

'There have to be other houses. There's been such a shortage since the war, the newspapers are full of advertisements for cooks and other domestic staff.'

'They wouldn't be no better.' Lucy put her bowl down on the table. 'I don't want to be bossed around by some snotty-nosed housekeeper, or Cook, like I used to be. At least nowadays I've got a bit of elbow room here. No one to tell me what to do every minute of the day. Lets me work out my own system.'

Her voice wavered dangerously. 'I only had my own

home for such a short time, you see, before the news came about my Albert.' She swallowed. 'Well, once I came back to myself again, I knew it were either go back and be a drudge for Mum until she wore me out to nothing, or come back here. Don't you worry, Miss, I knew what I were letting myself in for. And besides, I didn't want to leave. My Albert might be buried out in France, but he's here. With me.'

'Oh, Lucy.' Rosalind put her arms around her as the maid's face collapsed, holding her tight.

'It's the places I used to go with him, see. We started courting here. He used to meet me, out of sight of the house so neither of us would be dismissed. Mr Arden was strict about the maids having no followers. When I smell grass after its been mown, or watch the sunset through the trees, like I did when I was with him, well he's still there with me. Oh, I know he isn't, not really.' She leant her face on Rosalind's shoulder, convulsing with deep, despairing sobs. 'But he still is.'

'It's all right,' said Rosalind gently. 'I know what you mean.'

'Blow me. Now I've messed up your nice blouse,' said Lucy, after a few minutes, and extracting herself and blowing her nose.

'That doesn't matter. Salt water never did anyone any harm.'

'Didn't do it no good, neither,' said Lucy. 'And now I've set you off, too.'

'No you didn't,' said Rosalind, with a watery smile. She glanced at Lucy's washed-out face as she reached for the mixing bowl. 'When did you have time for breakfast?'

'That's all right, Miss. Once I've got this in the oven, there'll be plenty.'

'No there won't.' Rosalind pushed the cake mixture out

of reach. 'And I bet you were up well before dawn.' She brushed herself down. 'Sit.'

'Pardon, Miss?'

'Sit.'

Lucy eyed her as if she was yet another Arden to lose their mind, but lowered herself warily onto the chair next to the table. Rosalind grinned. After her first weeks back at Arden, she had begun to feel increasingly distant from the daring journalist, who had swerved her motorcycle around all obstacles towards the flames of bombed-out buildings lighting up the sky, intent on finding her next story. It was good to feel she hadn't lost the habit of being decisive and doing what had to be done, even if it was the domestic sphere, rather than capturing the realities of dazed and bloodied families picking their way through the rubble of their homes.

'Ham or sausage? Actually, why not both?'

'Miss—'

'No arguing. I'm going to cook you breakfast.'

'Rations...' protested Lucy faintly.

'There will still be enough meat left for tonight and I promise I'll personally dig up all the potatoes you need to hide any shortfall. A handful of beans and no one will notice.'

Lucy gave a stifled giggle. She sat quietly as Rosalind reached down a clean frying pan from the shelves, before melting a knob of precious butter to fry slices of ham and sausage, adding cooked potato she found in the larder, along with a few spoonfuls of last night's kedgeree. Once the concoction was heated through to her satisfaction, she bound it together with eggs to make a solid omelette, at the last minute throwing on a handful of fresh spinach, sitting in a bowl to be added to the evening's pie. Turning the final dish neatly onto a plate, she placed it in front of Lucy, along with a jar of homemade pickles.

Lucy stared at the finished dish with undisguised astonishment. 'Where d'you learn to do that?'

'I had my own room in London. I shared one electric ring and a couple of pans on a landing with the other girls, but it's amazing what you can do, when push comes to shove.'

'That weren't me prying. It was just, well I got used to cooking with whatever was to hand in those months I had my Albert. It brought back memories. Good ones,' she added hastily.

'Yes, me too,' Rosalind replied, with a smile. She scrubbed the pan clean and took up the mixing bowl, beating the rest of the eggs into the butter and sugar as Lucy made short work of her omelette.

'I'm not sure I'll be able to move if I finish this,' sighed Lucy at last.

'I shall be mortally offended if you don't.'

Lucy laughed. 'Don't you worry, Miss. I've no intention of leaving none.'

'That looks good,' remarked Alma, appearing with a tray of empty dishes. 'Smells delicious, too.'

'Miss Rosalind has become quite the cook.'

'I wouldn't say that. You haven't yet had a chance to discover the severe limitation of my dishes, Lucy. I'm afraid they are mainly a variety of the same thing. And toast. And I've been informed I make an excellent Welsh rarebit with the smallest amount of cheese possible, although since I've no idea how they are supposed to be, I couldn't possibly comment.'

'Well, you've done Jamie good just being here,' said Alma, emptying the tray with a smile, and finishing the washing of the dishes with the air of a woman accustomed to being up to her elbows in suds. 'He's definitely taking more interest in things. I left him reading the reports of the finds made at Sutton Hoo that Miss Parsons saved for him.'

'Thank goodness,' said Rosalind, relief flooding through her.

'See? You're doing him good already,' replied Alma.

'That's enough beating, Miss, or it will go the other way,' said Lucy, finishing her final mouthful and taking possession of the cake mixture. Already there was more colour in her cheeks as she set to draining and folding in the preserved cherries with a slightly less manic air.

Alma finished the dishes and dried her hands. 'Are you serious about photographing people in the village, Rosy?'

'It's what I promised my editor. It was the only way she said she'd let me stay here for more than a couple of weeks and keep my job. I need to start sending her something, or she'll be on the telephone every morning to nag me.'

'Well, in that case, perhaps you'd like to join me this evening. There's a rehearsal of the village choral society. We're busy preparing for the harvest festival, of course, but we're also starting on the carols for Christmas.'

'I didn't know you had joined the choir.'

'Oh, it was one of those things, during the war.' A touch of colour appeared on Alma's pale cheeks. 'I used to hear them when I was volunteering for the WI, so one day I stayed behind. I didn't really think I'd enjoy singing, but it feels so therapeutic.'

'Just the thing,' said Lucy, deep in her cake, with just the faintest hint of a smile.

Later that afternoon, Rosalind set out with her stepmother through the fields to Brierley-in-Arden.

There was a quiet bustle in the village, with the familiar Saturday afternoon relaxation of the working week. Women chatted to each other over walls as they tackled endless piles of mending in the sunshine, while their husbands dug gardens and harvested marrows and squashes that, along with wigwams of late peas and raspberries, supplemented the tedium of their rations and meagre incomes. Children played on the green by the pond, or in the little side alley-ways, their laughter interspersed with the occasional squab-ble, echoing into the air.

Brierley village hall was much as Rosalind remembered, small and plain, with creaking floorboards underfoot and a low stage at the far end, supporting the same, slightly moth-eaten, red velvet curtains hanging on either side. Just below the stage was an ancient upright piano, a dark-haired man in his early forties perched on a somewhat rickety chair, sounding the keys carefully, followed by a run of scales, before breaking into a rather wistful rendition of 'Jerusalem'.

'It sounds as if the piano has survived its tuning, Mr Fair-field,' remarked Alma, as Mr Parry's hymn came to a halt at 'dark satanic mills'.

'So it has, Mrs Arden,' he replied, looking up with a smile, revealing a pleasant, open face, marred by a deep scar running across one eye, leaving it opaque and sightless.

'I don't believe you've met my stepdaughter.'

'Good afternoon, Miss Arden.' His good eye, Rosalind found, was a deep green and clear as could be.

'Pleased to meet you, Mr Fairfield,' she replied.

He turned back to the piano, concealing the scarred side of his face as if conscious of her gaze, the keys breaking jaun-tily into 'What Shall we do with the Drunken Sailor'. 'I understand you're a photographer, Miss Arden.'

'I'd certainly like to photograph the choir, if you've no objections.'

'None at all,' he replied, leaving the drunken sailor to his fate and turning back to face her. 'The publicity will be welcome. We could do with more members.'

'The stage used to be filled with singers when I was child.'

'I remember. I used to walk miles with my dad from the farm to come and listen. It seems a long time ago. It's good to see it getting back on its feet again.'

Rosalind retreated to the back of the hall as a steady stream of slightly hesitant arrivals began to appear, men and women of all ages, some clutching children, perching themselves on the chairs with an expectant air.

Soon the rehearsal was in full swing. A full-throated rendition of 'London Bridge is Falling Down' and 'What Shall we do with the Drunken Sailor' subsided into the wistfulness of 'Danny Boy', followed by the familiar folk songs and sea shanties the Brierley choir had sung from time immemorial.

Alma, she found, wasn't the only well-dressed woman from the big houses round about joining the poorer members of the community, who arrived as soon as they had finished their chores or their work in the fields. Before long, it seemed half of Brierley was there, escaping the monotony of everyday life in a country wracked by shortages and loss with a good sing-song in the village hall, just like there always used to be. Small children ran between the chairs before being swept up and shushed by aunts and grandmothers. Before the war, the singers had been almost equally made up of both sexes, but like so many things now, it was mainly women, with mostly older men taking the parts of the tenors and baritones and just a few younger men scattered in between.

Rosalind concentrated on getting the best pictures she could in the uncertain light. She first photographed the choir following Mr Fairfield, as he nodded his head in encourage-ment from the piano. A short break in proceedings to stretch aching backs and legs allowed her to take a formal portrait of them all, slightly self-conscious, but buoyed by a particularly rousing rendition of 'Men of Harlech', before seeking out volunteers for individual portraits.

Just as she thought no one was going to brave the lime-light, two schoolgirls extricated themselves from the back row of the altos, with the air of having egged each other on.

'Are they really going to go in a magazine, Miss?'

'I'll send all the ones that come out, although it's up to the editor which one she chooses.'

'You mean, a proper magazine, not like the parish news-letter?' The first girl nudged her friend. 'Like them actresses from Hollywood?'

'Lauren Bacall,' sighed her companion, eyes glazed with hero-worship.

'Or Dorothy Lamour,' added the first girl, equally star struck.

'Something like that. Although maybe without the diamonds.'

The two giggled, intertwining arms with the ease of best friends as she took their portrait. Emboldened by example, Rosalind managed to persuade a shy and lanky young man, cheeks flushed as much from wind and weather as embarrassment, to gaze solemnly into the lens, followed by a group of middle-aged housewives, who were not about to be outdone by the youngsters having all the glory. By the time she had finished her rolls of film, she could spot several with regret on their faces at not having jumped in on time.

'I'll be back again, if I may,' she said. 'I need to check that I've got everything right, and I can't see that until I've developed my film and printed the pictures. But I've every intention of taking more.'

'And when we perform for the village?' demanded a girl from the back. 'We'll have our best clothes on then.'

'Definitely. If Mr Fairfield doesn't mind.'

'Not in the least,' he replied, already shooing his charges back on stage, to resume their slightly tentative attempts at 'Jerusalem', which was to be the climax of the performance for the village for the harvest festival in a few weeks' time.

The mellowness of a warm September evening was falling as Rosalind and Alma took the path through the kissing gate back towards Arden House.

'It's good to see the village looking almost like it used to be,' said Rosalind.

'The choir's made a difference,' said Alma. 'We're lucky to have Mr Fairfield come back to teach at the village school, after he was invalided out of the fighting, and start it up again. I don't think we'll ever be as ambitious as the choral society used to be before the war, but it's enjoyable and that's what counts.'

'Well, I'm glad it's back now,' said Rosalind. She could see that Alma's face had relaxed and there was more vigour in her step. It didn't matter if the somewhat ragged singing, coaxed into slightly more tuneful renditions by Mr Fairfield from the piano, would never reach the heights of *The Messiah* or Gilbert and Sullivan. Mr Fairfield had sighed that there was no soloist to take the place of Clive Leverson, who had been one of those who had not made it back from Dunkirk, the liquid beauty of his voice forever silenced amongst the stars.

All the same, she had seen the enjoyment on their faces, from the deep yearning of the 'Skye Boat Song' to the collapsing into giggles as they became hopelessly entangled in the round of 'Frère Jacques', with no one knowing who was starting and who finishing and who was still in the middle. It was a stepping out for a short while from grief, from memories of recent fear, and from the daily, and tediously familiar, battle with shortages and ways of mending everything from trousers to wheelbarrows, and with another winter soon approaching.

The two came to a halt as the path reached the garden walls and the remains of the excavation.

'I'm not sure this will ever be completed,' said Alma, regretfully. 'Kate seems so determined to stay in Italy, I'm not sure she will ever come home.'

'Jamie may soon become well enough again to continue.'

'Perhaps...' replied Alma, sounding uncertain again as the shadow of the house loomed up above them. 'I hope so.'

There was a distant crackling in the hedgerow, followed by the click of the gate and the sound of whistling. They both turned as a man emerged on the far side of the field, a small child on his shoulders, followed by a woman accompanied by a girl of about six. As they set off, following the path up the small incline towards the farms beyond the burial mound, the girl began to flag. The man turned back, taking one small hand, the woman the other, the girl helped along between them. The whistling started up again, louder this time. 'And did those feet in ancient time,' went the tuneful sound, echoing in the clear air, 'walk upon England's mountains green', Blake's clouded hills and dark satanic mills gradually fading into the distance.

'Sometimes,' said Alma, sounding utterly unlike her usual self. 'Life can be unbearably cruel.'

'I'm sorry...' said Rosalind, uncertainly.

Alma blew her nose. 'Don't mind me, my dear. I'm being selfish. I've such a comfortable existence, compared with so many. I really have no cause to complain.'

Rosalind winced. *What was there to say?*

The sky had cleared to a pure blue, revealing a crescent moon hanging above the trees as a myriad of stars began to appear. Tiny pipistrelle bats began their nightly dance above her head, swerving delicately here and there in search of insects.

'D'you know,' said Alma, thoughtfully, gazing down towards the half-uncovered tails of dolphins engaged in their eternal dance, 'I might start persuading Jamie to venture a little further with his walks. I rather think he could benefit from taking up his archaeology again.'

'I feel sure he will,' replied Rosalind, slipping her arm through that of her stepmother, as they made their way home through the gathering dark.

Chapter Twenty-Seven

To Rosalind's relief, the photographs of the choir were clear, capturing the faces of the singers, both in passionate concentration and smiling slightly self-consciously at the camera. She had also caught the two friends at just the right moment to reveal their mischievous glee.

Being a perfectionist, she found some angles she would like to attempt again, and others in which the light did not fall quite as she wished it, but there were enough that worked to send to Ginny to accompany her article on how the choral society was being reformed, with a hint of a traditional Christmas to come.

A few days later, Rosalind parcelled them up and sent them to *Woman's Time*, fighting down her disappointment that there was no letter from Guy waiting for her at the Post Office, despite knowing that it was still too early to expect anything.

While she waited for a reply, she joined Alma in encouraging Jamie to walk a little further from the house each day. He remained closed on himself for much of the time, refusing any suggestion of joining the rest of the family for meals, or evenings around the fire in the living room, but at least his physical strength was beginning to return.

To her relief, the members of the choral society were delighted with their portraits, joining a steady stream of the curious to peer at the pictures hung on the walls of the little museum. Even more to the point, Ginny was enthused by her first offerings, setting up a dedicated section she named 'Scenes from an English Village', and instantly demanding more of the same.

Relieved that she wasn't about to be given her marching orders, and that, for the moment, she still had a job to go back to, Rosalind set to work with new vigour. Over the next weeks, she had few difficulties in persuading villagers to pose, or at least ignore her as she found the right angle or waited for the best light. By the end of September, she had sent Ginny photographs of girls playing hopscotch on the street, accompanied by one of small boys brandishing makeshift bows and arrows, ambushing each other from behind garden fences. In another, Mrs Ackrite posed, arms akimbo, in front of her grocer's, not to be outdone by the rest of the shops in the row.

These were followed in turn by the village carpenter, proudly displaying his half-finished cabinet and surrounded by his tools, and the farmer with his dog, bringing in the cows for milking. Montague the cat, suitably bribed with scraps of chicken, sat regally in front of the museum with an air of ownership of the entire village. She even persuaded Mrs Bray the washerwoman to let her photograph her boiling up clothes in the copper in the back garden, before hanging out great lines of sheets to dry. Although, for decency's sake, Mrs Bray point blank refused to add the bundle of bloomers, bodices and petticoats until the final picture had been taken.

On the other hand, it was no good telling Papa of Jamie's gradual improvement; he stubbornly refused to listen to Alma's cheerful reports, while barely acknowledging Rosalind's presence, instead full of complaints that Oswald was likely to be in London on business for at least the next month and so quite unable to relieve the tedium.

But even their father could not resist when Bianca, emboldened by Oswald's continued absence, brought George and Hubert to visit, even daring to leave their nanny behind.

'I do hope they won't break anything,' she sighed, as she ushered in George, who, far from being a rumbustious little boy, clung to her skirts, overcome with shyness, while Hubert remained in her arms eyeing the proceedings solemnly with large brown eyes.

'Of course they won't,' said Alma, coaxing George into taking an interest in the ancient Noah's ark Rosalind remembered from her own childhood and had brought down from the attic for the occasion. 'And anyhow, if there is an accident, what does it matter, so long as they are not hurt? They are only children, after all.'

George, who had sat down next to the ark and was tentatively stroking the back of one of the elephants, looked up at this, as if attempting to determine the expression on her face, and worried he might be about to be punished for some unknown misdemeanour.

'Well, yes,' said Bianca, relaxing a little.

'Now then,' Alma continued, handing George a wooden giraffe, 'how about we find the other one, and for all of them, so they can go in two by two?'

'Yes,' he whispered eagerly, reaching out hesitantly towards the collection of carved animals, as if half-expecting to be reprimanded for being too fast, or too slow, or too careless. Rosalind crouched down next to her nephew as Bianca perched baby Hubert on his grandfather's knee to be admired.

'Poor squashed little things,' muttered Alma under her breath, as George, blossoming in being left to his own devices, grew more confident by the minute. Rosalind helped him arrange the brightly-painted creatures in line, ready to enter a less than seaworthy ark, with a large hole below the waterline where, she remembered with a pang of grief in her heart, Will had once grown impatient with such a childish game.

If I ever have children, I'll let them run wild, determined Rosalind, watching the cautious face, hazel eyes looking so anxiously to her for approval after each move, while gradually relaxing at the encouragement of her smile.

'It's alright,' she said, as George silently handed her a horse with its tail missing. 'That happened years ago. Your Uncle Will broke it when he trod on it by accident. I'm sure Uncle Jamie can repair it, he was always good at things like that.'

George nodded, and was soon absorbed in making the horse trot around the rest of the animals, lost in a story of his own.

'He's being so good,' exclaimed Bianca, pausing in keeping Hubert entertained and his chubby fingers from tugging at their father's unkempt hair.

'He's a pleasure,' said Alma firmly. 'They both are. You're welcome to bring them at any time.'

'Thank you,' said Bianca, the enjoyment fading from her face. *Not when Oswald is at home*, read her expression.

Rosalind winced. Bianca had always been the one most eager to please Papa, to be the quiet, self-effacing daughter they all knew they were meant to be. Now, it seemed, that had helped to mould her into the accommodating wife a man like Oswald required. *The sky changes when they are wives…*

I'll fight tooth and nail for my children, thought Rosalind, fiercely. Easier said than done, she recognised with a stab to the heart. Who was she to criticise her sister, who was completely dependent on her husband for every means of existence, for both her and her offspring? For all the opulence of Bianca's life, Rosalind would not have changed it for any of her own scraping together to afford new boots and carefully saving her clothing ration for a winter coat.

The money she earned from her photography might not be much, but when she had lived in London she had learnt to stretch it as far as it would go. Besides, it was her own, and she had a recognised skill – even a modest kind of standing in her profession, despite the handicap of being born female. From the moment she had left Arden House, she had directed her own life, answerable to no one, apart from her employer, and even then, when she went home at night, her life was hers to do with as she pleased.

'Hippopotamus,' she replied to George's enquiring look, as he held up the fat-bellied creature for her inspection.

'Hippot…'

'Hip-po-potamus,' she repeated gently.

'Hippop-potamus,' repeated George, grinning triumphantly. His nose and brows were those of Oswald, but the smile and the soft brown of his hair were so like Will she almost cried out. She caught Alma's eye. Her stepmother had seen it, too, with the mixture of pain and gratitude for the weaving of family resemblance that kept a part of Will still remaining within the family line.

'Let's see if Uncle Jamie is ready for his walk,' said Alma quietly. 'He can show you the dolphins, George.'

'Dolphins?'

'They are in a kind of picture, in the ground,' Rosalind said. How little she knew of children, she wasn't even sure how to explain something so simple as a mosaic so he could understand. 'Would you like to see them?'

George glanced towards his mother, who was busy extracting a velvet tassel, of unknown origin, from Hubert's mouth. 'Yes please,' he mouthed.

Alma met Rosalind's eyes. Now all they had to do was persuade Jamie, who would surely gain some comfort from the presence of his small nephew. *It's worth a try*, went the message between them.

Rosalind kept George entertained while Alma vanished upstairs. For a while, it seemed Jamie would not appear, but then a movement on the lawns caught Rosalind's attention.

'We're going to play outside,' she announced to Bianca.

'Outside,' repeated George, who had clearly learnt better in his short life than to mention such unlikely things as finding dolphins. Rosalind gave the small hand placed confidentially in hers a reassuring squeeze.

'Do take care,' called Bianca after them, as they disappeared, flustered at Hubert's insistence at not letting go of the offending tassel. 'And don't forget your coat, darling.'

They set off slowly, Jamie concentrating on walking to the exclusion of everything else, George far too in awe of this unknown relative to do more than trot along, holding Rosalind's hand tight. As they reached the path running alongside the walled garden, Jamie paused to catch his breath. His eyes fell on George, who was watching him solemnly.

'Hello,' he said.

'Hello.' George took a deep breath. 'It this the dolphins?'

'Dolphins?' Jamie glanced towards Alma.

'In the mosaic,' Alma explained. She smiled at George. 'It's not far, sweetheart. Just a few minutes more.'

Rosalind found Jamie was still watching his nephew, a troubled expression on his face. Did he also find shades of Will in the small features? Or was it the children he had seen in France, the innocents caught up in a conflict that was not of their making, and in which they were the most vulnerable, who still haunted him? Alma had told her it was the children's faces, both the living and the dead, he could not get out of his mind. Rosalind watched him sadly. She could understand those visions, remembering the faces of the children and babies she had seen in the devastation of the London Blitz that still sent her awake in the darkness, caught in the horror as if it was still there, all around her.

Jamie shook himself, as if to banish any remaining ghosts. 'So, young man, you would like to see the dolphins?'

George nodded. 'Please. Please, Uncle James,' he added hastily, no doubt feeling the fell hand of his father, or possibly his nanny, on his shoulder at any lack of politeness.

'Very well.' Jamie smiled with the same old tenderness Rosalind had seen in him when he picked up a stray lamb, or rescued bees trapped in the watery hollow of the marble birdbath in the centre of the lawn. 'Only some of them are hidden.'

'Oh.'

'But we can make them appear, if you help me.'

'Yes please,' said George, abandoning Rosalind in favour of the man of the party, who, despite the stick and the slightly odd air about him, had turned out to be not so alarming, after all. 'What's a dolphin?' he enquired, as they rounded the corner, making their way towards the Roman villa.

. . .

'That was a good idea of yours to bring Jamie,' said Rosalind, as she stood with her stepmother, while Jamie lifted George down into the excavation to inspect the tiles more closely.

'I had a horrible feeling it might do more harm than good,' Alma replied. She smiled at the sound of George's chatter, interspersed with Jamie's voice, speaking more fluently than they had heard before, as if catching the child's lack of self-consciousness. 'But they seem to be helping each other.'

'I think they are.'

Alma took out a large keyring from her pocket, containing two rather rusty keys. 'Now then, one of these is to the door of the walled garden nearest the house, so the other must be to the smaller one beneath the ivy somewhere.'

A few minutes searching revealed a wooden door, its blue paint faded and peeling. A bit of jiggling and the key turned, opening up into a mass of trees and brambles, with a weather-beaten shed to one side.

'That's where the gardeners kept their tools, there must be some in there Jamie can use for the excavation. I meant to sort it out once the Land Girls left, but somehow I never got the time.'

They returned to the site of the excavation just as Jamie lifted George back onto the neighbouring grass. Rosalind could see her brother was beginning to look exhausted at the unaccustomed exercise and answering a small boy who, freed from his customary constraints, was replete with questions.

'We can come back, George, the next time you visit,' said Alma, as Jamie pulled himself wearily from the excavation. 'There might even be more to see by then.'

'Octo-pus,' said George, rolling his new word around his mouth.

'There might be another,' said Jamie, retrieving his stick. 'And more fishes.'

He stumbled slightly as they set off back, leaning heavily on his support, but he listened closely to George, who was now glued to his side with distinct intimations of hero-worship. He showed no signs of flagging in his answers, being instead energised by his small nephew's interest.

'Well, I never,' said Alma, slipping her arm through Rosalind's as they followed on behind. 'Who would have thought it would be a child to bring Jamie back to himself.'

'You did have something to do with it, Mama,' said Rosalind, kissing her. 'And Jamie now has something to work towards with the excavation. We just have to persuade Bianca to bring the children again, so he can show George any new finds.'

'I do so hope Jamie is on the mend,' replied Alma, sounding as if she was holding back tears. 'Dear Lord, I hope so.'

The next morning, Rosalind found Jamie already at work on the mosaic, digging with a garden spade at the patch of ground next to the existing trench.

'There are plenty of trowels as well as spades,' said Alma, emerging from the little door into the walled garden. 'And more paintbrushes.'

'Those'll be useful,' said Jamie, pausing, breathless, to remove his jacket.

'Where was it you wanted us to take off the top soil, darling?' asked Alma.

'On the other side.' He frowned at them both. 'If you're sure.'

'Completely,' said Rosalind, firmly. 'We've both dug up more potatoes than you can count over the past weeks, since Papa doesn't seem to be able to replace the Land Girls. So you call us the weaker sex at your peril.'

Jamie grinned and returned to his new section, starting the slow, laborious business of scraping the earth away from what he hoped still lay beneath.

Rosalind helped Alma clear their designated patch of earth. Although neither of them turned to look, they could both hear Jamie as he continued to dig, pausing every few minutes to recover himself. As the sun rose high above them, the digging grew ever more intermittent, before finally ceasing all together.

'Leave him be,' said Alma, as Rosalind rose to her feet.

Rosalind turned to find that, rather than collapsed in a heap and more than ready to be helped back to his room, Jamie was building a small heap of sticks in the blackened ground at the edges of the field, where bonfires had been lit each autumn as more land was cleared to grow vegetables.

He worked slowly, methodically, lost in a world of his own. Within minutes, there was a crackling of fire and a thin line of smoke sailing up into the air. Rosalind returned Alma's smile. Even from this distance, she could see the relaxation on her brother's face, concentrating on his task, oblivious to anything else. He hadn't entirely lost his haunted look, but the absorption resembled a kind of peace.

As the fire began to collapse in on itself, glowing white hot in the centre, Jamie disappeared through the garden door, reappearing minutes later with an ancient Kelly kettle and a battered collection of tin mugs once used by the gardeners.

Producing a tin from his pocket, he spooned a dark powder into each of the mugs.

'Washington's Instant Coffee,' he explained, as Rosalind sniffed warily at the contents. 'The Americans drank it all the time.' A faint smile appeared at her grimace. 'Then, it tasted better than champagne.'

The three of them drank the fortifying hot liquid that did indeed bring the flavour of coffee, saying little, watching the flames die down to an orange glow. Rosalind could tell from the hunch of Jamie's shoulders that the morning's effort had completely exhausted him but that his pride wouldn't allow two women to work when he sat idle.

'I'm glad you found the kettle,' she said.

'It was where the gardeners left it. Where it always was.' He stirred the embers with a long stick. 'They thought they'd be home in months.'

'We all did, Jamie. None of us were to know.'

'Maybe.' He was lost in thought again.

As the bonfire died down, Jamie returned the Kelly kettle to the gardener's shed, along with his tin of instant coffee.

'That means he intends to come back,' whispered Alma, as she and Rosalind cleaned the earth from their spades. 'I do wish I knew more about Roman mosaics and archaeology.'

'I met Edmund Ford here when I first came back, looking at the mosaic. He told me he was interested in archaeology. I'm sure he might be willing to help uncover the Roman villa.'

'Edmund?' Alma frowned at her. 'You do know he's employed by Oswald?'

'Oswald?' It was a jolt to the stomach. *So that's how he knew so much about the road...* Rosalind's plans, her favourable impression of Edmund, turned somersaults in her mind. She settled them down, drawing on the instinct refined during her days and nights photographing the Blitz, when she had learnt to make snap judgements of who to trust and who not. Women's intuition, they called it. But there was nothing magical or mysterious about it, rather the rapid analysis of each clue observed, combined with every lesson she had ever learnt about human nature.

Rosalind concentrated her thoughts, trying to be as honest and impartial as possible, unswayed by a handsome face. There was nothing about the engineer that had repelled her in the way Oswald had done at their very first meeting. She had felt no alarm at finding herself alone with Edmund that morning, despite being out of earshot of the house.

She straightened her shoulders. She had risked bombs and shrapnel, along with fire and falling buildings, for her journalism. This was for Jamie. She could take a chance and trust that her instincts were right.

'Even if he is employed by Oswald,' she remarked, 'there's nothing to say that Edmund shouldn't indulge his interest in archaeology, especially if it might help Jamie. Surely that's in the best interest of everybody?'

'I'm not sure what your father would say. Oswald was telling him throughout the war that it was a waste of good growing land not to cultivate right up to the mosaic.'

'Does Papa always agree with everything Oswald thinks?'

'He does have some very practical ideas...' began Alma, before coming to a halt. 'He listens to him, like he did with poor Will. Sometimes I think he sees Oswald as a kind of replacement. Oh, I don't mean for Will,' she added quickly. 'More like a male figure he can rely on.'

Alma's eyes travelled to where Jamie had returned to

stand at the edges if the excavation, shading his eyes against the low slant of the afternoon sun as he gazed up at the burial mound, deep in thought. 'Someone he feels he'd be able to pass on responsibility for Arden, if Jamie...' Her words drifted into silence.

Rosalind considered her. All her preconceptions about her stepmother from her childhood seemed to have been overturned in the past weeks. *Or had they?*

'Do you mind Oswald being treated as the heir apparent?'

Alma flinched. 'He's very capable. When everyone thought Jamie must be dead as well as Will, I could see it gave your father comfort, especially as there was no one else. There was a distant cousin of your papa's who might have inherited, but he was killed in the fighting in Italy, at Monte Cassino. At least Bianca's sons have Arden blood in their veins.'

'And now?'

Her stepmother didn't reply.

Rosalind tried again. 'Now that Jamie's back, do you think Oswald will relinquish his position?'

'If Jamie isn't capable—' began Alma.

'But if he is?'

Alma chewed at her lips, without replying.

'Do you want him to?' persisted Rosalind.

Silence. Maybe she had been mistaken, and the Alma who had blossomed during the war was not ready to break from her husband's thrall. Jamie was going to have to fight this one on his own.

'Not that it matters,' Rosalind continued gently. 'I'm sure things will take their course—'

'I hate him.' The words burst out of Alma like an explosion.

'Sorry?'

'Oswald. I hate him. There, now I've said it. I hate him. I loathe him more than I've ever loathed anyone in my life. He doesn't care about your father, or about Arden. I've tried so hard to make Leo see, but he won't. I've never minded that he doesn't listen to me, he's so much older and he knows so much more. But with Oswald, it's as if Leo is utterly blind. Oswald has him totally in his thrall; he knows exactly how to play on his weakness...'

She came to a halt, a look of horror overcoming her face at what she had just said.

'I didn't mean that.' Her chin jutted defiantly. 'That's a lie. Yes, I did. I meant every single word. My dear, you must forgive me, but I'm tired of being dismissed as a fool.'

'No one should ever say you're a fool, Mama.'

Alma pulled a handkerchief from her pocket. 'That's the awful part. I am. I was. If I'd had a shred of sense of self-worth, I would never have allowed myself to be persuaded by that wretched aunt of mine, who only ever found me a burden after Mama died. I should never...' She swallowed, the unthinkable, the unspeakable, thought hanging in the air between them. She sniffed, defiantly. 'I always knew I should have been a seamstress or a milliner. Even if I'd ended up in the workhouse, at least I could have said I tried.'

'Well, I'm glad you didn't,' said Rosalind, abandoning her spade and kissing her. 'You always did your best for us. I don't know what we would have done without you.'

'Thank you,' said Alma, blowing her nose and sounding more than a little unconvinced.

'And you've built a life for yourself. I could see that when you joined in with the choir.'

'That's true.' Alma brightened. 'I'm a dreadful singer,' she added gloomily. 'I can barely hold a tune.'

'Rubbish. And anyhow, it's not about being perfect, it's about bringing everyone together.'

'I'm sorry my dear, take no notice of me, I think we all feel a little fragile at times, and I'm sure you saw far worse things in London than we did here. I saw some of the photographs you took in the midst of the bombing, and when people were being pulled out of the rubble. Some of them I couldn't bear to look at. I could never be that brave.'

'You saw my photographs of the Blitz?'

'Miss Parsons has every copy of *Woman's Time* from the war. She cut them out and put them up in the museum for all to see. Mostly the ones of the King and Queen inspecting the bomb damage at Buckingham Palace of course, and those you took of Mr Churchill, and that lovely one of Princess Elizabeth in her ATS uniform. But she put the others on display as well. It gave us a real insight of what it must have been like to be in the East End in all that horror, and made us think of what it must have been like in France and Germany after the allied bombing raids. All those poor people. Miss Parsons is very proud of you, my dear, and so am I. And I'm sure your papa would be...' She coloured.

'If he hadn't disowned me for daring to follow my own path, you mean.'

'He does still love you,' said Alma anxiously. 'You have to believe that. He just finds it hard to back down, even when he knows in his heart that he's in the wrong. He's just not always the wisest of men, I'm afraid, especially when he thinks he's being disobeyed.'

'That's where Oswald is so very clever, he works on him, bit by bit, until Leo is convinced the idea was his own. This whole thing about tearing up the village for a road, and building great mansions for Oswald's rich clients on Arden land – well, your father would never have given anything like that a second thought if he'd been in his right mind. At least, I hope he wouldn't,' she added, gloomily, her eyes straying back towards Jamie, who was still gazing up at the burial mound, lost in his own world.

'Then Jamie has to get well,' said Rosalind.

'That's our only chance, I'm afraid,' agreed Alma. 'But I can't bear to put such a burden on him.'

'Except he might wish to take over, if he gets stronger,' said Rosalind.

'But for that he's going to need help.'

Alma sighed. 'Which brings us back to Edmund. You're right about his interest in archaeology. The talk in the village is that he was forever finding things in the fields, bits of pot, old coins, parts of clay pipes, things like that.'

'In that case, he could be just the person to help Jamie. I'm certain that would help him more than anything, and I've a feeling he might be more at ease working here with a man, especially one who has been through similar experiences during the war.'

'Maybe.' Alma gathered up the cleaned spades to return to the garden shed. 'The talk in the village is also that Edmund is ambitious. Very ambitious. There are few who remain long in Oswald's employment. I've heard more than one of the engineers in the choral society suggest Edmund must be prepared to cut corners on Oswald's say so, among other things, to have stayed so long. I'm not sure we could entirely trust him.'

Doubt shot through Rosalind's mind. Maybe she had been mistaken. What if Edmund was, in truth, the cleverest dissembler of them all? She went back to her instincts. They were still to give him the benefit of the doubt, even if it was only up to a point.

'But that would be the same with anyone who came to

help, Mama. Besides, the field can be clearly seen from the village, if Jamie continues to work on the Roman villa, or makes an exploratory trench in the burial mound, Oswald is bound to find out, sooner or later.'

'I suppose so,' said Alma, sounding uneasy.

'We could always ask old Mr Ford's advice about the gardens,' suggested Rosalind. 'Papa can't let them be abandoned forever. And if we happen to mention that Jamie is reopening the excavation, well then Edmund can make up his own mind. At least that would show he has an interest, rather than being totally at Oswald's beck and call.'

Alma's face brightened. 'I suppose it wouldn't do any harm to consult Mr Ford. He's the logical person to ask for advice about the best way of planting now the Land Girls have left and Leo is ignoring the issue completely. To be honest, I've been thinking I can't just stand by and leave the gardens to your father to sort out, when there's no sign of shortages easing any time soon. We supplemented the rations for half the village, as well as ourselves, during the war. It would be foolish, in fact downright irresponsible, to give up now.'

'Exactly,' said Rosalind, smiling. 'Besides, Mr Ford might be able to suggest men Papa could employ. There has to be someone in the village with the right skills to make sure there are enough vegetables in there to tide everyone over until rationing eases? Not even Papa can object to that, surely.'

'Especially if it's a *fait accompli*,' said Alma, her mouth setting in a determined line.

Chapter Twenty-Eight

The following afternoon, as soon as Jamie had returned from a morning working on the mosaic to rest, Rosalind and Alma set out on the path towards the village.

Alma led the way to a small, slightly tumbledown, row of brick cottages by the stream that wound its way through water meadows on the far side of the village. As they reached the end dwelling, Rosalind could make out Edmund balancing perilously on a wooden ladder, fixing the roof.

'Afternoon, Mrs Arden, Miss Arden,' he remarked, with only the slightest indication of surprise, driving in a final nail to hold a recalcitrant tile in place.

'I hope we're not disturbing you, Mr Ford.'

'Not at all.'

'We'd like to consult your father, if we may,' said Alma. 'We'd like his advice on the walled garden at Arden.'

'Nothing will give him more pleasure,' said Edmund, before descending the ladder to reach them. He pulled on the grey woollen jacket hanging over a beer barrel now used as a water butt and led the way inside.

The Fords' cottage was tiny, dark and cramped, with the airless feel of a place where windows were rarely opened. It was clean and neat, but the ancient range was somewhat the worse for wear and the jumble of crockery on the shelves looked as if they hadn't been moved from their dusty resting places for years. A house without a woman's touch. Rosalind had heard that expression often enough, but it hadn't struck her what that meant before. The absence of care and activity, all the little details that make a life, yet are barely noticed until they are gone.

Edmund led them out into a small yard at the back of the cottage, where an elderly man with thinning grey hair and the reddened cheeks of one who had spent a lifetime working in all weathers, was sitting on a bench, dozing in the sun.

'Dad, you have visitors. You remember Mrs Arden.'

The old man jerked upright. 'Good lord. Afternoon, Mrs Arden. Miss Rosy. Why I'd know you anywhere, Miss Rosy, you haven't changed a bit. Apart from being taller and quite the young woman, that is.'

'I'm glad to hear it, Mr Ford. I remember you very well. I was so sorry to hear about Mrs Ford.'

'Had her head screwed on,' sighed the old man. 'It should have been me the tuberculosis took, not my Susan. She'd have been right as rain without me.'

'Nonsense, Dad. And you're not doing so badly.'

'He looks after me alright, does Edmund,' said Mr Ford, proudly. 'Though I'm still not sure I like you working for Mr Gorwell. Begging your pardon, Mrs Arden, and you, Miss Rosy. Gorwell might have married Miss Bianca, but he don't want to be part of the village. Looks down on us, that he does.'

'He's just a businessman, Dad,' put in Edmund, sounding

more than a little irritated. 'And a rich one at that. Brierley could do with some more riches.'

'Not the kind that takes out the heart of it,' Mr Ford retorted. 'It's the heart that counts; all the riches in the world can't bring that back, whatever he's promising. Couldn't find a heart even if he could hear it beating inside him, that one.'

Edmund frowned. 'You don't know that, Dad.'

'Aye well, when you've lived as long as I have, maybe you won't be saying that. Out for the main chance, that's what he is. Always was. Always did have his mind set on that place, right from when he first clapped eyes on it. The kind that knows the price of everything and the value of nothing.'

'Mrs Arden has come to ask about the gardens at Arden house,' said Edmund, colouring slightly.

'Ah, yes. The garden.' Mr Ford shook his head. 'Pity, that. It were a good place. We grew more than enough for the family in my day, and plenty left over to help the village. They're all gone now, the lads who worked there. Dead. And the ones who ain't won't be back. Youngsters don't want to do that kind of work no more. Too hard. Too long hours.'

'And too poorly paid and no security,' added Edmund tartly.

'We're looking for your advice, Mr Ford,' said Alma, charm itself. 'We need to find reliable gardeners to take over now the Land Girls have gone home. My husband feels that you're the best person to recommend young men who might be suitable, and the best crops we should be growing.'

'There's one or two I can think of. I'll put my thinking cap on.' He nodded approvingly. 'So, vegetables is it? And salad greens?'

'Yes. Anything that we can use to supplement rationing.'

'It'll all be there. There's always seed saved in the drawers in the shed, Edmund can show you where. All in paper bags, all labelled. If you need more, I can give you the name of suppliers. Jacksons is the best, if they survived the war. Honest. That's what you need. Don't use Raverskills from Coventry, they offer stuff cheap, but it's rubbish. You'll find half doesn't take. They may have changed, but I'd not be taking the risk.' He grinned. 'Besides, Jacksons is in Stratford – too close to start any funny business, they'll want to keep Mr Arden sweet.'

'Thank you, Mr Ford,' said Alma, smile broadening. 'I'll remember to order anything we need from Jacksons.'

'Hmm. Not above taking advice, then. Not like a usual Arden. Or a woman, for that matter.'

'Dad!' Edmund was mortified.

'I hope I can recognise advice well given,' replied Alma, solemnly.

Mr Ford gave a grudging smile. 'I'll ask around about possible gardeners, and make a list for Jacksons.' He cleared his throat. 'Edmund can bring it. My eyesight's not as good as it was.'

'Yes, of course,' put in Rosalind quickly, earning herself an unexpected look of gratitude from Edmund for not embarrassing a man who had been sent out to work with only a few years of indifferent schooling behind him and could most probably barely recognise his own name.

She couldn't blame Edmund working for Oswald, she thought as he accompanied them back to the front door. Not when it gave him a chance to escape the work that had bent his father over with arthritis, and no doubt in constant pain, without the means to trouble the doctor.

'I can bring the list tomorrow afternoon,' said Edmund. 'If that's convenient. I can show you where the seeds are usually hidden away from the mice.'

'Thank you,' said Alma. 'We'll appreciate your help.'

He eyed them both consideringly. 'Just Dad's advice, was it?'

'Not exactly—' confessed Alma.

'No—' said Rosalind, at the same time.

'I did wonder.' He cleared his throat, finding a sudden fascination with the crow observing them from a nearby wall, head on one side in case of the appearance of scraps. 'There's been talk in the village of work having been recently resumed on the Roman mosaic.'

'Has there?' said Rosalind, exchanging glances with Alma.

He grinned. 'I won't be running to Gorwell, if that's what you're thinking. And nor will anyone else in the village, come to that.'

'Thank you.' Alma coughed. 'The truth is, we were wondering if you might be interested in helping Jamie yourself?'

'Only now and again,' put in Rosalind hastily. 'We understand you have very little spare time.'

'Does he think there might be more of the mosaic?'

'It looks like it,' said Rosalind. 'We've done our best to help Jamie, but he could do with someone who knows what they are doing. Perhaps you might speak to him when you bring the list of seeds?'

'I'll think about it,' he muttered, sounding more than a little like his father.

'He will,' said Alma, as they made their way back towards the centre of the village. 'Edmund won't be able to resist working on the excavation. You could see it in his face.'

'But he may be worried about how Oswald might react?'

Alma came to a halt. 'I should have thought of that. Good

jobs like his are hard to come by, I remember it being the talk of the village when Edmund was taken on, it was a huge advancement. It's usually through recommendation or being a friend of the family. Oswald is an important man around here; if it suited him, he could easily make sure Edmund can't find other work close enough where he could look after his father.'

Guilt shot through Rosalind. She had been so focussed on the best way of ensuring Jamie became well, and keeping Arden safe from Oswald's machinations, she hadn't thought too closely of the reality of Edmund's position, or his family responsibilities. 'I wouldn't want that.'

'Nor would I.'

'So we mustn't be too disappointed if he feels he can't help Jamie. We'll just have to do our best.'

They continued in thoughtful silence, passing rows of narrow terraced brick houses, crumbling around the edges but their windows spotlessly clean, doors and window frames freshly painted. In the neat patches of front garden, tight crimson bells of fuchsias hung amongst the fading greenery, between the remains of lavender and late roses humming with bees. Smoke rose from a dozen chimneys, as evening meals were cooked, ready for families to gather around the fire once the day's work was done. Groups of children played between houses spreading outwards from the main street, their laughter echoing between sun-warmed walls.

As they passed the tiny museum set next to the church hall, Montague, who appeared to have survived the shortages with ease, his ginger coat sleek and distinctly well-fed, paused in stalking a family of sparrows squabbling in the nearest hedge, to wind himself, purring, around Rosalind's legs. She bent to stroke the appreciative head, which butted insistently against her hand, before turning to stroll lazily, tail snaking upright, towards the museum. The door was slightly ajar, allowing the tail to vanish inside, and sending out a hum of female voices, interspersed with bursts of notes from the piano.

'D'you mind if we go in for a minute, Mama? I've never had time when I've been there taking photographs, but I'd love to see the exhibitions again.'

Alma smiled, the worried expression easing from her face. 'I'm quite sure we do. In fact, I could do with speaking to the WI ladies.'

They stepped inside. As her eyes adjusted to darkness, Rosalind drew in the familiar musty smell of ancient bones and treasures preserved safe beneath the earth.

The museum appeared even smaller than she remembered, and more closely packed. She could make out the familiar weathered remains of gargoyles that had fascinated and terrified her in equal measure as a child, along with stone carvings of leaves and flowers, the only traces of the original Anglo-Saxon church uncovered during renovations long before she was born. Next was a suggestion of a something far older, with a female figure, barely visible in the weather-worn stone Miss Parsons had been convinced represented a Roman river goddess.

A little cabinet, made from the remains of old doors and a cut down glass frame, contained a flint tool, chipped so thin the light glowed through. Next to it were the fossilised remains of plants and creatures from an even older time and the entire skeleton of some kind of ancient sea monster found in the lime quarries at Wilmcote.

The deep rumble of renewed purring prompted movement in the shadows. It was not Miss Parsons, but Mr Fairfield, hastily folding up a letter and stuffing it into the inner pocket of his jacket.

'I'm sorry, I didn't realise anyone had come in. I thought it was just Montague on his usual hunt for scraps from the kitchen. He's a bit of a terror, especially when the Women's Institute are cooking fish for their soup kitchen.' He scratched the nearest ginger ear, now engaged in rubbing itself ingratiatingly against his ankle. 'I'm afraid he's charmed them all into submission.'

At which Montague instantly lost interest, making an unabashed beeline for the door to the kitchens.

'If you're looking for Miss Parsons, she'll be back in a minute.' He smiled. 'I hope you're thinking of joining us for the rehearsal this evening, Mrs Arden, I thought we might try another Irish folk song today, after the success of "Danny Boy". I've had the lyrics printed for "She Moved Through the Fair".'

'I should get back,' said Alma, blushing slightly.

'We can stay a little while, surely?' said Rosalind. 'It's a pity not to learn a new song. And I'd like to look round the museum a bit longer.'

'Very well,' said Alma, needing no further persuasion.

'Shameless!' They swung round as one, as Miss Parsons appeared at the door leading into the village hall. 'Montague,' she added to their enquiring faces. 'He just wormed half a tin of canned salmon out of Mrs Hays, and she always declares she hates felines. No wonder he's such a hopeless ratter. Thank you, Mr Fairfield. I'd better not keep you any longer, your singers are arriving.'

As Mr Fairfield and Alma made their way into the main part of the hall, Rosalind continued to inspect the little museum.

'You've so many new exhibits, Miss Parsons. I thought nothing would have been found during the war.'

'On the contrary, my dear. There was so much brought

up when the Land Girls were ploughing the fields around Arden we couldn't keep up.'

Rosalind's eyes were caught by a small glass cabinet made out of odd ends of wooden planks, and what looked like panes from a greenhouse. 'You've got some of the tiles from the Roman villa!'

'Not as many as I'd like. Miss Kate brought these, just before she left. She said these were loose, and she didn't want them to be lost, and she hoped the rest of it would be displayed in here one day.'

Rosalind sighed. Where was Kate now? Was she so determined not to come back to Arden, even to the excavations for which she had once shared such a passionate interest with their brother, that she preferred the war-torn ruins of Italy? Rosalind had read about the eruption of Vesuvius in the papers last year. While not nearly as extreme as the one that had buried Pompeii in Roman times, the violent explosion had still rained down ash and destruction on the neighbouring countryside.

She had felt such pity for the villagers of San Sebastiano when she had watched the newsreel of their evacuation from the volcano's slopes, carrying everything they could manage as the relentless river of burning lava oozed towards them to engulf their homes. At the time, it had never crossed her mind that her sister might be there amongst refugees, not of war, but of nature's violence from deep within the earth. The newsreel had said the residents were helped to safety by allied soldiers, both British and Americans, stationed there after the liberation of Naples the previous year.

Surely not even Kate would dare to travel to such a hostile environment? Unless, Rosalind acknowledged with a sliver of fear, Kate had found something in her volume of Shakespeare that had compelled her, even more than the prospect of joining the dig at Pompeii, towards the Amalfi coast.

'They are even more beautiful than I thought,' she said wistfully, gazing at the cleaned tiles that looked as if they were made yesterday. 'I didn't think the colours would stay so vivid after being in the earth so long.'

'People came in to see them, all through the war. I think it was a source of comfort, knowing how long people have lived here, and survived war and pestilence.' Miss Parsons indicated the larger cabinet next door. 'This is part of a sword that the Archaeology Department of Birmingham University said most probably come from the time of King Alfred the Great, when he was protecting this part of the world from Viking invaders.'

'It's wonderful.'

Miss Parsons grinned. 'So it is. Mind you, I like to think it was more likely to be from when Alfred's daughter Æthelflæd was queen and valiantly putting paid to Viking attacks.' She sighed. 'I was hoping we might be able to prove that old story of a female leader who followed her queen's example and kept Brierley safe, but there's been nothing that old. Although I'm still amazed at what appears whenever a field is turned or an alteration to one of the cottages is made and brings up layers from the past. I suppose if this road is built it will uncover things that might not otherwise have been found.'

'But destroy even more?'

Miss Parsons sighed. 'I'm afraid so. I wouldn't mind if it was the new housing the village so desperately needs, or even mending the cottages that are falling down from neglect. I wonder how many of my pupils will remain, even if Mr Gorwell's new mansions require plenty of domestic staff – especially if there's better paid work in shops and factories in

Birmingham.' She shook herself. 'I've put your photographs from the war in this part, so they can be seen all together.'

Rosalind followed her to a separate section at one side of the main room, where framed copies of the local newspaper, one the front page announcing the outbreak of war, another marking its end, were displayed, interspersed with clippings with obituaries of local men who had been killed in the fighting.

'You've put up so many!' Rosalind peered at the remainder of the cuttings covering every available space.

'You don't think I could resist displaying the work of someone from Brierley, do you?' said Miss Parsons. 'Even though they did terrify your stepmother when she saw them. You were incredibly brave, my dear.'

'Not really. I didn't have time to think about it. And none of us were safe.'

'Not even here,' agreed Miss Parsons, sadly. 'We might have been largely spared from such destruction, but not from the grief. So much has been lost, this all feels more precious than ever. And especially these.'

A further wall contained prints of the photographs Rosalind had taken before the war. She paused in front of the picture of Hal the elderly blacksmith, long since retired, proudly demonstrating the shoeing of a horse. Her eyes travelled to the adjacent view of the high street, empty and dusty, undisturbed by more than the occasional cart and the slow amble of ponies. Already it looked like a lost world.

'Mrs Arden brought them in,' said Miss Parsons. 'People like coming to see them as well as the artefacts. And not just from Brierley, a few have come in from Stratford. There aren't many reminders of how things used to be before the war. Many come in over and over again. They find it a source of comfort. No, more than that. Pride.'

'Pride?'

'That their lives were seen as being of value. Usually it's just the politicians and the aristocracy who have their portraits taken and their doings recorded for posterity. This redresses the balance, it's their stories being told.'

'Exactly,' said Rosalind.

'Of course,' said Miss Parsons, 'the world is still changing. It will never go back to the way it was. It seems a pity if it is lost, without any record.'

'I'll print you copies of the photographs I send to my editor, if you would like, and I've more as well that I didn't think were right for the magazine but your visitors might like.'

'That will be lovely, my dear.' She sighed. 'It will serve to remind Brierley of what we have to lose, if Gorwell gets his way. The war might have knocked the stuffing out of us – that's what he's is relying on – but I bet there's fight in at least some of us yet.'

In the hall, the wistful tune of the 'The Oak and the Ash' ended, with the north country maid's longing to return from London to her own country. Mr Fairfield set the singers off again, this time on the yearning simplicity of 'She Moved Through the Fair', with the ghost of lost love returning to haunt the beloved. As the singers found the tune, there was a haunting sense of a thousand griefs as the final lines, with their promise of being reunited in the afterlife, faded into silence.

Rosalind hugged herself. She had still not received a letter from Guy. She couldn't help a feeling of dread that she had already been left behind, a part of the past so intricately entwined with the traumas of war the mind could not bear to dwell on it for long. Surely she had to hear from him soon?

Chapter Twenty-Nine

Edmund was as good as his word, appearing the following afternoon at the site of the Roman villa, list in hand, a bulging knapsack slung over one shoulder.

'I copied it out for Dad. It's all here. He's still asking about possible workers. Mainly in the White Hart, I'm afraid. Although that's as good a place as any to get news.' He glanced over to where Jamie was continuing his patient scraping at the mosaic, as if he had not observed the new arrival. 'I've brought a couple of trowels and small brushes. I thought they might prove useful.'

'Yes, of course.' Alma smiled. 'Thank you for the list. Perhaps you'd like to have a look at how far Jamie has come?'

Edmund nodded. For all he was attempting to keep his dignity and appear indifferent, he headed over to the excavation without any need for further prompting.

'At least that's a start,' said Alma, as Edmund squatted down on the edge of the trench to talk to Jamie. Within minutes, he had jumped in to join him.

Rosalind should have felt relief when the sound of

scraping resumed, interspersed with the low hum of male voices discussing first one point, then another. But there had been something in Edmund's gaze that left her uneasy.

After a while, she joined them, taking mugs of fresh tea. Edmund was in the hole scraping away at the Roman mosaic, while Jamie was a little further along the small trench, investigating a line of stone wall.

'It's definitely Poseidon, or some other Roman sea god,' remarked Edmund, pulling himself up to sit on the end of the trench. 'That's quite a storm he's creating.'

In his shirtsleeves, collar undone, he had an even more rakish air than before. As Rosalind handed him the steaming tea he smiled, softening the determined lines of his face with unexpected charm, leaving her nonplussed and not quite sure what to say. She was no better than a giggling schoolgirl, she scolded herself, as the hairs on her arms instinctively lifted in response. Not to mention that he probably had a pretty good idea of the effect of his dark eyes on any woman he cared to bestow his attention. She turned quickly towards Jamie, who was arriving to join them.

'The mosaic might be even bigger than we thought,' he said, taking the proffered tea. 'Looks like it might be a whole room. There maybe more, as well.'

As Rosalind left, they returned to their work in companionable silence, interspersed with a comment now and again. It felt peaceful, the two of them absorbed in their task. Maybe she was wrong. Maybe all would be well.

The weather held for the remainder of September and into October, allowing the excavation to continue with only the occasional shower sending them under the shelter of the trees. Edmund joined them as often as he could, trowel and paintbrush at the ready, deep in discussion with Jamie between revealing writhing sea snakes and sharp-toothed fish.

But the sunshine couldn't last, not with the ever-flowing changes across the landscape, bringing intermittent bursts of rain. By the middle of October, the cloud thickened, sending heavy downpours most days, which slowed the work, leaving the earth thick with mud and a fine drizzle hanging in the air.

Despite Alma's optimism at Jamie growing physically stronger by the day, and conversing with increasing ease with Edmund, he still disappeared into his room as soon as they returned. For his part, Papa never asked after him or mentioned his name. Since their father was, much to their stepmother's distress, still barely acknowledging her own presence, Rosalind found any attempts to raise the subject brushed aside as if she hadn't spoken.

She was thankful her time was fully taken up with helping Jamie, between assisting Lucy and Alma with the running of the house and slipping out to take photographs in any spare moments. It made her forget the feeling of no longer truly belonging to her childhood home.

At least Ginny continued to show enthusiasm for her articles and accompanying photographs, sending instructions to expand her coverage to Stratford and the surrounding villages, travelling as far as she could on the Triumph whenever her petrol ration allowed.

The corn dollies that had been piled up between displays of fruit and vegetables in the church to accompany the joyous singing of the harvest festival were, by now, a distant memory. Slowly, the first hints of winter began to creep in. As mists lingered in the early morning light and left droplets hanging from the remains of blackberries and rosehips, the church hall resounded with the choir's preparations for Christmas carols.

Then, finally, in late October the longed-for letter from Guy arrived. Rosalind grabbed the envelope without ceremony, hurrying, despite a chill onslaught of rain, to the kissing gate, where she tore it open, caught between elation and dread.

All was well. She sank down onto the nearest stone in relief. Guy's words were as loving as she could have hoped for. He was growing accustomed to his new surroundings, and had found an apartment in New York. Finally, he was getting to grips with his work and his studies. She could hear his voice in every word, just as she remembered it. He missed her, he wrote, more than he could express. He took solace in walking through the turning leaves of Central Park, as a reminder of Arden. He lived for the day they could meet up again.

Rosalind breathed in deep as she folded up the letter safely in her pocket, tears mingling with the drizzle dampening her face. As she rose to her feet, the rain began to ease. Clouds parted to allow tall pillars of sun to illuminate distant fields into a sudden brilliance, catching her eye as the kind of light to capture the atmosphere of the English countryside. Calm now, finally reassured that she was not forgotten, her mind was instantly back on her work.

The scene in her mind would be a perfect accompaniment to her photographs of the villagers, especially as her next project was to photograph the Brierley Players as they began rehearsing in earnest for their performance of *As You Like It*, to take place on Christmas Eve. She knew exactly where the best viewpoint would be to make the most of the dramatic light. Adjusting her camera case over her shoulder, Rosalind set off across the fields and up to the burial mound.

A fence had been placed around the base of the mound, sometime after she had left for London, complete with a rusted gate that swung open, protesting loudly into the silence. Rosalind pushed through into the scrub of ancient woodland, feet crunching through the desiccated remains of leaves. The sun came out once more, its faint warmth stealing through the remains of the canopy above her, which had now turned to a deep gold between the dark skeleton fingers of denuded branches. An autumnal scent of fungi and the rotting of fallen crab apples hung in the air.

A pang went through her. The last time she had been here had been with Guy, the tentative beginnings of a love that they both knew to face insurmountable odds, and threatened by the oncoming of war, yet determined to find a way through. She could still feel the warmth of his hand on her back, the beat of his heart against her, the deepening passion of their first kiss. All so new, so full of promise. So devoid of questions and doubt.

She touched the letter in her pocket. Seeing his handwriting had made the reminder of his physical absence an agony, and yet one that already felt a part of her past, like the loss of Will, and the vanishing of Kate and Cordelia, now following their own paths abroad. The breaking up of their childhood world that each of the survivors must accept and live with, as they forged a new path, into their individual futures.

But her letter told her he still loved her, she reminded herself, trying to recapture the certainty of a few minutes ago. Guy loved her just as she loved him. It was a love that had survived the violence and uncertainty of war. Surely it could survive this current parting, when it was only establishing a means of supporting them, and family obligation, keeping them apart? It was only for a short while, and they would soon be together again.

Blinking away tears, Rosalind followed the stony path leading to the top of the little rise. As she reached the summit, she found the Warwickshire landscape stretched out around her, the patchwork of rolling fields, crops long gathered in and now waiting for next year's planting, interspersed with farmsteads and tiny hamlets of no more than a few houses. The smoke fires of Brierley hung in the air as the day began to chill towards evening, surrounded by church spires of distant villages stretching to the gleam of the River Avon winding its way from Stratford towards the sea.

As the light shifted yet again, Rosalind found the right position and waited for the sun to return. A sweep of rain sent her scrambling back down beneath the nearest tree for shelter, heavy drops bouncing off the greenery around her feet, turning the path into a stream. Then it was gone.

She clambered up the steep sides again, breathing in the scent of newly dampened earth, back to the viewpoint. There, she waited patiently, as the tall pillars of light strode across the countryside, following the clouds, guiding sunlight on the wind towards Brierley. As the rays reached the church tower she pressed the shutter, hoping she had caught the effect she strived for. If she had her settings and her focus right, and pressed the shutter at exactly the right moment, Brierley-in-Arden would be spotlighted in sun, highlighted within the landscape.

Mission completed, she stood for a while, watching sunlight race across the fields, breathing in the clear air, before turning to make her way back towards the little path.

It was such a peaceful place, surrounded by the chatter of birds, with just the occasional sound of a motor as a tractor or motorcar made its way along the lanes.

Memories from childhood were all around, painful as well as warm, of sneaking in amongst the trees with Will and Jamie, to become a lowly follower of Robin Hood (Will having naturally reserved the leading role for himself) ready to rob the rich, or a Viking (of the disposable kind, expected to roll over at Will's first wave of a makeshift spear) pursuing King Alfred the Great.

But there was something else as well. She had felt it as a child, elusive, just beyond her grasp. It was there in the atmosphere of peace and stillness as the sun crept in through the branches. An ancient landscape, holding its secrets, along with the memory of all the footsteps that had trodden here, all the ambitions and sorrows and dreams. And losses too, the kind that were commemorated in memorials to men fallen in countless wars.

The sun vanished again, wind stirring the branches like long-forgotten whispers. Maybe the feeling was simply due to the gentle closing in of life on itself, in preparation for the hibernation of winter and gathering strength for the new bloom of the following spring. Whatever it was, there was nothing haunted about this place, just a feeling of gentleness and calm.

She pulled out her camera, protected from the rain under the folds of her coat, and walked around the edges of the site, trying to find the right angle to catch the atmosphere. This was part of Brierley, too. She could see in her mind's eye that the photograph would need to be taken from near the ground, the effect of the lens showing the unnatural rounding of the top of the mound surrounded by the silhouettes of branches already denuded by the wind, the few remaining leaves illuminated against the sky to hint at the vibrant reds and golds in the variations of grey of the final picture.

At last she found the position that gave the dramatic effect she sought. She stepped back, right to the edge, balancing the camera as low to the ground as she dared. As she did so, the heel of her walking boot caught on a stone, sending her overbalancing, tumbling and sliding down the slope with perilous speed.

'Damn.' It was a tree trunk, rotted and fallen, that broke her fall. For a few minutes she lay there, barely daring to move. What had she been thinking? She'd told no one where she was going. No one from the house even knew to look for her in the direction of the village. If she couldn't get out under her own steam, it might be hours, days even, before she was found.

'Don't be an idiot,' she scolded herself. She'd been in worse places than this. There were no bombers droning overhead, ready to obliterate her existence in a moment. She'd move on her belly, and in agony, if she had to. There had to be a dwelling near that might hear her shouts.

First things first. She experimented with the arm that had slammed into the tree. It moved. Painful, but at least the kind that promised an impressive bruise by tomorrow morning rather than anything broken. She wriggled her toes. Nothing obviously agonising. Cautiously, she used the tree to pull herself to her feet, battered and shaken, but thankfully in one piece. Later on she could let herself think about how much worse it might have been, but for now she just needed to get back to solid ground.

On the other hand, she wasn't leaving without taking her photograph, not after nearly breaking a leg, or even her neck, for her pains. Her camera! It was still there, on the top of the mound, tipped on its side, but at least appearing undamaged. She breathed a sigh of relief and bent to adjust the laces of her walking boot, which had come loose in her fall. The last thing she needed was to slip again.

As she pulled the laces tight, something glinted at the edges of her vision. In the gloom underneath the network of branches, there was nothing to be seen. She blinked, trying to adjust her eyes. The sun flitted briefly through the clouds, and there it was again. She brushed away at the dampness of leaves, but the glint had vanished. It was probably nothing, she couldn't waste any more time. Besides, if there had been anything there, surely someone would have found it by now. She could feel the glow of the sun about to clear clouds again. All right, one last chance.

Sure enough, there it was again, a definite glint. Possibly metallic? Heart racing, she brushed the leaves aside. This time the sun stayed long enough for her fingers to close over something cold and hard. As she gently freed the object from an intertwining cage of tree roots, it was smaller than she had expected, small enough to fit inside the palm of her hand. Clutching her find tightly, she clambered up to her camera, on the edges of the circle of trees.

Positioning herself more securely this time, she opened her hand. A dull gleam of gold pushed through the clinging mud and earth. She brushed the nearest bit gently away, revealing intricate pattens set with a deep red stone. She had seen enough at Miss Parson's museum to recognise it as an ancient treasure, of the kind that appeared through the earth, now and again.

A patch of blue had appeared above. She carefully wrapped the object in her handkerchief and thrust it deep in her pocket, to concentrate on preparing the camera for when the sun arrived in full strength. Picture taken, she placed the camera back in her shoulder bag, brushed herself down as well as she could, and hurried her way towards home.

Chapter Thirty

'Anglo-Saxon,' said Jamie, carefully inspecting her find. 'Could be a brooch or a fastening for clothing, a later version of the kind of thing Kate found amongst the mosaic. That inlaid enamel looks as if could have been done yesterday. Incredible workmanship. I've a feeling it might just rival anything that was found at Sutton Hoo.'

'Would you be able to clean it up a little so I can photograph it? You know what you're doing, I'd be scared of damaging something so delicate.'

He nodded, a smile of pleasure lifting the tense thinness of his face. 'Looks high status, even more so than the things found in the fields during the war. Where's it from?'

'The burial mound. It was quite by accident, I was up on the top photographing the landscape when I slipped. It must have been the rain that dislodged it.'

'Those look like garnets,' he said, brushing away gently at the earth. His hands, she saw, were perfectly steady. He reached into his knapsack, kept next to his chair, for a small paintbrush. A few strokes revealed the deep red of an enamelled inlay, set between delicate patterns of gold wires surrounding the deep shine of garnets. 'Beautiful,' he breathed. 'Kate would love this.'

Her heart twisted, remembering the excitement he had shared with their sister at the prospect of excavating the burial mound, in the days when their existence at Arden – when life itself – had seemed to stretch on forever.

'Someone has to know if she's still in Naples? We could try again to find her, and entice her back.'

He shook his head, still brushing at the gold wires. 'It took her long enough to escape, she won't return. Or Cordelia.' His head bent closer to the brooch. 'They've more sense.'

She fought down rising tears. 'Just you and me then.'

'So it seems,' he murmured, his face closing in on itself again.

The following afternoon, Rosalind slipped out to the Post Office, her next packages of photographs and articles in her bag, along with a letter to Guy.

The museum door was open as she passed on her return, with Montague positioned in the sunniest spot, engaged in washing his face with the air of a cat who has just wrestled a morsel of chicken skin at the very least, if not the odd tail of fish.

A flicker of excitement went through her. Despite the sadness stirred by the find at the burial mound, she sensed it was a good story, the kind Ginny would love. She could feel it in her bones, with the familiar tingle that had overcome terror at the thought of what she might face as she swerved her motorcycle through darkened London streets, lit only by the distant glow of destruction.

There had to be something there. With the fascination at the finds at Sutton Hoo returning to prominence after the war, especially with the restoration of the exquisite artefacts, there had to be interest in anything hinting that similar Anglo-Saxon treasures might be found in Brierley. What better way of putting Arden on the map?

Besides, it might, after all, be the kind of find to tempt Kate back, if only for a little while. At least then they would know she was safe. The silence was the worst bit, bringing reminders of the time Jamie was missing. If Kate returned, then surely Cordelia would not be able to resist visiting?

She missed her sisters, with a deep ache in her heart, clinging to memories of their childhood held deep within Arden's walls.

The best way to ensure such a project was to obtain the support of Miss Parsons, and therefore the village. She stepped over Montague, who paused in attending to his whiskers to see if she had any offerings of cheese to complete his day, but being too full to push the matter, settled down for a snooze instead.

Inside the village hall, the customary chatter of the Women's Institute setting their trestle tables for their weekly sorting out of donated clothing and the cooking of hot soup had faded to a murmur. Each one, Rosalind saw, was agog with following the conversation taking place in front of them.

'My dear lady...' Rosalind came to a halt at the sight of the large figure of Oswald holding forth in the centre of the hall, with Edmund by his side, who was trying to appear stern, in an ill-at-ease kind of a way, under the collective glare of the WI, who were making no bones about skewering the traitor in their midst with their eyes. Oswald ignored the eruption of muttered protests. 'I can assure you, ladies, that the roof is utterly unsafe. It could fall down on your heads at any moment. Or on a child. And how do you think the parents would feel then?'

'I understood it to be sound enough,' returned Miss Parsons, in the dogged manner of a woman standing her ground.

Oswald waved his hand expansively, like a parliamentary candidate faced with a particularly recalcitrant selection of voters. 'It may look like that to the untrained eye, but my men have been up there and found it in a shocking state. The entire building may need to be demolished.'

'Demolished?'

'If it's found to be beyond repair. With Mr Arden's planned improvements to the surrounding area I shall, of course, be offering to build a new hall, as my contribution to the village And at my own expense, naturally.'

'Are you, now,' said Miss Parsons, sounding singularly unimpressed. 'Well, you must do as you see fit, Mr Gorwell.' She sniffed, loudly. 'Although some,' she added with an emphasis that sent Edmund colouring to the roots of his hair, 'might consider wholesale removal of a community that has been here since the dawn of time an act of sacrilege.'

'Progress, my dear lady,' said Oswald blandly. 'Progress. Besides, no one said anything about removal. Just a temporary inconvenience. Surely a sensible woman like yourself would not wish to stand in the way of such a benefit to the village? Ford here will inform you of the details, once they are ready.'

Point made, Oswald swept out, barely acknowledging Rosalind as he passed. Edmund followed in his wake, avoiding her eye, a look of mortification overtaking his face as he realised she had been there to witness this exchange.

'Drat the man,' muttered Miss Parsons, collapsing down onto the nearest chair. 'Doesn't he ever give up?'

Rosalind went over to join her. 'I didn't know there was a problem with the roof.'

'Oh, hello, my dear. So you heard all that. Well, to be honest, I'm not sure there is. No one mentioned it until a few days ago, when Mr Gorwell returned from London and sent his men up there to inspect its condition. Of course, the village could insist there's a second opinion, but no tradesman is going to want to go against a man with so much influence as Mr Gorwell. Work is hard enough to come by as it is, and just one bad word can ruin a man's reputation.'

'So Oswald is free to say it's unsafe and have the place knocked down.'

'With a promise of building another, which, even if it never materialises, will be enough to stop the village trying to replace it ourselves. Clever.'

'He can't get away with that! I'll speak to Papa.'

'Best to stay out of this, my dear. I'm afraid that brother-in-law of yours will make sure it only ends in tears.'

Rosalind clenched her fists. 'But you can't just give up!'

'Who said anything about giving up?' A gleam appeared in Miss Parsons' eyes. 'You don't think Brierley is going to surrender to the enemy without a fight, do you?'

Her voice deepened into a surprisingly life-like approximation of Mr Churchill. *'We shall fight on the beaches, we shall fight on the landing grounds, we shall fight in the fields and in the streets, we shall fight in the hills; we shall never surrender.'* She paused to take a bow in acknowledgement of the round of hearty applause emanating from the WI ladies. 'My dear, Gorwell might think this is the end, but I can assure you, it's just the beginning.'

. . .

The October afternoon was beginning to fade as Rosalind left Miss Parsons deep in discussion of tactics with the WI (plans she felt it was probably best not to overhear, particularly once boiling oil was mentioned) and set off back, through the kissing gate, following the path along the fields. She had crossed the first field and was pushing through the gate into the next, when she came to a halt.

'Can't go through there, Miss.' The man blocking her way was tall, smartly dressed and burly, and most definitely meant business. 'Private land.'

'People have walked these paths for generations.'

'Not any more. Once work starts it will be too dangerous.'

'Work?' Her eyes fell on several men inspecting the ground, with much making of notes and consultation. 'Surely the houses won't come this far. And you can't mean the new road.'

'None of your concern, Miss. Just move along and take the lane, as you should, like a good girl.'

His patronising air sent her temper flaring. 'I most certainly will not take the lane. I'm going home in the way I've always done, and you'll allow the members of the choral society to get back this way, too. You can't just ride roughshod over traditional footpaths.' She pushed her way through the gate. 'And if you've any objections you can take it up with Mr Arden.'

'You little— you can't just—'

She ducked under the outstretched arm, colliding almost instantly with a rather less substantial body.

'Oh.' She scowled at Edmund, who, she was glad to see, was looking even more ill-at-ease than he had done in the hall. 'And I suppose you're going to tell me to take the lane, too.'

'Certainly not.' His eyes travelled beyond her towards the sound of heavy footsteps. 'It's all right, Clarke. I think Miss Arden can be permitted to cross her own land.'

The burly man stopped in his tracks. 'Beg pardon, Miss.'

'It doesn't matter. I trust you won't stop anyone else.'

Clarke shuffled awkwardly. 'Orders,' he muttered.

'Get back to your work, Clarke,' said Edmund. 'I'll deal with this, just keep an eye on the men, will you. And tell them not to trample over the excavation near the garden wall. It's not to be disturbed, d'you hear?'

'As you wish, Mr Ford.'

As Clarke beat a hasty retreat, Rosalind recovered herself. 'Thank you.'

'There's no need.' He was still not meeting her eyes. 'You have the right, but you can't expect the men to allow anyone else to cross against orders. It's more than their jobs are worth.'

'I'm going to speak to Papa. He can't have intended people to be prevented from using paths they've followed for generations, especially as the lanes take most of them miles out of their way.'

Edmund flinched slightly. 'It's a question of safety.'

'Even you can't believe that. They're not idiots, and they've little time enough as it is to rehearse, and they've not got that many weeks left before Christmas.'

He glanced back towards the men, who were throwing curious glances in their direction. 'Look, I can't go against my employer, but I'll do my best to see the paths are kept as they've always been, at least until the work starts. For the villagers' sake, if nothing else. I don't promise anything else.' He cleared his throat. 'And you can reassure Jamie I'll keep the archaeology intact for as long as possible and do my best to ensure there's a proper investigation if we uncover anything else.'

Her anger burst. She could see Edmund attempting to keep an inner wrestle of emotions from his face and not quite succeeding. If she walked away from Arden, she would leave free of responsibilities. He, on the other hand, had his father to keep from the workhouse, and so a blacklisting from Oswald to fear more than any gunfire he had once faced in France. She could sense the pincer movement closing in around him, as effective as any German tank encirclement, and could have wept at her own feeling of utter powerlessness.

'Thank you.'

'That's all right,' he muttered. 'Look, I don't like this any more than you. I never thought Mr Arden would give permission for any of this. But Gorwell swears he has, so here we are. I'm not jeopardising the roof over my dad's head.'

'I would never expect you to do that. I can't believe my father agreed to all this either.'

He grimaced. 'If I know the way Gorwell works, he'll have got agreement to build on the land next to the village, and he's taking it further up here, knowing your father is still pretty immobile and can't get out to check for himself what's happening. Once he's extended the road and built the houses, what's anyone going to do about it? You can't exactly put the field back to the way it was.' Edmund's eyes fixed on a spot somewhere beyond her shoulder. 'I didn't tell you that.'

'I didn't hear a thing.'

'Thank you.' He nodded, his face easing slightly as his eyes met hers, a softening in their depths, the kind that could catch any woman unawares. 'Believe me, I hope with all my heart that it can be sorted out for the best. I've a job to do, but

I'm also afraid Dad will never forgive me if I'm party to tearing the heart out of Brierley, whatever the consequences. Rock and a hard place, eh?'

'I'll do my best to find a solution,' she replied.

'I didn't mean...' His pride was back.

'I know you didn't, you idiot. That doesn't mean I don't want to help if I can.' She was uncomfortably aware of the men now openly watching them and drawing their own conclusions and felt the heat rising in her face. 'Good day, Mr Ford,' she said loudly, turning away to hide her sudden confusion, hurrying back towards home.

Chapter Thirty-One

Rosalind arrived at Arden House to find it even more than usually silent, panelling creaking in protest as she passed. Alma had already left to join the evening's rehearsal, including an adventurous foray into the 'Hallelujah' chorus, in preparation for the carol service on Christmas Eve. Lucy was spending her day off with her sister in Stratford, so there was not even the sound of clattering in the kitchens to break the lack of life.

There had been no sign of Jamie at the dig as she passed, and the little door into the walled garden was locked. With a rising sense of unease, she made her way upstairs to his room. The door was half open. She could see he was back in his armchair facing the window, gazing outside as if he had never risen in the first place.

'May I come in?'

'If you wish.' On the table to one side, a bowl of soup lay congealing, along with several untouched slices of buttered toast. Her heart sank.

'I looked for you as I was coming back from the village. I saw the men, they are just surveying the ground for the moment. If you keep on working...'

He shook his head. 'You should have seen them stare. They all wanted a glimpse of the lunatic. I can't go back, not if they are there.'

'I'm sure they don't! They are bound to be curious, as you're the next Arden to take over the estate. But if you're working on the archaeology, they'll forget you're there. I'll come with you, if you like?'

'No.'

Curse Oswald. This wasn't even about the village. This was about Jamie, when he had been doing so well.

'I'm going to develop some more of my photographs this evening after dinner. Maybe you'd like to help me?'

'Maybe.' But his voice was blank, shutting her out, back lost in the world she had found him when she first arrived.

'I'll bring you a cup of tea,' she said, overwhelmed by despair.

'I'm sure you're mistaken, my dear,' said Papa, as she steeled herself to make him listen to her and took the remainder of the tea into the library. 'Oswald reassured me it would not disrupt anything. He needs to discover if the land is suitable if we choose to build one or two new houses on the outskirts of the village.'

He sat up straight in his chair, complacency spreading over his face. 'There are several very respectable families eager to join our select social circle already, you know, and we could do with more of the higher class of neighbour. You can be certain Oswald will only produce the finest of mansions. He's quite right, the fields are of little use, especially now the war is ended. Besides, the profit will allow us to bring Arden up to modern standards. There's no need for anyone to come so near to the house. They must have been testing for water, or checking the lay of the land. Something like that.'

'They were inspecting the field right up to the walls of the garden. I saw it with my own eyes.'

'Oswald would have informed me if he was going to build so close. I'll have a word with him, and he can put your mind at rest.'

Exasperation overcame her. 'Does he tell you everything, or just what he thinks you want to hear?'

'What nonsense, my dear. He's a professional man. An honest man, highly regarded by all. I'll speak to him about the paths, if that will make you feel happier.'

'It's not just the paths, Papa. Jamie was enjoying getting back into the excavation of the Roman villa, it's made his recovery come on in leaps and bounds. He was almost back to his old self. Now he feels he can't carry on.'

There was a tightening of her father's jaw. 'If he can't cope with a few workmen, how is he ever to deal with anything else?'

'He just needs time. Does Oswald have to do this work now? Surely it could wait a few more weeks, at least until after Christmas. There's bound to be snow on the ground soon.'

'I know you wish for the best, my dear, but this would have no effect on Jamie, if he was really recovering.'

'If only you would speak to him, you could see how much he has improved. I know he isn't Will, Papa, but you may find you have more in common than you think.'

'Will is gone. I can't replace him. It would be an insult to his memory to try.'

'I'm not suggesting you replace him, just that you see if you can build a different kind of connection with Jamie. He's been through so much, and he has such deep ties to this place. You might find him easier to convince to see your side of things than Oswald, especially as Oswald has his own business to run so can't put all of his attention towards Arden.'

'When is Lucy back?'

So that was that. She had failed. The stubborn expression had returned to her father's face, the kind that always rendered him deaf to any information he didn't wish to enter into his consciousness. She knew from experience that if she tried again, he would only fly into a temper as a means of avoiding the issue. She was going to have to try some other approach. For now, all she could do was to keep the peace, so at least he didn't forbid her for a second time to never darken Arden ground again. It was becoming the story of her life.

'Not until tomorrow morning,' she replied. 'She's staying with her sister in Stratford. She's left rabbit pie for tonight's dinner, for when Mama returns. Perhaps we could persuade Jamie to join us?'

'Doubt it,' said her father, gesturing for her to cut another slice of Lucy's apple cake, which miraculously tasted as if it had never met a carrot or a turnip in its life. He sniffed. 'I don't see why your stepmother has gained this sudden obsession with singing.'

'It's good to see some of the old traditions coming back to life after all that's happened. The village is starting to feel alive again. It sounds as if Christmas Eve will be almost like old times, with a play and then carols in the church.'

But Papa wasn't listening. 'And folksongs of all things. It's not even as if she can sing.'

It was hopeless. She could talk all the sense in the world

and he was never going to listen to her, or Alma, come to that. As she escaped to her room before her temper began to crack, Rosalind had never felt more alone.

The impulse to speak to Guy was overwhelming. She hastily scribbled a letter to him, desperate to pour out her feelings, but at the same time not wishing to burden him in his own struggle to build a new life for them both. Tonight, despite his loving words, he felt infinitely far away. The dread was back that she would never see him again.

She shook herself firmly. She was in no position to feel sorry for herself. At least Guy had returned from war. At least they had a chance of a future together, however far away that might seem now. That made her luckier than so many women who had lost husbands and sweethearts. Her mind strayed back to the rose placed so faithfully on the park bench in London. The unknown woman marking a favourite meeting place, gone forever, and all the other women surviving with broken hearts, making lives for themselves.

As she sealed the letter, ready to take down to the Post Office the next morning, there came the rumble of a car making its way up the drive. Curious, Rosalind reached the window in time to see a battered Morris – it had definitely seen better days – pulling up in front of the house. Minutes later, Alma emerged, thanking the driver in a low voice. Her stepmother then stood, watched as the Morris retreated, until it reached the lane and vanished, engine chugging its way towards Brierley, and then turned with unmistakeable weariness towards the house.

As Rosalind reached the landing, she found Alma removing the pins from her hat in front of the mirror encased within the umbrella stand in the hallway, a preoccupied expression on her face.

'Hello, my dear,' she said, as Rosalind joined her. 'I'm

afraid I'm rather late, the singing overran – we forgot the time. It was very good of Mr Fairfield to drive me home, or I should have been even more late. I'm sure your Papa is eager for dinner to be served.'

'I'm certain he's not noticed, Mama. He's had tea, and plenty of Lucy's apple cake, so he can't complain of being starved.'

'Thank you, darling.' Alma brightened. 'It's just, I wouldn't like to think he was worrying.'

'He's fully occupied re-reading Grandfather's history of the Arden Estate,' Rosalind reassured her. 'And the dinner is ready, it just needs heating up. I'll come down and help you, if I may?'

'Yes, of course, my dear.' Alma flushed with pleasure. Her face, despite its strain, had regained an air of youthful animation.

Rosalind could have kicked herself. How had she not noticed the delicate prettiness of her stepmother's features before? Because she had not viewed her with an adult's eyes – no longer as the stepmother who was weak and silly, and easy to disobey, but a woman caught in an impossible situation, between the demands of an autocratic old man and his wilful children.

'I'd like to.'

'I wish Jamie would feel able to join us. He has been so much better these past weeks.'

'It was good to see him grow stronger every day,' sighed Rosalind. *At least until Oswald began sending his men to disturb the peace that he had found in uncovering the Roman villa*, she thought, gloomily. But there was no need to burden Alma with this new worry. If Jamie's recovery had suffered a permanent setback from Oswald's machinations, they would just have to cross that bridge when they came to it.

. . .

Later that night, after the agonisingly stilted dinner was over, Rosalind returned to Jamie's room.

'May I come in?'

'Yes, of course.' His voice was stronger than she feared, and to her relief his eyes had regained some of their light. 'I was just coming to show you. I've cleaned your find as much as I can. Take a look.'

'It's beautiful.' She stared in astonishment at the brooch, lying on a small table, now free of dirt and sparkling in the dim light. 'I'd no idea it would be so sophisticated.'

'Definitely high status,' said Jamie, thoughtfully. 'I know Miss Parsons would love to display it in her museum, but I've a feeling Birmingham University, or even the British Museum in London, might be interested, especially given the interest around the artefacts found at Sutton Hoo.'

Her heart began to beat fast. So, after all, there might be a solution to Oswald sweet-talking Papa into allowing him to take over the field. 'Which might also mean at least one of them could be interested in supporting you to explore the surrounding archaeology?'

'Possibly. From the articles Miss Parsons found, there's a real interest being sparked in Anglo-Saxon art. It seems the Dark Ages might not have been as dark as we believed. Fascinating.'

Thank goodness the enthusiasm was back in his voice. She had to keep his mind on the brooch, blotting out the memory of Oswald's men staring at him. If Jamie had a purpose, that must surely help him to overcome his fear of how others might view him. He might yet grow strong enough to be able to face their father.

'If I photograph it, we can send it to anyone you think

might be interested.' She hesitated. 'Miss Blake at the magazine is always asking for new proposals for stories. I could send copies to her as well. I'm sure she would be interested if I suggested a series following an excavation of the burial mound. I could photograph it from the very start, then if you found signs that there is more there, it would be a proper story, the kind readers love. It might attract even more interest as well.'

'The burial mound...'

'Where no one can see you working. Why don't you concentrate on digging there for now? Only you and I need to know, at least until I'm certain Miss Blake is interested.'

He turned the brooch slowly in his hands. She could tell from the expression on his face he was finding the prospect of uncovering more, or even a major archaeological site, one he wasn't able to resist.

'I'll fetch my camera,' she said.

Rosalind worked through the night, printing the best versions of the photographs of the brooch and writing up her proposal for Miss Blake. She trusted the editor's eye for a potential exclusive would prevent her from sending in reporters and treasure hunters, although she took the precaution of mentioning that it was on private land, just in case she might be tempted.

As dawn broke, there was a stirring in the room along the corridor. A few minutes later, she heard Jamie quietly leave the house. From her window, she watched as he made his way between the wisping mist lying across the fields before Oswald's men arrived.

Smiling to herself despite her exhaustion, she parcelled up her proposal, placing it in her shoulder bag, along with her letter to Guy, ready to slip away to the Post Office. Oswald might not know it yet, but it was not just the village who were about to fight him on the beaches, not to mention the fields and the streets. It was a battle she was determined, for all their sakes, he would not win.

Chapter Thirty-Two

All through the damp mistiness of that November, Jamie spent entire days absorbed in excavating the burial mound.

Rosalind couldn't resist daily visits to the Post Office, before joining Jamie on the way back. She carefully avoided being seen by Oswald's men by skirting the fields on the far side and approaching the burial mound thorough the woods. Not that, so far, there had been much to photograph. Jamie found very little in his exploratory trench, apart from a few discarded clay pipes and a Victorian penny, but she could see him growing stronger once more, his confidence increasing by the hour.

Like Papa, he threw himself into things with a passion, driven to succeed. It was clearly a family trait. Even if the brooch had been a fluke – or as Jamie warned her, had been overlooked by grave robbers who had taken anything they considered of value – the time was not wasted.

Once he was back in Arden House, Jamie still avoided their father as much as Papa went out of his way not to meet him. But as she watched her brother's irritation with the activity of the men in the field increase, she had a glimmer of hope that his old spirit was returning.

'I'd forgotten it was so beautiful here,' Jamie remarked late one afternoon, gazing thoughtfully out of his bedroom window as Rosalind brought him a cup of tea.

'So it is.' She smiled, pushing aside the disappointment of yet another fruitless journey to the Post Office. Ginny, it seemed, was ignoring her, and there was no word from Guy. The twinge of loss sat permanently in her heart these days, she couldn't help concluding that she had, after all, slipped out of his life. 'I thought the same when I came back. It's seeing it with new eyes. We took it all for granted when we were children; we knew nothing else.'

Jamie sighed. 'Will was always taking about scaling the Alps, or great game hunting in Africa, as if he couldn't wait to escape. But he never could really tear himself away, even to escape Papa. At least not until the war, and then it wasn't exactly a choice.' He lit a cigarette, hands shaking ever so slightly. 'It was the responsibility of this place.'

So that was what was on his mind. She should have guessed. Rosalind longed to hug him, to tell him everything would be alright, but the last thing she suspected Jamie needed at this moment was his dignity compromised, even by a sister.

'You don't have to take over Arden, Jamie. Some of my friends who work for magazines in London are always writing about big old houses being lost, some turned into hotels or guesthouses, others divided into more manageable apartments. The truth is, places like this belong to the world before the wars. I don't think things will ever quite be the same again.'

'Indeed.' He smoked for a few minutes in silence. 'I know Oswald would be more than happy if I vanished and opened the way for him to talk Papa into let him take over and suck what profit he can out of the Arden estate. It's all right, Rosy, I've seen enough over the past months to guess what he's up to.'

'I didn't want to worry you,' she confessed, torn between hope that the village might have an ally and fear that confronting Oswald might yet be too much for him. 'And it's not certain he'll succeed.'

Jamie grimaced. 'I wouldn't mind if I thought he was going to use those fields to build housing for the village, or even turn the house into apartments for those who have no home. I wouldn't even object if he was planning to put up a village of prefabs until more permanent housing can be built. But there's no money in any of that, is there?'

'I'm afraid not.'

He was silent for a few minutes while he lit a second cigarette from the glowing stub of the first before extinguishing the remains. 'Besides, whatever he might be telling Papa, I'm quite sure Oswald is the kind to make sure he takes the lion's share of any profits. I don't like the thought of Arden House being surrounded by summer homes for London society and Brierley being wiped off the map, at least as far as a living, breathing community is concerned. I'm not like Papa, I don't want to be grand, or have anything to do with high society. I prefer quiet and obscurity and being covered in mud.'

'Then perhaps that's what Arden should allow you to be.'

'And you think Papa will listen to me?'

'You could try reasoning with him. If you give him an alternative plan, he might well listen. I'm sure deep down he loves us all in his own way, just as he loves everything about Arden. He's just not very good at acting on it.'

Jamie sighed. 'That's all very well, but you know what he's like. He just shuts off if anyone tries to argue, or gets cross.'

'But Oswald isn't blood.'

'There's George. He's got Arden blood in his veins.'

'If you leave it up to poor George, there will be no Arden left by the time he takes over,' she retorted.

'I can't help that.' Jamie's face had closed in on itself again, but this time it gave her an idea.

'I'm not sure I'd want to be Oswald's son,' she remarked. 'George really comes out of his shell whenever he's been here, and Bianca seems happier, too. There's no reason why you shouldn't be a benevolent uncle and take George and Hubert under your wing. I don't mean to live here, or as your heirs,' she added at his frown. 'And certainly not to take the place of your own children, when you have them. But it might be a way of giving them, and Bianca, a means of refuge from time to time. Isn't that what families do for each other?'

'I suppose,' he said, sounding unconvinced.

She tried again. 'All I remember of our grandfather is that he was a bully. And a little unhinged. It can't have been easy for Papa with him for a father, any more than it was for us growing up with Papa.'

Jamie took a long drag of his cigarette. 'I hadn't thought of it like that.'

'Neither had I until I came back and could see it all as if from a distance.' She hesitated. Sometimes the truth was as hard to say as it was to hear. 'Papa isn't nearly as confident as he makes out. You don't have to model yourself in his image. In fact, it seems to me it might do Arden good to throw out all those portraits of our grand Tudor ancestors and try something different. Or at least banish them to the attic,' she added as he appeared mildly scandalised at this sacrilege.

'Mrs Pretty at Sutton Hoo was a landowner and an archaeol-ogist combined. There's no reason why you shouldn't organise things differently from Papa and follow in her footsteps.'

'The village,' he muttered.

'I think, left to its own devices, and with a little help, Brierley can look after itself. Sell some land, by all means, repair the cottages, build some new ones with running water and proper bathrooms. Put up prefabs on the field by the kissing gate. I'm sure that given a sound roof over their heads Brierley can take its fate into its own hands. Everyone I've met while taking my photographs has been clever and hard-working and wonderfully ingenious at making the best of what they've got. You don't need to be responsible for every-thing, Jamie.'

'Maybe,' he muttered, distracted by the familiar roar of Oswald's Bentley, which had turned in from the lane and was starting to make its dignified progress up the drive. An impatient blast from the horn caused Lucy, who was returning from her weekly visit to her sister in Stratford, to jump onto the grass, nearly falling over in her haste.

'*Now* what does he want?' Rosalind exclaimed in exas-peration. Her heart sank. 'I bet he's planning to get Papa on his own. He only comes here to try and make Papa agree to the road and any houses he might choose to build. You're the only one who can stop him, Jamie.'

'Rosy—'

'Do you want Oswald to win? If you ask me, he's deter-mined to take over as much as he can, and Bianca will back up everything he says and does, or her life won't be worth living. This isn't just about you, or me, or Papa. If Oswald builds grand houses on the Arden estate and puts a road through the village, Brierley won't exist anymore. I'm sorry

Jamie. I thought we had more time, but I've a horrible feeling it could be now or never.'

'I'm not sure I can do anything.'

'You can look out for Papa's best interests. You may not be able to stop him, but at least you will have tried.' From downstairs came the clattering of pans, followed by the unmistakable aroma of judiciously burnt toast. 'I'd better help Lucy. There's no cake left, and I can't let her take that toast in, she's done that deliberately, and she might give him a piece of her mind as well after he nearly ran her over, which won't help anything.'

She raced downstairs to the kitchen, forestalling Lucy, who appeared tempted to add the bowl of fresh peelings to the tea tray, as decoration to Oswald's neatly oiled head.

'And you can tell him to bugger off, and all,' said Lucy, regretfully removing the worst of the blackened toast. 'They've already had one lot, so that's today's loaf all gone, and there's not a touch of butter or jam left, and if they're expecting to stay to a dinner I don't what to give them, that mutton Mrs Arden got from Hambledon Farm won't stretch to his majesty as well.'

'I'm sure there's something we can find, Lucy,' said Rosalind, soothingly. 'As soon as this is done, I'll collect whatever I can find from the garden, and I'm sure Mama can check the ration cards to see if we can still get anything you might need.'

'Arsenic,' said Lucy darkly, turning her attention to the kettle now coming to the boil.

Teapot filled, Rosalind balanced the tray along the corridor to the library, stopping only to remove two only slightly less singed pieces of toast that Lucy had managed to smuggle beneath the others, throwing them out of the nearest window for the benefit of the birds. The household might be about to fall apart, but they couldn't afford to lose Lucy – although how much longer she would stay if this continued was anyone's guess.

'Oh.' As Rosalind pushed through the door, she came to a halt. Papa had abandoned his toast, Oswald looked as if his coffee was of the bitterest, while Bianca was dabbing nervously with her napkin at the corner of her mouth. Across the room, Alma met her eyes, braving the faintest of smiles.

'I thought it was time I joined you all,' said Jamie, who was taking his seat in the armchair next to their father, directly opposite Oswald. He was white as a sheet, and the slightest of hesitation haunted his words, but his mouth was set in Papa's own determined line. He reached for a piece of toast, set out on a small table within easy reach of them all, placing it calmly on his plate and buttering it with barely a tremor.

'You're very welcome, my dear,' said Alma gently.

'Yes, of course,' muttered Papa. 'Good to see you feeling better, my boy.'

'And you, sir. I think we've both taken time to get back on our feet.'

'Yes, indeed.' Papa resumed chewing on his toast, covered with the last of Lucy's raspberry jam, made with the minimum of sugar and so showing a tendency to acquire an interesting bloom of mould, given half a chance. 'Good work you've done with that excavation of yours, I hear.'

'It has helped me, sir, as well as being fascinating in its own right.'

'Yes, yes, I can see that's so.' Their father put down his toast, expression warming. 'The garden always was the place I turned to myself, to soothe the soul. I need to get this damned leg of mine back to strength and start overseeing what's what in there. Can't get workmen for love nor money, you know.'

A faint smile appeared on Jamie's face. 'I've been given the names of one or two promising gardeners from the village, Papa. They are young, with not much experience, but perhaps under your guidance...'

Rosalind stifled a sudden explosion of laughter bubbling to the surface, avoiding Oswald's suspicious glare in her direction. It appeared that, for all his self-doubts, Jamie knew exactly how to deal with their father.

'Well,' Papa was replying, straightening his shoulders. 'If you think they are worth a try.'

'I have it on good authority that they are hardworking and eager, and will only be lost to places like Kew, or the Birmingham Botanical Gardens. We can at least give them a trial. If we are to plant in time for next year, we should be starting to clear the walled garden as soon as possible, don't you think? If we leave it much longer, the frosts will be too hard on the ground.'

'Yes, yes indeed.'

'It's marvellous to see you up and about, Jamie, dear,' put in Bianca, who was starting to look more cheerful. 'And George is so looking forward to visiting his grandfather again.'

'My nephews are welcome to visit at any time, isn't that so, Papa?'

'Yes, yes indeed.' Their father's expression softened, as it rarely did apart from in the presence of his grandsons.

'That's good to hear,' said Oswald, not quite able to disguise his irritation. 'Good to see you ready to go out into the world, James. Off to university, wasn't it? That was what you were planning before hostilities broke out? Ancient Greece, if I remember correctly.'

'Archaeology. It was Will who studied Classics. I prefer history that's closer to home.'

'Really.'

'The kind that belongs to all of us, the village as well. It seems such a pity you're building all over the field with the Roman villa without a chance to finish seeing what's there first.'

'Roman villa?' Papa sat up straight. 'You didn't tell me you were going as far as that, Oswald.'

'My men are just surveying the land, that's all. In case of hidden streams. Or mine shafts.'

'Mine shafts.' Papa snorted. 'There's been no mine workings here, I could have told you that. Quarrying, yes. But nowhere that near Brierley, and if you think you might stumble across coal, you're mistaken.'

'Safety,' muttered Oswald, slowly turning a dark shade of puce.

'And in any case, there has been no mention in your plans of any houses reaching this far,' put in Jamie. 'Are you intending to double the size of the village?'

'We can go through the plans, James. I can explain it to you. We have discussed the possibility of a road. It would be far more convenient than the lane between here and Brierley.'

'Convenient for what?' demanded Jamie.

Rosalind rose to meet Lucy at the door to take a second teapot and hide her grin. As she passed, she could see from Jamie's expression that he was beginning to relax. He retained Papa's determined set of the mouth as he continued to question Oswald, not letting him escape by changing the subject, while their father followed every word, eyes darting between them, but coming to rest each time a little longer on Jamie's face. Alma watched them with equal attention, as she sipped her tea, the lines on her face easing into an increasingly youthful glow.

'Miss,' hissed Lucy, as she handed over the teapot, beckoning urgently with her head for Rosalind to join her. Rosalind placed the teapot next to Alma, and returned hastily to the corridor muttering something about fetching cake. Lucy was already at the far end, out of earshot of the library, hopping anxiously from one foot to another. To Rosalind's dismay, she found Lucy extracting an envelope from her pocket.

'Don't tell me that's your notice? Not that I blame you—'

'Me? Oh Lord no. Better the devil you know, and all that. It's for you, Miss. He was on the way to the Post Office in Stratford, only, I spotted him and promised I'd bring it back with me, so you got it today.'

Blood was thudding in her ears, turning her dizzy. 'Who, Lucy?'

'Mr Thompson, of course. Who else?' She caught the look on Rosalind's face. 'Didn't you know, Miss? It's all around Stratford. Old Mr Thompson was taken bad last week, right after I'd visited Martha, and now they are saying he hasn't got long. Days, rather than weeks. Mr Guy arrived back from America last night.'

'Thank you,' said Rosalind, taking the letter, mind numb with the fact that he was so close, yet so out of reach, relief that she was not forgotten, after all, and aching for the heartbreak he must be facing.

'Miss?' Lucy paused in turning towards the kitchen.

'Yes, Lucy?'

'The thing is, I don't mean to pry, and I told Mr Guy as much, only, as he can't leave his dad's bedside for long, and you have that motorcycle, I did happen to mention that I thought you might be able to get to Stratford. He said he'd do his best to take a walk over Clopton Bridge each day, to clear his head, like. At noon.'

'Lucy.' Rosalind hugged the maid so hard she was afraid of knocking the breath from her body.

'That's alright, Miss,' said Lucy, eyes suspiciously glossy. 'I'm glad I weren't wrong. It were just you understanding so much about my Albert, I thought there had to be somebody. The moment I saw his face when he recognised me from all those years ago, well, only a fool could miss it.' She returned towards the kitchen, blowing her nose loudly as she went, while Rosalind raced upstairs, where she could read Guy's note safely in the privacy of her room.

Chapter Thirty-Three

The next morning, Rosalind wheeled the Triumph from its place of safety in the stables that in her grandfather's time had housed the carriage horses, and set off through the lanes towards Stratford.

At least none of the family had thought to question her further at breakfast when she muttered vaguely about taking pictures of Holy Trinity Church, to show the resting place of Shakespeare as context for her village photographs. Papa, once the thought had entered his head, was impatient to visit the walled garden, insisting on walking from the library to the dining room with the assistance of a walking stick on one side, Jamie's arm on the other. Alma, too, was preoccupied, vanishing immediately after the dishes were cleared away, declaring she was off to join the inevitable queues at Mrs Ackrite's and the butcher's, in a valiant attempt to stretch the family's ration books to replenish he inroads made on their supplies by the Gorwells' unexpected visit.

'Off,' Lucy had declared, when Rosalind attempted to help her with the washing up. 'I've plenty of time while the bread's proving, Miss, and while I work out what to do with all them cabbages.'

Outside, the late November chill hit Rosalind deep in her chest. Mist hung over the fields, extinguishing the burial mound in an ethereal orange glow from the sun as it rose above the trees. Frost glistened at the edges of the driveway, forcing her to swerve to miss the ghostly blooms of ice set in every pothole, ready to trap the unwary. The lane outside was equally frozen, causing her to slow to a minimum to avoid slipping out of control, dreading meeting any vehicle coming from the opposite direction. Around her, brambles arched white in the hedges, while the fields beyond glistened as swathes of frosted greenery turned to dew.

With the constraints of petrol rationing, she had not yet taken the Triumph as far as Stratford, and it was soon obvious that this morning's icy journey was going to take far longer than she had bargained for. Rosalind wound the Triumph through the lanes as fast as she dared, cursing each leisurely wagon with its slow clip clop of a horse, or the cumbersome lumbering of a tractor, impatiently seeking out the widening of the road allowing her to pass.

She could see from the church clock that it was well past noon when she reached Stratford, racing between the half-timbered houses until she found the river. She drew up next to Clopton Bridge, abandoning the Triumph and unfastening her helmet as she rushed towards the centre.

The bridge was empty.

She stood there, the bitter cold from the river rising up to settle on her limbs, eyes seeking desperately, hoping against hope, that she had not missed him. Perhaps he was simply keeping the blood moving by walking along the riverside. But there was just the usual kind of traffic making its way in and out of Stratford-upon-Avon, and a couple walking along the river bank, breath rising in clouds as they hurried towards some destination and welcome warmth.

As the mist finally began to lift, a rower passed under the Medieval arches, with the even pull of oars against the stream, gliding along on the mirrored waters, calm, eternal. Ducks waited expectantly by the shore. On both banks, she saw more men and women appearing to stroll along the paths, enjoying the fragile sunshine under a perfect blue sky. A burst of laughter echoed from one of the boats moored a little upstream.

But there was no sign of Guy. She must have missed him, or he had been unable to get away. Or it could be his father was too near the end to be left, even for a few moments. Slowly, she turned back towards her motorcycle. She had nearly reached it, when a figure in a greatcoat appeared through the mist still lingering in the streets beyond.

'Rosy!' Guy reached her in moments. 'Thank goodness, I thought you must have gone by now.'

'Never,' she replied, walking into the warmth of his embrace. 'You'd have to freeze my blood first.'

'Dear Rosy, dearest, dearest Rosy.' She felt the grief wrack his body and held him tight. 'I haven't long,' he said, as he raised his head from her shoulder, showing his face pale and drained, dazed exhaustion in every pore. 'I promised Mum I wouldn't leave her for more than half an hour. Dad's still hanging on in there, but it won't be long.'

'I'm so sorry.'

He turned away briefly to dash the back of his hand across his face. 'At least I was in time to see him, and to make a kind of peace.'

Rosalind slipped her arm under his, as they walked

slowly towards the centre of the bridge, saying little, just holding each other close, savouring every brief moment, caught in the whirlwind of the ending of a life.

'I'm glad with all my heart that you had that chance to get here in time,' she said, as they paused before turning unwillingly towards the inevitable return as the precious minutes ran their course.

Guy's arm tightened on hers. 'This isn't the way it was meant to be, Rosy. I'd written to you, I so wanted to talk to you. There was so much I wanted to tell you, so much I wanted to say. But not like this.'

'It doesn't matter,' she said. 'Not for now. Your family is what counts. There will be time enough for everything else.'

'Dear Rosy.' He stopped to gaze into her face, as if he couldn't bear to let her out of his sight. 'We all lived for each moment during the war, when we might have died at any time. I forgot that intensity as soon as the fighting stopped. Time seemed to stretch on forever. I thought there was time to make a fortune on my own terms, to make peace with Dad, and for us...' He swallowed. 'I was so afraid I had missed you today, or that in my stupidity I had already lost you.'

Rosalind kissed him. 'You won't lose me, Guy.'

'But if I had, it would be my own selfish, hard-headed fault for rushing off halfway around the world, on some dream of becoming another Lutyens.'

'And I'd have still dashed off to help Jamie, and you'd have only made it worse by trying to make Papa understand.'

His eyes lingered sorrowfully on her face. 'I should have stayed close by and been a support to you.'

'It's my family, Guy. It was always something I had to do on my own, and I love you all the more for not forcing me to choose between you.'

In the distance, a church bell struck the hour. Rosalind felt Guy's arms tighten around her. 'I have to go.'

'I know.'

'There's so much I want to tell you.'

'Don't worry, it will keep. Write to me when you're ready.' She could feel him locked away in the separate world of grief that only families can share. A twinge of fear, however selfish, went through her. 'Promise you won't leave without seeing me.'

'I won't leave,' he replied quietly, holding her close.

They had by now reached the Triumph, surrounded by a small group of admiring lads, who scuttled to a safe distance as they approached. There was no time, no privacy, to say goodbye. With a final squeeze of Guy's hand, Rosalind strapped on her helmet, ignoring the scandalised whispers of their audience at the sight of any female being allowed in charge of such a powerful machine, and wheeled the Triumph round to face in the direction of Brierley. As she set off, Guy was already hurrying between the houses, the strained anticipation of what he was returning to clear on his face. He turned to wave briefly as she passed, and then was gone.

Rosalind rode home through brilliant winter sunshine, whose fragile warmth had already melted the ice patches on the road and turned the fields to faded green, or rows of tawny stubble between the ploughed lines of red earth. It was a sight she had taken for granted all her life, but now every colour, every pocket of chill air in the road, every shadow radiating from the skeletons of trees, and every distant hint of bonfires held the vibrancy of knowing life must end. Guy was right. They had all lived that intensity during every day of war, when each hour could have been their last, each farewell a final parting. She didn't want to lose that now.

Reaching Brierley, she could not resist a hasty visit to the Post Office, finding a letter from Guy, posted from New York, waiting for her, along with one from Ginny Blake. She returned to the bench near the pond on the green, eagerly devouring Guy's message of love and of missing her and the promise to write again soon. It had so clearly been written before the news of his father had reached him, her heart ached with the thought that his words belonged to the final hours before his world changed forever.

She rose stiffly to her feet. She needed to get back before anyone started to ask why she had been away so long, but she couldn't resist a quick peek at Ginny's letter. Thank goodness, she found as she scanned it quickly, Ginny had jumped at the idea of following the excavation of the burial mound. In her usual enthusiasm, she appeared to view this as likely to be another Sutton Hoo. Rosalind smiled, hoping her editor would retain the same passion once she accepted that Sutton Hoo was an incredibly rare find and anything matching, or even surpassing, the ship burial was highly unlikely.

Rosalind began to fold up the letter. She would read the rest later. But her eyes had already fallen on the next paragraph, the words sucking her in, not letting her go. Slowly, she sank back on the bench, hurrying through the remainder of Ginny's hasty scrawl, then reading through again more closely.

So that was what had taken her so long to reply. With Christmas only weeks away, Ginny was already thinking of the dawn of 1946, and the year ahead. Despite herself, Rosalind couldn't help the familiar flicker of excitement in her belly at the plans laid out for her on her return to London, fighting a guilt that she should feel anything of the sort, or that her brain was already buzzing with ideas, especially when Guy was facing such turmoil.

Taking a deep breath, Rosalind folded the letters away, deep inside her leather jacket, her eyes falling on the familiar bustle of Brierley going about its business. It wasn't just the approaching end of the old year, but also the prospect of the new, the first without the weight of war hanging over them for so long she could barely remember the feeling.

All around her, change was stirring, moving on to a new future. Whatever happened with Guy, whatever path she chose to follow, she could feel the world turning on its slow, unstoppable axis and knew that nothing would ever be the same again.

Chapter Thirty-Four

Guy's father died before the week was out.

'Sad, very sad,' remarked Papa, shaking his head over the obituary in the local paper. 'Thompson & Son was remarkably successful during the war. Must have been one of the most profitable in Stratford.' He coughed, as if suddenly remembering his second daughter's unfortunate association with the troublesome son. 'Mind you, much of that will change now there will be less of a call for these Spitfires. Wouldn't be surprised if the business closes down, now Thompson isn't at the helm.'

Rosalind pretended not to hear, concentrating instead on Alma's working out of what might be possible for Christmas, given the conflict between the continuing shortages and the general desire to have some celebration for the first Christmas of the peace. Her body ached to rush and hold Guy and ease his pain, but the rational part of her knew that her presence, appearing out of nowhere, would only add to his burden. This was his family, his loss and, for now, the only way she could help him was to leave them in peace to deal with their sorrow together.

Shortly after the funeral, on a damp and misty December afternoon, Rosalind rode the Triumph once more through the lanes to Stratford. This time they had arranged to meet under the high vaulted ceilings of Holy Trinity Church, where Rosalind could photograph Shakespeare's tomb, to satisfy anyone who might be curious to see the results of her supposed mission. The last thing either of them needed at this moment was a fight with Papa.

There was no point in fooling herself, she acknowledged as she paused in front of the carved image of Shakespeare, quill in one hand, paper in the other. Her father might be rapidly transferring his blind admiration of Oswald to an absorption into Jamie's plans for making the most of the walled garden and his hopes for the excavation of the burial mound, but his remarks about Henry Luscombe were still there, lurking, ready to rise to the surface on any occasion. Papa had accepted her presence but, she recognised with a sadness in her heart, he still viewed her as the Arden's channel back to becoming a part of the aristocracy. Her blood was only worthy of his if it was to be mixed with blue, to produce an heir to a dukedom, one who could rapidly overtake George and Hubert in his affections.

Rosalind hastily completed her photograph of Shakespeare's monument, followed by the stone slab of his tomb in front of the altar, with its familiar curse on anyone disturbing the interred bones. All done, she ducked between the visitors paying their respects to the playwright, to the pew where Guy was quietly taking a seat.

In the softly coloured beams streaking through the stained-glass windows, she could make out that he was still pale and gaunt, but he had lost the shell-shocked look that she had found when they had met on Clopton Bridge. His expression was more one of deep sorrow turning towards acceptance, while his smile as he greeted her was the same as it had always been.

'That will keep them happy at home, in case anyone asks awkward questions,' she said, barely above a whisper, so as not to disturb the echo of footsteps between the arched Medieval pillars, accompanied by the occasional cough reverberating around the ancient walls, and the reverend murmur of voices. She busied herself packing away her camera into her knapsack. 'And if the pictures come out well enough, I could send them to Ginny Blake.'

'You should,' he replied, equally quietly. 'My sister sent me copies of the magazine with your photographs of the choir and the amateur dramatics society in Brierley-in-Arden. I think Gwen hoped to make me homesick,' he added to her inquiring glance. They sat back, as if admiring the light streaming through into the chancel. 'Which they did,' he added, his hand brushing hers. 'More than Gwen could ever have believed.'

Warmth flooded through Rosalind, filling every part of her. 'Let's get out of here,' she whispered, as yet more pilgrims arrived to view the tomb. They slipped out and through the churchyard, making their way to the path alongside the river, where there was a little more privacy, and none of their fellow strollers took much notice of a couple walking close together, slowly, aimlessly, wrapped up in each other in the winter gloom.

They had so little time, thought Rosalind. They had to be practical, with little time for emotion. 'When are you going back?'

'Back?'

'To New York.'

'I'm not sure.' He walked a few paces in silence. 'Rosy, would you mind if I don't return to America? At least not for now. I love it over there, and I'm sure you would too, it's so vibrant, with new ideas and opportunities. But things have changed.'

She couldn't help it, her initial relief that he was not planning to be half a world away was extinguished by dread that family duty might still drag them apart. 'You mean, you're taking over the business?'

'It's what Dad wanted, to make sure Mum and my sisters are provided for.'

It seemed an ultimatum was about to face her, after all. 'I see.'

He came to a halt. 'I'm not returning to Thompson & Son, Rosy. Gwen and Laura ran it perfectly well between them when Dad was ill. I can see how much Laura needs it, especially after Dad. It's brought back all the grief of losing her fiancé in the landings on D-Day.'

Guilt shot through Rosalind at not having considered that Guy's family may well have suffered their own losses in the war. 'I'm sorry, that must have been terrible.'

'The worst of it is that I didn't even know she had been engaged until I came back from New York. She hadn't wanted to worry me. Any of us. I can see it's helping her, now she's putting all her energies into turning Thompson & Son back to civilian purposes. Mum is worried that with so many men lost, Gwen might never marry and, as a woman, she could barely make ends meet as an accountant, despite all her training. I'm well aware that she was really the brains behind the firm's recovery, even though Dad would never admit it. I can't take that away from them, even if I wanted to.'

A mixture of emotions raced through her. 'So you're still free to become an architect.'

'Maybe.' He pulled her gently towards a bench set at the side of the path. 'I've put by enough savings to set up my own practice.'

'Then you should!'

'Or I could use it to rent a house in London for a year or so, maybe more.'

She scanned his face, unsure of his expression, wishing she could read deep into the truth of his heart.

'London?'

'Or Birmingham, if you prefer. I've been talking to architects working in both. There's a real move to improve housing stock after the destruction of the war, especially the old slums.'

'But you were so set on establishing your own design practice.'

'I still could, one day. Maybe.' He turned to gaze over the river. 'Dad would laugh. I had such grand dreams before the war of becoming a famous architect like Edwin Lutyens or Frank Lloyd Wright. Now, I find I prefer domestic architecture for ordinary families. I've seen the difference it makes, having simple things like a bathroom and a proper kitchen, and electric lighting.' He gave a wry grin.

'My sisters are discussing turning the workshops to making pipes for plumbing in readiness for a wave of new government building work. I'm tired, Rosy. I'm tired of death and destruction. I want to see a better material world, the kind that promotes health and happiness and prosperity. When the plane flew into London, I saw the vast swathes of destruction laid out below me. I'd seen photographs, but that really brought the scale of the task home. It's a sight I'll never forget.'

He meant it. Rosalind steeled herself. Even now, it was almost impossible to overcome a lifetime of training to be accommodating, the figure in the background, the one who had no right to demand her own place in the sun.

She could already feel her choices shrinking in the very way she had always dreaded, her energies consumed by the demands of creating a comfortable home for Guy to return to each evening, and an ever-expanding brood of small children around her feet. It wasn't that she had no desire for a home, for children, or for love. But she wanted a life of her own to live, too.

Was that so very much to ask? She had fought so hard to give herself that chance, she couldn't bear to throw it all away. Not even for Guy. Not even for love. That might make her an unnatural woman, but it was who she was. She couldn't deny it, and especially not to herself.

That way madness lies, came the thought, clear in her head, wrestling with the love in her heart. For her, at least. True, disintegrating insanity – like King Lear in the wildness of the storm, raving against the world, lost forever. The feeling of being stretched impossibly thin was back, stronger than ever, tearing her apart.

She could never be Alma, stumbling into a promise of security to find herself in a mire of emptiness and frustration. It had to be said.

'Ginny Blake is expecting me back in London after Christmas. Well... demanding I'm back, with menaces. She's determined not to lose me, and I don't want to leave my job. It's what I was born to do, Guy.'

'I remember. London it is.'

She wouldn't be female if guilt didn't instantly overtake her. 'But your mother and sisters—'

'There are trains between Birmingham and London.

351

Besides, I have enough to afford a car, and petrol rationing can't last forever. Surely you'll want to see your family, too?'

'Of course. If Papa is still speaking to me, that is,' she added, gloomily.

He cleared his throat. 'Rosy, I don't want to presume...' His voice drifted into uncertainty.

That was the moment she knew. The pieces whirling inside her mind, the possibilities of a myriad of futures, coalescing into one clear path. He could feel her doubts, her questions, and he was trying to understand, with the few clues any man was given into the reality of a woman's mind. She could feel him hesitating, not wanting to be clumsy and offend her, and loved him even more for it.

'The thing is,' she said in a rush. 'Ginny has made me a proposal. I wasn't sure about it at first, but the more I've thought of it, the more I like it.' She bit her lip, but this part also had to be said. They needed to understand each other before their fates were tied inextricably together. Besides, she wasn't the self-sacrificing kind. 'It means I'll be working flat out for months, maybe even a year or so. Guy, I so want to do this. It could be the making of me as a reporter and a photographer.'

'I see.' He sounded faintly hurt. 'Then you should go for it.'

'I will.' Now it came to it, her courage almost failed her. She took a deep breath. 'Ginny has her ear pretty much to the ground. Or rather, she has good contacts, the kind she'll never divulge. She's quite certain the King and Queen will be announcing the engagement of Princess Elizabeth to Prince Phillip of Greece within the next year.'

'Oh?' He thought she was changing the subject, discussion closed.

'If I was the princess,' she added, in an attempt to lighten the mood, 'I'd certainly insist on the most handsome prince to be found.'

'Yes, of course.' He was still grave, uncertain.

Couldn't he see? Love, mixed with exasperation, made her bold. After all, one of them had to come to the point, or they would be meeting secretly on benches in the rain and snow forever.

'You see, Ginny is determined to make the most of it, and after my photographs of the choir and the Brierley Players have proved so popular, she wants me to photograph other young women as they become engaged and prepare for a wedding under rationing, as best they can. She's convinced it's just the thing everyone needs, something joyful and posi-tive and looking to the future after the war.'

'So you'll be based in London?'

'Mostly. Ginny wants me to mix society ladies with girls in towns and villages all over the countryside, or at least as far as trains and the petrol ration can reach.' It was now or never. 'The thing is, it seems to me that it might be a wonderfully joyful addition if one of brides were to be the photographer herself.'

Her breath froze at the blank expression on his face. She had misunderstood his heart, his intentions, his reference to the house in London. It was too soon after his father's death. He had never intended to marry her. Mortified, she began to disengage her hand from his. But his grip tightened, pulling her closer, his eyes seeking out hers. In them, she saw only love and understanding, the kind that never dies.

'I'm an idiot,' he said. 'Yes, dearest, darling Rosy. Yes, of course, with all my heart.' He released her hastily from his kiss only at the outraged tutting of a passing nanny, pushing a vast perambulator and with two small children in tow.

He grinned as Rosalind did her best not to giggle, and so

seal her reputation as a married woman shamelessly cavorting with her lover (doubtless one of many) for all to see. 'I'm tired of all this hiding away in corners. Perhaps you would like to come and see my mother and sisters? They would love to meet you, and we don't have to tell them anything yet, not until we're ready. It's only a short walk away.'

'There's nothing I'd like more,' she said, tucking her arm through his.

'Although I should warn you, once they hear their brother is engaged, my sisters will insist on being brides-maids, and once they've set their minds to something, there's no arguing.'

'I like the sound of them already,' she replied. 'And as long as they don't attempt to truss me up in lace and net, I'm happy to let them fight it out with every one of my sisters for whatever finery they please.'

Rosalind returned to Arden just as dusk was beginning to gather around the house. She wheeled her motorcycle into the stables and made her way to the front door, passing the dark shadow of Oswald's Bentley parked in the driveway. No one had mentioned such a visit this afternoon and her mind was in such a whirl all she wanted was to escape to her room and absorb the events of the day. But hopefully it meant Bianca had brought George and Hubert to visit, despite Lucy's inevitable frustration at being expected to yet again produce cake out of nothing and with no warning.

Rosalind looked up at the familiar Tudor façade. She loved Arden House, and all those kept safe within its walls as much as ever, but at the same time she felt a strange kind of detachment. Her mind was already moving on to a future where, however much she visited Arden, the core of her life would be elsewhere.

Her heart still glowed with the warmth of the welcome from Guy's mother and sisters, their grief-lined faces visibly brightening as Guy introduced her as the creator of the photographs in *Woman's Time*. She had caught the instant 'told you so' look pass between his sisters and blushed so furiously there was no point in hiding anything. Guy's mother, a small, grey-haired woman with intelligent eyes, so like her son's, had embraced her without a word, smiling through her tears.

She was still filled with astonishment that already the half-timbered house in Stratford, shabby with the haste of busy female lives, arranged for comfort and convenience rather than a desire to impress, had become a part of her. From now on, it always would be, as much as London's streets, the home she and Guy would build together, and wherever in the world Ginny might choose to send her.

As she slipped quietly inside the front door, tactfully left open for her return, she could hear the familiar clatter of pans in the kitchen and the quiet murmur of voices from the library.

'That one!' came George's cry, with the excitement of a small boy engaged in a game. 'That one, Uncle James.'

Smiling with anticipation of seeing her nephews again, Rosalind raced up to her room, changing her muddy slacks and leather jacket for a skirt and her neatest Fair Isle cardigan, before returning downstairs to join them.

'Ah, Rosalind.' It was her father beaming at her broadly from his place next to the fire that gave her the first inkling of unease. 'You're such a good girl with all your charity work for the unfortunate of the village.'

'I wasn't—' she began, stumbling to a halt at such

unlikely praise, and with an instant desire to vanish into the ether.

Rising to his feet from the place of honour in the armchair on the opposite side of the fire to Papa, was Henry Luscombe. The complacency of his expression sent shivers down her spine, the joy of the day evaporating, instantly out of reach.

'Henry has generously offered to financially support us in improvements to the village, Rosalind,' remarked Oswald, in a manner so pointed it was impossible to miss, let alone the fact that he had deigned to acknowledge her presence at all. 'It will mean there may not be the need to build houses over the Roman villa, or for any road to go through the village. And it will mean your father can be made comfortable in Arden, after all.'

'Very generous,' added Papa.

Oswald's smile broadened, with a triumph that send the hairs on the back of her neck rising. 'And then there is Jamie's find.'

'Find?'

Jamie was still engaged in playing pick-up-sticks with George, without meeting her eyes. Something had changed in the household, she could feel it in the air.

'The burial mound,' said Jamie. 'There's definitely a burial in there, after all. From the remains of the skull, I'd say it was someone fairly elderly. The wisdom teeth are through, and there's quite a bit of wear on the molars.'

'And you're sure it's not someone recent,' said Oswald, sounding slightly disappointed.

'Quite sure,' said Jamie. 'The police have been notified and there will need to be a treasure trove inquest, like there was at Sutton Hoo, if there are valuable grave goods that have survived the attentions of thieves. But all the evidence points to her being at least Medieval, if not earlier.'

'Her?'

'I'm certain the brows don't look heavy enough to be male. The experts from the university will be able to say more, but it looks like a woman to me. From the brooch Rosy found, any grave goods could be magnificent. It's the kind of thing that could really put Brierley on the map, Papa. After all, visitors flock to Stonehenge, not to mention the Egyptian antiquities.'

'Yes indeed,' muttered their father. 'Yes, indeed.' He smiled at Rosalind. 'We're fortunate Henry has also just promised to support any excavation.'

'Oh,' said Rosalind.

Jamie had gone back to entertaining George, firmly avoiding her eyes. Bianca was shushing Hubert, who had begun to whimper in the over-tired manner of a baby kept up too late and with too many new experiences. Alma was pretending to be completely absorbed in embroidering a child's smock. The rest was expectation hanging thick in the air, her fate already sealed.

Nothing like guilt, and being the one to save the family, both financially and emotionally, to bring a wayward woman to heel. The realisation sent the breath from her body, her mind a cornered blank. The betrayal hurt like a knife. How could Jamie, who knew what Henry was like, who despised him for his treatment of women, even think of trying to blackmail her into putting her own future, her own dreams, aside so he could follow his own interests?

Henry's complacent smile, accompanied by an enjoyment in his eyes she didn't want to think about, turned her stomach. The memory of their encounter in the drawing room still made her blood run cold. She was under no illusion that time would have made him forget her escape that day, let alone forgive.

She had lived through so much since he had attempted to bend her to his will, she could barely recognise the girl in the flimsy dress he had forced up against the wall, but one look at his face told her that nothing had touched him. He was incapable of change. If anything, it mattered even less to him who he was to present as his socially acceptable veneer of a wife, and she had a horrible feeling the attraction of one he would have the pleasure of tormenting, paying her back with interest for the humiliation she had inflicted on him for the rest of her days, would be irresistible.

Forget the grandiose villains, it was the petty that were the most terrifying.

His smile deepened, enjoying her discomfiture, even more so for the secret moment of violence seared into both their memories, invisible to all around them, and now sealed – as far as he was concerned – as an inevitable part of her fate.

Chapter Thirty Five

A few days before Christmas, Rosalind paced her room in frustration, wishing she could simply jump on the Triumph and flee, and avoid the family battle that had been brewing since Henry had departed with a promise to join them for the New Year. At least the festive season, with its family demands, and promise of agreeable entertainment in London, had given her a short respite from Henry's attentions.

She would spend Christmas with her family and share in the honouring of Will's passing, leaving Guy in peace with his family to deal with their own difficult memories. Whatever Henry might believe, by the time Papa turned on the wireless to hear the chimes of Big Ben bring in the beginning of 1946, she was determined she would be gone.

Guy had already left for London to meet his prospective new employers. He was returning to spend Christmas with his mother and sisters, but not before securing a temporary home for when Rosalind accompanied him, all ready to start their new life together, however long it took for their actual wedding to take place.

She had been careful not to mention anything about Guy to her family, although she had returned Lucy's quizzical look with a smile so broad Lucy had danced in silent glee around the kitchen, finger on lips to signal her continued secrecy.

Peace. All Rosalind wanted was peace, and to secure a way of being able to return again to Arden to visit Alma and Jamie and her sisters, and catch up with Lucy, even if Papa chose to never speak to her for the rest of his days. She didn't want to leave Arden House as she had done before, without any prospect of seeing any of them again. She couldn't live the rest of her life like that, visiting Guy's family in Stratford as often as they could, while banished from her own.

However much her urge to flee, she couldn't miss this final celebration in memory of her brother, and the life that had been when he had been the one choosing the Christmas tree and directing operations.

Kate and Cordelia had to be there, they couldn't miss this Christmas, even if it was to be the final one they would ever spend together. Alma had finally managed to find an address for Kate from the farm in Cornwall where she had worked during the war. As yet, there had been no word back from Italy, but a letter had come from Paris, to say that Cordelia would be arriving in a few days. Rosalind couldn't help remembering the weeping she had heard from Kate's room, the day Miss Parsons had given them the volumes of Shakespeare and wonder if she would ever see her adopted sister again.

Once, nothing could tear us apart, thought Rosalind. But now they had all set out on their own paths. There was so little left of their childhood world, of the summers swimming in the lake and sitting out on the grass on the lawn, as Papa worked in the gardens and Alma took tea under the trees. The world that had turned so securely, amidst the slow clop of horses' hooves between fields, the rhythm of ploughing and harvesting. Such an innocent time it felt now, before the world changed, leaving its memory of grief and horrors in every cottage and mansion, and in the drift of the young and the able towards the cities.

There seemed little reason for the family to meet up again, the connection that had once been so strong, so intimately tied up with Arden House, with its fields and its hedgerows and the little village between its rolling fields, lost forever.

All she had to do was to keep Henry at bay until Christmas was over and she could return to London under the pretext of fulfilling her employer's demands and not wishing to bring the house of Arden into disrepute through a broken contract.

All the same, Rosalind could feel the old trap opening up. It was there in the way Papa finally welcomed her company, insisting that she sat next to him in the place of honour by the fire in the library. Alma was already fussing with altering her voluminous old gowns to echo the sleek utility style in preparation for Henry's next visit, while Jamie was avoiding Rosalind, spending as much of his time as he could working on the burial mound or closeted in endless discussions with their father.

The sense of something not being quite right was growing stronger. She could feel it in her bones. But she also knew all too well how the Arden mind could, on occasions, fool itself into believing what was convenient, and how little the world was seen through a woman's eyes.

Rosalind stopped her pacing. The walls of the house were closing in even tighter around her. She couldn't breathe. Grabbing her camera, she shot down through the house, pausing only to slip on her coat and boots, and set off through the gloom of a winter afternoon, through the fields to Brierley-in-Arden.

Once she reached the village hall, she paused to drink in the familiar scene. A little way down the street women were deep in discussion, putting the world to rights, in the usual village hum of the day slowing towards night. A ripple of piano echoed from the village hall, sending 'Greensleeves' to echo amongst the indignant protests of mallards, as Montague passed through the village green on his daily stroll, setting moorhens darting amongst the reeds in panic. Montague ignored them, following instead the aroma of the WI's fish stew lingering around the village hall.

Rosalind glanced up towards the Gorwells' house, its large glass windows blazing out the brilliance of electric light into the softness of the ending of the day. Shadows passed to and fro across the windows, followed by a burst of laughter erupting into the quiet.

She bent to stroke the warm head of Montague, who was now winding himself lovingly around her skirts, just in case she was in the habit of keeping a stash of fresh kidneys in her pockets. Rosalind drew in the familiarity of Brierley-in-Arden around her like a beloved shawl, warm and secure, and ached, deep in her heart, for it to stay like that forever.

There was another burst of laughter from Oswald's guests, now spilling into the grounds, the lamps set around the garden catching the crystal gleam of champagne flutes in their hands.

'He clearly thinks it's a done deal.' She looked round as Miss Parsons emerged through the door of the museum.

'Oswald, you mean?'

'Indeed. Cassie, the Gorwells' undermaid, said those are business associates being wined and dined up there tonight. The kind who'll make a killing if the Arden grounds are developed into country retreats for the rich and powerful.'

'But I thought that was all settled? Papa was listening to Jamie rather than Oswald only a few days ago.'

'Well he's not anymore. Gorwell is back to insisting the road through the village goes ahead.'

She couldn't believe it. And yet remembering Oswald's confidence and Jamie's withdrawal from any kind of communication, she had to accept it was true. There was a twist, deep in her belly. What on earth could Oswald be holding over Jamie to make him give up the fight so easily? There had to be something.

'So Oswald has won,' she said.

'Oh, I don't know,' replied Miss Parsons, thoughtfully. 'I have the skull Jamie found locked away in my museum for safekeeping until the Archaeology Department can get here, and we might have a trick or two up our sleeves yet.'

Around them, the choir had begun to arrive for the evening's rehearsal, more than one humming along with 'Greensleeves' on their way in. Before long, it would be 'Away in a Manger' and 'Once in Royal David's City' spilling out between renditions of 'John Barleycorn' and 'Scarborough Fair' into the frosty night skies, as they made their preparations for the Christmas Eve concert, now only days away.

'After all those centuries a church has stood amongst these fields,' said Miss Parsons quietly, 'and after all those pagan temples that stood for time immemorial before that, I could not bear to think that this might be the last Christmas celebrated in Brierley-in-Arden. The final turning of the year.'

'Hopefully not,' came a new voice. Rosalind started as Edmund emerged from the museum, swinging a knapsack over one shoulder. 'Digging in its heels is the Brierley way.' He pulled a pair of bicycle clips from his pocket, fitting them round the ankles of his trousers. 'And surprisingly effective, all things considered.'

'Thank you, my dear,' said Miss Parsons, patting him gently on one arm. 'This won't be forgotten.'

'That's all right,' he muttered, fiddling with the securing of his clips.

Miss Parsons vanished inside, leaving behind an awkward silence.

'Did you hear that Jamie uncovered a skull at the burial mound?' said Rosalind, as Edmund began to push his bicycle towards the Ford's cottage with the air of a man wishing to flee as fast as possible. 'It looks as if there might be something exciting down there, after all.'

'I heard.'

Edmund too. She could hear the wish to avoid her in his voice. 'I'm certain the professor taking over the dig would welcome volunteers.'

'I'm sure they will have plenty already. But tell Jamie good luck.' He came to a halt. 'Look, you'll hear soon enough. I'm no longer employed in Brierley. I've accepted a post in Stratford.'

'Oh,' said Rosalind. Guilt shot through her. 'It isn't because Oswald dismissed you, is it? For helping Jamie, I mean.'

'No,' he replied, shortly. He set off again pushing his bicycle, then came to a halt. 'I've done my best. I tried to warn Jamie, but he was so caught up with his excavation,

I'm not sure he was listening. Or maybe it was already too late.'

He finally met her eyes. 'Believe me, I've seen the way Gorwell works. He has a way of tricking those employed by him to do things that could put shame on their family. Then he uses that threat of exposure to get them to do other things, the kind that, if they ever come to light, really can ruin a family or put a man behind bars for the rest of his life. Meanwhile, Gorwell gets off scot-free, enjoying the profit and starting the process all over again.'

It was a jolt of understanding, straight to her belly. Papa under Oswald's spell once more, Jamie avoiding her, not wishing – not daring? – to confront Henry Luscombe. Oswald's complacent smile. Nausea rose inside her.

'Do you mean to tell me that's what he has done to Papa?'

'Possibly.' His voice was wary. 'I'm sorry, Rosalind, I've done what I can. Now I've got to do what is best for Dad.' His hand rested briefly on hers. 'Get out of this while you can. Don't get caught up in Gorwell's schemes. Your family are not you. You owe them nothing.'

'You're a fine one to talk.'

He gave a sad smile. 'It's different with me and Dad. I owe him for his insistence I got an education, even if he didn't see the point of people like us going to university. I know he hasn't got many years left, and he has so little, even after a lifetime of working his fingers to the bone. I will have the rest of my life once he's gone.

'It's not the same as binding yourself to a man like Henry Luscombe. I've seen the enjoyment he takes in destroying women, especially those strong enough to stand up against him. Your family may yet be in far too deep to get out of this, but you still can. You're worth more than this. I wish...' His eyes lingered on hers. 'Or maybe not. I have a suspicion it would be my heart that would be broken.'

With that, he was gone, flying through the streets on his bicycle without a backward glance, as if the devil himself were at his heels.

Light shone out from several windows as Rosalind arrived back at Arden House. The events of the evening had left her shaken, her mind in a whirl. As she made her way inside, the sound of voices, loud, enthusiastic, came from the library. She could make out Jamie amongst them.

'Darling!' It was Alma, appearing on the stairs. 'Thank goodness you're here. I've been looking out for you. Jamie said you had complained of a headache and must have gone for a walk. I'd have come with you if I'd known.'

'I just needed some fresh air, Mama.'

'Well, you're back now. It's quite extraordinary. Several members from the Archaeology Department have arrived from Birmingham University, they are talking to your papa now. They think the burial mound might be an important site. They want to do a proper excavation. It sounds really quite exciting.

'They agree with Jamie that the skull looks as if it could be that of a woman. In which case it really could bear out that old story, and be the burial of an Anglo-Saxon ruler from the time of King Alfred the Great, or even Queen Æthelflæd, the leader who protected Brierley from Viking invaders all those centuries ago. It could mean that, if they have survived, the grave goods are some of the finest ever found in Warwickshire. Who on earth would have thought? It will be so wonderful for Arden, and the village. And it's good to see Jamie so energised. I think finally your father is starting to listen to him.'

Rosalind swallowed. She should have been equally excited by the news, and wished for nothing more than to brave the academics – who might tolerate her presence, if not her opinions – to hear more. Instead, all she wished for was to escape to the privacy of her own room.

'That's just what Arden needs,' she murmured.

'And the village,' sighed Alma. 'It's good to see the streets coming back to life, too. I'd forgotten how much I missed it. But then I suppose I didn't do as much before we were all thrown together during the war. I'm not sure I can just go back to just doing good deeds once a week. The choir has given me a new lease of life.'

'I'm glad, Mama.'

'And I won't give it up, I don't care what anyone thinks. I did try so very hard with your sister, with all of you. But I'm afraid, despite all her advantages, Bianca has become, well, just a little spiteful at times. I hate to say it, but it's the truth. I'm not sure pushing her towards Oswald Gorwell was the best thing to do, he seems to have brought out the worst in her.'

'You did what you thought was right at the time, Mama.'

'I've always tried to do what I thought was right. Although maybe... well, it has struck me recently, that I might not have admitted to myself that it was more for my own benefit.'

Rosalind paused in moving past her. It seemed it was a day for events falling into place with a horrible clarity. In a pause in the conversation spilling out from the library, silence fell, echoing through the house, tightening around them.

'It was you,' said Rosalind, slowly, realisation dawning. 'You gave the letter from Guy to Papa, all those years ago.'

Alma blanched. 'I was only trying to protect you. Your father had told you explicitly he was an unsuitable young man, and you knew so little of the world.'

'So I am not to be trusted with my own happiness?'

Alma did not reply.

'But... it's not like Ginny Blake was an unsuitable young man set to ruin me. I take it you destroyed the letter she sent offering me a commission as well?'

'My dear, a journalist! They keep such dreadful society, quite frightful.'

'It's a magazine for women, written by women, with an editor who is a woman. Just how was that supposed to jeopardise my reputation, or lead me astray? It certainly hasn't since.'

'Darling—'

'If you thought me that predisposed to vice, it was a wonder you ever let me out of your sight!'

'I didn't. I wouldn't.' Alma dissolved into tears, but Rosalind was beyond being kind. Fury went through her, the quiet, despairing kind of fury that was ruthless in its clarity. Yet another betrayal. Over the past weeks, she had come to believe once more Alma had their best interests at heart, that she could trust her. The disillusion went through her, like a knife.

'So now you're once again prepared to throw me to Henry Luscombe. I'm not a child. You know what he tried to do to me and how I felt. And you can never make me deny that, just because it's inconvenient for Papa.'

Alma reached for her handkerchief. 'I'm sorry. You're right. Sometimes I think – now I'm too old to do anything

368

about it – that I too should have fought more for my own happiness.'

Rosalind's fury burst. 'You're not too old, Mama. You're never too old.'

'Darling!' Alma paused in dabbing her eyes and stared at her, scandalised.

'I love Papa with all my heart, but that doesn't prevent me from observing that he's a selfish and self-absorbed old man, who isn't always wise. I wouldn't love him if I didn't at least give him the justice of seeing him clearly, or if I flattered him just to get my way, as Bianca does. But I've no intention of living with him for the rest of my life, dancing around his moods and his vanity and his determination to see all females as silly and naturally his inferior.'

Alma winced. 'So you're leaving.'

'Do I have any other choice? If you love me at all, Mama, surely you wouldn't want to see me throw myself into the power of a man who will delight in tormenting me for the rest of my life?'

'No,' said Alma. 'Darling, I love you with all my heart. You and your brothers and sisters have made my life worthwhile, even though you have caused me heartache at times. You have made my world a richer place. The Shakespeare sisters are the one thing I will never regret.'

'Thank you,' said Rosalind, kissing her.

Alma's arms came around her. 'What will you do?'

'Make my own happiness.' She stopped. She still didn't trust Alma enough to confide in her.

One hint to Papa that she was planning to marry the very man he had forbidden all that time ago, and she could be spending Christmas climbing out of her room at midnight, dangling from the end of knotted sheets. At the very least, she would ruin it by being nagged at every available opportunity to recant from such marital heresy, especially when she was all set to spend her life as a duchess.

'Darling...'

'For one thing, I shall continue to work for Miss Blake's magazine. So I'm warning you I'm intending to travel as far as Pompeii to find Kate, if she doesn't answer your letter. Or even to photograph the antiquities of Egypt, if Miss Blake chooses to send me there.'

'Egypt? Oh my goodness. So very far away. Aren't there snakes?'

Rosalind hugged her. 'And very unsuitable men. Who I'm told are very beautiful.'

'Rosy!'

'I'm joking, Mama.' Despite herself, her eyes welled up.

'Love is a strange thing,' sighed Alma. 'And can arrive in the most unexpected of places. I've come to think that true love really does exist, after all. It may be a rare thing, but all the more worth fighting for.'

'And we shall keep on fighting,' said Rosalind firmly, smiling at her through her tears. 'And never give up.'

Chapter Thirty-Six

Cordelia arrived the day before Christmas Eve, giving enough warning of her arrival to enable Rosalind to fetch her from the railway station in Stratford in Jamie's Austin.

There was little opportunity for conversation as they drove carefully back through the low slanting light of the midwinter afternoon, with pockets of mist forming in dips in the road and frost already glistening on the hedgerow.

'No sign of Kate then?' said Cordelia, once they reached the familiar winding lanes leading to Brierley-in-Arden.

'None. Not even when I wrote to her at the address Alma was given to tell her about Jamie's find and that Birmingham University think the burial mound might be an important archaeological site.'

Cordelia sighed. 'I've heard nothing either. As far as I know, she's still living in Naples, but she's told me nothing of what she's doing, beyond helping with the excavation of Pompeii. Reading between the lines, I've a feeling that there's a man involved, but of course, because of Papa, she would never say. I suppose Christmas wasn't ever going to be the same again, not without Will.'

'No.' Rosalind concentrated on a stretch of road with ice forming over the puddles where last night's ice had melted.

'I expect Oswald and Bianca will be there.'

'They decided not to join us, after all. They are taking the boys to the Riviera to spend Christmas with Oswald's mother in some fancy hotel.'

'Poor Mama, I thought they might be more considerate, especially as this Christmas is supposed to be in memory of Will and might be our last chance of ever being together.'

'Although it might possibly be more peaceful...'

Cordelia laughed. 'Don't ever change, Rosy. Whatever happens.'

'That, I can promise,' replied Rosalind, smiling.

Alma was waiting for them as they reached the house, pulling on her coat as she hurried down the steps. 'Come on in, you must both be frozen. Lucy has put the kettle on and there are fires in your rooms. I swear I can smell snow in the air.'

Cordelia stepped out of the passenger side. 'Hello Mama,' she said, standing awkwardly.

'Darling.' Alma hugged her tight. 'It's so good to see you.' She stepped back to inspect her. 'Paris clearly suits you.'

'Having an occupation suits me,' replied Cordelia.

'It's such a pity about having no word from Kate, and Bianca being so far away. But at least there will be two Shakespeare sisters at Arden this Christmas.'

'Is Jamie here?'

'Yes, darling. He's in his room, he's so looking forward to seeing you.'

'I'll go and say hello.'

'Of course. And your papa...'

'I'll come down straight away. Tell Papa I've gone to change, if he asks.'

'Yes...' said Alma, as Cordelia brushed past her into the house.

'She doesn't mean to be rude,' said Rosalind, at the sight of the hurt on her stepmother's face. 'The last time she saw Jamie he was still in the hospital in France, when they thought he might never recover. I think she just wants to check his progress for herself. She's probably afraid we've been exaggerating.'

Alma forced a smile. 'That's understandable. I'll help you with the luggage. I'm sure by then tea will be ready, and we can all go in together.'

Papa was sitting in state in his favourite chair by the fire as Rosalind helped Lucy take in the tea tray.

'I take it she's arrived.'

'Yes, Papa. Cordelia just wanted to make herself look presentable.'

He sniffed. 'There's no need for that here.'

'It's a long train journey, Papa.'

'Ah, here she is,' said Alma quickly, as Cordelia appeared, her crumpled skirt exchanged for a woollen dress of deep green, the cut skimming her figure perfectly, accompanied by Jamie.

'You're going to have to show me,' Cordelia was saying. 'You really think there might be a chariot under there?'

'It's a possibility.'

'And all those times we played up there, we never knew.' She came to a halt at the doorway, chin lifting slightly. 'Good evening, Papa.'

He didn't look up from the fire. 'You considered it worth your while coming to visit us for Christmas, then.'

'I came to see you, Papa,' replied Cordelia. 'There have

been too many Christmases when we were unable to be together, or to celebrate because of the war. I'm glad some of us can be here this year. It's the best way to remember Will.'

'Hrmph,' growled their father, clearly irritated at being schooled by a daughter, and a mere chit of a girl, at that.

Across the room, Rosalind met her sister's eyes and smiled. Now she could see her clearly, Cordelia's stance had become self-assured. Even Papa seemed to sense that he had lost some of his power over her, any reprimand he might have been about to give dying on his lips.

'It's good to have you here,' said Jamie.

'And it's so good to see you looking so much better,' said Cordelia. 'Arden House has clearly done you the world of good. And the excavation, of course.'

'I don't see why Oswald and Bianca decided to go to France,' said Papa, irritably.

'I'm sure they have their reasons,' replied Jamie.

'I thought there was Christmas cake?'

'Lucy is just fetching it,' said Alma, rising from her seat, a slightly fraught look on her face. 'I'll go and help her. She has quite enough to do without waiting on us hand and foot.'

'What else is she employed for?' he snapped.

'As a cook,' said Jamie, ignoring their father's ill humour. 'Lucy has turned out to be an excellent cook. We should really be thinking of employing someone to help her and allow her to concentrate on what she does best. There are several hotels in Stratford advertising for cooks and at far higher wages than we could ever afford. We'll be lucky not to lose her.'

'Village food,' he muttered.

'Not everyone requires a French chef, Papa, and I'm sure Alma has plenty to do running the house without being required to become a cook as well.'

'Might keep her occupied,' he retorted, with a sniff. 'Instead of wandering off in the village, all hours. People will start to talk.'

There was a moment's silence. Rosalind gazed around at the familiar scene of the family gathering for Christmas. It was one she had longed for, all the years of the war, the fire sending warm light to illuminate the shelves of books adorning the walls of the library, the heavy brocade curtains drawn to keep in the warmth.

Alma had already brought out the nativity scene, which had been lovingly carved and painted by a Victorian ances-tor, and was now illuminated by a small candle. It had always been too precious to touch when they were children.

Rosalind remembered gazing mesmerised at the little scene each Christmas; at the sheep and cattle, and the small terrier Papa said had been made in honour of a beloved family pet, now buried in the animal cemetery in the grounds under the headstone declaring *Romeo, most faithful of friends.* Each year she would press her nose as close as she could get it, entranced by the flicker of candlelight over the attentive faces. How long ago that now seemed.

'I'm looking forward to hearing the choir,' said Cordelia, slightly wistfully. 'And Rosy said the Brierley Players are putting on a performance of *As You Like It* for Christmas.'

Papa sniffed. 'I expect you will be saying you're used to only the best and village fare isn't good enough for you now.'

Exasperation passed over Cordelia's face, quickly suppressed. *Cordelia has changed too*, thought Rosalind, free to scrutinise her sister's face from the shadows. There were fine creases at the corner of her eyes Rosalind had not seen before. Lines of strain and maybe also of sorrow. Cordelia had said very little about her life in France, apart from that she was working to help refugees from the fighting, and that she had plans to support herself with her dress-making skills, once things got more back to normal, with an ambition to make costumes for theatres, maybe even Hollywood, one day.

'I may be used to the best, Papa,' said Cordelia, quietly, 'but not so much that I can't appreciate seeing people I know and love doing their best.'

He looked up at that. 'Paris has made you forward. Not an attractive thing in a woman. No man will look at you twice.'

'You don't know that!'

'You sound very confident of the fact.' His eyes narrowed. 'In that case you had better stay here, where your stepmother can teach you how to behave.'

'I'm sure that can wait,' put in Jamie, with a quick shake of his head at Cordelia, who looked about to explode. 'We can decide on that after Christmas, surely, Papa? A new year, a new start. We've enough to get ready if we're to help Lucy and decorate the house as it used to be.'

'I'm not sure we should,' he replied, grumpily. 'Not respectful.'

'We agreed it was the best way to pay our respects to Will,' said Jamie.

'So we did, my dear,' added Alma, gently. 'To celebrate in Will's memory, just as the village is celebrating the memories of all those who have been lost.'

'Yes, that's true.' Papa's face eased. 'You're quite right, my boy. We'll celebrate Christmas in peace.' His eyes rested on Cordelia once more, before travelling to Rosalind. 'Then we'll start the new year with the household as it is meant to be.'

. . .

'He hasn't changed,' said Cordelia, when she and Rosalind finally escaped upstairs. 'He never will. You can see he's planning that neither of us will leave. He just wants us back under his control. I wish I'd never come.'

'It doesn't mean we have to do what he wants,' said Rosalind. 'We're both capable of earning our own living. Besides, I have my motorcycle, so you can always ride pillion as we do a midnight flit.'

Cordelia giggled. 'I like the idea of a moonlit flit.'

'Don't worry. He's been in a terrible temper since Bianca and Oswald said they were going to spend Christmas in the south of France.'

'I wish Kate was here, but the only thing I really want is for this Christmas, at least, to be peaceful.'

'So do I,' sighed Rosalind.

The morning of Christmas Eve dawned bright and clear, with a deep chill that sent frost flowers whitening the inside of the windows with exotic patterns, to melt into nothing as the sun rose in the sky. A scattering of snow had fallen overnight, crunching under foot as Rosalind joined Jamie and Cordelia heading to the small forest to collect the Christmas tree, to be decorated all ready for Christmas Eve itself.

The three fell silent as they reached the small glade of pines, first planted by their great-grandfather when Queen Victoria had brought in the fashion for Christmas trees, and grown for the purpose over the years.

'It was always Will who chose the tree,' said Cordelia at last. 'I'm not sure where we start.'

'It doesn't feel quite right,' agreed Rosalind.

Jamie gazed at the shapes of the boughs, needles glistening with frozen snow, eyes travelling from one to the other. 'Remember Will always made sure he chose the one for the next year too, so none of us could argue? That one over there, with the snow just starting to melt – I'm certain that was the one he selected, the last Christmas before the war.'

'So, it is,' said Cordelia. 'I remember we had an argument because it's slightly lopsided, but Will never would change his mind. He was always so like Papa. It's grown huge!'

'It feels right to let Will choose the tree this one last time.'

'Agreed.'

'Then I'll start. You'd better stand back, both of you.'

A snort erupted behind them. 'If you try to drop that, it'll fall on your heads.'

'Kate!' Rosalind swung round, blinking at the apparition appearing through the snow. 'When did you arrive?'

'Just now. You aren't the only one who can drive, Rosy.' Their sister cut a distinctive figure as she strode to join them, black hair as short as ever, a long trench coat flapping behind her, revealing a pair of men's trousers, oversized and kept up at the waist by a study belt. 'Lucy told me you'd come to get the tree. You're in luck, I worked as a woodsman for a while during the war. I can drop a tree within inches of where I choose.'

'If you're sure,' said her brother, uncertainly.

'Now don't disappoint me, Jamie, darling. You sound almost like Papa, and Will, trying to be his shadow. You never were like either of them.'

'I never could be.'

'Which is why I love you most of all,' said Kate, smile turning irresistible. 'I'm sure you're not too proud to admit that you might be infinitely more skilled than me at uncovering what lies beneath the earth, but I'm more knowledge-able about chopping down the things that stand above.'

Jamie laughed, the unexpected sound echoing around the snow-silent trees. Rosalind held back tears, aware of Cordelia hastily banishing her own. Kate's smile barely flickered, but the swallow in her throat told its own story.

'How can I resist that challenge?' he said, sounding more like the Jamie of before the war, the quiet one of the family, who had adored his elder brother above all things, but had always been more comfortable in the company of his sisters, and in the quiet grubbing of the earth to reveal its secrets.

'Good,' replied Kate, taking the axe. Just for a second, her air of bravado cracked a little. 'I'm glad I decided to come, after all. You should never be afraid of what you might find. We're all stronger than we think, when it comes to it.'

'I hope we are,' said Jamie quietly. 'Even when broken.'

She and Jamie took turns to cut grooves under her instruction, forming a triangular shape, until the pine finally dropped neatly into a patch of grass at one side.

'Perfect. At least now I know I haven't lost the knack,' said Kate, breathing hard as she eyed her handiwork with satisfaction. 'I'd say I've earnt my Christmas dinner, and if Papa tries bossing me around I'm leaving. I'll sleep in my van again, if needs be.'

'I'm glad you came,' said Rosalind. 'It wouldn't be the same without you.'

'As I said, I only really came to see this archaeological dig you've all been telling me about,' Kate muttered, awkwardly.

Jamie took hold of the trunk, with its resin scent of cut pine filling the air. 'I'll take you up to the burial mound once we've got the tree back to the house.'

'But you've got to be back in time to help us decorate it,' said Cordelia. 'We're not breaking tradition and doing it without you, Kate. The tree always was the domain of the Shakespeare sisters. Although I think we can forgive Bianca this year.'

'It's freezing up there,' said Jamie with a smile. 'Don't worry, we couldn't do any digging, even if we wanted to. We'll be back in plenty of time.'

Little was said as they dragged the tree back to the house, with none of the noisy triumph of childhood Christmases, when it had always been Papa, then Will, taking sole charge of the tree, the rest of them tagging along behind as witnesses. The rest of Christmas, the preparation of cakes and mince pies and the decorating of the tree, had always been a feminine affair, with the males of the household resting on their laurels for the rest of the festive period, bringing in great logs, ready seasoned, for the fire, and shepherding them all down through even the thickest of snow to Brierley-in-Arden for the latest offering from the Brierley Players, followed by carols at midnight.

'The delivery from Mrs Ackrite's has got through after all,' said Jamie as they reached the driveway. 'Alma was sure it would be too icy.'

Rosalind let go of her branch. 'That's far too smart a car for Mrs Ackrite.'

'Oh, my lord,' whispered Cordelia. 'That's Oswald.'

'It can't be,' said Jamie in undisguised dismay. 'They're in France.'

'Obviously not,' said Kate, darkly, as a large greatcoat emerged from the driver's side, opening the passenger door to allow the extravagant fox fur of Bianca to slide out elegantly, with a distinct lack of enthusiasm.

'Looks like they are planning to stay,' said Rosalind, as

the two made their way to the front door, leaving the new nursemaid, barely more than a child herself, to struggle out with the boys and follow in their wake.

The dragging of the tree slowed to a crawl.

'Turning up at all hours used to be bad enough,' exclaimed Lucy, spotting them and shooting over with the air of a woman in dire need of giving vent to her feelings. 'But inviting themselves for Christmas, right up to New Year, that takes the biscuit. With that posh home to go to, and no warning, neither. Not to mention throwing out orders about bringing in the cases.'

'We'll do that,' said Rosalind. 'The tree can wait, we're not decorating it until this evening.'

'Well, I wouldn't say no,' said Lucy. 'Lord knows if we've enough in, even after saving up all we could from the rations and getting extra in from the farms. It feels like more snow on the way, and the delivery from the village's not come.'

'The sun's melting the ice, and Oswald and Kate got through,' said Jamie. 'There are plenty of stores left in the kitchen garden and I'll walk down and see if the grocer's in Brierley has anything left.'

'I'll drive you down,' said Kate. 'My van's ex-army – it can deal with ice, and it has plenty of storage. I'm sure we can find an additional half a pig from one of the farms on the way. That should keep them quiet.'

'I'm not spending Christmas sawing up beasts,' said Lucy firmly.

'Don't worry, we'll stick to a haunch,' replied Jamie, with a grin. 'And if the worst comes to the worst, we'll go out and hunt our own venison.'

'Then you're cooking it,' retorted Lucy, returning inside with what sounded suspiciously like a chuckle.

The back of the car was crammed full of smart suitcases

and boxes, accompanied by bags of parcels wrapped with expensive-looking wrapping paper.

'Well, those will put our home-made gifts to shame,' said Cordelia dryly.

'And my framed illustrations,' added Kate. 'I'm not sure why I bothered dragging them all the way here.'

'They've been made with love and that's what counts,' said Rosalind firmly. 'Although the question is, what on earth are they doing here, when they should be lording it up a fashionable hotel with their rich friends and Hollywood movie stars?'

Jamie pulled out a large, wrapped parcel in the unmistakeable shape of a rocking horse. 'I can't help having a bad feeling about this,' he said.

Chapter Thirty-Seven

Rosalind paused at the library door, tea tray in hand. Oswald and Bianca were settled in their customary armchairs, Bianca next to Papa and Oswald directly opposite, between the three of them almost blocking out the warmth of the fire, despite the additional logs brought in from the forest to celebrate the season.

'You shouldn't be doing that, my dear,' said Papa, looking up with a frown. 'Where's Lucy?'

'Preparing tonight's meal and working out how to stretch all our rations to make additional pies for Christmas dinner,' said Rosalind, pointedly. 'Mama is helping her. Did you know Kate has arrived?'

'She hasn't been in to see me,' he complained.

'She'll be in soon. She's gone with Jamie to see if Mrs Ackrite has anything left that's off the ration. They said they might have a look at the work on the burial mound on the way back, while the light lasts.'

'We brought wine,' said Bianca stiffly, cheeks turning a

bright pink that had nothing to do with the heat of the fire. 'And Cook's plum pudding we were taking with us to France.'

'And brandy, the finest from our cellar,' put in Oswald, smiling blandly at Papa. 'I know you appreciate a good brandy, sir.'

'Yes, indeed.' Pride soothed, Papa forgot Kate's lack of suitable fealty. 'We haven't had brandy, or wine come to that, all the years of the war. Most appreciated. Most unfortunate, the circumstances, but we're glad to see you.'

Rosalind laid down the tray. 'Unfortunate?'

'The shipping company mislaid our booking,' said Oswald. 'Incompetent fools. And every berth taken. I shall be sending in a strongly worded complaint in the morning. They offered to recompense us, of course, and to put us on the next liner out. Far too late. I've no intention of spending Christmas in some inferior guesthouse. And besides, Bianca never made a secret of preferring to spend Christmas here, did you, my dear.'

'No indeed,' said Bianca, shuffling uncomfortably in her seat. 'And how could I not wish to spend it with you, Papa? Especially as this is a commemoration for our poor dear Will.'

'Yes indeed,' sighed Papa, patting her hand. 'You're a good girl.'

'I'm sure there are many others who would like to celebrate poor William's life,' added Oswald. 'Everyone who knew him admired and respected him.'

'So they did. Villages are already putting up commemorations to the men who were lost, alongside those from the Great War. We should do that in Brierley, too. Things will never be the same.'

'No indeed,' said Oswald, 'your words are very perceptive sir, as they always are.'

Rosalind busied herself pouring tea and handing round a plate of Lucy's ginger biscuits, made from a suspiciously large bag of flour Kate had brought with her, accompanied by butter and the miracle of oranges. Kate had forbidden an open-mouthed Lucy to ask questions – *and no, she didn't sell her body for any of them, she wasn't that daft.* Bianca, she saw, was back to shuffling.

'Don't you agree, my dear Bianca?' added Oswald, voice sharpening. The shuffling ceased.

'Yes, of course.' Bianca sat up straight, the crimson velvet of her gown, too full to owe anything to rationing, sweeping in folds around her. 'Darling Papa, we always relied on you for your wisdom.'

This was a bit much, even for their father.

'Well, none of you ever took a blind bit of notice when you lived here,' he retorted, taking a large bite of biscuit.

Bianca smiled. 'I hope we have learnt better now. Don't you think, Rosalind?'

'I feel certain we must have all grown wiser,' replied Rosalind, blandly. Oswald's eyes narrowed.

'Are you going to decorate the tree this evening?' put in Bianca hastily. 'I'm sure George would love to see the decorations go up, just like Will did, when he was a child.'

'Yes, indeed,' said Papa.

'And Hubert has started to take so much more notice of his surroundings. Your only grandchildren, dear Papa,' added Bianca. 'The ones who will carry on the bloodline, whatever happens. It must be *such* a comfort.'

'Indeed.'

'I'll fetch another pot of tea,' said Rosalind, fleeing with the tray as fast as her heels could take her.

'Well?' demanded Lucy, looking up from her efficient rolling out of pastry.

'No idea,' replied Rosalind. 'But they are up to something.'

Lucy transferred the pastry to a large pie tin with a flourish. 'And ain't that a surprise.'

'What kind of something?' demanded Alma, busily chopping cabbage and turnip to go with the meat sizzling in a pan, in a bid to supplement the small amount of lamb already gently roasting in the oven with as many potatoes as could be fitted alongside.

'No idea, but I'm ashamed to say Papa is lapping it up.'

'I can imagine. But why didn't they go to France?' said Alma. 'That's what I want to know. Bianca told me some story about a lost booking, but someone as rich and important as Oswald isn't going to be turned away. They'd throw some lesser mortals off first before risking losing his custom, if you ask me.'

'Well,' said Lucy, conspiratorially, 'I took the liberty of taking a cup of tea and some toast up to the nursemaid. She looked frozen and half famished, poor thing, she's only been with them a month, and trying to deal with two young boys ain't the easiest at the best of times. What Florrie said was that they never got near no boat. Didn't get further than the Gorwells' fancy house in London. There was a terrible row between Mr Gorwell and his father, that's what she said. Something about bringing the family name into disrepute.'

'It probably means he has a particularly notorious mistress,' said Alma, gloomily. 'It usually does. Poor Bianca.'

'Wasn't that,' said Lucy, who was clearly enjoying herself. 'Florrie wouldn't say exactly. But she did ask me if there was any employment going here. Now she wouldn't be asking that for no reason, would she?'

'She could just want to stop being a nursemaid?' said Rosalind.

Lucy grinned. 'Or he could have gone bust.'

'Oswald?' Alma's knife bounced from the frostbitten carrot she was slicing, clattering onto the flagstones. 'That's impossible.'

'Is it?' Through the steam rising from her pan, Lucy's smile was positively devilish. 'There was talk in the village, only I thought it were just Brierley gossip, and that can get out of hand. Like that one about there being a pair of star-crossed lovers buried in that mound, when everyone knows Kitty Evans and Charlie Smeaton are living in Manchester, and not a thing that bully of a husband of hers can do about it. Bet Evans wishes he throttled her when he had the chance, instead of only half doing the job and going down the White Hart, giving her the chance to run—'

'Oh my goodness,' said Alma, turning bright red as she bent to retrieve the knife. 'How dreadful.'

'Not for Kitty, did her a favour, giving her no choice if she loved life as well as Charlie. Last I heard, her and Charlie were doing so well in their business they'd even bought their own house, and had six kiddies between them, and all. While old Herbert Evans is still as miserable as sin—'

'So what did you hear about Oswald?' put in Rosalind hastily, as Lucy appeared to launch into even more lurid details.

'Shoddy work. Too fond of cutting corners, and got away with it so long he was cocky with it. And underhand dealings, and all.' Lucy was definitely enjoying herself. 'Might have got away with it this time, too, but he tried it with that big house he was building for the artist in Stratford. Someone told the client. Gorwell tried to get out of it, but there was paperwork to back it up.'

She lowered her voice. 'Which must mean it was someone he employed, who had a grudge, or didn't like what he was doing. Of course, saying no names, but there are one or two guesses in the village. Old Mr Ford found a ham and a real plum pudding on his doorstep yesterday. And a bottle of whisky, and all. If you take my meaning.'

'Surely a scandal like that would have found its way into the papers,' said Alma, dubiously.

'Stratford is small fry,' replied Lucy. 'If you ask me, it's the rest of his work in London that really counts. And that new hotel he told the vicar he was building for some Hollywood movie star in France. He always did look down his nose at artists, didn't see how you could make a fortune with just blobs of paint and scrawls. I expect he thought Mr Keithley was the type to have inherited his fortune, when everyone in Brierley could have told him that Mr Keithley is so famous he knows everybody who's anybody, and his wife was a lady-in-waiting when he married her and knows even more. Rumour is, he's been commissioned to paint a portrait of Mr Churchill, and you can't get more connected than that. If you ask me, no one will touch Oswald Gorwell with a bargepole. Like I said, bust.'

'Oh,' said Alma. 'Well, if that's the case—'

'Which it is.'

'—Then he must be looking for work to salvage his fortune, if not his reputation.'

Rosalind paused in swilling out the teapot. 'Which is why he must be insisting on the old scheme for building a whole host of grand summer houses on Arden land.'

'And the road,' said Lucy. 'When I saw Miss Parsons yesterday, she said she'd been given notice the hall and the museum would be demolished straight after New Year.'

'He can't do that!' exclaimed Alma.

'If Papa agrees, he can,' said Rosalind, slowly. 'And not even Jamie can do anything about it if he won't – or can't – listen. The village is on Arden land. Papa can do as he pleases.'

'Then it's my fault,' said Alma, bursting into tears. 'Leo hated me going to singing so often, even if it was just once a week, and a few times more over the past month to get ready for Christmas. He was always trying to dissuade me. I'm sure he thinks if the village hall is gone, there'll be nowhere for the singers to meet and I'll be back at home looking after him day and night, with no interests of my own.'

'Don't worry, Mrs Arden,' said Lucy, 'we'll work something out.' She bent down to check the roast. 'And Mr Fairfield isn't one to give up so easily.'

'No, no, that is definitely true,' murmured Alma, returning to her vegetables, face hidden.

'Bankrupt?' exclaimed Kate, warming her hands against the fire in Rosalind's bedroom. 'Really? Oswald? How perfectly delicious.'

'Not for Bianca, or for those poor boys, who never asked for anything of this,' retorted Cordelia.

'I'll feel sorry for George and Hubert,' Kate conceded, reaching for the toasting fork hung up at the side of the fireplace. 'And I'd even have some sympathy for Bianca, if she wasn't still hinting Jamie should be confined to an asylum. She collared me just now, as we were unloading the van, and I'm sure she was well aware Jamie was within hearing.'

'Those poor boys,' sighed Cordelia. 'No wonder you said they are like Jack-in-the-boxes as soon as their parents are out of sight, Rosy. Imagine having to live with all that scheming day and night.'

'I'm sure Bianca is fond of them,' replied Rosalind. 'But she doesn't seem to have much time to even listen to them.'

'And poor Jamie,' said Kate, stabbing one of Lucy's fluffiest crumpets with the toasting fork, as if wishing it was piercing a heart instead. 'You should have seen him at the burial mound, he was quite like he used to be. And yet not – Bianca can say what she likes, but he seemed more self-assured than I've ever seen him.' She held the pitted round to the flames. 'A man rather than a boy, I suppose.'

'Just as we are no longer girls,' said Rosalind.

The three of them crouched around the fire in silence, as Kate's blue fingers turned to a more healthy shade and the smell of toasting filled the air.

Cordelia sighed, wistfully. 'We used to do this when we were in disgrace and Papa wouldn't let us join them for dinner.'

'And I was always the one sent to worm bread and butter for toast from Cook,' said Rosalind.

'Well, you were the best at persuading her,' Kate pointed out. 'And you usually came back with teacake and muffins as well. With all the shortages and everything, I bet none of us have had teacake in years.' She dislodged the crumpet onto the waiting plate, next to the butter dish, and speared her next offering. 'It seems so long ago. Of course it won't ever be the same again, however hard we pretend. It does feel like an ending.'

'I'd rather think of it as a beginning,' said Cordelia, taking charge of the buttering. 'The war is over. Things will get back more to normal soon, despite all the destruction and the suffering. We've got the rest of our lives ahead of us.'

'And surely between us we can stop Oswald from tearing the heart out of Brierley,' said Rosalind. 'I'm hoping now he won't have the means, however much he tries to persuade

Papa.' *Which is why he needs Henry*, came the thought, unbidden, into her mind.

The three sat silently for a while, basking in the warmth of the fire and the unfamiliar luxury of the buttery stickiness of toasted crumpets.

'Whatever Papa thinks, I'm going back to France. I'm not going to stay here,' said Cordelia, at last, sucking the last of the butter appreciatively from her fingers.

'No one can force you to stay,' said Rosalind.

'Except Papa keeps on about the three of us disgracing the family by not being here so he can keep an eye on our morals, and Alma looking panicky whenever I mention Paris, as if she thinks it's the road to becoming a prostitute. I've tried to tell her I'm on a reasonable income and I'm working far too hard to even think about sex, but you can see she thinks it's her duty to keep me a virginal prisoner here.'

'I'd say that was the best argument for leaving,' said Rosalind.

'Will you?' demanded Kate, eyeing her curiously.

Rosalind looked around the room, with its security and its familiarity. In this brief moment of life held at bay, as snow and Christmas festivities took over, she could have stayed forever. But even without the prospect of Henry Luscombe appearing for New Year, she could feel the house closing around her as the short day sank towards darkness, and, even in the stillness, the beams in the rafters began to creak.

'I can't stay here, either, once Christmas is over,' she said. 'Even if I'm never allowed home again. I feel sorry for Alma, but I need to live own life, and Papa will never let me do that, not in a million years.'

Kate poked the fire into a scattering of sparks, followed

by a deep orange glow of flames at its heart. 'I'm returning to Italy. For now, at least.'

'But then?' demanded Cordelia.

There was a moment's silence. Kate had told them very little about her life in Naples. Rosalind could sense emotions wrestling inside her, ones she was not ready to share. *Another story, for another time*, was the unspoken message in their sister's change of subject whenever her work during the war, or her life now, was raised.

'You're right about Shakespeare being in the blood,' Kate said, at last. 'I'd like to know more about those volumes your mother left to all of us and who illustrated them.' She fell silent again, into the embers. 'And why I was included.'

'You're our sister,' said Cordelia, stoutly.

'Am I?' She pulled her thick cardigan around her, as if still not quite able to banish the chill that had entered her bones from staying too long in the snow at the burial mound. 'Do you remember, Miss Parsons said your mother loved me as much as if I was her own. But I'm not her own. I remember my real mother. English isn't even my native tongue. I need to know why I was left a volume that contains all the varieties of love. Don't you see, I have to find out, if I can? I'm not even sure I know the country I come from, or who I am. Or if I can call myself a Shakespeare sister at all.'

'Darling Kate, you'll always be one of us,' exclaimed Cordelia, hugging her tightly.

'Of course you will,' added Rosalind.

Kate looked up at that, tears glistening in her eyes. 'I don't deserve it, and especially from you, Rosy, I was so horrible to you before you left. I was envious. I thought I'd never be free. I never thought it would be such a terrible thing as a war that would give me my freedom. Will used to drive me mad, but now I'd give anything to have him back, and for Jamie to be just as he used to be, and nothing to have changed.'

'I feel the same,' said Rosalind, putting her arms around her. 'And you were right, I wasn't thinking of you, or Cordelia; I was so desperate to escape. I suppose we all were, in our own way. And you might not be able to help Will, none of us can, but you've helped Jamie in the best way anyone could by coming back and going to see the burial mound. You're the one who always shared his love of archae-ology. I love what he finds, but I don't have the knowledge, not like you do.'

'And I haven't a clue,' confessed Cordelia.

Kate sighed. 'I'm not sure I've really done anything. You're making me feel guilty for abandoning you all.'

'Of course you didn't!' said Rosalind. 'And none of us can expect you to stay. Just being here for this Christmas, when we are remembering Will, and letting Jamie show you the burial mound is enough. Don't you see, it's Jamie's passion for this place, and for uncovering the burial mound that is bringing him back to himself. It might not be the old Jamie, but I have a feeling that he's stronger and more compas-sionate that he might ever have been.'

'If we can just make Papa see it,' said Cordelia, gloomily. 'So much for *"we that are young shall never see so much, nor live so long".'*

'Well, I'm not sure King Lear was always very wise,' returned Rosalind, smiling. 'Although at least he learnt to be simply human at the end. Sometimes, I can see Papa almost throwing off his own illusions of grandeur, but there's always something that pulls him back. Usually Oswald and Bianca. They really do bring out the worst in him.'

'I wish he could see all that posturing doesn't matter,' said Cordelia. 'That we'd love him just as much if he wasn't always trying to play God. Probably even more, if he would let us.'

'Don't hold your breath,' snorted Kate.

'I didn't find anything,' said Cordelia, abruptly.

Kate frowned at her. 'Anything?'

'In the books of Shakespeare plays Miss Parsons gave us. She said there were messages for us, remember? I've looked and looked, but there's nothing there.'

'You might have missed it,' muttered Kate, busily stirring the logs on the dying fire back into crackling life, before adding more from the basket by the fireplace.

Cordelia shook her head. 'I've read the plays through, time and time again.'

'Have you thought about the illustrations?' said Rosalind. Kate's newest addition tumbled from the flames in a swirl of smoke, narrowly missing singeing the threadbare Persian rug.

'The illustrations?' exclaimed Cordelia, as Kate busied herself replacing the fallen log and inspecting the rug for any sparks that might yet send it up in flames, her face hidden from view. 'Of course! Why didn't I think of that? I was so sure there was something hidden in the binding, and I bet it was there in front of my nose, all along.'

'You never know,' replied Rosalind.

Cordelia's head tilted to one side, like a Robin sizing up the worm-providing possibilities of the nearest human. 'So, is that how found your message?'

'I'm not sure,' replied Rosalind, fighting down a blush. She began tidying away the plates and knives, aware of her sisters waiting, not daring to ask, in that silent agreement of theirs, unless she volunteered the information.

Not yet. The hints she had found in Rosalind and Orlando's courtship were too close to her own heart to confess without disclosing a far larger secret, one too big for the three of them to keep for the whole of Christmas Day without someone guessing, and risking Papa's incandescent fury.

Not now. Not yet.

This Christmas was about remembering Will and all the Christmases they had ever shared. Her own future, with its potential to rip the family apart, had to wait until it was over.

Most of all, she could not share the final indentation she had found below the illustration of Rosalind, cropped hair curling around her face as she gazed passionately into the distance, above the quotation exclaiming *'how many fathom deep I am in love!'* The very memory set her heart racing uncontrollably.

Rosalind hastily finished her clearing away, ignoring her sisters' curiosity, and jumped to her feet. 'Come on, it's time to decorate the tree, or it will never be done, and I'm sure George will love to be allowed to join in.'

As the three raced down to join the rest of the family, they found Jamie had already secured the Christmas tree in the hallway. With the afternoon beginning to fade, they helped George and Hubert place decorations from the box, filled with memories of the times they had done so as children, each one a memory of a Christmas past. Some were of delicately blown glass baubles, brought back from Venice by their grandfather, others of painted papier mâché created by their mother, amongst the stars and the angels they had each made as children. Finally, they clipped on the metal candle holders with their tall red candles, all ready to be lit.

'Now it begins to feel like Christmas,' said Alma, emerging hot and flushed from the kitchen. 'I believe we finally have enough to feed everyone handsomely and that tree is as beautiful as any I remember.'

'There are just these,' said Cordelia, taking a wooden box from the small trunk where the Arden decorations had been kept for generations.

Alma swallowed. 'Perhaps we shouldn't.'

'I think we should,' said Cordelia.

'It's going to be upsetting whether they are there or not,' said Rosalind, gently. 'There's nothing that can ever bring Will back. Just for this once, for one last time.'

Alma nodded. Cordelia opened the box to reveal a miniature hot air balloon, along with perfect miniature replicas of Spitfires and a Lancaster bomber carved out of wood, accompanied by a tiny Bentley.

'Will had quite a talent,' said Cordelia, as each one was carefully hung in pride of place, where they would catch the best light from the candles.

'Funny how we never noticed how skilled he was at making things when he was telling us how brilliant he was at everything else,' sighed Kate.

'At least we can appreciate it now,' said Rosalind.

'Very pretty.' The front door opened, allowing in a cold wind, accompanied by a swirl of snow, and Oswald swept through, enveloped by a long fur coat. 'At least the Shakespeare sisters have some talent, even if it is only for decoration.'

From the corner of her eye, Rosalind saw Cordelia tread firmly on Kate's foot, stilling the explosion rising to her lips.

'It's time for tea, before we go down to the village,' she said. 'I'll let Lucy know that you're back.'

'And lay an additional place.' Oswald's face was a smirk.

'Additional?'

'Didn't your father tell you? We're lucky to have an honoured guest, perfect for a celebration of William's life.'

Rosalind turned as Papa stomped out of the library,

leaning on his walking stick. 'Good, good.' He said, smiling complacently. 'Come on in, come on in. As I told you, Rosalind is the most excellent manager, she has created a perfect Christmas from nothing.'

'So I see,' said Henry Luscombe, stepping inside.

Chapter Thirty-Eight

She had to make him see sense, if it was the last thing she did. Rosalind gritted her teeth and slipped into the library, while the rest of the household prepared to take the brief journey down to the village for the Brierley Players' performance of *As You Like It*, followed by Christmas carols.

'Papa, I'm not going to marry Henry Luscombe, however long he stays. Besides, shouldn't he be spending Christmas with his own family, rather than being cooped up here with us? We all worked so hard to get the Arden family together to remember Will and celebrate that Jamie is so recovered.'

'My dear,' returned her father, without looking up from the fire. 'I know you have done your very best for your brother, as a good sister should, but I'm afraid we're going to have to face the fact that Jamie is never going to be strong.'

'But you've seen for yourself that's not true!'

He shuffled uneasily, dignity as thin as paper. A man with no choices left, and far too proud to admit the fact, even to himself. With a sinking heart, she saw that Papa had thrown his belief behind Oswald, considering the alternative too dreadful to consider.

What on earth had Oswald done?

'When it comes to the mind, that is,' he muttered. 'I've agreed that Jamie should begin his studies with the Archae-ology Department of Birmingham University next year, once they have completed the excavation of the burial mound and Oswald is able to start work. He's being very patient about waiting, he truly cares for Jamie, as well as the family. He's suggesting a life in academia may well be the best to preserve poor Jamie's mental state. Digging in the past, that sort of thing.'

'That's Jamie's passion, but it's not all his life, Papa!' She controlled an urge to shake some sense into him. 'Don't you see? Jamie loves the past because it's Brierley's past, and that of the Ardens and Arden House. It's the past that made us all. The beautiful and the vile, the kind and the unspeakably cruel. Jamie loves this land more than any of us have ever done, even Will. He's been through so much, and dug so deep to return to us, he won't need rich socialites in fancy summer houses to look down on us to keep Arden and Brierley safe. However hopeless things might look now, he'll find another way. That's what love does.'

Papa was silent. She saw his shoulders stiffen, the twisting struggle inside him between the vanity fed so care-fully by Oswald and Bianca, and the words she knew had hit home. Deep inside, the heart of the romantic young man who had once married for love and had been loved through all his weaknesses, his changes and his petty tyrannies, still recog-nised the truth.

She loved him at that moment more than she had ever done. She wished more than anything to hold onto the man who might have been, who was more like his younger son than he would ever admit. Who had once, with love, had the capacity to become the finest of human beings, filled with an adoration of beauty, tempered with compassion, content in the privileges of this small portion of the vast world he had inherited.

At the same time, she despaired.

'George and young Hubert are fine boys,' he said at last. 'They've Arden blood in them, after all. Bianca is right. They'll be the ones to keep Arden safe. It is up to us – all of us – to support their future in the best way we can.' His shoulders shrunk in on themselves, as if he had plunged an invisible knife into his own heart.

There was nothing to be said. Grief went in deep through Rosalind, with a terrible finality. Not even love could save him from himself. That was the truth of that last vision of her mother, pale on the bed, the fight gone out of her as fever raged through her body. She must have used the last of her strength to summon Miss Parsons, to leave the last messages for her daughters, trusting that one day they would understand. The things she could not say, maybe could never have said, had she lived. A truth too deep and too agonising to be spoken face to face. Of love freely given, and love stifled. Of the deep human desire to be free, to make sense of the one life given, the one life lived, the passion that still burns within, however much it is extinguished. And of the life-giving power of true love, in all its glorious and infinitely varied forms.

'Yes, Papa,' she said quietly.

He straightened. The world was ordered as it should be, he was lord of his domain once more. She wondered, in his avoidance of her gaze, if he also, somewhere in his heart, understood the love he had thrown away. 'We should be getting ready, it'll soon be time to attend the village performance.'

'I'll see if Mama has finished helping Lucy.'

He coughed. 'I'm not sure we should stay to hear the carols in the church. Your mama will be a little disappointed not to join in, but her duty is here with her family. It looks as if it might well snow, and we don't want to be stuck in the village on Christmas Eve.'

There was nothing to say. She had no fight left. Rosalind fled before tears overwhelmed her.

Snow was already beginning to fall as they took the short walk to the village. Oswald and Bianca made their way down in style, despite the lane already almost too slippery for the Bentley. Of Jamie, there was no sign.

The sinking sun sent a pinkish glow across the swathes of white covering the roll of the fields and muffling the surrounding woodland. Rosalind glanced up at the burial mound, now sharply etched in white between the dark fingers of branches. To her relief, there was no sound of digging or scraping in the still air. So, Jamie had not retreated into his private world, unable to face their unexpected visitor. Surely Jamie would never give up so easily and allow Oswald and Henry to manipulate their father into doing their bidding?

In a flash, she remembered Edmund emerging from the museum, and his warning as he rode off into the night. Miss Parsons thanking him. The gifts placed outside his father's cottage. Something fell into place, with the faintest spark of hope. All was not lost. Not yet.

The village always did have the quiet kind of rebellion that has nothing to do with pitchforks and cannonballs, or even the screaming of insults, but rebellion good and proper, all the same. Brierley-in-Arden had never been known for armed resistance, not having anything remotely military (apart from the odd farmer's gun of the generally unpredictable variety) to hand. Digging its heels in was more the Brierley way. Silent, stubborn, unmoveable resistance, of the kind difficult to identify as such, let alone justify sending in the constables. Might just make a fool of any man who tried.

The village was where Jamie had gone, she felt certain. He knew something. He had to. And she was just as sure any answers lay hidden deep within Miss Parson's museum, where Oswald, who considered it beneath his dignity to acknowledge that middle-aged schoolmistresses existed at all, would never think of looking. At this moment, Rosalind loved the village more than she had ever done.

'Take care!' She had been distracted too long. The others had moved a few steps ahead in the narrowest part of the path, with the sharp thorns of sloes on either side forcing them to go in single file, and her arm was being firmly seized. 'You could break an ankle.'

'In walking boots, hardly,' she retorted, shaking off Henry, whose own highly polished shoes were slipping and sliding on the snow as if he had chosen to skate.

'I'm glad to see you chose to stay at Arden House for Christmas. I would have hated to have missed you. Now we will be under the same roof for the entire festive season, plenty of time for me to make you see sense.'

Cold fury went through her. But that's what he wanted, to intimidate her, make her lose her temper. She wasn't about to give him the pleasure.

'I doubt it,' she replied, coolly.

'Oh, come on, don't be like that. You know you're going to have to give in. Women always do. They make a fuss first –

that's what makes the chase so exciting.' He seized her arm once more, despite the catching of his expensive coat on the most protruding of the thorns. 'Come on, Rosy, we're both adults. I can see you're not the innocent little chit who so charmed me before the war. London has hardened you. I'm well aware of the kind of things you girls got up to during the, shall we say, rather more lax times of blackouts, and the like.'

'You don't say.' They were nearly at the village. In a few moments the path would widen again and she could escape his proximity.

'Not that it matters to me. Lessens the piquance of the wedding night, but then we both know that's not what this is about. Oswald made it quite clear this marriage is of a trans-actional nature.'

Her determination to ignore him evaporated. *Of all the—* 'You've arranged to marry me with *Oswald*?'

'Of course. As nominal head of the family.'

'Then he lied to you. He's not nominal head of anything.'

'What with your father starting to lose his faculties, and your brother unable to face the world – that's what they are saying among his friends and in society. Now I can tell them it's the truth.'

'My father has as many faculties as he ever had, and it's plain to see that Jamie has recovered from his injuries and there's nothing wrong with his mind. I've had enough of your insults, I'm joining my sisters.'

'I'm sure you wouldn't want to see your family bankrupt.' That worked, as he must know it would. 'Imagine the shame, all over the papers, the whisper in every corner. Your father would never be able to hold up his head in society, not after losing the Arden Estate, possibly to be forced to live out his declining years in one of his own cottages. If he's lucky and it's not the workhouse. I wouldn't be surprised if the shame didn't kill him. And not to mention your sisters – do you really want a life of penury for them?'

'I'm not interested in your blackmail.'

'Even if it's the truth? You must have heard rumours about Oswald's, shall we say, slight difficulties?'

'That's Oswald's business. That's nothing to do with the Ardens. I'm sorry for Bianca, but it's not my concern.'

'As I said, as nominal, and presumably so soon to be, head of the Arden family, Oswald should be your concern. Your first consideration. The fact that your father has signed papers to allow Oswald to take responsibility of the estate, and fulfil his debts, so forfeiting Arden should Oswald's business fail, how can that not be your consideration?'

Rosalind came to a halt, her worst fears shooting through her body. 'Papa would never endanger Arden. He'd never sign the estate away, however much he trusted Oswald. If that's true, Oswald must have tricked him.'

'The signature is genuine, I can assure you. And witnessed by Gorwell's solicitor. An excellent fellow. I use him myself. There was no question your father was in command of his faculties when he signed. So that, you see, my dear Rosy, is the transaction. I bail Oswald out from his current financial difficulties, and provide the backing for him to turn the Arden Estate into a summer retreat for those wealthy enough to afford it, so allowing your father to live in the house for as long as he's capable of recognising his surroundings.

'I've informed Oswald that all he needs in turn is to provide me with a wife. A nice, quiet little wife, who knows it's in her best interest, as well as that of her family, to keep my dear Papa, and my acquaintances – maybe even the law – convinced that I am a happily married man. You can do that, can't you, my dear?'

'Don't be ridiculous. If we're going to be honest about it, you dislike me just as much as I loathe you. Of course I'm not going to marry you.'

'A pity. In that case, I might choose to withdraw my financial backing, meaning your father and stepmother could well be cast out into the cold before the year is out.'

'And I suppose you think threats make you more of a man?' Rosalind retorted. 'Well, you can't bully me into ruining the rest of my life.'

The path had widened, Rosalind pulled herself free joining Cordelia, doing her best to calm her breathing. He had to be bluffing. Surely?

Within minutes they had reached the village, picking their way through the winding streets with glow of candles from downstairs windows on either side, as families gathered for Christmas Eve. All was still and quiet, with none of the merriment spilling out from the White Hart as there had been before the war. It was more a sombre air, in memory of all those who had been lost, than wild celebration.

As they reached the village hall, Miss Parsons greeted them, looking slightly anxious. 'I'm so sorry, Mr Arden, I was just about to send someone to meet you, to let you know.' Glancing beyond her, Rosalind could see that, rather than being filled with the usual audience breathless with anticipation for the evening's play, the hall was empty, apart from Mr Fairfield, who was sitting at the piano, ten or so of his choral society gathered around, going through 'In the Bleak Midwinter'.

'Let me know?' Papa was clearly standing on his dignity.

'I'm afraid we have had to postpone this evening's play. The snow is already too deep to expect the performers from the outlying farms to risk being stranded here and missing Christmas with their families.'

'*What shall I give him?*' came hushed tones, as the singers at the piano reached the final verse, followed by the triumphant reply, '*Give him my heart.*'

Miss Parsons cleared her throat. 'Mr Fairfield thinks he might be able to manage a short carol service at midnight, with just the singers who live in the village, but of course that won't be for some time yet. It seems a pity to break with tradition and not sing in the turning of Christmas Eve into Christmas.'

'*Si-i-lent night,*' began the choir. '*Ho-o-ly night, all is still, all is bright...*'

'Mr Gorwell has gone to see if he can secure the main room at the White Hart, so you can rest and warm up before he takes you home.'

'A public house?' Their father sounded horrified at such an indignity foisted on the lord of Arden.

'Well, I'm frozen,' announced Kate. 'I think we should go to the White Hart and warm up a bit, so we can get back before we're completely cut off.'

'We can always read *As You Like It* to you, Papa,' said Cordelia, taking his arm and steering him towards the door. 'Like we used to read plays at Christmas, when Will was alive.'

'It's all right,' said Jamie, arriving breathlessly through the door, a scattering of snow caking his hair. 'Mr Fairfield has offered me the use of his car to take you home, Papa. The roads are just about passable, but we will need to go straight away.'

'Yes, of course.' Their father was steered firmly towards the door, helped by the fact that trudging through the snow had clearly exhausted him. 'That's very good of you my boy, very good of you indeed.'

'Not at all, sir. Besides, there's a matter I wish to discuss with you, which I'd rather we undertook in private. I'm sure it can be sorted out between us.'

'Well, yes, of course...' At the door, the old man looked back helplessly towards Alma, who had joined the carol singers as they resumed their practice of 'Silent Night', with '*sleep in heavenly pe-eace, slee-ep in Heav-en-ly peace,*' before Jamie propelled him purposefully outside.

Chapter Thirty-Nine

As the lights of Mr Fairfield's Morris disappeared, flicking between the trees of the little lane, Rosalind hurried to catch up with the rest of the party, heading for the White Hart. She found Kate waiting for her, in a tiny pool of light from her torch, stomping her feet in the snow.

'Where's Cordelia?'

'I thought she was with you,' said Kate.

'Rosalind felt a twinge of unease. 'I haven't seen her since she made sure Papa left with Jamie.'

'She must have gone back to Arden with Jamie.'

'Jamie wanted to have Papa on his own, where he couldn't escape – it's the only way he's going to talk any sense into him. The last time I saw her, she was at the hall door, speaking to Henry Luscombe.'

'She was talking to Henry?' Rosalind's stomach lurched.

'Looked like she was trying to get away from him. He's slimier than ever, you know. I was going to help scare him off, but when I looked back they had gone.'

'You mean she left with him?'

'Surely not. She can't stand him. And anyhow, Henry's still only got eyes for you.'

'He needs one of us. I'm not sure he minds which.'

'Rosy!' Kate sounded horrified.

'I mean it. And it's not just to satisfy his family. He and Oswald have the future of Arden and Brierley worked out between them. If they win, Oswald will make a fortune and Henry can carry on doing exactly as he pleases, with a squashed little wife to keep his family happy and cover his tracks. If Cordelia is with him, we need to find them, and fast.'

Rosalind swept her flashlight around them, urging the beam to reach as far as it would go. The streets were empty. The village green deserted. Deep silence hung in the muffling of the now rapidly falling snow.

'Cordelia!' she yelled with all her might.

'They can't have gone far,' said Kate, swinging her own beam around her.

They called and called, searching for any sign. A curtain was drawn back, a door opened to allow the warmth of light to fall onto the frozen streets with the murmur of curious voices. But there was no sign of Cordelia.

'Over here,' exclaimed Kate, concentrating her torch on indentations in the snow where the village green began. Already half-obliterated in the fresh fall of snowflakes, a weaving line of footsteps, one set large and clear, the other smaller and less distinct, as if dragged unwillingly, were making their way across the pristine centre of the green.

As they followed the footsteps, calling as they went, more doors opened, the message of a young woman missing in the darkness, with its instant overtones of alarm, passing rapidly from house to house, street to street. Lamps and flashlights began to appear around them, beams probing into the chilly darkness.

'She has to be here somewhere,' said Kate, in desperation, as they reached the far side of the green.

'We'll find her,' said Rosalind, following the prints, now heading into one of the alleyways leading towards the seclusion of the bridge and the vast darkness of the water meadows beyond.

Halfway down the alleyway, a door was flung open, sending out a stream of light.

'Oi, you!' A man's voice echoed between stone walls. 'Filthy bugger, what d'you think you're doing?'

There was a convulsion of shadows, just outside the beam of the man's torch, followed by a man's yelp of agony, then a woman's scream.

'Cordelia!' Rosalind caught the figure racing towards her, stumbling in the snow, her breath harsh with terror. 'Cordelia, thank goodness.'

'She bit me, the little bitch!' Henry was not far behind.

'Then I hope you've got fingers missing,' retorted Kate, placing herself in front of her sisters, preventing him from taking a step closer.

'She came perfectly willingly.'

'I did nothing of the kind,' gasped Cordelia, voice shaking but clear. 'You dragged me out. I know what you were up to.'

Henry pushed Kate aside.

'Don't you touch her,' said Rosalind, holding Cordelia tight. Beams of light streaked across them from every angle as the searchers converged on the commotion. Henry hesitated. She could see the fury contorting his face. Then he turned, vanishing into the darkness. In her arms, Cordelia began to tremble.

'Are you all right?' demanded Kate.

'Yes.' Cordelia's teeth were chattering. 'Thanks to you. I couldn't get free...'

'Let's get you inside,' said Rosalind. 'You must be frozen.'

Already, immediate crisis over, the villagers were beginning to return to the warmth of their homes. A few of the young men stayed to direct their torches into corners, but there was no sign of Henry.

They began to help Cordelia, who was now trembling uncontrollably, along the street towards the welcoming lights of the pub.

'You don't think that's him, do you?' said Kate, at the distant whine of car wheels as they attempted to gain a grip on the snow.

'Let's hope so,' said Rosalind. 'I don't care where he goes, as long as it's as far away from us as possible.'

But Henry's car was at Arden. Had Oswald come to his rescue? A new dread went through her. Rosalind allowed her sisters to go on ahead, turning to peer into the darkness. She could hear the distant wheels finally getting traction, the car moving. The beam of headlights danced crazily between the huge flakes of rapidly falling snow, revealing the vehicle heading towards her, into the heart of the village, rather than away.

'Not so fast.' Her arm was gripped from behind, her flashlight sent spinning wildly, beam dying as it crashed through the snow.

'Henry!' she exclaimed. 'Try anything, and I'll scream the place down.'

'Damn you.' Henry's voice was low with temper, the dangerous kind that no longer cares for any consequences. 'If you think I'm leaving empty-handed, you little tart, you've another thing coming. It seems it'll have to be you, after all, my dear.'

'I'll jump off a cliff first,' she retorted, twisting in his grasp, until she felt her coat tear.

'That can be arranged. In time. With pleasure.'

Her boot caught his shin. Rosalind pulled herself free, stumbling across the roadway towards the safety of the White Hart, sliding on the trodden snow. He caught her, just as the lights of the approaching motorcar reached them, dragging her straight into its path.

Chapter Forty

Instinctively, Rosalind flung her free arm across her head as the lights veered crazily towards her with the squeal of brakes. At the last moment, the driver turned just enough to stop within inches. She could feel the heat on her skin, the stench of fumes surrounded her.

'Bastard!' The driver jumped out, grabbing Henry, a single blow sending him sprawling into the snow. 'You could have killed her.'

Rosalind struggled against the slithering of ice, trying to get to her feet, still blinded by the headlights as her rescuer reached her.

'Rosy? Rosy, thank God, I was so afraid I smashed into you.'

'I'm not hurt.' She felt the familiar greatcoat as the beloved warmth of Guy enveloped her, steadying her as she clambered to her feet.

'Thank heaven.' He held her tight. She could feel his entire body shaking. 'When I saw you in the headlights, when I saw what the bastard was doing...'

'You stopped in time,' she said, returning his embrace. 'That's what matters.'

'Is he dead?' demanded Guy, turning towards his passenger, who was now bending over Henry's prone figure.

'No, more's the pity.' It was Edmund's voice coming from the shadows at the edge of the headlights. 'A few more inches and his head would have cracked on the edge of the war memorial. He's out cold enough, though.'

'I can't say I'm sorry, but I suppose I could do without facing down the English aristocracy on a charge of murder,' replied Guy.

Rosalind shuddered. 'Much as I loathe Henry, I couldn't bear the thought of losing you because of him. That would be too cruel.' Her breathing was beginning to even out a little, her legs, though like lead, steadying. 'What on earth are you doing here?'

'Meeting Jamie. He telephoned a short time ago. It sounded urgent. Besides, it seemed unfair to leave Edmund to cycle home in the snow after we'd detained him so late on Christmas Eve.' He turned back to Edmund. 'What do you suggest we do with Luscombe?'

'The police cells tend to be quiet on Christmas Eve,' said Edmund. 'Seems the best place for him to cool his heels, at least until the snow melts. Fetch the constable, would you, Jones?' he called to the men spilling out of the White Hart to watch the drama. 'Can't have old Mr Arden distressed by fraudsters and blackmailers on Christmas Eve.' He reached into the car to switch off the engine. 'I'm afraid this isn't going to move for a while, especially now it's starting to freeze.'

As several of the revellers arrived to noisily take charge of a now-stirring Henry, dragging him with little care for his expensive shoes towards the tiny police station behind the

High Street, Edmund released the straps securing his bicycle to the roof rack. 'You're welcome to stay with me and Dad if you find yourself stuck,' he added, a little gruffly.

'Thank you,' replied Guy. 'But I'm sure there will be room for me at the inn. Have a peaceful Christmas.'

'And you,' said Edmund, nodding in Rosalind's direction.

'He's a good man,' said Guy, his eyes following Edmund as he pushed his bicycle through the snow, following in the ignominious wake of Henry, whose unconscious form was disappearing into darkness, heels bumping along the ice, accompanied by sounds of merriment from his captors. 'You can see his heart will always be here in Brierley, however much he might wish to escape.' He cleared his throat. 'I see also that he was worried about you.'

'And I'm grateful,' she replied, meeting his eyes.

'Oh... Rosy—'

'Don't be an idiot,' she returned, kissing him. 'If you think I'm going to fall head over heels for every handsome face I meet, we'll never get anywhere.'

Guy laughed and retrieved a knapsack from the back of the car. 'Quite. You must be frozen. At least it will be warm in the White Hart. Jamie said he'd meet me there after the play.'

'The performance was cancelled. Papa was exhausted so Jamie's taken him home, but the rest of them are there.'

'Including Gorwell?'

'Yes.'

'He's the only one I need.' Guy took a flashlight from his pocket. 'Rosy, I promised I'd leave Edmund out of this. He might not work for Gorwell anymore, but his dad still lives here.'

'I won't say a word.' She frowned at him. 'Are you telling me that Edmund's new employer is Thompson & Son?'

'My sisters were looking for engineers, particularly those with experience in domestic settings. It's a small world round here, word gets about if someone is good at their job. And, to be honest, there aren't many men happy to work for a couple of women.'

'Good for Edmund,' she replied.

They began to make their way through the hardening snow, between cottages glowing from within with fires in the hearths and candles flickering on the windowsills, until they reached the White Hart.

'Rosalind!' She was caught in Kate's arms and hugged tightly the moment they emerged into the lamps of the White Hart's best room. 'We were just coming to look for you—' She came to a halt as her eyes fell on Guy. 'Hello, Mr Thompson.' She smiled, eyes filling with tears. 'It seems such a long time ago, that day we first met you when you came with Will to swim in the lake.'

'So it is,' he replied, gravely.

'Thompson.' Oswald put down his brandy. 'James said you had a matter to discuss with me. It must be something urgent, to make your way here on Christmas Eve.'

'Jamie thought it couldn't wait,' replied Guy, removing a large file from his knapsack and laying it on the low table in front of Oswald.

Oswald visibly relaxed. He took his time to light a musty-smelling cigar, after the manner of Mr Churchill, and leant back in his chair. 'My good man. It's Christmas Eve. I've no desire to entertain a business proposal. James would have been better instructing you to approach me after the festive season has passed.'

Guy ignored him. 'I don't believe you've ever met my sister Gwen, who runs the accounts for Thompson & Co in Stratford?'

'I'm sure I would remember the honour,' Oswald replied smoothly. He turned towards Bianca. 'Perhaps, my dear, if you're sufficiently recovered, we should make our way to Arden House. I'm sure with all this snow, Mr Thompson will need to find a room for the night.' His smiled deepened. 'If any are available.'

'Jamie has invited Guy to stay at Arden House,' said Rosalind, firmly.

'I'm sure that's not necessary. This year's celebration is for family only.'

Guy opened the first file. 'My sister was employed during the war by a company investigating fraud, including for the War Damage Commission.'

Oswald set down his brandy so hard the liquid nearly escaped the round bowl of the glass. 'I really don't see—'

'Gwen was very good at her job. One of the best. She has an eye for detail, a tenacious memory, and once started, she never lets go. She was known for being able to spot almost immediately the tiny details that revealed when a claim for bomb damage wasn't quite right, and especially if it formed part of an established pattern, designed to defraud the authorities. She's recently been using her skills to help investigate a pattern of deliberately shoddy work, aimed at defrauding private investors. Organised crime, some might call it.'

'My good man, I'm quite sure—'

Guy laid a headed paper next to the abandoned glass, followed by a second. 'I've more. And a comprehensive list. Dates, times, claims. Monies paid...'

'How much.'

Guy straightened. 'I beg your pardon?'

'How much do you intend to get out of me with this crude attempt at blackmail?'

'My dear...' Bianca put a tentative hand on Oswald's arm, which was immediately struck away.

'How much?'

'Not a penny,' replied Guy.

Oswald snorted. 'What, then? A valuable contract, an introduction...?'

Guy placed a final paper in front of him. There was a moment's silence. Rosalind could see the fury, mixed with something that strongly resembled fear, slowly dawning on Oswald's face.

'You can't put that on me.' He blustered, rising to his feet. 'The responsibility is not mine. That paper was signed of my father-in-law's own free will. He knew what he was doing. With James incapable of running the estate, it was only right, as Bianca's husband, the father of his grandsons, that old Arden should make over the responsibility to me. The place was going to rack and ruin.' He turned to Bianca. 'Isn't that so, my dear?'

'Yes,' said Bianca, sounding strangled. Rosalind saw her hand clench the arm of the chair. 'Although I do think we were a little hasty—'

'Perhaps we should discuss this in private,' said Guy.

'I see no reason—' began Oswald loudly. He came to a halt as the door opened to reveal a white snowman of a figure, coat and boots laced with ice.

'Well, I do,' said Jamie, as drips began to splash all around him.

It took less than half an hour before the three men returned from the small snug, hastily cleared by the landlord as a private meeting room.

Oswald was dignity itself. 'We will not trouble you any

further, James. I'm sure this misunderstanding will soon be cleared up.'

'I very much doubt it,' replied Jamie.

Oswald straightened his shoulders. 'My dear, given the circumstances, I suggest we spend Christmas in our own home.'

Bianca turned pale. 'But it's shut up. There are no staff. We let Chef go, and even the maids have gone. Besides, the children are at Arden...'

'We needn't disturb them,' said Oswald, heavily. 'They are well enough where they are with the nursemaid, and Alma will enjoy taking care of them. I'm sure your father will be delighted to have children in the house for Christmas. I rather think that from now on we should spend far more time in our London house. The society here is so shockingly unsuitable, especially for our boys. And the amenities totally inadequate. I always said London society was the thing. I'm certain you agree, my dear.'

'Bianca comes back with us to Arden tonight,' said Jamie firmly. 'That is part of the deal. Will was her brother, too. Besides, I feel sure you can't wish to deprive children of their mother on Christmas Eve?'

'I—' Oswald glared around him, his attention finally coming to rest on Bianca, who sat rigid in her chair, eyes clenched tight shut. 'I won't forget this,' he declared, gathering up his dignity and sweeping out.

'He's not going to sleep in the snow, is he?' whispered Bianca, as soon as he was safely out of earshot.

'Don't be silly, I'll arrange a room for him here,' said Jamie. 'I'm sure the landlord can do with the custom. And it will be a good deal more comfortable than joining his accomplice in a police cell,' he added, causing Bianca to dissolve into hysterics.

'She'll be alright,' said Kate, gruffly. 'She's tougher than she looks. But it might be best if we get her home, and Cordelia.'

'You, too, Guy,' said Jamie, as the party began shuffling to their feet.

'I don't want to put you to that trouble,' said Guy, awkwardly. 'I'm sure I can find a room.'

'Rubbish,' said Jamie. 'You left your own Christmas with your family to help us save Arden. The least we can do to thank you is a bed for the night, and for as long as you need if the snow doesn't melt. So you're coming with us.'

'Please do,' said Rosalind quickly.

'You have to, Guy,' added Kate, 'especially now you've saved the day.' Her eyes filled with unexpected tears. 'We all deserve to be with those we love on Christmas Day, and if not, well then at least a house full of warmth and kindness. She blew her nose loudly. 'Besides, Papa is going to have to get used to the idea some time.'

'Get used to what?' demanded Bianca, suspiciously.

'Well, I thought that was obvious,' said Cordelia, sitting up straight, bright and alert once more.

'If even Jamie can work it out,' added Kate, 'I'm sure the rest of us should be able to, at some time or other.'

'What they mean,' said Rosalind, slipping her arm through Guy's, 'is that it looks as if I may have found myself a respectable husband, after all.'

In Arden House, Jamie lit the final candle on the Christmas tree, sending a warm glow into the hallway.

With Bianca showing signs of recovery from the trudge back through deep drifts, accompanied by huge swirling flakes descending from above, Florrie the nursemaid had brought both boys, who were far too excited to sleep, down to watch the lighting of the tree at midnight, and the welcoming in of Christmas Day.

In the pause in the reading of scenes from *As You Like It*, sherry and a fair approximation of mince pies were handed round. Even Lucy obeyed to the pressure to sit down with a sherry and bask in the sensation of preparations all completed, the more difficult members of the family removed, and a promising Christmas Day in prospect.

The sound of laughter and conversation filled the room. Even Papa, installed next to the fire with a fine selection of mince pies and brandy, was looking reasonably benign, having – after a strong talking-to from Jamie – resigned himself to the fact that a passable husband for Rosalind was better than none at all. Jamie was still uncertain whether their father had allowed himself to fully comprehend the catastrophe he had so nearly allowed himself to be lured into by Oswald, which didn't exactly bode well for the future, but at least Jamie was forewarned.

Unnoticed, Rosalind followed her stepmother out to the front of the house to watch the snow, which was by now falling thick and fast.

'They'll be drawing to the end of the carol service in the church,' said Alma, wistfully.

Rosalind tucked her arm inside that of her stepmother. 'They'll soon be preparing for Easter, Mama.'

'I suppose they will. I'm glad to see you happy, my dear. You always did know your own mind. I'm not sure any of us should have interfered.' She brightened. 'Do you really think there will be a wedding for Princess Elizabeth before too long?'

'Ginny Blake is convinced, and she's rarely wrong.' She eyed her stepmother. 'If it does take place, why don't you come and watch the wedding procession through London? I'm certain to be there with my camera, catching the reaction of the crowd. You could always accompany me.'

'Go to London? On my own?' Alma looked thoughtful.

'I don't see why not, Mama.' Rosalind bit her lip. 'And I hope I will be able to come back here, and visit you at Arden House.'

Alma kissed her. 'My darling, you will always belong here. You and your husband, and one day your children, will always be welcome. I'll make sure of that.'

In the distance, echoing through the snow, there came the murmur of voices. The opening lines of 'Once in Royal David's City' drifted towards them on the still air.

'It's the choir,' exclaimed Alma. 'They are singing outside in the snow. They must be frozen.'

'They are singing for you, Mama, because they know you can't join them.'

As Rosalind hugged her stepmother tightly, Alma's eyes filled with tears. 'Do you know, my dear, I rather think they are.'

Then it was time to return to the warmth of the fire for the Shakespeare sisters to finish the reading of the final scenes of *As You Like It*, each of them taking the different parts with abandon.

'*To you I give myself,*' said Rosalind, smiling at Guy. '*To you I give myself for I am yours.*' She could see the love in his eyes as he smiled back, sending her heart racing.

'*How many fathom deep I am in love...*' he replied.

'Epilogue,' commanded Papa, as the play ended with true love united and general joyfulness. 'Don't you think, Jamie? It feels appropriate.'

'I think it's up to Rosy,' replied Jamie.

'Yes, true, true. Although I would like to hear it again. It reminds me so much—' He glanced at Alma, who was still a little tearful and cleared his throat. 'It's good to be reminded,' he murmured.

'With the greatest of pleasure,' said Rosalind. 'I couldn't think of anything better to begin Christmas.'

As her sisters took their places amongst the little audience, Rosalind resumed her position on the makeshift stage in front of the Christmas Tree, opened her volume of Shakespeare's comedies once more, and began.

A Letter from the Author

Dear reader,

Huge thanks for reading *The Shakespeare Sisters*, I hope you were hooked on Rosalind's journey and enjoyed being with her, every step of the way. If you'd like to join other readers in hearing all about my new releases (and don't forget the bonus content!), you can sign up for my newsletter.

www.stormpublishing.co/juliet-greenwood

If you enjoyed this book, and could spare a few moments to leave a review, that would be amazing. I love seeing what my readers think, and even a short review (it only needs to be a few words!) can make all the difference in encouraging another reader to discover my books for the first time. Thank you so much!

I loved writing *The Shakespeare Sisters*. It's a story I've always wanted to tell and I've been incredibly excited to be able to work with Storm to finally bring it to life. It was inspired by growing up in the beautiful English countryside near Stratford-upon-Avon and my family's passion for Shakespeare. While Mum sang in an amateur choir, Dad (who, like Edmund, bore a passing resemblance to Errol Flynn in his youth) had a passion for amateur dramatics. I still remember the tins of greasepaint lying around the house when I was growing up!

My grandad might not have owned a grand ancestral home (he worked in a factory), but he did get up early to read his beloved Shakespeare before going to work each morning and he named his daughters after Shakespearean characters. My mum was called Audrey, after the character in *As You Like It* – a tradition she clearly passed on when she named me.

Most of all, the story grew out of the family's illustrated and leatherbound copies of Shakespeare's plays that I have now inherited. They might be battered, but they bring back wonderful memories of childhood, when the Victorian illustrations first drew me into Shakespeare's tales, making me fall in love with storytelling and words, and stirring my first love of writing. They also remind me of my grandparents, who lived through the horrors of two world wars, and dreamed so passionately of making a better life for their descendants.

I'm now excited at seeing where Rosalind's sisters find their volumes of Shakespeare take them, and uncover the secrets they hold...

Thanks again for being part of this amazing journey with me and I hope you'll stay in touch – I have so many more stories and ideas to entertain you with!

Juliet

www.julietgreenwood.co.uk

facebook.com/juliet.greenwood

twitter.com/julietgreenwood

instagram.com/julietgreenwood

linkedin.com/in/juliet-greenwood-28770536

Acknowledgments

First of all, I would like to thank Kathryn Taussig for being such a brilliant and enthusiastic editor, and taking me on the learning journey of my life. Thank you also to everyone at Storm – it's a huge pleasure working with you. I'm both honoured and excited, and can't wait to see where this takes us all.

Thanks also to my wonderful and steadfast agent, Judith Murdoch, for the help and suggestions, and taking an idea and running with it, while pushing me to be the very best I can, even when I think I can't. (And despite my occasional gibbering in a corner).

Thank you, as ever, to my friends and family for their patience and understanding, and for dragging me out for walks (or cake/wine), especially when I disappear too long down the writing or editing hole. Thank you to Trisha Ashley and Louise Marley for keeping the inspiration going, even when it isn't, and the members of Novelistas Ink for coffee and writerly conversations. Thanks also to fellow author Carol Lovekin for the regular exchange of ideas, along with laughter and making sure that word count keeps growing. And finally, as ever, *diolch* – thank you – to Dave and Nerys, Catrin and Delyth, for being the best of neighbours – a strong community is the greatest gift of all.

Printed in Great Britain
by Amazon